By Kris Tualla:

Loving the Norseman
Loving the Knight
In the Norseman's House

A Nordic Knight in Henry's Court
A Nordic Knight of the Golden Fleece
A Nordic Knight and his Spanish Wife

A Discreet Gentleman of Discovery
A Discreet Gentleman of Matrimony
A Discreet Gentleman of Consequence
A Discreet Gentleman of Intrigue
A Discreet Gentleman of Mystery

Leaving Norway
Finding Sovereignty
Kirsten's Journal

A Woman of Choice
A Prince of Norway
A Matter of Principle

The Norsemen's War: Enemies and Traitors
The Norsemen's War: Battles Abroad
The Norsemen's War: Finding Norway

An Unexpected Viking
A Restored Viking
A Modern Viking

*****

A Primer for Beginning Authors
Becoming an Authorpreneur

Battles Abroad

THE NORSEMEN'S WAR

Book 2:
Tor & Kyle

Kris Tualla

Battles Abroad: The Norsemen's War is a work of fiction. Names, characters, places and incidents are products of the author's imagination or are used fictitiously and are not to be construed as real. Any resemblance to actual events, locales, organizations, or persons, living or dead, is entirely coincidental.

Published in the United States of America.

© 2016 by Kris Tualla

All rights reserved. No part of this book may be used or reproduced in any form or by any means without the prior written consent of the Publisher, except for brief quotations used in critical articles or reviews.

ISBN-13: 978-1541380745
ISBN-10: 1541380746

*This book is dedicated to the competitive skiers
from America and Europe
whose careers were derailed by World War II,
and who responded by enlisting
in the United States Army
to teach our soldiers how to ski.*

*To the newly formed Tenth Mountain Division
which trained in Camp Hale, Colorado,
and the Women's Army Corp members
who served in rugged conditions alongside them.
Thank you for your service.*

*And to the readers who might be discovering this bit
of American history for the first time:
all the events in this story did happen,
but not everything that happened
is in this book.*

CHAPTER ONE

November 18, 1943
Denver, Colorado

Captain Tor Hansen of the Norwegian Army had been delayed in getting to America and he was as tense and fidgety as a man standing on the edge of a cracking glacier. After eight months of red tape and passports and military negotiations he was finally about to land in Denver, Colorado and take up his commission as an adjunct to the United States Army.

Seems that the American soldiers need to learn how to ski.

And after being denied the chance to compete in the cancelled nineteen-forty Winter Olympic Games—thanks to that bastard Adolf Hitler starting this war—Tor was itching to get back on the slopes and show off his skills.

But as he stared out the window of the airplane from the cramped, far-too-small-for-his-frame seat, the prospect of finding those slopes seemed unlikely. Since leaving Chicago on this third and final leg of his long and exhausting journey from London, Tor saw nothing below him except miles and miles of flat ground.

Sure, a hill rose up now and then. And the farmland was occasionally relieved by clusters of denuded trees or small grayish-green lakes. But the further west they flew, the farms gave way to vast expanses of yellow-grassed prairie land. Not a mountain in sight.

Where in hell are we supposed to ski?

His travel-weary body must have succumbed to a light sleep because he was jerked awake by the sudden and plane-jolting rise and drop of the aircraft. He grabbed the arms of his seat and looked around to see if anyone else seemed concerned as their path became increasingly turbulent.

His head grew dizzy from the constant motion. His belly, so disrupted by the last twenty-four hours' time-of-day shifts, sporadic sleep, and unfamiliar food, threatened to empty whatever it still held onto Tor's lap. He reached into the seat pocket in front of him and fumbled for the little waxed sack.

"It's always like this coming into Denver," his seatmate assured him. "It's because the airport is so close to the mountains."

Mountains?

Tor turned back to the window. All he could see was the unending roll of the prairie.

He faced the man beside him again. "What mountains?"

"The Rocky Mountains." The man smiled knowingly. "Wait until we turn around to land. You'll see them then."

In Tor's experience, a landscape never just shifted from vast plains to tall mountains without many miles of gradually increasing foothills. He saw no sign of the sort of foothills that would lead to mountains high enough to require his expertise.

His view disappeared as the two-propeller wing lifted and the plane dipped to its left. Looking across to the windows on the other side, all he could see was brown, snow-dusted ground.

And then, the aircraft leveled out.

Tor's jaw dropped. Rising suddenly from the plains as if all the land had been scraped from the east to form them, the majestic Rockies stretched north, south, and west as far as he could see.

Jagged peaks were crowned in glorious white—the kind that never melts completely away. They both dwarfed and protected the city that knelt at their feet. As the plane continued its bone-shaking bounces and violent swerves on its downward path, Tor smiled in spite of his discomfort.

This was what he expected to see. This was the sort of landscape he was familiar with.

I'm home.

He hurriedly opened the wax sack and completely emptied his stomach into it.

И И И

Tor straightened his drab-green Norwegian Army captain's uniform with its three-starred collars and King Haakon the Seventh's crest on his arm, and checked once more for any stray flecks of vomit that might have missed the sack. It wouldn't do to give his hosts a bad impression at first glance.

Satisfied that he looked presentable, he settled his cap on his head and stepped into the aisle to gratefully exit the airplane. Bitterly cold wind slapped his bare face as he carefully descended the steps to the frosted tarmac and followed the other passengers into the terminal. His scarf was in his duffel bag. He didn't care; it was a short walk.

Thank God my feet are on the ground.

Once inside, he swept a gaze over the crowd which was waiting for the deplaning passengers. He was supposed to be met by an American soldier from his destination, Camp Hale—a Lieutenant Kyle Solberg. Tor had no idea what the man looked like but figured that, as the only Norwegian soldier on the flight, he stood out enough for the man to find him.

When he saw no one who fit the bill, he turned to follow the baggage collection signs, assuming the lieutenant was waiting there for him.

"*Unnskyld meg, sir,*" The feminine voice at his shoulder addressed him in Norsk. "*Er du Kaptein Hansen?*"

Tor stopped and looked down at the blonde woman in what he believed was a lieutenant's uniform based on the information he was given during his cross-cultural training.

"Yes, I am," he answered in the same language. "And you are?"

She flashed a relieved smile and saluted him before continuing their conversation in Norsk. "I'm Lieutenant Kyle Solberg. I'll be your translator while you're stationed at Camp Hale."

Translator?
And Kyle Solberg is a woman?

Under different circumstances, Tor might have admitted that he spoke English fairly well after training in England for a cumulative fourteen months over the last three years. But at the moment he was far from his best.

His head pounded and he was still woozy from motion sickness. His empty stomach simultaneously begged for food while promising to reject anything that might appear. He was so tired from lack of sleep he was ready to topple over. And every muscle in his tall frame was cramped and aching.

So instead, all he said was, "I'm glad to meet you, Lieutenant."

She extended one hand in the direction of the baggage claim. "Shall we collect your bags?"

⚔ ⚔ ⚔

Once his heavily stuffed duffel bag was retrieved and crammed into the trunk of the lieutenant's little black sedan, Tor folded himself into the passenger seat.

Lieutenant Solberg noticed. "There's room to slide the seat back," she offered. "How tall are you, exactly?"

"Six feet and six inches. Just like my younger brother."

Now why did I mention him?

That was only going to lead to small talk. Tor pressed his lips together and pulled the door closed to shut off the windy blast that swept over the parking lot. Clouds scudded across the sky as if undecided whether to gather or move on.

Solberg started the engine. Cold air blew from the car's vents; he found it refreshing.

"It should warm up soon."

Relieved that she was going to ignore the comment about his brother, Tor said truthfully, "It's fine. I like it cold."

She reached down and turned a knob. "It's a three hour drive to the camp. Are you hungry?"

"Not at the moment."

"Okay. Then I guess we're on our way." She backed out of the parking space and turned the car toward the exit. "We should get there before supper is served at six, but if you want to stop along the road just let me know."

"Thank you." Tor shifted his weight, trying to straighten his legs without success.

"So is your brother in the Norwegian Army, too?"

Damn.

He looked at the lieutenant. Her profile was classically Norse: high brow, high cheekbones, straight nose. She was actually very attractive. In another setting...

Stop.

"No. But he's a sergeant in Milorg. That's short for Military Organization."

"The Resistance?" she clarified.

"Yes."

"Does he look like you, too?"

Tor blinked heavily. The motion of the car was already making him sleepy. "The truth is we've often been mistaken for twins. The most obvious difference in our appearance is that he has green eyes and mine are blue."

Solberg briefly glanced at him. "I always wanted blue eyes."

He couldn't see the color of her eyes when she faced the road, but he thought he saw they were gray. Maybe greenish gray. He yawned.

She noticed that, too. "It's okay if you want to grab a nap. The seat leans pretty far back."

"If you don't mind..." Tor felt for the lever. "I've been traveling since sometime yesterday."

"Not at all, sir."

He found the lever and pulled it. The back of his seat fell backwards to a forty-five-degree angle. He resettled and closed his eyes.

What should he do about Lieutenant Kyle Solberg?

The idea that he would be provided a translator surprised

him initially, but as he thought about it the accommodation made sense. He didn't mean to puff himself up, but he held a significant military rank and he was an exceptional skier. For him to come to America and teach others to ski as well as he did was sort of a big deal.

And of course no one would assume he knew English; he hailed from a proud but small and internationally unimportant kingdom.

Hell, Hitler walked in and claimed the entire country in just a five hour siege.

There was resistance now, sure, but no battles. No actual war. Most of the world probably had no idea what was going on in Norway for that matter.

So—here he was with a translator. A woman. An attractive woman. He'd be a fool to put a stop to this before he got a chance to know her.

She spoke Norsk like a native. He'd have to ask her about that. In the meantime, a lot could be gained by not admitting he understood the conversations that took place around him.

Tor smiled inwardly.

This could be fun.

Thus resolved to continue the ruse and speak nothing but Norsk for as long as it suited him, he shifted his position in the car once again before allowing the steady hum of the engine and the gentle motion of the vehicle to lull him into a much-needed nap.

Ν Ν Ν

Kyle listened to the captain's soft snores as she drove into the shadows of the Rocky Mountains. Night came swiftly here, the sun hidden long before it fell level with the valleys. The fact that he slept, trusting her with his life, warmed her heart in a stupid, silly way.

He's just exhausted, she told herself. *Who wouldn't be?*

She looked over at him again, before the interior of the car grew too dark for her to see his face.

Damn, he's handsome.

Kyle never swore out loud—it wasn't acceptable for women in her mind, even in the military. But since joining the Women's Army Corps as a translator and being stationed at Camp Hale she'd certainly heard an abundance of colorful language.

The fact that Captain Tor Hansen was an exceptionally good looking individual wasn't going to be helpful in her situation. She couldn't allow herself to become infatuated with the Norseman because she was engaged to be married. Hopefully he'd turn out to annoying enough to keep any unwanted attraction from forming.

When the war ended Kyle would return home to Viking, the tiny town in northern Minnesota where she was born, and marry Erik Olsen. She would live on his farm and together they'd eke out a decent living. They'd grow a variety of grains during the fleeting summer months and tend cows and pigs indoors when the sub-arctic winds froze everything solid.

That was what was expected from her.

When she saw the ad in the paper asking for a translator for a Norwegian officer, Kyle answered on a whim, not expecting anything to come from the interview. And then the notice arrived instructing her to go to Minneapolis and accept her commission.

Four weeks of basic training was easy for a farm girl.

And the weather in the Colorado mountains wasn't any worse than Minnesota so far.

She slid into the role with intriguing ease.

Captain Hansen sat up, halting her musings. "Where are we?"

"We have about half an hour to go." She looked at him in the dusk. He was frowning a little and seemed uneasy. "Do you need something?"

"I need to piss."

Kyle blushed, glad that he couldn't see it in the car's dim interior. "I'll pull over."

She stopped the car well on the shoulder. Tor opened the passenger door and exited in a blast of frigid air sprinkled with tiny dancing snow pellets. She watched in the car's mirrors as he moved to the back of the sedan, fidgeted with his clothes, and then stood still.

He didn't move for at least half a minute. When he did, he put himself back together before squatting and scooping up a double handful of snow which he scrubbed against his face and rubbed between his hands. Then he dragged his fingers over his cropped military haircut before he turned around and came back inside the car to reclaim his seat.

His cheeks were damp and reddened and he looked more awake than he had in the airport. "Thank you."

"Yes, sir." Kyle shifted and pressed on the gas. "Did the nap help?"

"Yes." He smiled at her. "At least my face won't fall in my soup."

"After you taste Cooky's soup, you might regret that," Kyle teased, surprised at her sudden temerity. "Let's hope for the best."

Captain Tor Hansen's head fell back and he loosed a deep, delighted laugh.

Damn, he's handsome.

CHAPTER TWO

"Do you have any questions about the camp?" Kyle asked as she resumed their drive.

Tor chuckled. "Yes. But more than half an hour's worth, I think."

Kyle smiled, her eyes still fixed on the winding wintry road ahead. "Start with one. Let's see how far we get."

Basic information, then. Tor twisted in his seat so he could look at her. "How big is the camp?"

"In area? About two-hundred-thousand acres."

That was surprising. But, "I was thinking about men."

"Men?" Now Kyle chuckled. "There are over eight thousand."

Tor tilted his head. "Why do you laugh?"

"I'm not a man."

"Well, that's pleasantly obvious," he complimented. "Are you saying there are women at the camp as well?"

Kyle's jaw clenched a little before she answered. "There are two-hundred-and-fifty-three members of the Woman's Army Corps stationed at Camp Hale."

"Really?" Tor was impressed. "I didn't know that."

"We're responsible for a variety of non-combat functions within the Army. But we are full military." She glanced at him. By the light of the headlights her eyes were colorless. *I'm curious what color these non-blue eyes actually are.* Her eyes shifted back to the road. "And by that I mean we all went through basic training and still have a training regimen. We had military schooling. We follow military order and discipline." Kyle gave a little shrug. "We just don't go into combat."

Tor wondered if she was challenging Norway's situation. "We don't have women in our army, but tens of thousands of them do serve in Milorg."

Kyle bounced a small nod. "Understood."

Tor leaned back again and considered the lieutenant. He was intrigued. "So what made you enlist?"

She drew a deep breath and blew it through loose lips. "I did it on a whim, I guess."

"A whim?" This was a pretty big decision to make without a plan. "What sort of whim?"

"I'm from a tiny town in northern Minnesota. Not too far from the Canadian border." She glanced at him again. "I'd never been anywhere else, and it didn't look like I was going to."

Eyes back on the road. "Then I saw an ad for someone to act as translator for a Norwegian ski instructor. I applied."

"And here you are."

She smiled a little. "And here I am."

Tor thought of a million questions but decided to start with, "What did your husband think of this?"

Kyle wiggled the fingers of her gloved left hand. "I'm not married."

"How is that possible?"

Another glance under a lowered brow. "What do you mean?"

"I mean you seem to be a very attractive, intelligent, and capable woman in her… mid-twenties," Tor guessed. "Why are you still single?"

Kyle's jaw clenched again. "I'm engaged. Are you married?"

Interesting. "No, but—"

"Why are *you* still single?"

Tor's jaw dropped. "Because I'm busy fighting a war."

This time, Kyle turned her face toward his and glared at him. "And so am I."

※ ※ ※

Pompous ass.
Kyle gripped the steering wheel and stared at the snow-banked road. Her relationship with the handsome captain was already taking an unpleasant turn.
She needed to pull it back around before she lost the position. She'd joined the WAC for an opportunity to travel and see something of the world beyond her tiny hometown and that was still her goal.
And to be honest, as a chance to win some independence from both her family's and Erik's expectations. Before she settled down to marry him, she needed to sow some oats of her own. Get it out of her system. Be ready for life as a farm wife in Viking.
"Of course you are," Tor said softly. "It was not my place to ask you such a question."
"It's fine." Kyle shook her head to clear her thoughts. "We're going to be spending a lot of time together, so we might as well learn to be honest with each other without getting bent out of shape over it."
The captain's brows lifted as if her answer surprised him. "Agreed."
"So, to finish answering your question." Kyle pulled a deep breath. "I replied to the ad on a whim, but I enlisted on purpose. I was excited for the opportunity to serve my country and help the war effort."
"I feel the same way," Tor said soberly. "When Hitler invaded Norway I enlisted that same day. Within a week I was..." He paused. "I was taking my training."
This is good, Kyle thought.
We're being friendly again.
Kyle slowed the car to make a turn. "We're almost there. Time for one more question."
Tor smiled. "How do you say 'I don't speak English'?"

⋈ ⋈ ⋈

Tor listened to Kyle's answer carefully, noting the broad, flat accent of her American English. He repeated the words several times until he eliminated the rounded British tones of the language he'd learned during his training in England.

He almost gave the game away before it began.

Once he admitted he'd spent so much time in England, his ignorance of their language would become suspect. And he was so intrigued by the feisty female lieutenant that his decision to hide his understanding remained as solid as the mountains surrounding them.

Kyle steered the car toward a large lighted building labeled *Camp Hale Headquarters* and stopped in front of it. "Here we are."

Tor opened the door of the parked car and gratefully exited the small sedan.

"I'm going to take you inside to meet Major General Lloyd Jones," Kyle said as she walked around the car. "He was given command of the Mountain Training Center because he specialized in winter operations and mountain warfare."

Tor did a slow turn. They were surrounded by hundreds of one and two-story building, all well lit inside and out.

How strange it was to be at war in such a safe location.

"How long has the camp been here?" he asked.

"Just over a year." Kyle pointed her thumb back at the car. "We'll drive to your barracks and unload after you meet the general. Follow me. Uh, sir."

Tor flashed a crooked grin. After their spirited conversation in the car, Lieutenant Solberg had already dropped her guard. It was a good beginning.

Inside the heated building, Tor removed his calf-length wool coat and handed it to the receptionist—another woman in uniform.

"The general is expecting you," she said. "Go on in."

Kyle handed the woman her coat as well before walking to the partially opened door.

Tor leapt forward, grabbed the knob, and opened it.

"After you, Lieutenant."

The general, a middle-aged military man with average looks and a solidly trim frame, was sitting at a massive oak desk. He looked up when Kyle walked into the office. She halted at attention in front of the desk and saluted.

Tor followed her example.

"At ease, soldiers. Please have a seat."

Kyle took one heavy wooden chair facing the desk and Tor took the other.

General Jones set down his pen. "Welcome to Camp Hale, Captain Hansen. We're glad to have you."

"*Takk.*" Tor leaned his head toward Kyle's and murmured in Norsk, "I understood that, of course."

Kyle simply nodded.

"The willingness of so many men from Norway, Sweden, Denmark, and even Germany, to come to America and enlist in our armed services is gratifying, as you can well imagine."

Tor struggled not to react until Kyle spoke the general's words to him. He needed his position in the Norwegian Army to be made clear.

"Remind him that I am not enlisted here. I'm still a Captain in Norway and plan to return there after the war" he said carefully. "I am here as an adjunct."

Kyle did.

"Of course." Jones put up one palm. "I was clumsily trying to thank you on behalf of all our Scandinavian friends."

Tor smiled and nodded after Kyle's translation was complete.

"We have another one of your countrymen here who you might know." Jones paused while Kyle spoke. "A champion ski jumper by the name of Torger Tokle."

Tor nodded when he heard the name. "*Han er her?*" Is he here?

"Yes. In fact he's assigned to the Eighty-sixth Infantry Regiment—the same regiment that you'll be attached to."

Tor looked at Kyle. "Does he have a translator?"

She shook her head. "He came over in thirty-nine. Went through basic in California before he was assigned here. Speaks pretty good English now."

Tor nodded. "Tell the general I do know him."

"Excellent!" Jones smiled. "So are you prepared to train our men in ski combat?"

Tor tried not to act like that was a stupid question. "Please tell him that in the Norwegian Army *all* soldiers are trained in ski combat."

Kyle softened his words a little, but the point was essentially the same.

"Great. Let's get you settled in." General Jones looked at his watch. "The officer's supper shift has just been served. Lieutenant Solberg, why don't you take the captain to eat first, and to his barracks afterwards?"

⚜ ⚜ ⚜

Kyle's boots crunched the snow underfoot in tandem with Tor's as they crossed the camp to the huge mess hall. "How do you know Torger Tokle?"

"We were both on the nineteen-forty Winter Olympics team. Plus, Norway isn't a big country. If you compete, you know each other."

"But he left Norway a year before Hitler invaded?" Kyle wondered at that moment why Tor hadn't done the same. "Before the Games were cancelled?"

"Yeah." Tor shrugged. "I guess he figured out what was coming and bolted while he still had a career."

"But you stayed."

What she could see of Tor's expression by the camp lights was grim. "I did."

Did he regret that?

Don't ask him now.

Kyle led the way into the mess hall. "The officers sit at the tables at the other end."

Tor saw the ski-jumper at one of the tables. "What rank is Tokle?"

Kyle grinned up at him. "Sergeant."

Tor grinned back and winked.

As the pair approached the bank of tables, Tokle looked up and saw Tor. His face split into a broad grin.

"Tor Hansen! I heard you were coming!"

Kyle stepped out of the way before the ski jumper knocked her over. He and Tor pounded each other's shoulders like they were old buddies.

"That's Captain Hansen to you, Sergeant," Tor teased in Norsk. "It's good to see you, man!"

Kyle settled into an empty seat at Tokle's table. Tor dropped into the seat beside her and Torger moved his tray so that he was facing Tor. The pair of Norsemen engaged in an animated conversation that she understood, but did not try to become a part of.

Meanwhile the other officers at the table stared at the men in bemusement.

An American sergeant turned to her. "Can you follow what they're saying?"

"Of course." She laughed at the man's surprised expression. "Norwegian was my first language."

Tor glanced at her, momentarily halting his conversation with Torger. When she shot him an inquisitive glance he just smiled and resumed his reunion.

✣ ✣ ✣

Tor left the table with Kyle to get his food. He returned to the table with his tray, his stomach finally settled and eager to dig in.

"This isn't bad," he said to Torger with his mouth full. "How's the food overall?"

"Lacking in fish, I'm afraid," the Norseman answered. "But we do have meat everyday."

That's a blessing.

"It's tough at home," Tor said softly.

"I know." Torger lowered his eyes. "I get letters sometimes."

Tor chewed a piece of beef. It was a little overcooked, but he savored it anyway. It had been a long time since he enjoyed such a luxury.

"So. You have a translator." Torger's mischievous gaze moved to Kyle who didn't seem to hear him. "You're a lucky man."

Tor didn't know how to respond to that, other than to say, "I appreciate the general thinking of it."

"It's too bad you didn't come sooner."

I tried. "Why?"

"There was a group of a thousand Norsk-speaking American soldiers training here." Torger grinned. "They were called the 'Viking' battalion. But they deployed in September."

Tor stared at his friend, wondering if his leg was being pulled. "Are you serious? *Viking?*"

"Ask your lieutenant." Torger scooped the last bite of apple pie into his mouth. "Anyway, you'll learn English soon enough. It's easy to pick up."

Tor kept his eyes lowered and focused on his food. In light of Torger's words—which he was certain that Kyle heard and understood—he wondered how long he could maintain his ruse.

"We'll see then."

Tor lifted his cup of black coffee and inhaled the aroma. The fact that his coffee was actually black and not transparent brown was encouraging. He couldn't remember the last time he had a strong, hot cup of coffee.

The first sip did not disappoint.

"Ahhh…" he sighed aloud. "This is good."

He turned to look at Kyle, and she met his eyes.

Mostly gray.

With green around the pupil.

Satisfied, Tor returned his attention to his coffee.

CHAPTER THREE

Kyle wasn't allowed inside the men's barracks, so she asked one of the guards on duty to escort Tor to his room on the second floor. Officers were billeted in the same barracks as the enlisted men in their units but in a separate area.

"The other ski instructors are billeted at the Mountain Training Center, but I'm afraid it's full," Kyle apologized. "But this building is closer to the camp's amenities."

She handed him the key to his room. "I'll see you tomorrow when I pick you up for breakfast. Officers eat at eight."

Tor palmed the brass key, warmed by her hand. "What will we do tomorrow?"

"I'll take you on a tour of the camp before lunch. Then we'll get you kitted out afterwards."

"Thank you, Lieutenant."

Kyle smiled. "My pleasure, sir."

Tor faced the guard and motioned for the man to lead him. He hefted his duffel bag onto his shoulder and followed the soldier up the wooden stairs to the second floor. His room was at the far end of the hall.

"*Tusen takk*," he said to the guard, who saluted sharply before walking away.

Tor shut the door and considered his Spartan but clean quarters. The small room had a single bed, a metal desk, and wooden dresser. The closet didn't have a door, just a sturdy rod in the carved out rectangle. There was more than enough room to hang his uniforms, so whatever garments he received the next day should fit as well.

"Welcome home, soldier," he muttered while he unpacked his bag and tucked everything neatly away.

The task complete, he yawned and stretched. The more than twenty-four hours of travel hit him hard all of a sudden, and the weight of his exhaustion drained the strength from him.

Time for bed.

After stripping to trousers, t-shirt, and slippers, Tor grabbed his shaving kit and one of the two towels that were folded on the bed and headed back down the hall to the shared latrine. He counted rooms along the way—eight on each side. If half the rooms held junior officers at two per room, then there were twenty-four men sharing the second-floor facilities.

That would do.

Tor relieved himself before he washed his face and brushed his teeth. A few other officers wandered in to do the same. They nodded a greeting, but didn't say anything.

Tor nodded back.

They know who I am, he realized. And they don't think I know English.

Perfect.

November 19, 1943
Camp Hale, Colorado

Kyle drove an open jeep today and kept up her patter as she drove Tor around the spread-out camp.

"The Tenth Light Division has eighty-five hundred troops here. The Tenth is comprised of three Infantry Regiments: the Eighty-fifth, Eighty-sixth, and Eighty-seventh."

She looked at him. "You're assigned to the Eighty-sixth."

"I remember."

She smiled slyly. "Just making sure."

Tor rolled his eyes. "I'm fine."

Just because he slept like a dead man, missing breakfast and coming late to lunch, didn't mean he'd lost his memory or his mind.

"Well, you wouldn't have seen this, anyway," Kyle waved a gloved hand around them. "You can't tell now, but this morning the clouds covered the mountains more than halfway down."

Tor looked at the mountains completely surrounding the flat valley where Camp Hale was constructed. They looked adequate for training purposes.

He consulted the map of the camp that Kyle gave him. They drove past building after building while she named them off in quick succession.

"Motor Vehicle Repair. Fuel, coal, and water storage. Sewage treatment. Ordnance warehouses. Fire Station Number One. Hospital, infirmary, dental office."

"Number one?" Tor looked up from the map. "How many fire stations are there?"

"Two." Kyle turned the wheel. "You've seen the main administration building. This is the auxiliary one."

He stared at the map again. "How long did it take for you to learn all of this?"

"A couple weeks." She chuckled. "Once I was able to drive around instead of walk around, I learned a lot faster."

"This camp is bigger than most of the towns in Norway." A new thought occurred. "Will you always be driving me around?"

"I expect so." Kyle steered the jeep onto a road. "Cooper Hill is about five or six miles from the camp. That's where the MTC is and the other instructors."

Mountain Training Center.

Right.

Kyle sped down the road before making a sharp turn. She slowed the jeep to a stop and turned off the engine.

She looked at him, clearly concerned. "I won't be going up the mountain with you. Is that going to cause a problem?"

Tor shook his head. He'd already thought about that, should the question arise.

"Skiing is about demonstrating, not talking. I'll be fine."
"Good." Kyle jumped out of the vehicle. "Come on."
Tor did the same. "Where are we going?"
"This is Cooper Hill. I want to show you the T-bar." She walked away from him obviously expecting him to follow.
"This is where you go up to the top," she said over her shoulder. "The T-bar goes seven miles an hour, and pulls two men at a time up the mile-and-a-quarter to the top."
Tor caught up with her in three strides. He'd heard of systems like that and was eager to see this one.
He heard men's voices coming from straight ahead. Boisterous and booming, he caught a few words before the masculine sound was swallowed by snow and trees.
And there it was. He walked forward and watched as two men at a time sat on the inverted metal Ts and slid on their skis up the slope and out of sight.
Tor faced Kyle, excited. "How high?"
"It goes to eleven thousand feet. Almost two thousand above where we are now. This particular lift is one of the most powerful and efficient in the world." Kyle's voice held unmistakable pride. "As soon as we get you kitted out, you can come back and try it."
Tor whirled around. "Then let's go!"
He started jogging back to the jeep, assuming Kyle would catch up. He didn't expect her to run past him.
"Altitude training," she said when he reached the jeep after her, panting heavily. "You'll get used to it."
Tor nodded, scooping deep breaths of the thin air. "I was delayed—too long in—coming here. Out—of condition."
Kyle drove him past more buildings: bakery, cold storage, post office, and surprisingly a stable and blacksmith with grain and hay storage nearby.
"We use mules to carry supplies up the mountain." She patted the dashboard of the jeep. "These guys are great down here but they'd never make it up."
Tor pointed to a group of low buildings at the outer edge of the camp. They were surrounded by tall fences topped with thick spirals of barbed wire. "What's over there?"

Kyle steered the jeep closer and slowed to a stop. "Those are our German prisoners of war."

"Here?" Tor faced Kyle, gobsmacked. "You send the Nazis this far?"

"I guess." Her expression darkened as the men on the other side of the fence glared at her. "It's pretty secure here. If they tried to escape, they'd probably die in the mountains before getting anywhere."

True.

Unless someone broke them out.

One of the men shouted something very crude. Several others laughed before adding their own comments and gestures.

Tor's anger swelled and his fists clenched.

Filthy Nazi bastards.

He considered Kyle carefully. "Do you speak German?"

"No. But it's just as well." She shifted the jeep's gears and started moving again. "I can tell by their expressions and the tone of their voices that they aren't exactly complimenting my job or my parentage."

Tor looked back over his shoulder as they drove away, shocked at his strong reaction to the prisoners' taunts and insults.

Harm her and you'll answer to me.

ん ん ん

Tor rode the T-bar to the top of the mountain. His heart raced with anticipation. Even the seven miles an hour seemed too slow.

It took two hours for him to collect all the clothing and paraphernalia that made up his kit and now there was only sunlight enough for one downhill run. He carried the seven-foot skis and four-and-a-half foot poles on his shoulder as he hurried from his barracks to the mountain.

At the bottom of the lift, he strapped and buckled the toes of his new hiking boots in place on the white-topped skis. Next he slid their heavy heels against the coiled-spring catch and clamped them snugly.

And then he impatiently joined the line of men waiting their

turn to ride to the top.
There was no skiing in England while he waited for his delayed deployment. Since arriving in this freezing, snowy camp the urge to fly down a mountain grew stronger by the minute. Almost like an addiction. Tor smiled.
I am addicted.
The soldier sharing his seat tried to start a conversation on the way up, but Tor shrugged and concentrated on quashing his British accent.
"I don't speak English."
"Oh. Sorry."
When they reached the top of the lift, Tor slid off the bar just as the men in front of him had. He wondered if they were expected to wait and ski down in the same order as they came up.
When some of the men showed no sign of starting their descent, Tor moved to the head of the swath of open snow and pushed off.
Heaven.
Crouching on bent and flexing knees he quickly picked up glorious speed. His adrenalin surged as his body remembered what it loved to do.
Snow flew as he slalomed from right to left and back again. Around trees. Between trees. Taking small jumps over moguls.
God, how I've missed this!
The sting of snow on his cheeks. The cold wind in his face. The feel of the ground below as he flew over its icy coating. He never wanted the feeling to end.
It was always like this for him. A beautiful mix of power and skill, of control and freedom, so compelling that for the several minutes it took him to reach the bottom, nothing else in the world existed.
Only him and the mountain and the snow.

ᚾ ᚾ ᚾ

Kyle waited for Tor at one of the officers' tables. "I was afraid you were going to miss another meal. Were you able to take a ski run?"

She asked even though his face had changed so startlingly that she knew the answer. Tor Hansen looked alive. Exhilarated. Satisfied.

"Yes. And it was spectacular." He claimed the chair opposite hers. "God, how I've missed that."

That was an odd comment; the man lived in Norway. "How long has it been since you skied?"

Tor blinked at her. "What?"

"When did you ski last?"

"Last winter." He looked around. "What's for dinner tonight?"

"Meatloaf." Kyle was still confused. "You mean there wasn't any snow in Norway from September through November this year?"

Now Tor looked confused. "What is meatloaf?"

"It's like a Swedish meatball that's the size of a loaf of bread," she answered impatiently. "Why haven't you skied this season?"

"Is it good?"

Good Lord, the man was annoying at the moment. "Do you *like* Swedish meatballs?"

He wagged his head undecidedly. "They're all right."

"Same with meatloaf." Kyle leaned forward. "Why haven't you been skiing?"

Tor's shoulders slumped and he seemed frustrated. "My deployment was delayed. I was stuck where there were no mountains."

Something about that explanation didn't ring true.

Let it go for now.

"Let's get our food."

When they returned to the table, Tor put a bite of meatloaf into his mouth and chewed thoughtfully. Then he nodded.

"I like this."

"Notify the press everyone," Kyle mumbled. She hadn't known the man for long, but his moods and actions were proving a bit unpredictable.

Tor frowned at her. "What did you say?"

Kyle realized she grumbled in English. "Nothing important. Just English slang. How are the potatoes?"

"Mushy."

"They're mashed potatoes."

He shrugged, his eyes twinkling. "I like potatoes which require teeth."

Kyle burst into laughter. Tor's reaction was—perfect. "Oh, gosh. Tor. That's hilarious."

He grinned at her. "Thank you."

Two WAC nurses, officers who oversaw shifts in the hospital, approached their table. Both of them were staring at the tall, handsome, and occasionally charming Norwegian captain.

"Excuse us," one said. "May we interrupt?"

Tor rose to his feet and turned toward the woman, smiling. Both nurses stared up at Tor in awe. "I'm Sergeant Delores Brown, and this is Sergeant Helen Johnston."

Helen Johnston blushed and her eyelids fluttered.

Kyle groaned inwardly.

Is she having a seizure?

"He doesn't speak English," Kyle interrupted the dual assault. "So that's about as far as your conversation can go without me."

That was obviously disheartening news to Sergeant Brown, but apparently Sergeant Johnston was up to the challenge.

"Oh, I'm sure an officer of Captain Hansen's—stature," more eyelash works ensued, "can communicate just fine when he needs to."

Helen rested her hand against Tor's chest and cooed, "Isn't that right? Sir?"

Kyle switched to Norsk. "Watch yourself, Captain. This one's got a reputation."

Tor's expression didn't give away his words. "And very well-earned, I'll wager."

"What do you want me to say to them?"

He shifted his smile to her. "Tell them *I'm* not a whore."

Kyle literally choked on her swallowed guffaw and started to cough.

Tor handed her his glass of water. "Are you all right?"

"No," she squawked when she could manage any sound at all. "I'm going to kill you."

Tor cocked one amused eyebrow. "You shouldn't threaten an officer."

Kyle turned to the befuddled sergeants. "He says he's flattered, but needs time to adjust to his position before he can consider any social engagements."

She set the glass down hard. "You're on your own now. Sir."

CHAPTER FOUR

December 18, 1943

During the past month, Tor slid into the rhythm of the camp. He and an American First Lieutenant named Frank Collins shared a platoon of thirty-eight men who had skills of various levels. After the first two days, they split the men into two groups with Tor volunteering to take the novices.

"Learn the basics well from the start and you've got a solid foundation to build on," he told Kyle. "Collins can take it from there."

Teaching sixteen beginning skiers was a challenge, there was no doubt about it. The skiers would train for eight weeks at time, six hours a day, for six days a week. If they were fit to move on, then they did. If not, they started over.

Tor started with simply walking on the skis. After that came gliding—the simple two-step movement of his countrymen's cross-country skiing. Eventually the men would be coordinated enough to move like they were skating over the snow.

And there would be no T-bar in the Italian Alps, so the ability to climb up the side of a mountain without sliding backwards into your fellows was extremely important.

Tor started with the herringbone, making a V with his skis

spread at the tips and almost touching in the back as the men walked straight up the slope. Next was the traverse, walking at an upward angle across the mountain's face. Last came the side step—which was exactly what it sounded like.

"How do we know which one to use?" one of the men asked. Another punched his arm. "He doesn't speak English, moron."

And here's the glitch in my plan.

A man in the back called out, "Do the one that works." Problem solved.

For the moment.

Tor motioned to the men to practice, holding up three fingers and attaching one to each method he had demonstrated. As they did, he watched, stepping in when he was needed.

Which was sadly more often than he expected.

When he told Kyle about the about-face maneuvers, he laughed so hard he nearly wet himself.

"You are supposed to move like this." Tor lifted one leg straight out in front of him. "Once the back of the ski is resting on the ground beside you, you rotate it outwards, like this."

Kyle started to giggle. "I can see where this is going."

Tor started laughing again. "Once that ski is on the ground, parallel to the other, you just step over it and there you are."

"And you're training *men!*" Kyle laughed and clapped her hands. "I bet they fell all over themselves—like pins in bowling!"

So many parts of that sentence confused him. "What pins in bowling?"

"Bowling." Kyle wiped her eyes and kept chuckling. "You know—those lanes in the Rec Center where people throw balls to knock over those… well, pins. At the ends."

The presence of a huge recreational center at one end of the camp was Tor's biggest surprise since arriving. Sure, the idyllic setting and wealth of services was offset by long and grueling training sessions in bitter cold for six days out of the week. But America was at war.

A war not being fought on her land.

And that made all the difference.

"Why men?" he asked.

Kyle immediately put her feet alongside each other, heel to toe and grinned up at him. "Fifth position. Any little girl who's had a ballet class knows this."

Huh.

Today was the last Saturday before Christmas. The soldiers in camp were offered three-day passes, staggered so they'd leave on the twenty-third, twenty-fourth, and twenty-fifth, and return to camp on the twenty-sixth, twenty-seventh and twenty-eighth. Any soldier who could make it home and back in that timeframe accepted the pass and their resultant distraction was driving Tor to the brink of his patience.

He'd shout at them if he could. Cussing them out in Norwegian would have to do.

"Such language, Captain." Kyle chided when he climbed into the jeep waiting near the bottom of the lift.

"They're lucky I didn't strangle their scrawny necks," Tor grumbled. "How do you get *worse* after four weeks of training?"

Kyle slipped the jeep into reverse and backed up. "They'll be better when they get back."

Tor considered the lieutenant. "What are you doing tonight?"

"Well..." Kyle shifted into first and drove toward Tor's barracks. "A few of the nurses and I are going into Leadville. Why?"

Tor pulled off his gloves. "I feel the need for a distraction of my own."

"Do you want to come with us?" she offered without looking at him. "There's a camp bus that goes back and forth."

"I know." For some reason he didn't feel like sharing her company with anyone else.

But her invitation was so completely unexpected he thought he should accept before she retracted it.

Lately, Kyle had been a bit cool towards him. When he asked her what was bothering her, her response caught him off his guard.

"You flirt with every woman who shows an interest in you, and it means nothing. You're playing games. It's so ridiculous. It's beneath you, Captain."

"Beneath me?" Tor scoffed. "They *are* games, Lieutenant. Just a diversion to pass the time. Why does that bother you?"

"It shows a lack of... depth," she said haughtily. "A depth of character."

Tor stared at her hard. "Are you accusing me of being shallow?"

Kyle didn't answer at first. Then she said, "No. I know you're not. But it's so darn irritating."

Tor had let the subject drop, but her comments remained in his head. That made up his mind.

"Yeah. I guess I'll go along tonight."

ᚾ ᚾ ᚾ

Oh, no. Why did I invite him?

Over and over again for the last month Kyle had seen how women responded to the six-foot-six, sandy blond Norwegian with the bright blue eyes. Every single female who crossed Tor's path seemed to stop and stare at him, like he was some sort of Norse god or something.

Sure, he was gorgeous. Probably the handsomest man Kyle had ever seen. But he was also painfully human. And their constant fawning over him grated on her nerves.

Kyle glanced over at him. "Gee. Don't get too excited, soldier."

Tor grunted. "Where are you going?"

"To a bar that caters to servicemen. And women." She paused, trying to decide whether to play it up or down. Which would discourage him? "Nothing fancy. It's just drinks and dancing."

His head snapped around. "Dancing?"

Was he happy about that? "Do you dance?"

"Not much. But I saw some wild moves when I was in London." He made a dismissive gesture. "I was there, uh, for a few days. Waiting for my flight to New York."

His curious gaze pinned hers. "Do you dance?"

Kyle tried to sound modest. "I've picked up the basics of the jitterbug. But I'm no expert."

Kyle pulled up in front of Tor's barracks and waited for him to get out of the jeep.

He sat still for a minute, staring at his gloves. "I think it will be good for me to go." Kyle told herself the evening was still going to be fine even with the captain in tow. "All right, then. We'll leave at seven-thirty."

Tor nodded slowly. "A last chance to cut loose before you go home for Christmas."

Kyle's heart lurched. "I'm not going home."

Tor's eyes lifted to hers and his brows pulled together. "Why not?"

Tell him the truth.

"Because I've already spent one lifetime in Viking and when the war ends I'll be going back for another. This is my only chance to spend Christmas somewhere else."

Tor blinked. "Viking?"

"That's the name of my hometown."

Now his brows shot up in disbelief. "Viking? They call a town Viking?"

Kyle rolled her eyes. "I know—it's a verb. It's like calling a town Raiding or Pillaging."

Tor laughed. "So you are avoiding Viking this year. I understand."

"What about you?" she asked. "Would you go home if you could?"

Tor's demeanor sobered. "I haven't spent Christmas with my parents since nineteen-thirty-nine. Not since the occupation."

"So you haven't been home at all?" Even in her desire to break free, at least for a while, Kyle thought that was tragic.

"I've been home a few times. I've seen them," he corrected. "Just not at Christmas."

Kyle relaxed. "Understood."

Tor opened the jeep door. "I'll see you at supper, Lieutenant."

She smiled a little. "Yes, Sir."

ℳ ℳ ℳ

The Pastime Bar was dark and crowded, filled with men and women dressed in civilian clothes. It was impossible to tell who was from Camp Hale and who was local.

"Do you want a beer?" Tor asked Kyle.

She looked up at him. "I'll get it myself. We're not on a date."

Kyle's friends Frances and Florence—"Call me Flo."—were all over him in the bus. Even though he was conscious of Kyle's constant and disapproving attention, Tor played along as best he could without displaying any English understanding. He knew without any doubt that if he wanted to bed either woman tonight that opportunity was going to present itself.

Why shouldn't he accept? He hadn't been with a woman since leaving Norway. That was a long dry spell for him.

He watched Kyle make her way to the bar and saw men notice her along the way. She was tall for an American woman, he guessed five-foot-eight, and the blonde in her hair was natural, not the result of peroxide.

When a small table opened up, Tor grabbed it and waved to Kyle when she turned around. She was holding two beers.

"Here you are, Captain." She set one of the glasses in front of him. "A delayed welcome to America."

"I'll buy the next round," he declared, a little irritated at her. "I am a gentleman, after all."

"What's he sayin' to you, honey?" The man approaching clearly had a head start on the evening's alcohol consumption, and the glass in his hand was nearly empty. "Do you understand his gibberish?"

Kyle shot the man such a cold look that Tor felt a shiver run up his spine.

"It's not gibberish, it's Norwegian," she answered in stern English. "This man is an Olympic skier who's come to Camp Hale to teach our soldiers how to ski."

Kyle.
Be quiet.

"Well la-dee-dah." The man wiggled the fingers of his empty hand in the air and then fixed Tor with a sarcastic look.

"Since you don't speak American, it won't do me any good to tell you I'm borrowing this little lady for a while."

"No thank you." Kyle leaned away from the man's reach. "I'm staying right where I'm at."

Tor saw clear signs that this man was not at all dissuaded. He slid off his stool and stood looking down at the top of the man's head.

"Tor Hansen," he growled. "*Du?*"

"Dale." He lifted his chin angrily. "Dale Maple."

"Dale." Tor pointed at Kyle, then at himself. Then he made shooing motions at Dale.

Dale frowned. "I'll go when I'm good and ready."

Tor clenched his fists in front of his chest. He threw an inquisitive look at Dale.

Dale sniffed and spat at Tor's feet. "Fucking foreigner."

As he turned his back to walk away Tor quivered with the desire to smash his heavy boot squarely into the man's back.

Kyle laid her hand on his arm. "He's gone."

Tor perched back on his stool and drained his beer in one long pull. He slammed the glass on the round tabletop.

"I'll be back."

CHAPTER FIVE

Kyle watched Tor like a hawk, afraid he was going to pick a fight with Dale, but the Norseman was only headed to the bar. He returned with a beer and a shot glass of some amber liquor.

"*Skål.*" He threw back the shot and followed it with a gulp of beer.

Kyle looked toward the dance floor in the center of the bar and then turned back to Tor. "Want to dance?"

"No. You go. I'll watch."

"Are you sure?"

He nodded determinedly. "I need to cool off."

Kyle hopped down from the chair and wiggled through the crowd to where Frances and Flo were doing the jitterbug with each other. A soldier she recognized from the camp grabbed her hand and started dancing with her—and he was good. It wasn't long before the crowd opened around them and cheered them on.

Kyle loved to dance. She watched others and practiced the moves in her room at night, though as a second lieutenant she had a roommate.

But Marguerite was seldom around. Where she snuck off to after dark was none of Kyle's business. And if she was having a torrid affair with some soldier in the camp, her frequent disappearances gave Kyle that much more privacy.

Kyle danced with the soldier—whose name was Charles—through three consecutive songs before begging for a break. "Come back, beautiful," he called after her. "You sure know how to cut a rug!"

Kyle laughed and turned toward Tor.

A glaring Dale stood square in her path.

⁂

Tor was fascinated as he watched Kyle dance. Her sense of rhythm and graceful moves had him spellbound. The most amazing thing was her incredible smile—it lit up the entire dance floor as far as he was concerned.

Knowing she must be working up a thirst, Tor went back to the bar to buy Kyle the beer he promised her. When he set it on the table beside her almost empty glass, he looked up to find her.

Oh no.

Though Kyle was facing him, her way was blocked by that same Dale who was disrespectful to both of them earlier.

Before Tor could act, Kyle shoved Dale aside and marched to the table.

"Some people," she growled. She looked up at Tor. "Thanks for the beer."

"Do I need to step in?" he asked.

She brushed a lock of damp hair off her forehead and took a decent drink from the cold fresh beer before she answered him.

"Please don't. He's not worth getting the MPs involved."

Tor glanced across the bar at the two soldiers with white holsters strapped across their chests and the letters M and P emblazoned on their arms.

He returned his angry gaze to Kyle's. "Only if it becomes necessary."

Dale didn't seem to know how to take *no* for an answer. He and a couple buddies planted themselves at a nearby table with refilled drinks. They sneered at Tor as if challenging him to engage in battle.

While they drank, they talked. Loudly.

About Kyle."

"A sweet mouth like that? I bet she gives it to him real good." One of the men made a rude gesture with his tongue hanging out.

"I'd bet he spent all his time growing that body and there weren't nothin' left over for wood, if you know what I mean."

"She'd know!"

"Look at her squirm—she's hot for it right now."

Another rude gesture. "I got what you want right here. Come and get it."

Tor stood. Rage was turning his vision red.

Kyle's hand clamped down on his forearm. He paused and looked into her eyes.

"Let's go somewhere else." She downed her beer and slid from the stool. "Come on."

Tor reluctantly followed Kyle on her winding path through the bar crowd. When they reached the door, Tor stopped.

He met the MP's eyes with an intense glare. Then he shifted that glare to the table of taunting assholes. And then back to the MP.

The policeman narrowed his gaze as if taking Tor's measure. Tor gave a little nod, then left the bar with Kyle.

"Jeez it's cold." Kyle buttoned the double-breasted front of her Army-issue woolen coat. "Where should we go now?"

"I don't know this town," he pointed out. "You choose."

Kyle wrapped her scarf around her neck. "Well... there's a pizza place—"

"You whoring for foreigners tonight, bitch?"

Tor stepped between Kyle and the challenge. He figured the three men must have left the bar from a back door so they wouldn't cross paths with the MPs at the front.

"Hey, buddy. Get out of the way." Dale sauntered unevenly toward Tor, flanked by his motley back-up crew. "My date's waiting behind you. Gonna give her the time of her life."

"Let's go," Kyle tugged on his arm.

Tor held his ground. Every single insult he wanted to throw at the trio of idiots rumbled around in his head and sent steel into his fists.

Come and get me.
If you dare.
"He's an officer," Kyle shouted from behind him. "You're only enlisted men."
"Yeah? I don't see no stripes." Dale sniffed and spat again.
"Come on, Tor!" Kyle yanked on his arm. "He's not worth it!"
"You haven't tried me yet, honey. You don't know what I'm worth." Dale grabbed his own crotch and his laugh taunted Tor. "I'll make you scream little lady. You'll get so hot—"
Dale's words were smashed from existence by Tor's fists in a one-two attack. He dropped like a rock.
"Lieutenant, get the MPs out here, now!" Tor barked the order and jumped over the fallen man.
He raised his fists again as he stepped toward the other two. "*Ja? JA?*"
They backed away.
"Hey, we didn't mean anything."
"Nah, just having a little fun."
Fun? FUN?
These Neanderthal assholes considered harassing a woman with sexual taunts *fun?*
I should beat them half to death for even thinking like that.
Tor leapt forward.
The two cowards turned tail and ran.
He heard heavy footsteps behind him. Dale moaned pitifully. Tor turned to face the MPs and put his hands in the air.

ⵥ ⵥ ⵥ

Kyle sat with Tor in the infirmary and dabbed a stinging antiseptic on his split and swollen knuckles.
"It's a good thing you got the MP's attention before we left the bar," she conceded. "It was easy for me to convince them you weren't at fault."
Tor winced as Kyle replenished the medicine on her cotton ball. "No man, for any reason, should ever speak to any woman like they spoke to you. There is no excuse."

Kyle froze, the cotton ball suspended over Tor's hand. "How do you know what they said?"

Damn.

"I'm a man," he began carefully. "I understood the expressions on their faces and the tone of their voices. And if there was any doubt at all, when Dale grabbed himself that doubt disappeared."

Kyle's gaze moved away from his and she resumed the cleaning of his wounds. "What a way to spend our last Saturday before Christmas, huh?"

"Have you heard from your family?" Tor intentionally changed the subject.

"My parents sent me a package." Kyle dropped the spent cotton ball into the waste can. "That should do it. Let me wrap it so you don't bleed on your clothes."

Tor did let her. Being alone in the quiet with her was nice after the crowded and loud bar. "What about your fiancé?"

"Nothing yet." Her tone sounded strained. "I think he's jealous."

Tor recoiled. "Jealous of what?"

Interesting gray eyes with green centers met his. "Of you. What else?"

"Me?" Tor looked at her like she just told him his hair was on fire. "Why on earth? What did you say?"

"Nothing, really. I only said that you were interesting to talk to." She looked like she might cry. "I didn't even tell him what you look like."

Tor held his breath while he tried to figure out what *that* meant. He let it out in a whoosh when another thought arose.

"Does he want you to go back to Viking?"

Still a stupid name for a town.

"Of course he does." Kyle tied off the bandage. "But I reminded him that I enlisted for a two year tour of duty."

She rose from her seat and put the antiseptic and unused bandages back in the first aid kit.

Tor gingerly flexed his hand but stopped when spots of red appeared through the gauze wrapping. "Will you honor your engagement?"

"I'm a woman of my word." Kyle turned back to face him. "And I love him."

"I've never been in love," he confessed. "Someday you should tell me what it's like."

December 25, 1943

Dinner in the mess hall was a small affair with so many soldiers gone. When most of the officers had finished eating and left, Torger Tokle dropped into a seat at Tor's table.

Kyle excused herself, saying she'd be back. Tor watched her exit the mess hall wondering if everything was well with her.

"*God jul*, Tor."

Tor shifted his regard back to his companion, smiled, and answered in Norsk. "Happy Christmas, Torger."

Torger flashed a conspiratorial grin and pulled a flask from his pocket. "Want some aquavit in your coffee?"

"God, yes." Tor pushed his cup toward his countryman. "Thanks."

Torger poured a substantial amount into Tor's cup. "How is it going for you so far?"

Tor glanced at the small gathering of novice skiers several tables away. "Better than them, I think."

The other man turned around to look, and then faced Tor again. He nodded his agreement as he capped his flask and tucked it away.

"For you and me the mountain is our beloved friend. For them, it's still their adversary."

"True." Tor inhaled the steam rising from his fortified coffee before taking a delicious sip. "Ah. That's good."

Torger lifted his mug. "A toast? To being safe and warm this Christmas."

Tor touched his mug to Torger's. He kept his thoughts about Torger never actually seeing any of the war to himself.

He took another sip of the coffee, savoring its aroma and flavor, before changing the subject. "So what is it like when you jump?"

"You mean when I fly?"

Tor paused, his cup suspended in front of him. "Is that what it's like?"

Torger's eyes brightened. "No. It's what it *is*. I crouch low and tight as I slide down, my muscles coiled and ready to leap. And then, at the perfect moment..." He swooped one hand down and up as he talked. "I launch myself into the air. And for those few seconds there is nothing in my sight but my skis and the far horizon."

Tor was spellbound by the description.

"Then I see the ground and I prepare to land." Torger wagged his head reverently. "But until I do, I'm a bird of prey, Tor. Flying over everyone."

Tor took a gulp of coffee, contemplating Torger's words. "What about you?"

The question broke into Tor's thoughts. "Me?"

"Yes, you. When you fly down the side." Torger smiled. "What's it like for you?"

Tor saw the picture in his mind's eye. "First I stand on top of the world, you know? I can see everything just as you do."

Torger grinned. "Yes."

"And then... I guess I'm like a bird, too. But one that flies low over the sea, and dives for its prey." Tor liked his impromptu analogy. "I skim effortlessly over the surface, swerving this way and that. I take jumps over waves of snow. I change direction to follow my prey."

"The bottom of the mountain."

"Yes." Tor gave Torger a wistful look. "Don't you wish the journey took longer?"

"Every single time."

The men clunked their mugs again and took another sip.

◆ ◆ ◆

"What are you guys talking about?" one of Tor's students, a novice named Kossin, stood beside their table. Four men stood behind him.

On a crazy impulse Tor climbed on top of the table. He

pointed at Torger and then began to mime the actions the ski jumper had just described. He narrated in Norsk, knowing that though the soldiers wouldn't understand his words, they would understand the excited expression in his voice.

The men began to chuckle.

Tor flexed his knees, then straightened, leaning as far forward as he could and blinking frantically like wind was in his eyes.

The chuckles turned to laughter.

Tor crouched and wobbled, mimicking the landing.

"Well done, Captain!" Kossin shouted clapping his hands. Even Torger applauded.

As Tor climbed down, the ski jumper pretended to hang multiple medals around his neck.

"My turn," he said in English. "This is the famous Tor Hansen, Norway's downhill champion."

Torger moved to the aisle between tables. He grabbed a couple forks to indicate ski poles.

He paused and looked down and around as if surveying his kingdom. Then using the forks, he mimed pushing off with the poles.

Torger swerved on his ankles as he shouted, "Around that tree, over this rock, take that jump! I'm faster than a mountain lion and twice as pretty!" Then he swung around and faced the opposite direction. "I'm so good I can do it backwards!"

The men were doubled over with laughter.

Tor had to sit he was laughing so hard. "*Stoppe! Jeg kan ikke puste!*" Stop! I can't breathe!

Then he jumped up and pointed at Kossin. "*Ja?*"

"Yes!" the soldiers chorused.

Tor walked to the spot Torger vacated. Torger handed him the fork props. Tor stood still and took a deep breath, staring straight ahead. Everyone waited, silent.

Tor slid one foot forward, looked panicked, wind-milled his arms frantically, and dropped to the floor.

Raucous hilarity filled the hall, with Kossin laughing the loudest of all.

CHAPTER SIX

Kyle heard the men's laughter and decided not to go back inside. She would be out of place. Besides that, her mood was sour and she didn't want to have to feign cheerfulness.

She opened the package from her parents that morning. Bless their hearts, they tried. But no matter how many times Kyle told them that she was safe and well-supplied, they listened to reports of soldiers overseas and assumed she had the same needs.

Socks. Always socks.

And chocolate bars.

At least her mom's letter was long and chatty. Pappa was fine, her seventeen-year-old brother Lars had hit his growth spurt finally and was as tall as her father, and twenty-year-old Ingrid was being courted by a Swenson boy who returned from the war after losing a finger to a grenade. Her closing was as plaintive as it could be:

> *We miss you so much. Please promise you'll be home with us next Christmas.*
> *Love, Mamma and Pappa*

Kyle felt a stab of guilt when she read it, but it dissipated quickly. If she were being honest the letter and the gifts made the differences between life in Viking and life in Colorado that much more stark.

Erik's correspondence—or lack of it—angered her. He sent her a card. *A card*. Signed it: *Love, Erik*.

"Does he really love me?" she asked the dark and perpetually coal-smoke-hazed sky.

If he did, wouldn't he be trying to convince her to return to him? Talk about the great life they were going to share when she did?

She had so many things she wanted to say to him that she left the mess hall after dinner to try and sort them out. She didn't want to react in anger, but she had to let him know she was hurt.

Kyle wondered for the hundredth time whether Erik was jealous of her. Coming late in his parents' marriage, thirty-two-year-old Erik was their only child and the sole support of his aging parents. For that reason he was exempt from the draft. However, he was free to enlist if he chose to.

There was no way he could make that choice.

Kyle knew it. She understood it. Erik knew it as well; but that didn't mean he didn't resent his inability to fight for his country.

Or resent Kyle for enlisting in the WAC.

Maybe he actually was jealous of Tor Hansen. But why? Kyle had purposely been very vague in describing the captain and kept her mention of him minimal in her letters.

She turned toward the women's barracks and walked away from the hilarity inside the mess hall. She wouldn't sleep until she wrote the letter, so she might as well get on with it.

ᚾ ᚾ ᚾ

Warmed by the aquavit and camaraderie of the shared laughter, Tor eventually left the mess hall and went in search of Kyle. Something was bothering the lieutenant during supper and he wanted to make sure she was all right.

She wasn't in sight, so he walked toward her barracks. As he got closer he saw a single figure walking ahead of him.

"Lieutenant Solberg."

She stopped and turned around. "Yes, Sir?"

Tor closed the gap between them. "Is there something wrong?"

She shook her head. "No. I'm just feeling a little homesick. I'm going to write Erik a letter."

The fiancée.

"If you're sure that's all?"

Her smile was joyless and resolute. "I'm sure."

If he was a betting man, then he'd bet Kyle just lied to him.

"I'll see you tomorrow, then." He wanted to pat her shoulder but retrained the urge. "Happy Christmas, Kyle."

Her eyes widened when he called her by her first name. "Happy Christmas to you, too."

Tor turned around and walked away, heading nowhere in particular and wondering if he had just made a mistake.

Since arriving at Camp Hale more than a month ago, other than Torger he'd restricted himself to conversations either with his translator or conversations where she was present. He'd spoken to her more than he'd talked to any one person in months.

He realized that he considered her a friend.

Did she feel the same way?

Tor heard men's voices. He looked up in his wandering and realized he was near the POW enclosure. He stepped behind a shed and listened, breathing softly and closing his eyes so he could concentrate.

"Six more weeks."

"Why so long?"

"He says his contact is slow to answer."

"Are we sure we can trust him?"

"What choice do we have?"

"None, I guess."

The voices disappeared with the crunch of boots in snow. Tor's pulse surged. Were the Germans talking about escape? If so, he had six weeks to try and discover more—even though he had no idea how to go about it.

He could report what he heard to Major General Jones, but he'd need Kyle to go with him and he didn't want to involve her if he could avoid it. The German prisoners had already threatened and insulted her in words no gentleman would ever use—much like Dale Maple in the bar. Tor was determined to protect her from any further encounters.

No. I'll wait. Keep my ears open.

And he wouldn't tell anyone he spoke fluent German until he needed to.

January 3, 1944

Kyle snuggled into her woolen coat as she waited to pick up Tor in the covered jeep at the bottom of the lift. The mittens and scarf her mother knit and sent to her were thick and warm and kept her from freezing while she sat.

She mailed her letter to Erik the day after Christmas and she received his rather harsh reply yesterday. All day today Kyle had been consumed by his words echoing in her head, and wondered what she should do next.

Should I ask Tor what he thinks?

Ever since he called her Kyle instead of Lieutenant, she allowed herself to think of him as Tor. They were becoming friends, after all, not only colleagues. Six weeks of constant conversation couldn't help but push them in that direction.

The captain's scowl as he climbed into the jeep and slammed the door shouted that her concerns needed to wait for a better time.

"Did everyone live?" Her tone held no trace of amusement.

"Barely."

Kyle started the engine and shifted into reverse.

Tor was silent as they drove to headquarters. When she parked he asked, "Why are we here?"

"The general wants to meet with some of the instructors." Kyle shut off the engine. "He didn't say why."

She removed her scarf and mittens and started to open the door when Tor grabbed her hand to stop her. "Is it bad news?"

She frowned a little. "I don't think so. Why?"
"Because you haven't been the same person since Christmas." Tor leaned forward. "What's wrong?"
Kyle's shoulders slumped. "I'm not sure. But can we talk about it later? Not now."
"Are you ill?"
"No."
"Has someone mistreated you?" he pressed, his face a mask of concern.
She hesitated. "No one in Colorado has."
"Ah." His expression eased. "Erik."
"Later, Captain," she snapped. "We have business to attend to. *Sir.*"
Tor seemed pleased at her outburst, for some reason. His blue eyes held a puckish glint. "Yes, Lieutenant. We certainly do."
He opened his door.
Two dozen ski instructors, including Torger Tokle, waited around the huge table in the headquarters' conference room. The room was overheated, as usual, and Kyle shrugged out of her coat.
Tor grabbed it and folded it over his forearm.
"I can—"
"Shh." Tor pointed to the front of the room.
Major General Jones strode to the head of the conference table.
Tor leaned down to her, his eyes focused on the general. "Should I tell him his fly's open or do you want to?"
Kyle's horrified glance dropped to the area in question, then snapped up to the general's face. She fought the urge to laugh.
"Be quiet," she warned. "I have to listen to him."
"But everyone assembled here can see his unmentionables." Tor paused. "On the other hand, thank God he's wearing some."
Kyle glared up at Tor, her lips unfortunately twitching. "Stop it. I mean it."
"Lieutenant Solberg, is there a problem?" General Jones was staring at her.
Her face flamed. Tor disguised a snicker as a serious throat

clearing. If the general wasn't watching her she'd jam an elbow deep into his belly.

"No, sir. Captain Hansen was correcting my grammar."

The general nodded, his irritation clear. "I've called you men here today to get a reading on how well our soldiers are progressing in their training."

Kyle struggled to keep up with the explanations and discussions so Tor wouldn't fall behind. Thankfully he behaved and listened without comment until he was asked a direct question.

Kyle translated his response: "Half of their men will be ready next month. The other half still need a lot more work."

The general nodded. "Thank you, Captain."

"Your fly is still open."

Jones's brows lifted and he looked at Kyle. "Yes?"

She bit her tongue so she wouldn't laugh.

I'm really going to kill him.

"He says you're welcome, Sir."

Ν Ν Ν

"What the *hell* was that about?" Kyle stomped around the jeep and threw the door open. "Are you trying to get me fired?"

"Not at all. You saw it for yourself—the general's fly was gaping open." Tor opened his door and dropped into his seat. "And I don't believe I've ever heard you swear before."

Kyle slammed her door and glared at him. She looked more alive than she had in a week. "I don't swear. Or I didn't. But your behavior was intolerable."

Tor faced her. "This is the first time you've been honest with me since Christmas. It was worth it."

Kyle stuck her tongue out at him. "*Sir.*"

Tor laughed. "I deserved that."

"More than," she muttered and started the engine.

"Let's go somewhere," he said suddenly. "Somewhere we can talk privately."

Kyle looked at her watch, not sure how she felt about that suggestion.

"We have two full hours until dinner," Tor pointed out. "Where should we go?"

The lieutenant was clearly making up her mind whether or not to agree. "No. We have one hour and fifty minutes."

Tor gave her a kind smile. "Then we better hurry."

※ ※ ※

Kyle and Tor sat on piles of cleared snow alongside the driveway into the camp.

"Were these signs here the night we arrived?" he asked.

Kyle looked at the two caricatures of Adolf Hitler on the wooden boards. One was a fist labeled *Camp Hale* knocking the Fuhrer backwards into Japan's Hideki Tojo.

The other declared, "We've got a date with this sonofabitch. Let's be on time!"

"Yeah. They've been here since I got here."

"That's probably why Jones's meeting with the instructors," Tor suggested. "*Is* the Tenth Division's activation date set?"

"I don't know," Kyle answered truthfully.

The pair sat quietly for a moment and then both of them spoke at once.

"You go first," Kyle urged. She still wasn't sure exactly what she was going to say.

Tor flashed a wry smile. "I was going to ask you why you've been in such a funk lately."

"Oh." How should she describe it? "I guess the easiest explanation is that no one back in Viking seems to understand why I'm here."

Tor looked pensive. "Your parents?"

"My mother sends me socks and chocolate, convinced that my situation here is the same as if I was in Europe." Kyle flipped back the cuff of her gloves and rubbed her chilled nose with the heel of her hand. "But at the same time she moans about the fact that I can't just up and go home."

"You could have gone home for Christmas if you wanted to," he reminded her. "Is she upset because you chose to stay here?"

"She doesn't know I had a choice," Kyle confessed. "It would have been cruel to tell her."

"I suppose that's true."

"Why is it so hard for people to understand that I want to experience more of the world before I lock myself on the farm?"

Tor's brows flew upward. "Lock yourself? That's a very strong statement,"

"I didn't mean locked like a prisoner," she deflected. "I just couldn't think of the right word."

"Freud would disagree."

Kyle threw a gloveful of snow at him. "You're impossible."

Tor chuckled and brushed the snow from the front of his coat. "So what did Erik send you for Christmas?"

Kyle sighed. "A card."

Tor looked surprised. "That's all?"

"Well, he signed it *love, Erik*," she said sarcastically. "What else could I possibly want?"

Tor's mouth worked like he was chewing up words instead of spitting them out.

"Oh just say it!" she huffed.

"Can I be honest?"

"You better be," she declared. "I can't imagine what I'd do if you ever lied to me."

A shadow crossed his face and his gaze dropped.

"What?" she demanded.

Tor put up his hands and seemed to change gears.

"It's nothing. Just that…" He looked at her again. "If you were my fiancée, I'd want you to be content with the life I could give you."

Her heart skipped. "And if I wasn't content?"

"Then I'm not the man for you."

CHAPTER SEVEN

"Come out with us tonight," Marguerite urged. "You need to get your mind off that hick up north."

"He's not a hick," Kyle grumbled. "He's a farmer. He owns his family's farm."

"Whatever you say." Marguerite turned away from their shared makeup mirror. "But he obviously doesn't realize what a catch you are. Maybe you should meet someone who does."

Flo was waiting for Marguerite, perched impatiently on the foot of her bed. She twiddled the cigarette Kyle forbade her to light in the room and giggled.

"What?" Kyle's glance bounced between Flo and Frances, who sat at the foot of Kyle's bed.

Frances shrugged, her expression mischievous. "We all wonder if you already have."

"Me?" Kyle scoffed. "Of course. That's why I'm engaged!"

"To a hick," Marguerite countered through pursed lips. She capped her lipstick and looked at Kyle again. "But you spend an awful lot of time with the Norse God."

"Oh, please." Kyle looked at the three women, appalled. "Is that what you call him?"

"We're not blind," Flo stated. "And I don't think you are

either."

Kyle felt her cheeks redden. "Yes. He's a very handsome man, I'll give you that."

Marguerite swung around in her chair to face Kyle. "And?" Kyle figured she knew what Marguerite was asking but still replied with, "And what?"

"And is he making advances?"

Kyle actually had to stop and think about that. Marguerite's question made her suddenly question every conversation she'd had with the captain.

"No."

"Are you sure?" Flo asked. "Because you don't look sure."

Florence wagged a pointed finger at her. "He decked that Maple guy when he harassed you last time we went out together."

Kyle waved the finger away. "He's a gentleman. He'd have done that for anyone."

"Maybe…" Marguerite said slowly. "Or maybe not."

Kyle scowled. "Don't be ridiculous."

"Why didn't you go home for Christmas?" Marguerite pressed.

"Because I was needed here," Kyle deflected.

"Needed by the N.G." Flo giggled again and leaned forward and spoke conspiratorially. "That's shorthand for Norse God."

"Yeah." Kyle mimicked her tone. "I got that."

"So N.G. one, hick zero." Marguerite grinned. "But if the captain doesn't do it for you—"

"Can I have him?" Frances blurted.

Flo reached over and smacked Frances on the knee. "What about Fred?"

Frances blushed. "He's a sexy flirtation. Same as Luddy and Gerry."

Kyle noticed Marguerite stiffen. Her roommate's expression hardened.

"Gerry is serious about me," Marguerite stated. "And I'm just as serious about him."

Flo looked at Marguerite like she was a child. "I'm sure you are, sweetie."

Marguerite scowled. "Don't talk to me in that tone. When the war's over we're going to get married."

Kyle looked at Marguerite. "Why are you waiting?"

"He's not free to—I mean his situation is—complicated," she stammered.

"Oh no," Kyle moaned. "Is he married?"

"No!" Marguerite paused as though the thought was a new one. "I don't think so."

"Let's be honest, girls." Flo sat up straighter. "We're all engaging in a little wartime fun for now, aren't we?"

Frances nodded resignedly.

Marguerite looked like she could strangle Flo.

"It's romantic and fun and it gives all parties involved a diversion from what's going on in the rest of the world." Flo patted Marguerite's arm. "And who knows. It could turn out to be true love in the end."

"It is," Marguerite insisted. "I love him and he loves me. I have the notes to prove it."

Frances scooted forward so her feet hit the floor beside Kyle's bed and she could see Marguerite clearly. "He wrote *I love you* in one of his notes?"

"He did." Marguerite lifted her chin. "And I wrote back that I loved him, too."

Why were they passing notes?

Is this high school?

"Has he said it to your face?" Kyle asked.

"Not yet." Marguerite drew a deep breath. "But I know he will."

Kyle made up her mind on the spot. "If you're meeting your guys tonight, then I'd rather stay home. No point in being a seventh wheel."

"Oh we're not," Frances blurted. "So do come."

"Are they on duty?" Kyle asked. "All three of them?"

The trio of nurses glanced at each other looking a little like trapped cats.

"To be honest..." Flo began. "They're more like pen pals at the moment."

"Pen pals?" Kyle was gobsmacked by the claim. "Have you actually met them?"

"Of course we have!" Marguerite snipped. "I'd never tell a man I loved him if I hadn't actually spoken to him face to face."

"So come with us," Flo urged, deflecting the direction of the conversation. "It'll do the N.G. good to show him you're not waiting for him."

"I'm *not* waiting for him," Kyle insisted. "I'm engaged."

"To a hick," Marguerite repeated.

Kyle's irritation bubbled up and spilled over. "He may be a hick in your eyes, Marguerite, but he's *my* hick. And he's *real*, and we're *engaged*."

"Our guys are real, too!" Frances stated hotly. "It's just that our futures aren't settled."

"Except for mine." Marguerite glared at her friend. "I'm marrying Gerry."

"Leave her alone, Fran," Flo stepped into the fray. "Gerry can certainly be serious about Marguerite, even if you and Fred aren't at that point yet."

"Let's just go. I need a drink." A somewhat placated Marguerite stood and looked down at Kyle. "So—are you coming?"

Kyle shook her head. "Thanks for the invitation, really, but I think I'll stay behind and write the hick a letter."

Marguerite shrugged. "Suit yourself."

The three nurses, all dressed to the nines, single-filed their way out of the room and shut the door behind them.

Kyle blew a sigh.

Now what do I say to Erik?

January 5, 1944

Kyle had never been so cold in her life. Turns out there was something very different about the cold here in the mountains from the cold in Minnesota. Maybe because Minnesota trees and lakes didn't radiate the same frigid conditions that the granite did.

Once that stone absorbed the chill, no amount of winter sun could coax all that cold back out. It was like living in a natural refrigerator at times.

But the sunny days in camp were miserable in their own way.

While the sun melted the thinner patches of snow and ice, its rays also reflected off the Camp Hale valley's white-covered walls, redoubling its efforts. The valley warmed surprisingly, but the heated air was trapped from above by the heavier frigid air that surrounded it.

And because the camp relied on burning coal for its primary source of energy, these winter air inversions held all the smoke and ash right over the camp, fouling the air.

That was decidedly not the case this morning. A nasty wind was blowing down the length of the valley from north to south. Kyle heard it buffeting her barracks as she dressed.

Her roommate Marguerite, who drew duty in the hospital last night, snuggled in her bed and pulled the blankets over her head. A mumbled *see you later* emanated from their depths.

Kyle's WAC-issued uniform matched the men's, down to her optional wool trousers. Someone somewhere realized that requiring the WACs to wear skirts in the camp's winter freezing temperatures—which dipped below zero degrees at night—wasn't the best idea.

Kyle zipped her trousers and sat on the edge of her bed to don her sturdy leather boots, glad for the heavy rubber tread on the soles which kept her from falling on the camp's icy paths. She pulled her knit cap down over her ears, grabbed her calf-length double-breasted wool coat from the hanger, and clomped out of the room.

At the door to her barracks she pulled on her gloves and wondered if she should brave the growing wind-sculpted snow drifts, or go back upstairs and get her bearpaws. Deciding she didn't really need the wood-and-mesh snow shoes quite yet, she wrapped her scarf around her face and stepped into the blast.

The world was still dark at seven in the morning as she trudged toward the motor pool, her first destination every day. When she reached her assigned jeep the first thing she did was start the engine. Once it turned over and hummed steadily, she lifted the hood and removed the heating kit that kept the engine from freezing during the night.

"You good to go this morning, Lieutenant?"

Kyle faced the chapped-faced private rubbing his hands together. "Yes, soldier. Thank you."

He gave her a casual salute and moved down the aisle to check on others.

There was a heater in the jeep, but it would only blow cold air at this point. Kyle sat inside the vehicle for a few minutes to allow the jeep's engine to wake up and settle in. Then she backed out of the assigned space and headed toward Tor's barracks.

Snow, which was riding the wind when she was walking to the motor pool, began to fall in earnest. Thick white flakes danced across her headlight beams in a frenzied horizontal formation.

It was still too dark to see the sky, but if the tops of the mountains were hidden by clouds there would be no skiing today. Weather like this made skiing so dangerous that even if similar conditions were met in the Italian Alps an attack would be delayed until visibility was restored.

Instead, the troops would probably practice cold-weather survival today, or maybe hold weapons practice. Or both.

Kyle drove the sturdy little jeep through the drifts that were shifting and settling across the camp's roads and slid to a stop in front of Tor's barracks door.

Moments later, the captain pulled the door open and ran down the four steps as if this was a delightful spring day.

"Good morning, Lieutenant," he practically chirped. "Isn't this a beautiful day?"

✴ ✴ ✴

Kyle glared at him. "Really?"

Tor laughed at her reaction. "I can't help it. I love snow."

"And mornings," she grumbled, slipping the jeep into gear.

"And mornings."

Tor always awoke before he needed to rise. He didn't mean to, it was just how his body functioned. He felt most alive in the morning. Ready to take on the world.

Kyle parked the jeep in front of the mess hall. The clouds above them were just beginning to lighten to a steely gray.

Tor stepped out of the jeep, ignoring the wind that whipped the hem of his coat around his legs and the snow that stung his eyes. He squinted at the mountains. He couldn't see their tops yet.

Kyle was already at the mess door. "You coming?"

Tor took big, leg-stretching strides toward her. "I guess we'll have to wait and see what the day brings us."

Kyle pulled the door open and Tor grabbed the edge, holding it while she entered in front of him.

The hall was slowly filling with sullen-looking soldiers. They knew that the snowstorm meant they would be training in dreadful conditions and none of them looked happy about it.

"You know what the troops call this place?" Tor asked Kyle.

She looked up at him. "The mess hall or the camp?"

He chuckled. "The camp."

"Tell me."

Tor grinned. "Camp Hell."

Kyle huffed a laugh. "How'd you learn that?"

Uh, oh.

"Torger told me."

"Oh. That's funny." Kyle smiled and walked to the food line. "And true, I guess. The training here is pretty intense."

Tor took a seat across the table from his platoon's co-leader, First Lieutenant Frank Collins. He nodded his greeting, saying *god morgen* which sounded like *good morn* in English.

Frank nodded back. "Morning, Captain."

He waited for Kyle to get settled then said, "Would you ask Collins if he thinks we could take a couple of M29 Weasels out today?"

Collin's head snapped up. "The Weasel?"

"Yes," Kyle confirmed. "Captain Hansen wonders if your platoon could use them for training today."

"And do some cross-country skiing and hiking with the

bearpaws," Tor added.

Kyle translated.

Collins' cheeks split into a wide grin. "That's a great idea. I'll talk to the motor pool as soon as I'm done."

"*Takk du!*" Tor's mood brightened even further.

"Did you understand him?" Kyle sounded suspicious.

"I understood his smile and his enthusiasm, of course," Tor deflected. "Did I respond incorrectly?"

"No. That was fine." She returned her attention to her breakfast.

I need to be more careful.

CHAPTER EIGHT

The soldiers in their platoon actually cheered when the three Weasels pulled up. The tank-bottomed vehicles were designed for snow operation, and though they only had three passenger seats each, Tor figured they could squeeze at least six soldiers onto the open-topped transports.

Lieutenant Collins gave the instructions for the men to report back immediately with skis, poles, and bearpaws. The plan, as Kyle translated to Lieutenant Collins, was to drive Tor's half of the platoon two miles from the center of the camp and drop them off.

Collins' half would ski and hike to the drop-off point, following the Weasels' tracks.

Tor's men would then ski and hike back to camp, and Collins' men would ride back in the Weasels.

The snowstorm had not let up at all, so the layer beneath their skis was dry and powdery in the freezing air. When Collins quizzed the men, they correctly answered that the blue wax was needed and set to waxing the bottoms of their steel-edged skis.

"This will be a good change of pace for our men, I think," Lieutenant Collins stated. "Tell Hansen I'm glad he thought of it."

Kyle did, then asked Tor, "What should I do?"

Tor considered that for a moment, but he didn't see a reason for her to do anything.

"Again, it's showing, not talking. I don't need you to be there."

Her relief was clearly evident. "Do you want me to wait here for you?"

Tor nodded. "That would be good. And still keep your radio on, just in case. It won't be as dangerous as downhill skiing, but you never know what trouble some fool like Kossin will find himself in."

Tor really liked the novice—who claimed he could ski so he'd be assigned to the Tenth—but the man had never touched a ski in his life before arriving here.

Kyle flashed a crooked smile. "You have to admire his determination."

Tor chuckled. "Well, you have to admire something, I guess."

N N N

Kyle watched Tor pile his men precariously onto the three Weasels and drive away.

When Collins' men were ready and lined up by twos, their bearpaws strapped to their heavy boots and their white skis and white poles resting on their shoulders, they began their march along the Weasels' tracks.

Kyle turned up her radio. "Testing. Testing."

Tor's voice crackled back. "Roger, Lieutenant."

"Ten-four."

And now I wait.

N N N

Tor's group reappeared an hour and a half later. Covered head-to-toe in white from the unending blizzard, Tor dismissed them for the day before climbing into the jeep with Kyle.

He tugged off his gloves and the liners underneath, dropping them into his lap and blowing on his hands to warm them.

"That was brutal. We were headed into the wind the whole way."

Kyle handed him a thermos of hot coffee and a cup. "I figured you'd need this when you got back."

God bless you. "Thanks."

"Do you want to wait for Collins to get back?"

"Yes." Tor held the coffee cup with both hands. The heat stung his fingers at first. "Has he been on the radio?"

As if in answer to his query, Kyle's radio came to life.

"Collins here."

Kyle pressed the button on her transmitter. "Go ahead."

"On our way."

"Roger that." She hung the transmitter back on the jeep's radio. "Shouldn't be too long."

Tor winked at her. "Did you bring him coffee, too?"

"Only if you don't drink it all." She winked back.

When the Weasels pulled into view, Tor heaved himself out of the jeep to talk to Collins with Kyle in tow. His men looked as done in as Tor's were.

"Tell him I dismissed mine for the rest of the day," he instructed Kyle.

She did.

"Good idea." Collins spat the words against the stubborn snow-laden wind. He barked the order to his relieved men before facing Tor again. "Can I hitch a ride?"

"Sure!" Kyle answered for him.

The three piled inside the snug little vehicle. Tor handed Collins the remaining coffee and the second cup Kyle brought with it. Kyle headed toward Collins' barracks.

The First Lieutenant leaned forward.

"Ask him if he wants to meet and discuss the last two weeks of training."

"Over a drink," Tor replied. "Officer's club after lunch?"

Collins nodded as Kyle eased to a stop in front of his barracks. "Great. See you at two."

When the officer exited, Kyle turned to Tor. "How'd Kossin do?"

"Amazingly well, actually. He's definitely better on the level than the slope."

As Kyle drove to the next building, she asked, "What's it like to ski?"

Tor stared at her. "You've never skied?"

She shrugged a little. "No."

"Not even on the level?" he clarified. "Cross country?"

Her gray-green eyes met his. "Nope."

He was shocked. When the jeep stopped at the front door to his barracks he turned to face her.

"I need to understand this," he began. "So let me back up."

"Okay." Kyle put the jeep in neutral but kept the engine, and consequently the heater, running.

"First of all, you speak Norwegian like a native."

Her cheeks pinkened, but not from the cold. "It was my first language. My grandparents insisted on it."

"Did they come from Norway?"

She nodded. "From Solbergelva. About thirty miles west of Oslo. They took Solberg as their surname because it was easier for Americans to say and spell than Schjelderup."

True. "So your parents spoke both Norsk and English."

"Yes."

"Did your grandparents bring Norse traditions with them?"

Kyle rolled her eyes. "Sure they did. Food, holiday traditions, bunads, and rosemåling."

"But not skiing."

Kyle's brow wrinkled apologetically. "I guess they saw all types of skiing as just methods of transportation that they no longer needed."

Tor leaned back in his seat.

Just a method of transportation?

Skiing was *life*. There was nothing in the world as exhilarating as racing down the side of a mountain, being one with the creature on whose back he rode.

Nothing.

He watched Kyle's reaction carefully as he spoke. "I guess we'll need to find a way to remedy that."

January 9, 1944

That very next Sunday—on the soldiers' day off—Tor tied two pair of skis and poles to the top of Kyle's jeep.

"I'll train you the way I train the men," he said once they were on their way to the bottom of Cooper Hill. "Start with the basics and move you ahead as you learn."

Kyle grinned as she maneuvered the jeep over the plowed-but-slippery camp roads. "I'm excited to learn."

Once parked, Tor hefted the two pair of skis over one shoulder. "Will you bring the poles?"

"Sure." Kyle pulled them off the jeep's roof.

He led her to the benches at the bottom of the hill. They sat side-by-side while he showed her how to strap the skis to her dual-purpose Army boots.

"How does that feel?" he asked once she was on her feet. He handed her a pair of white poles.

"Okay, I guess." She slipped the straps over her hands and looked down at the seven-foot-long pieces of flat, steel-edged hickory strapped to her boots. "I never realized they were so long."

Tor stood next to her on his skis, poles at the ready. "Everyone gets the same size, no matter how tall they are."

Kyle squinted up at his six-and-a-half feet. "Not too long for you, though."

Tor chuckled. "True." He grabbed his goggles. "Goggles on."

Kyle settled her standard-issue goggles—green-tinted glass lenses for ultraviolet, infrared, and glare protection—over her eyes.

She looks adorable.

Tor smiled at her. "They suit you."

She grinned back. "I feel like a soldier."

"You look like one. Now let's see if you can ski like one. Watch me and do what I do. First we walk."

Tor strode forward, lifting his skis slightly off the snow. Then he turned to watch Kyle.

She was having trouble lifting the skis—which were sixteen

inches longer than she was tall. After trying to take six steps and only moving forward about three feet, Tor decided to skip that skill.

"Never mind," he said. "Can you slide forward? Use the poles for leverage."

She was next to him in a blink. "Gosh, that's so much easier."

He nodded. "Let's do that then. Try to keep up with me."

They skied the length of the bottom of the hill together before Tor showed her how to do the about face maneuver.

Kyle imitated his effortless movements and promptly tumbled to the ground in a tangle of skis and poles.

Tor helped her up and she tried again.

"Damn!" she blurted as she fell backwards. "The skis are too long..."

Tor helped her up and eventually got her turned around. "There you are."

"So much for my fifth position comment," she groused. "It's harder than it looks."

"You got the gliding part without falling down," he reminded her. "That's better than many of my men."

She heaved a frosty, resolute breath. "Okay. What's next?"

Tor was impressed. "Next? We start climbing."

He immediately decided that the herringbone was too hard for her with the seven-foot skis, and he decided to try the one climb that did not require her to turn around.

"Do this."

He put his right ski a shoulder length higher on the side of the slope than his left ski. "Bring the other ski alongside it."

Kyle imitated his motion.

"It's easier to lift the skis sideways than forward," she stated, taking a second step.

"Good! Keep going."

Tor stayed downhill from Kyle and followed her upward path—in case she slipped he could halt her unintended descent.

"How far?" she asked.

Tor considered the slope. From the point they had reached, Kyle could ski a ten-yard diagonal to the bottom.

"Let's stop here. Now you watch me, and then do what I do."

Tor planted his poles. "Aim this direction." He angled his skis down forty-five degrees from the slope. "Keep your skis about shoulder's width apart and parallel to each other."

Kyle copied his position. "Like this?"

"Yes. Good. Now, bend your knees a little. The faster you go, the more bounce you need to be ready for."

She looked startled. "How fast am I going to go?"

"Not very, don't worry," he assured her. "Once I reach the bottom, use your poles to push off. Like this."

Tor glided down the slope and skied in a semi circle to face her. He called out, "Your turn."

"I can't turn like you did," she called back.

"I'm going to catch you." He motioned to her. "Come on."

What he could see of Kyle's expression was the definition of determination. She dug her poles into the snow in front of her and gave herself a heroic shove.

Crouched over her skis, poles tucked under her arms, Kyle looked like a comedic slow-motion pro. Tor reached for her when she got close enough and grabbed her waist to slow her down.

"Well done, Lieutenant!"

Kyle laughed, clearly delighted. "Do you grab all of your students around the waist?"

"Only the cute ones," he teased. "But truthfully, you've moved several lessons ahead already."

"Can we do it again?" she bubbled. "But from farther up?"

"Yes—after I show you how to slow down." Tor moved the tips of his skis together. "This is called a snowplow for obvious reasons. Next time do this when you reach the bottom, and see if you can stop yourself."

"Got it." Kyle glided to the bottom of the slope and started side-stepping up.

Tor followed, surprised by this version of Kyle Solberg. She was playful. Almost childlike in her enthusiasm.

He liked it.

A lot.

"That's far enough," he said when she was twice as high as before. "Now back away from the center of the run."

She did.

"Angle your skis toward me once I get down there."

"Okay."

"Look at me, Kyle."

Wide eyes peered up at him through green glass that stole their color. "Yes?"

"The angle will be steeper because you're higher up," he cautioned. "You'll be going faster. Don't forget to snowplow at the bottom."

She gave her head a little shake. "I won't."

Tor resettled his goggles and skied to the bottom of the hill, once again turning around to face her. "Are you ready?"

Kyle called down, "When do I learn how to turn?"

He laughed. "Next time. First get down here safely."

Kyle adjusted her goggles, planted her poles and pushed. She picked up speed as she descended.

"Snowplow!"

Kyle struggled to angle her skis.

"SNOWPLOW!"

She can't do it.

Tor skied directly into her path to grab her.

She slammed into him, knocking them both to the ground, and landing on top of him.

With a wide grin, she reached up and lifted her goggles. "That was amazing!"

Tor removed his goggles as well. "Are you all right?"

"I'm perfect! Did I hurt you?"

Tor was lying on his back in the snow, skis and poles askew, with a beautiful woman lying on top of him. There was only one response worth making.

Tor grabbed the sides of Kyle's head and pulled her into his kiss.

CHAPTER NINE

Kyle stared down at the prostrate man. "Why did you do that?"

"To see if you'd kiss me back."

And I did.

She struggled to extricate herself from the captain, the skis, the poles, and her deep embarrassment until she was finally free of the tangle and sitting in the snow beside him.

"I didn't mean to," she objected. "I just got caught up in the moment."

Tor sat up without visible effort. "So did I. You were so happy and excited. You were glowing."

She frowned, knowing the tightness in her cheeks had nothing to do with the cold air. "So you would've just kissed anyone at that moment."

"Kyle," he said softly. "What do you think?"

She huffed. "Does it matter, Captain Hansen?"

He laughed at that. "Can I be honest with you?"

She raised her arms a little and then punched her fists into the snow on either side of her. "Why do you always ask me that? Yes! Yes—be honest with me!"

"All right." He rested his hands on his knees. "You are an

intriguing woman, and I'm very attracted to you."

All of the queries Marguerite and her friends threw at her slammed into Kyle's chest. "I'm engaged."

It sounded feeble, even to her.

"So you say."

Say?

"I am!" she snapped. "You need to remember that!"

"Maybe you need to remember." Tor pointed at her with one brow lifted in accusation. "You kissed me back."

"I didn't *mean* to. Especially since..." She stopped.

His eyes narrowed. "Since what?"

If he wanted honesty, she was going to give it to him.

In spades.

"Especially since every unmarried female in the camp is sniffing after you—and even some of the married ones, too. They drool when you walk by. They flirt and pose and smile and—ugh! It's disgusting."

Tor's crooked grin proved he'd noticed.

"Look at you—gloating over it!" Kyle punched the snow again. "The last thing I want to be is another one of your conquests. Another notch on your headboard."

"Conquests?" The smile disappeared and Tor looked puzzled. "What do you think of me?"

"I think of you as a man, obviously. One the ladies call the Nordic God. One who has opportunities galore laid at his feet. Or in his bed." Kyle fought the lump in her throat that her own words prompted. "Who *wouldn't* take advantage of all of that?"

Tor glared at her, his expression thunderous.

The truth hurts, doesn't it.

He uttered one angry word. "Me."

Kyle's jaw dropped, incredulous. "Come on, Captain. Do you really expect me to believe that you've been celibate since you arrived here? Be honest."

Tor gave her the tiniest shake of his head. "No. I haven't been celibate since I arrived here."

Kyle felt a pain in her chest. "I knew it."

"I have been celibate since last March." His bright blue gaze pinned hers. "Eight months before arriving here."

Kyle felt a different kind of pain. She couldn't muster any words at the moment.

"I am almost thirty-one years old, Kyle." His voice was low and steady, making his words that much more intense. "I am not a randy little boy looking to dock in any available port. I've explored enough. I'm done with that."

Her voice was very small. "Oh."

"The next woman I take to my bed will be my wife."

"So you're not…"

"Exactly."

Kyle felt the chill of the snow seeping through her clothes. "I guess we're done for the day."

"I guess we are."

A scowling Tor unstrapped her skis first, and then his own. Kyle scrambled to her feet and brushed the snow off her damp trousers and ski coat. She was way too embarrassed to say anything just yet, but she knew she owed Tor a sincere apology.

She offered it once they were in the jeep and the motor was running.

"I really am sorry," she reiterated. "I made an assumption, and that wasn't fair."

"No, it wasn't." He sighed. "What makes me angry is that you thought so little of me."

"I'm sorry." Kyle's lips twisted. "But you did kiss me."

"And you kissed me back."

Stop reminding me.

"That was wrong of me. It wasn't fair to Erik."

※ ※ ※

Please don't talk about him.

That was Tor's own fault. He pushed her on the kissing incident.

"I don't know Erik," he said carefully. "But I don't think you should marry him until you're certain he can make you happy."

Kyle stared at him. "What are you suggesting?"

"Nothing," he back-peddled, thinking quickly.

I'm not planning to take his place.

"But we are in a unique situation, you and I. Thrown closely together for an unknown length of time. And we've become friends. Haven't we?"

Kyle nodded soberly.

"I can't make plans with anyone—least of all you," he continued, making it up as he spoke. "And you already have plans with someone else."

"I do."

"So what if we shared an affectionate friendship?" he suggested, wondering of such a thing was even possible.

She looked skeptical. "*How* affectionate, exactly."

"The occasional hug. Maybe a kiss now and again. Just... comforting each other." That actually sounded nice. "Be a safe harbor for each other in this world gone mad."

"But no docking in anyone's port." One side of Kyle's mouth lifted. "Right?"

Tor chuckled. "Right."

Kyle chewed her lip. "I'd have to think about it."

Another thought occurred to him. "Maybe you could be my protection. Against all the sniffing, flirting, and posing."

Now she looked startled. "You mean kiss and hug in public so people think we're connected?"

Tor put up his hands. "Only if you're agreeable."

He could practically see the gears turning in her mind.

"As a favor." She chewed her lip again. "I could probably go along with that more readily than the other thing."

"Think about it. In the meantime, I do have another favor to ask. One that relates to your job."

"Ask me while we drive back." Kyle backed up and turned toward camp. "I'm freezing."

After he heard the German soldiers' esoteric conversation, Tor hadn't been able to get their words out of his mind. He'd made a transcript from memory, just in case he found out more. But even though he snuck back several times after that night, he never caught anyone discussing any plans again.

Three weeks had passed since he overheard the man say six more weeks and Tor figured his luck was running out.

Tor waited until they were halfway to the supply depot to

turn in Kyle's borrowed skis before he said, "I need you to tell Jones that I speak German."

Kyle slid the jeep to a stop, nearly killing the engine before she clutched, and turned to stare at him. "You do?"

"Yes."

Her eyes widened as her brows lowered. "Why does he need to know?"

"Because I overheard some of the prisoners talking."

"When?"

"Three weeks ago."

"Three weeks?" she yelped. "Why didn't you say something sooner?"

"Because they were being cryptic and the information was vague." He twisted in his seat to look at her. "I snuck back at night four or five times since then, but wasn't able to hear any more. But they said something about six weeks."

"Three weeks ago?"

"Yes."

Kyle shifted into first gear and turned the jeep toward Headquarters. "We're going now."

"I thought you were freezing."

"It's always overheated in there," she replied without looking at him. "I'll be fine."

N N N

They waited over half an hour to see the Major General who, because it was a Sunday, was catching up on correspondence and wasn't accepting any appointments. By then Tor's clothes were dry and both he and Kyle had shed all of their outer ski clothing.

"The General will give you ten minutes," the uniformed soldier at the desk said when Tor and Kyle were summoned to enter the office. "Make it brief."

Jones scribbled quickly on a paper in front of him and seemed irritated at the interruption as Kyle and Tor approached his desk. He asked, "How can I help you, Lieutenant?" without looking up.

"Captain Hansen has something important to tell you, Sir."

The general's head popped up and he fixed his gaze on Kyle. "Yes?"

"He wants you to know that he speaks German and he overheard two POWs making plans."

Jones looked at Tor. "What sort of plans."

Tor almost answered instead of waiting for Kyle to translate the question but caught himself. Barely.

"Tell him this is what I heard."

She did.

"The first man said six more weeks," Tor began. "The second man asked why so long?"

When the general didn't respond, Tor continued quoting. "He said his contact is slow to answer."

Kyle translated.

"Then the second man asked, are we sure we can trust him? And he said, what choice do we have?"

Major General Jones stared at Tor for a moment before barking, "Anything else?"

Tor kept his eyes on the general. "Tell him that was three weeks ago, so whatever they were planning is three weeks from now."

Jones nodded. "Thank you. I'll talk to my advisors."

Tor glanced at Kyle. "Is that all?"

She addressed the general. "Thank you, Sir."

"Dismissed."

Tor wanted to say something else, but he couldn't think of what. So he saluted, turned on his heel, and followed Kyle from the office.

"That was disappointing."

She handed him his coat, speaking flatly. "I'd say so."

Frustrated, Tor wrapped his scarf around his neck and demanded, "Well do you think he'll *do* anything?"

Kyle glanced toward the secretary who watched them curiously, and Tor immediately understood her reserve.

"I'm sorry," he said calmly and lifted his shoulders in and exaggerated shrug. "We'll talk outside."

Kyle gave him a tight-lipped smile and addressed the secretary. "Thank you for getting us in."

"You're welcome." The man pointed at Tor with his chin. "Those Norwegians get worked up don't they?"

Kyle looked up at Tor, who struggled not to react to her translation.

"Let's just call it stubborn," she answered.

"You're Norwegian, too," Tor reminded her.

Kyle smiled sweetly. "But he wasn't talking about me, was he?"

✯ ✯ ✯

After the disappointing audience with Major General Jones, Tor was determined to find out more about what the German prisoners were planning. That night he dressed in his white ski clothes and turned his reversible parka inside out so he would blend in with the snow. He also decided to wear his small emergency snowshoes so he wouldn't sink in the snow but would be able to move quickly if needed.

Under a faint crescent moon he walked slowly toward the POW enclosure, stopping often so he didn't draw attention if his movement was visible.

When he reached the far side of the fence, at the edge of the camp, he squatted behind a rock and waited.

An hour passed.

He shifted his body to a different position.

Another hour passed.

Tor faced the camp, watching for anyone approaching the enclosure as much as listening for conversation on the still and frigid night.

After a third hour, he was too cold and stiff to remain any longer. He stood slowly and retraced his path away from his hiding spot.

Voices ahead of him made him stop. He stepped behind a tree that didn't completely conceal him and stood absolutely still.

The voices were female.

What were women doing out here this late at night?

He slid a little to his left so he could see the barbed-wire-topped fence. There was movement inside the enclosure.

Three dark-clothed figures stepped up to the fence from the outside. Whoever they were, they hadn't been issued the white camouflage kit.

Or they're too stupid to know to wear it.

A huddle of figures appeared on the inside of the fence. Tor couldn't hear words from this far away, but snippets of definite conversation wafted to him on the frozen air. Something small was being exchanged through the spaces in the chained fence.

After a quarter of an hour at the most, the three females turned back and silently traipsed through the knee-high snow toward the camp.

Tor watched the huddle of prisoners split into three separate bodies who headed in three different directions.

In case one gets caught.

That was a common tactic.

Tor eased himself from his second hiding place and began his own slow return, his mind full of questions.

Did the three women have anything to do with the first conversation he'd heard?

If so, what?

And if not, was there another plot at hand?

The worst thing about witnessing what he had was that he couldn't identify any one of the people involved—on either side.

And I'm not running to Jones with another half-baked story, that's for certain.

His only option seemed to be discovering who these three women were. They were part of the camp, obviously. But which part? Kyle told him there were two hundred and some-odd women stationed at Camp Hale.

How could he ever pick three obscure needles out of such a large haystack?

CHAPTER TEN

January 13, 1944

In order to build camaraderie, at least that was the official explanation, the officer in charge of education and information decided that Tor should give a Norwegian Culture lecture.

"We have soldiers here from Norway, Denmark, and Sweden," he told Kyle. "It's interesting to our American soldiers to learn about our Scandinavian brother-in-arms."

"Can't Tokle do it?" Tor grumbled.

Kyle asked. Tor heard the answer, but waited for her to translate. "Apparently, he already did. But you're new since then and so are the recruits."

Tor sighed. "When?"

And that was how he found himself standing in front of a pair of microphones at a podium in the Rec Center the next night after supper.

His own sixteen trainees were present because he commanded them to be. There was nothing worse than throwing a lecture and no one showing up.

Frank Collins was also there with about a dozen members of the more skilled half of their shared platoon. And to Tor's surprise at least twenty other soldiers wandered in—including

Torger Tokle.

"Why are you here?" he asked the ski-jumper.

"Moral support." Tokle grinned. "Don't be boring."

Boring?

At that moment, Tor changed his mind about what he'd talk about.

He leaned over and said to Kyle, "Let me know if I go too fast for you. I just changed my speech. I'm not following the notes."

Concern furrowed her brow. "What are you going to do?"

"Educate," he replied. "Isn't that the point?"

"How—"

Tor stepped up to one of the microphones and started talking. "How many of you know what is happening in Norway with regards to the war?"

Kyle spoke into the second mike. "Our speaker tonight is Captain Tor Hansen of the Norwegian Army. Captain Hansen qualified for the nineteen-forty Olympics in downhill skiing. He is at Camp Hale as an adjunct and ski expert."

She paused and waited for the polite applause.

Tor nodded his acknowledgement. "Okay. Now that the formality is done, repeat my question."

When she did, the soldiers in the audience looked at each other as if wondering who might answer that.

When no one did, Tor flashed a grim smile. "Well let me tell you."

For the next quarter hour, Tor explained how the neutral Norway was subdued by five simultaneous German attacks on her major port cities and occupied the country in a matter of hours. He told them that King Haakon the Seventh escaped to England along with his son, Crown Prince Olav, and the government ministers.

"The best part, they were smart enough to bring the gold reserves with them." Tor smiled. "Norway has the best-funded resistance of all the occupied countries."

Encouraged by the attention he was being paid, Tor shifted to the traitorous Minister-President Vidkun Quisling. He explained how his own younger brother had been arrested and sent to a labor camp in the Arctic Circle.

"These men were teachers!" Tor nearly shouted. "They weren't trained for the dangerous work. And they were housed in cardboard-walled huts. In the Arctic."

"Is he still there?" a soldier called out.

Tor waited for Kyle's translation then answered, "No. The attempts to subdue the teachers failed and they were all sent home before the harshest part of winter set in. They were considered national heroes."

Tor turned to Kyle. "Ask if they have any other questions."

She did.

"Is he in the army, too?"

"He's a member of the Military Organization, Milorg for short," Tor explained. "He's an officer in the resistance."

"What did your brother teach?"

Tor slid his gaze to Kyle. "What difference does that make?"

"I don't know." She tried to look unfazed. "Was it science?"

"Secondary school chemistry."

Kyle translated his answer.

"Why didn't Norway fight back when they were invaded?"

Tor felt his national pride surge. "Because we were neutral, jackass. We weren't prepared."

Kyle left out the jackass part.

"But after that," the jackass pressed.

Tor was getting irritated. "What the hell do you think resistance is? Playing patty-cake with the Nazis?"

Kyle hesitated. "He said… that the resistance is… effective against the Nazis."

Tor looked at his translator. "What are you doing?"

"You can't say those things."

"Why not?"

"It's not polite."

"Polite?" Tor resisted pointing at the jackass, one of the random soldiers attending that night. "He's an idiot."

Kyle glanced at the offending soldier. "Even if he is."

Tor turned back to look at his audience. Several were smirking. He'd bet they knew Kyle was softening his answers;

they had to hear the tone of his voice even if they didn't understand his words.

"What does effective mean?" Clearly the jackass was not going to let go. "How many Nazis has your brother killed?"

Okay, buddy. You want to play bait the Norseman? Here goes.

"More than you, I guarantee it dumbass."

Kyle forced a smile. "He's not sure."

"But he has killed Nazis, right?"

Tor nodded. "Oh, sure. At least five before breakfast every morning."

Kyle glared at him. "Yes. But the Captain doesn't have an exact number."

Tor noticed that Torger Tokle's shoulders were shaking and he had his hand in front of his face.

"In fact…"

Kyle groaned. "Don't."

Tor grinned at her. "In *fact*, he built bombs and rigged them to blow up desks when the Nazi bastards opened the drawers."

Kyle's glare grew more intense. "Why are you doing this?"

"Translate it," Tor said. "That part is completely true."

"No…"

Tor put his hand on his heart. "Swear to God. I was in Bergen when one blew up. Now translate all of that."

She did.

The soldiers whooped their approval.

All except for Private Jackass. "I don't believe that. That's story's ridiculous."

Tor stepped out from behind the podium.

"Don't, Tor," Kyle warned. "Remember where you are."

Tor looked back and smiled at her. "I know."

He sauntered toward the private, who nervously straightened in his chair. "What are you doing?"

"I'm giving you an education," Tor said calmly.

Kyle translated that from the podium.

The private made a face. "By making up shit?"

"No." Tor kept his tone cool and his half-smile in place. "By showing you how to act toward someone who has more brains in his trousers than in his head."

Torger laughed so hard at that he fell off his chair.

The soldiers' attention bounced from Tor to Kyle to Torger and back.

"What'd he say?" several asked.

Kyle sputtered, "By—by showing the, um, private how to, uh, act…"

"How to act?" Jackass squeaked. "What the hell?"

Encouraging laughter erupted around Tor. He wasn't ready to let this go. Not by a long shot.

He leaned over the now-cowering private. "You, sir, are an ignorant ass. If I was your commanding officer I'd house you with the mules so you'd feel right at home."

The entire audience turned their heads back toward Kyle, expectant and eager.

She shook her head. "I—I can't."

Torger climbed to his feet. "But I can!"

Chairs clanked and rumbled as everyone present spun around to face the instructor in the back of the room.

Torger translated word for word.

The room exploded.

N N N

"I think that went well."

Kyle stopped walking and threw her arms out to the side. "Are you serious?"

Tor stopped as well and looked back at her. "It was educational. That was the point, right?"

She clapped her hands on her head. "You're impossible!"

"Not only that, but it was entertaining as well." Tor pointed a finger at her. "You have to admit it."

"Entertaining for you, sure." Kyle was so angry she was afraid she'd cry. "But what about me?"

Tor took a step toward her. "You?"

"Did you ever, even for one tiny little moment, stop to think about the position you put me in?" Kyle's body shook with rage.

"You mean translating?"

"Yes, translating, you thick Nordic ox!" She threw her hands wide again. "How can you expect me to stand there and repeat all those insulting things?"

Tor looked half confused, half contrite. "But they aren't your words. They're mine."

"But they're coming out of *my* mouth! Ugh!" Kyle stomped past Tor and marched angrily toward her barracks.

"Kyle, wait."

She jammed her hands in her coat pockets. "Leave me alone."

He didn't. She heard his boots crunching through the snow behind her.

When his words reached her they were gentle. "I've never had a translator before."

"Have you ever had a brain before?" she grumbled.

He sighed. "I guess I deserve that."

"Yes, you most certainly do." Kyle stopped about five yards from her barracks—close enough for the light to show Tor's face, but far enough from the door that their heated conversation wouldn't draw attention.

She turned to look at him. "You owe me an apology. A big one. *Sir.*"

The handsome planes of Tor's face were sculpted in shadow by the light over the barracks's door. In his somber mood he looked more vulnerable than she had ever seen him. And that made him even more attractive.

Kyle felt a dangerous rush of warmth toward the errant officer.

Keep your head on straight, Lieutenant.

"I'm waiting."

Tor took a step closer. "You're right."

She lifted her chin. "Go on."

"Never, not even for one tiny little moment, did I stop to think about the position I put you in."

Her brows plunged. "Are you mocking me?"

"No, not at all." He crossed his heart. "I'm very, very sorry, Kyle. And I ask you to forgive my behavior." He wagged his head slowly. "I was being just as big a jackass as that private."

Kyle drew a deep breath. "Well. Maybe."

"Maybe what?" Tor tilted his head. "Maybe you'll forgive me?"

"No. Maybe you were as big a jackass." She lifted one shoulder in a partial shrug. "Maybe not quite. He did start it."

Tor took another step closer. "Am I forgiven?"

"That depends." Kyle crossed her arms. "Do you promise not to do ever it again?"

The captain hesitated. "I'm not sure..."

Her mood, which had been lifting, dropped again. "What do you mean by that?"

"I mean there are times when I just need to say what's on my mind." He looked sincerely apologetic. "Every man does, Kyle. It's part of what makes us men. We can't always dance around ugly situations with pretty words."

Damn it.

He's right.

"I understand that," she offered. "But when that happens, can you please give me something else to say? I feel like an idiot scrambling for appropriate words when people are waiting and staring at me."

Tor nodded. "That's fair. Of course."

"In that case, I forgive you. But just tell me one thing." She closed the remaining gap between them. "The exploding desks? Was that really true?"

Tor smiled crookedly. "Completely. My brother was asked to use his chemistry knowledge to create a bomb, and then figure out a way to detonate it by opening or closing the center drawer."

"Huh." Kyle shivered a little.

"You're cold."

She nodded. "You know how you feel after something intense happens. Sort of drained."

Tor wrapped his arms around her and she let him. She rested her head on his shoulder, feeling protected and cared for—not at all what she'd felt a quarter hour before.

"I don't want to fight with you," she murmured.

"And I don't want to fight with you either." He sighed and

she felt his chest expand and shrink against hers. "There is the one thing, though."

"Hm?" She closed her eyes and relaxed in his grip. "What?"

"Making up." She slid her arms around his waist and hugged him. "Like this?"

"No." His gloved fingers slipped under her chin and tilted it upward so she was looking into his eyes. "Like this."

Tor's lips claimed hers. The kiss was soft and exploring to begin with. When she responded, it deepened. His tongue moved with hers in a sensuous waltz, one which swept her outside of herself.

Erik had never kissed her like this.

Kyle couldn't open her eyes at first when Tor ended the kiss. But when she heard someone giggle, they flew open.

"Congratulations, Second Lieutenant Solberg." The voice was her roommate's.

A beaming Marguerite passed them on her way into the barracks. "Well done."

Tor grinned down at her. "Two birds killed with one delicious kiss."

For a split second, Kyle wondered if Tor kissed her just because he knew there would be a witness. "Is anyone else coming?"

He looked around. "I don't see anyone."

"Good."

This time, she kissed him.

CHAPTER ELEVEN

Kyle threw her coat on her bed along with her scarf and gloves and sat on the wooden desk chair in front of the desk that she and Marguerite shared. As she opened the drawer to get out paper and pen, the refrain *what are you doing* played over and over in her head.

"I'm writing to Erik," she said aloud. "The man I love. The man I'm going to marry."

I am *going to marry him.*
When my enlistment ends.
Thirteen more months.

Kyle drew a steadying breath and shoved Tor and his decadent kisses out of her mind. She closed her eyes and thought about Erik's farm instead.

She pictured herself walking through his front door. The living room was on her right—she saw a cozy fire burning and smiled. The dining room was on the left and filled with Erik's grandmother's big Victorian table and chairs. The kitchen was beyond that, clean and bright with a little wooden table under the window. The bedrooms were upstairs.

And there was Erik, coming in from his labors and removing his boots and coat in the mudroom. His dark mop of hair was perpetually falling forward in the most charming way. His blue eyes were darker than Tor's—*stop it*—and Kyle hoped their children would inherit Erik's blue, not her gray-green. Erik's smile was slow to come and more than a little shy. It took him three months of casual conversations after the Lutheran church services before he got up the nerve to ask her on a date. But he took her out to dinner every week after that.

After a year, they began talking about their future, and the next Christmas he made it official with a small diamond ring that belonged to his father's mother.

Kyle opened her eyes and looked at her naked finger. She knew how much that ring meant to the Olsen family so she purposely left it behind when she joined the WAC. Erik was angry when she told him, saying that all the soldiers would think she was unattached.

"I'll *tell* them I'm engaged, Erik," she repeated every time he mentioned it. "I just can't risk anything happening to it."

When she got to basic training, she was glad she made that choice. She would've needed to remove the ring and leave in her kit everyday, and if it didn't get stolen, it easily could have gotten lost.

She wrote him and told him that.

He wrote back and said that if she hadn't enlisted, she wouldn't need to worry about it.

Oh, Erik.

Kyle stared at the blank paper in front of her. What should she write to him about tonight?

The culture lecture. And the questions Tor was asked. And his answers. And how hard it was for her to translate and be civil at the same time. And how angry she was.

With a resigned sigh, Kyle knew she couldn't write all that. In the first place, she kept the Norwegian captain out of her letters whenever possible. After writing about him when he first arrived, Erik's reply was blatantly jealous.

That was completely understandable. And he hadn't even seen the man.

Stop it.

Kyle also had to refrain from including too much about any

negative experiences she might have because Erik wasn't at all sympathetic. He used those as opportunities to remind her that she chose to enlist and move away.

And so a letter just about the culture lecture, including what Tor said about Norway's occupation, would have to do. Kyle pulled the end off the cartridge pen, put the date in the top right hand corner and wrote *Dear Erik*.

Tor's words flooded her brain: *Can I be completely honest with you?*

Kyle laid the pen down.

January 14, 1944

Tor needed to talk to his sixteen trainees so he told Kyle she needed to come with him to the base of the mountain. She stood next to him near the T-bar lift and the soldiers stood in a half-circle in front of them. She translated his words efficiently, and he didn't throw any surprises at her this morning.

"Men," Tor began. "We have just one week left until the ski tests which will determine whether you are accepted into the Tenth Division."

"What if we don't pass?" Kossin asked.

Tor shrugged. "Then you get to see my smiling face six days out of seven for another eight weeks."

The men groaned.

Kyle snickered.

Tor ignored that. "Today we go to into the high peaks. We'll be at thirteen thousand feet elevation. And you know that the weather there means we might be in the clouds, so let's get going while it's still clear."

He turned to Kyle. "Thank you."

"You're welcome." She smiled faintly. "I'll see you when you're done."

She saluted him and then headed back to the parked jeep. Tor watched her go, wondering how she was feeling about him this morning.

He honestly hadn't noticed that anyone was approaching last

night when he kissed her. He just really wanted to kiss her. Needed to.

The fact that Marguerite saw them together was a happy coincidence. Tor figured his assumed romance with his translator would spread through the WAC ranks fairly quickly, and then he would stop being a target for every lonely woman in the camp.

Fingers crossed.

The second kiss—the one Kyle initiated—was startling, to say the least. The deep passion she displayed aroused him more than he thought a kiss could, and that arousal moved through his thoughts and his body for the rest of the evening.

He assumed she was a virgin, of course. Kyle didn't strike him as the sort of woman who would jump ahead of the wedding, especially living in a small town where everyone was in each other's pockets. But he thought that the man who did finally bed her was going to be one lucky bastard.

Too bad it'll be Erik.

Tor couldn't help thinking that Kyle was destined for bigger and better things than life on a farm in Viking, Minnesota.

N N N

Thankfully the weather cooperated. Tor stood near the top of the run and watched through binoculars as his men skied past him one at a time down the slope. From his vantage point, he could watch them push off, ski down to him, and then make the curve to the left. From there he could watch them for another hundred-and-fifty yards.

When a soldier disappeared from his sight, he waved for the next man to start his descent.

Tor knew his men well, so he knew which ones were going to pass the test—and which ones weren't. Today he was making mental notes to give the strugglers some last-chance instructions in the hopes they might improve during the final week.

He looked up to see who was next.

Kossin.

Tor really liked the boy. He was always eager and never complained. Even his confession that he thought joining the ski division would be light duty was amusing.

Once Kossin realized what he was actually in for though, he'd squared his shoulders and buckled on his skis. If trying was all it took, this guy would earn flying colors.

Tor raised his arm.

Kossin settled his goggles in place, crouched, and used his poles to get started. He grinned when he skied past Tor.

Tor watched him descend, wondering what advice would best help the gangly soldier, when something went terribly wrong.

Kossin began to flail his arms, losing his balance. He tumbled over and rolled into the trees that lined the run.

And he didn't get up.

Skitt.

Without hesitating, Tor shouted to the men waiting above him. "Radio the base! Kossin's hurt! Have the medics meet me at the bottom!"

When they just stared at him, he shouted, "NOW!"

"Yes, sir!"

He pushed off and skied down to the soldier who still hadn't moved.

What he saw was bad.

Kossin's left leg was impossibly twisted below the knee, and he was unconscious and bleeding from the head.

I'll have to ski him down.

"Oh, God."

Tor turned to find two of his men had followed him down. They stared at Kossin, white-faced.

"I need to take off his skis," he barked while he knelt on his to undo the bindings. "I need his belt and one of yours."

"Yes, sir." One soldier—Smith—was unbuckling his belt.

The second man, Graves, dug through the layers of Kossin's clothes to find his belt, but gave up and yanked his own off.

"Use mine, sir."

"Thanks."

Tor laid Kossin's ski poles on either side of the twisted leg.

"We need to keep this leg from moving. Smith, buckle your belt around his thigh. I'll do his ankle." He pointed to Graves.

"Look in his eyes. Tell me if his pupils react."

Tor wrapped the belt around Kossin's ankle and the two poles to hold the leg in place. "What do you see, Graves?"

"His pupils are contracting, sir."

"Good." Tor stood, turned around, and squatted with his back to Kossin. "Get him on my back."

Smith and Graves lifted Kossin and draped one arm and his uninjured leg over Tor's shoulders. Tor gripped Kossin's wrist and ankle and settled the bleeding and unconscious private across his back.

"Help me up."

Each of them grabbed Tor's upper arm and lifted him high enough that he could get leverage to stand.

"You two can follow me down."

"What about your poles, sir?" Graves asked.

Tor shook his head. "Don't need 'em."

ᚾ ᚾ ᚾ

Summoned by the emergency call, Kyle skidded to a halt and bolted from the jeep before the cut engine stilled. She ran through the snow to the base of the mountain and squinted up the run.

The ambulance was already there. Four medics stood by, waiting.

When Tor skied into sight, the injured man draping heavily over his shoulders, she gasped. The captain had no poles. He held the injured man by the wrist and ankle, and skied with the power and precision that proved he was a champion.

Two soldiers trailed behind him, moving with the caution of novice skiers.

When he reached the bottom, Tor didn't snowplow to slow down like he taught her. Instead he turned his skis parallel to the base and dug the uphill edges in, sending up a frozen spray of white as he stopped.

The medics were on him instantly, easing the soldier off his back and onto a stretcher. Kyle's stomach clenched when she saw the man's twisted leg.

"What happened?" she asked Tor, her voice tense.
He looked at her, obviously startled.
"I got the call to come meet you," she explained. "When the emergency was radioed down."
"Oh. Good. That's good." He shook his head as if to clear his thoughts. "I saw him take a bad fall from higher up. I don't really know what happened."
Tor pointed to the radio. "Can you ask him to send the rest of my men down? We're done."
She did.
He waited there, not speaking to anyone, until all his men were accounted for.
Then he told Kyle, "I want to go to the hospital."
"There's blood all over the back of your coat, Captain."
Tor shrugged out of the parka. Steam from his heated body rose in the freezing air, but he seemed unfazed by the chill. He held up the coat and looked at the streaks of blood that ran down its length.
"*Skitt.*"

ⁿ ⁿ ⁿ

Kyle took Tor to his barracks to get his long woolen coat before she dropped him at the hospital. Then she took his parka to the laundry to see if they could get the blood out or if he would need the reversible parka replaced.

While she waited, the image of Tor effortlessly skiing down the mountain with the unconscious man slung across his back played over and over on her mind's screen.

He was so strong. So skilled. She glimpsed for the first time the champion that he truly was. Champion, and hero.

"You should have seen him, Lieutenant," Private Smith gushed when she returned to the hospital waiting room, Tor's new parka in hand. "He had us take off our belts and he strapped the poles to Kossin's leg like a pro."

"He didn't even blink, I don't think." Private Graves looked awestruck. "He knew exactly what to do."

"I imagine this isn't the first skiing accident he's seen," she

posited.
Smith wagged his head. "No ma'am. I reckon not."
Tor appeared in the doorway looking completely wrung out. He spoke Norwegian, but looked intently at Privates Smith and Graves, not at her. "He's in surgery. The doctor thinks he can save the leg, but it means weeks in traction."
Kyle translated.
The two privates nodded solemnly.
"Yes, sir."
"We understand, sir."
"Good." Tor did face Kyle then. "Is that my parka?"
"Yep. Your *new* parka." She held it up. "They said if they can get the blood out, you can keep both."
"Thanks." Tor rubbed his face with both hands. "Can you take me to my barracks? I want to change clothes and then come back."
Kyle knew that the captain was probably in the throes of an adrenaline crash. "How about a cup of coffee, too?"
He smiled faintly. "That sounds good."

CHAPTER TWELVE

January 15, 1944

Someone was shaking his shoulder. Tor opened his eyes and bolted upright on the couch.

Waiting room.

Right.

Standing in front of him were Smith, Graves, and the three other soldiers from his training group who were still at the top of the run when Kossin crashed.

He looked at his watch. It was one o'clock in the morning. Twelve hours since the accident. Why were they here?

"We need to talk to you, sir." Smith's expression was sober.

Tor stretched and looked around the otherwise empty room. "She's not here."

Tor recoiled a little and stared up at the five men. Had Kossin died?

"We won't beat around the bush," Smith said. "We know you speak English."

Tor was relieved that the injured soldier was still with this world, even if *he* was about to be metaphorically executed.

Tor pointed at some chairs. "Sit."

He hadn't meant to speak in English on the mountain; it was

a reflex. He needed to be understood when Kossin was hurt, so he started barking orders in that language without thinking about the consequences.

The truth was that until Kyle asked him in Norsk *hva skjedde*—what happened—that he realized which language he had used.

The five soldiers pulled their chairs close and huddled around him.

"Here's what we figured," Graves said, his voice low. "You showed up here and the army automatically gave you a translator. Didn't ask if you needed one. Just assigned one. Right?"

Tor nodded slowly.

Smith leaned forward. "So you take a good look at her and think, what's the harm in keeping her around? Yeah?"

Tor shrugged a little.

"So here's the thing," Smith continued. "You saved our buddy Kossin's life up there. You fixed him up real quick and got him down the mountain faster than I've ever seen anybody ski."

Graves looked gobsmacked. "Me and Smith couldn't even keep up with you."

"And you did it with that lunkhead on your back."

The other three men nodded their agreement.

"Wish I coulda seen it," the radio tech said.

Smith waved his hands. "Anyway, we all talked it over, and we made a decision."

Tor frowned, worried about what was coming next. "What decision?"

Smith sat back and folded his arms across his chest, grinning like the Cheshire cat. "We're gonna keep your secret."

Tor looked at each man in turn. "What's the catch?"

"No catch, Captain," the radio tech said. "It's our way of thanking you for all you've done."

"Yeah, you've been so patient with poor Kossin," Graves observed. "Hell, you've been patient with all of us, sir."

"None of us would still be here if it wasn't for you, sir."

Smith was still smiling. "And Second Lieutenant Solberg—

we gotta be honest, sir—she does brighten our days when she's around. I imagine you know what I mean."

Tor looked at each of the earnest faces in front of him. Could he trust them?

Did it matter? He'd blown his own cover. They were under no obligation to maintain it, and they weren't getting anything in return for doing it.

"Thank you," he said finally. "I appreciate this very much."

"We appreciate you, sir."

"And the other eleven of you grunts have no idea?" he clarified.

All five shook their heads. "No, sir."

"Besides," Graves said. "It's only for another week. Most of us will be moving on."

"That's true..." *This could work.*

"So that's what we came to tell you." Smith stood up and yawned. "Let's go."

"You coming, Captain?" the radio tech asked.

Tor shook his head and rose stiffly from the couch. "Not yet. I'm going to check in on Kossin again. I'll see you tomorrow."

Each of the five men extended a hand. When Tor shook them, every man said, "You have my word."

N N N

Kossin looked bad.

His hair was shaved around a ragged gash that was stitched together by black thread. Both of his eyes were swollen and underscored in vivid purple and red.

The soldier had been in surgery for several hours while the doctors realigned his broken tibia and fibula, and then ran long steel pins through them to keep them in place.

Now Kossin slept with the head of his bed raised and his right leg in traction, suspended in an impressively complex web over his hospital bed.

Tor took a chance in the ward full of sleeping men and lifted Kossin's medical chart from the foot of the bed. He opened the aluminum folder and started to read:

Severe concussion.
Scalp laceration, five inches.
Spiral fracture of the right tibia and fibula.
"What are you doing?"

Tor jumped. He hadn't heard the nurse enter the room.

She marched toward him, radiating her irritation. "You aren't supposed to be reading that."

Tor faced her and held out the folder. "*Spiralformet? Spiral formasjon?*"

"What? What are you trying to say?" She grabbed the chart but he held on and pointed to the words *spiral fracture*.

"Oh!" Her eyes widened with realization and she considered him with a different sort of interest. "You must be that Norwegian skier that everybody's been talking about today."

They've been talking about me?
Why?

He dipped his chin a little. "*Kaptein* Hansen."

She saluted him with her free hand. "Nurse Warren, sir."

Tor tapped at the chart again and continued the ruse, lifting his brows in question.

"Spiral fracture." She frowned. "What did you say?"

He refrained from heaving an annoyed sigh and spoke slowly. "*Spiral formasjon.*"

She nodded, her brows tugged together in thought. "Yes, I think that's probably the same thing."

Tor pointed to the word *laceration*. The Norsk word *sårskader* was too dissimilar for him to pretend to understand the English.

"Laceration." Nurse Warren traced Kossin's scar on her own head.

Tor nodded and pointed at *concussion*. There was no way he could get to the English word from *hjernerystelse*.

"Concussion." Nurse Warren mimed hitting herself in the head as she spoke. "That's a hard blow to the head."

Tor nodded and released the chart. Nurse Warren hooked it back onto the foot rail of the bed and then looked up at him with one hand jammed on her hip.

"You, Sir." She pointed at him, then threw a thumb over one

shoulder. "You need to leave."

"Først..." The word sounded enough like its English counterpart *first* that Tor expected Nurse Warren to understand.

"*Han er god?*" Tor gave the nurse a thumb up.

"*Han er dårlig?*" Tor turned his hand so the thumb pointed down.

"*Eller, så så?*" He wiggled his flat hand in front of him.

Her expression softened. It seemed that by showing concern for his soldier he earned at least partial forgiveness for the breach of regulations.

"So so," she repeated. "We'll know more tomorrow."

"*Takk du.*" Tor smiled grimly. "*God natt.*"

И И И

Though he was exhausted physically, Tor's mind wasn't restful. He walked toward the north end of the camp where the POWs were imprisoned, not really knowing why he was going there.

The camp was quiet; the sound of guards' conversations, snow shovels scraping paved sidewalks, and the occasional brays of a wakeful mule were muffled by the snow that started falling sometime between supper and now. Tor wished he smoked, because right now a cigarette seemed like the perfect way to occupy his hands and pass some time in thought.

The day had been hard. Obviously.

When Kossin was finally awake and coherent Tor hoped to find out what happened to send the man tumbling so horribly on a run he'd succeeded at dozens of times before. Sure, his form was bad and he never reached the bottom before time ran out. But he always reached the bottom.

Tor was walking with his head down, watching where he stepped and trying to stay on the freshly-snow-covered path, when someone walked right into his left shoulder.

Tor stumbled backwards. "Hey!"

The man caught his balance and looked up. In the dim light outside the door of a nearby building, Tor recognized him.

Dale Maple.

Maple looked frightened, like he was facing the devil himself. Without a word of greeting or apology, he turned around and continued on his hurried way.

What the hell?

Tor stood there for a minute, wondering if he should follow the jerk, but decided not to. No point in stirring anything up now, not in the middle of the night.

Wait.

It's the middle of the night.

In a moment of curious inspiration, Tor decided to follow Maple's tracks and see where he'd come from. Maybe find out what the man was up to.

It was easy in the fresh snow, even in the dim light. Tor walked the path that Maple laid out so clearly—and found himself at the fence of the POW enclosure.

Not only that, but there were multiple boot prints on the inside of the fence. It was clear that Maple was standing right here and conversing with more than one man on the other side.

Is Dale Maple the man the two prisoners were talking about?

The one whose contact was slow to answer?

And if so, what were they planning?

Tor turned around to retrace the steps one more time, thinking that coming on a walk to clear his mind only ended up creating more questions.

One thing was sure: Tor had to let Major General Jones know that Private Dale Maple was meeting with German POWs in the middle of the night. That had to be a breach of several regulations at the least, and probably something much more sinister judging by the man's character.

Maybe this time he'll listen.

ⵜ ⵜ ⵜ

Kyle turned over in bed again. Sleep eluded her tonight, because every time she closed her eyes she saw Private Kossin's impossibly twisted leg and profusely bleeding head. She didn't think she had a weak constitution—she was a farm girl, after all, and had seen animals butchered her whole life.

But it's different when it's a human being.
Of course, thinking of the injured private made her think of Tor Hansen, holding the injured soldier on his back, skiing straight to where the medics were, and skillfully coming to a dramatic stop right in front of them.

And thinking of Tor Hansen reminded her that she hadn't finished the letter to Erik yet. What was she going to say? Everything interesting that happened here was centered on the man she was assigned to translate for—and the captain, whom she passionately kissed, was the last thing she wanted to write to Erik about.

Damn.

She rolled over to lie on her back and stared at the ceiling in the dark.

"Can you please be still?" Marguerite mumbled from the other bed. "Your stupid bed springs keep waking me up."

"Sorry." *I'll try.*

"Man problems?"

"What else," Kyle admitted.

Marguerite heaved a resigned sigh. "Want to talk about it?"

She did, actually. "I'm having trouble writing letters to Erik that aren't full of Captain Hansen stories…"

Marguerite leaned up on one elbow. "What's up with you two, anyway?"

Kyle huffed. "Which two?"

"You and the Norse God."

Kyle rolled her eyes though Marguerite couldn't see. "Nothing, really."

"That's not what it looked like." Marguerite's tone scolded her. "Be honest."

"I *am*," Kyle insisted. "I'm engaged to Erik, and I'm going back home in thirteen months. Tor's either going to Italy with the Americans or back to Norway. Depends on how the war goes, I guess."

"But—"

"The point is," Kyle interrupted. "Whatever silliness we play at here will hopefully rescue him from all the women who go sniffing after him."

"Because he's apparently taken."

"Right."

Marguerite laid back down and was quiet for a while. Kyle wondered if she'd fallen back to sleep, so when she spoke again Kyle startled.

"Here's the problem with that. First of all, with all that kissing you're likely to fall hard for the Norse God."

"Stop calling him that," Kyle grumbled.

"And secondly, that plan's not going to keep anyone away."

Kyle frowned at the ceiling. "Why not?"

"Because..." Marguerite chuckled. "Any woman with eyes in her head is going to claw yours out to get to him."

Marguerite's bed creaked as she turned over to face the wall. "Sweet dreams."

CHAPTER THIRTEEN

January 15, 1944

Kyle stifled a yawn while she and Tor waited to see Major General Jones. She slept poorly last night once she finally drifted off—and then she *dreamt* that she was awake.

But Tor had a worse night than she did, and it showed. The captain had dark smudges under his eyes and his face was pale under his skier's tan.

When she picked him up this morning he told her about falling asleep at the hospital, awaking in the middle of the night, sneaking into the ward to see Kossin, and his cryptic conversation with the nurse on duty.

Then he told her about literally running into Dale Maple near the POWs, and following that man's tracks to the fence.

"When I finish today, we have to talk to Jones," he insisted. "Maybe this time I can convince him to investigate."

Kyle was impressed that Tor was still going to train his men today, considering yesterday's frightening accident.

"I have to," he said between sips of black coffee. "It'll be much worse in battle. They can't let anything like this shake their confidence."

That made sense.

"Besides that, it's too difficult to reschedule our time on the peaks." He set his cup down and rubbed his eyes before he continued. "With six dozen instructors and thirty-five platoons training, it gets crazy at times."

Jones's door opened and a major exited the office. He pointed at Tor and Kyle while he addressed the secretary. "The General says to give him two minutes and then send them in."

И И И

"So what is this about?" Jones asked as soon as Tor and Kyle sat down.

"Captain Hansen encountered Private Dale Maple last night leaving the POW area at approximately two in the morning," Kyle explained. "He followed Private Maple's tracks back and they led to the compound's fence where, judging by the tracks in the new snow, it appeared that Maple met with at least two of the prisoners."

Satisfied with Kyle's distillation of what he told her, Tor watched Jones's expression.

The general frowned. "And why was Captain Hansen in that area at such a suspicious hour?"

That reaction was not what Tor expected.

Kyle turned to Tor and translated the question. "What should I say?"

"Tell him what I told you about the hospital."

Kyle faced Jones again and did so, though Tor noticed she added a little embellishment about how heroic his actions were and how deeply he cared for the men under his command.

Tor bit his tongue to keep from smiling.

"I do appreciate all that Captain Hansen did under the circumstances, Lieutenant." Jones folded his hands on his desktop. "But I'm still not clear about *why* he went to the POW compound."

Tor waited for Kyle to translate, then said, "Tell him that I've visited that area frequently, hoping to overhear the Germans talk about their plans again."

Since he ignored my last report.

Jones grunted. "And has he heard anything new?"

Kyle checked her answer with him before she spoke. "Not until last night."

"But he didn't actually hear anything—he only ran into Private Maple exiting the area. Is that correct?"

"Yes, sir."

Tor was seething. Why weren't his words being trusted?

Jones looked at Tor. "While I agree that the evidence raises questions, the assumption that something covert is afoot is unsubstantiated. I will, however, have Maple interrogated."

Tor stared at the general while Kyle translated.

"Oh don't overexert yourself, Sir," Tor said. Then he pulled his eyes from Jones and looked at Kyle. "Sorry. Thank him for seeing me. Us."

ᴎ ᴎ ᴎ

Kyle was going to punch Tor in the chest when he made that snide remark but the captain apologized quickly, apparently remembering that he promised not to do that to her again.

"But I don't understand why he doesn't take this more seriously," he grumbled once they were outside.

"I assume it's because he isn't worried about anything happening." Kyle waved a hand at the low clouds which were once again shaking their frosty flakes all over the camp. "Look around. It's pretty secure here."

Tor looked up at the darkening sky. "How much snow does this camp get?"

"I'm not sure," Kyle admitted. "Thirteen or fourteen feet would be my guess."

"Snow won't deter the Germans." He looked at her again and winked. "Any more than it'll deter Norwegians."

"Captain Hansen!"

Kyle and Tor turned toward the voice. A soldier that Kyle recognized as one of Tor's trainees was hurrying toward them. He had several copies of the camp's weekly newspaper folded over his arm.

He was a little out of breath when he reached them. "Did you see the *Ski-Zette* today?"

He handed one of the copies to Tor and one to Kyle. "You're a hero, sir!"

Kyle looked at the headline and translated it out loud in Norwegian for Tor's sake. "Norwegian Olympic skier rescues injured soldier."

Tor was staring at his own copy, his eyes moving over the page under a lowered brow.

"Let me read it to you," Kyle said. "I can translate as I go."

That seemed to startle him. His gaze jumped to hers and he folded the camp newspaper and tucked it under his arm.

"Yes. Please."

Yesterday during routine downhill ski training, Private Keith Kossin of the 86th Infantry Division lost his balance and took a bad fall, breaking his right leg below the knee and cracking his head against a tree.

His commanding officer, Captain Tor Hansen from the Norwegian Army, wasted no time in reaching the unconscious soldier, and carried Kossin on his back as he skied the rest of the way down the mountain.

Medics had been alerted and were waiting to rush Kossin to the hospital where he underwent surgery to stabilize his leg. He is expected to make a full recovery, thanks in part to Captain Hansen's heroic rescue.

The private was beaming. "We're proud of you, sir."

Tor gave him a humble smile. "*Tusen takk.*"

Kyle's gaze shot to the captain. "Did you understand him?"

He looked at her like she was simple. "I've told you before, tone and expression can say as much as words. Thanking him could not have been an incorrect response."

"No, it wasn't," she conceded.

"Well, I gotta go give these to the other guys." The private saluted and Tor saluted back. "See ya tomorrow, Captain."

"Let's go to the mess hall and get some coffee," Tor suggested. "Then you can read this week's war news to me, if you don't mind. After talking to Jones, I could stand to hear about an Allied victory or two right about now."

Kyle nodded and pulled the collar of her coat tighter to keep the snow from falling down her neck. "Good idea, sir."

N N N

After supper, Kyle and Tor went to the hospital to see how Kossin was doing. Tor was hoping that one of Kyle's nurse friends was on duty in Kossin's ward so that they wouldn't be chased out too quickly.

Luck was on his side in two ways. First, Frances Bundorf, part of Kyle's group of friends—whom Tor labeled the *Terrible Trio* in his head—was head nurse in Kossin's ward tonight. And secondly Kyle told him Frances had a boyfriend named Fred with whom the nurse was completely smitten.

This was very important information, because after the *Ski-Zette* came out today Tor was besieged all throughout his supper by flirtatious WACs asking him to autograph their copies.

Tor looked at Kyle while she translated the first request, wondering if she was pulling a trick to get him back for his own shenanigans. "Is she serious? She really wants me to sign the newspaper?"

Kyle looked like she was enjoying his discomfort. "You're a famous skier. Remember?"

Taken aback at first, Tor eventually decided to save his copy and mail it to his parents.

"How's Kossin?" Kyle asked Frances.

"Awake." Frances held a tray of medications and pointed toward the private with her head. "But keep it brief. We don't want him to get too exhausted. He's got a lot of healing to do."

"Understood," Tor told Kyle. "I just want to find out if he remembers what happened."

Kossin looked up at Tor through his slightly less-swollen eyes and managed a crooked grin. He saluted weakly. "Hello Captain."

Tor sat next to the bed and Kyle stood behind him, translating quietly throughout their conversation to keep from disturbing the other patients.

"At ease, soldier." Tor smiled. "How are you feeling?"

"I've been better, sir."

"I was here last night checking on you. You've had the very best care they can give," Tor assured him.

Kossin was clearly surprised by that. "You were?"

"Of course. I'm your commanding officer, Private." Tor leaned a little closer. "I don't want to tire you out, but can you tell me what happened? Why you fell?"

Kossin's lips twisted. "Part of it. I don't remember anything after I started to fall until I woke up here."

"What do you remember?"

"The rabbit, sir."

Tor blinked. "Rabbit?"

"Yeah. It was huge and white and it ran out of the woods right in front of me."

"A rabbit did." Tor wagged his head, trying to imagine the scene. "Did you hit it?"

Kossin nodded a little. "I think so. I tried not to, but that's when everything went wrong."

Tor was relieved that the accident was triggered by an outside force, not Kossin just screwing up.

I'll need to add that to the training: hit the rabbit and save yourself.

Kossin turned his head a little. "Can I ask you some questions, sir?"

Tor nodded. "Of course."

"How did I get down the mountain? I mean…" He pointed at his suspended leg with the steel pins poking out of it. "I guess I was hurt pretty bad."

"Yes. You were." Tor shifted in his seat planning to downplay his actions. "I used your ski poles as braces to keep your leg secured and strapped them on with Smith and Graves' belts."

Kossin seemed impressed. "And then?"

"And then I, uh…" Tor cleared his throat. "I carried you the rest of the way down."

If the soldier could have opened his swollen eyes any wider,

Tor thought they might have rolled out of the private's head.

"You did? How?"

Tor shrugged. "On my back."

"Wow," Kossin breathed.

"It's a basic maneuver," Tor deflected. "Anyway, we radioed the medics so they were waiting at the bottom and they brought you here."

He stood more quickly than he meant to, so he smiled to soften his sudden exit. "I think that's enough for this visit, soldier. You keep healing. That's an order."

"One last question?"

Tor nodded. "Sure. But only one."

"What happens to me now? I mean, with the Mountain Division?"

Good question. "You'll come back to training when you're able—not for months, though—and we can start again." Tor paused. "That is, if you want to. Otherwise, I'm sure you could get a transfer to another unit somewhere."

Kossin's hands fisted by his side. "No, sir! I want to stay right here!"

Tor grinned. "Okay, Kossin. See you soon."

и и и

Kyle drove Tor to his barracks. "Get some sleep tonight. No more wandering around the camp. Sir."

Tor chuckled. "I'll say the same to you, Lieutenant. Sleep well."

He thought about kissing her but decided not to. He didn't want to turn their kisses into a habit—he wanted them to mean something. And he also didn't want to prompt any physical reaction that might keep him awake.

Upstairs in his room he changed out of his uniform and went to the latrine to wash his face and brush his teeth. That done, he settled into his bed and picked up the copy of the *Ski-Zette* newspaper that the private gave him.

Alone in his room, he didn't have to pretend he couldn't read it.

Tor's eyes grew thankfully heavy as he skimmed over the articles detailing camp happenings and schedule changes. He was about to drop the paper on the floor and switch off the light when a headline jolted him fully awake. He sat up in his bed.
Camp Hale Ski Team to compete in Salt Lake City.
Camp Hale has a ski team?
"Why don't I know about this?" he mumbled.
Because I don't speak English so I never get the paper.
Tor read the article twice through. The competition was twelve days away. Was it too late to join? The article didn't say.
How could he find out?
"Torger will know," Tor said to himself. "He's probably on the team."
Why didn't he invite me to be on it?
Probably because as far as anyone other than his little band of five knew, he didn't speak any English. That meant Kyle would have to travel with him. The only woman in a group of men. That situation presented more problems than it solved.

Tor made two decisions.

First, he'd find Torger Tokle tomorrow and ask him about the ski team.

Second, he'd ask Kyle to teach him English. He smiled as he put the paper away and turned off his light.

She just might discover I'm an excellent student.

CHAPTER FOURTEEN

January 17, 1944

Tor spotted Torger the minute the man entered the mess hall. "I have to talk to Tokle," he told Kyle as he set down his coffee cup and stood. "I'll be right back."

Tor wove his way through tables of rumbling conversations until he reached the ski jumper. "Can I talk to you?"

Torger shrugged. "Sure. Just let me get my tray first."

Tor got himself a fresh cup of coffee and followed Torger to a table. He sat down facing his fellow countryman.

Torger jabbed his fork into his eggs. "What's on your mind?"

"The Camp Hale Ski Team."

Torger grinned. "Just find out about that?"

Tor nodded. "There was an article in the *Ski-Zette* yesterday."

"Which you saw because you were the headline." Torger wagged his head. "You really should keep up, Hansen."

"I'm going to learn English," he replied defensively. "But tell me about the team. Are you on it?"

Torger made a face. "Of course I am."

"Can I join?" Tor pressed.

"You'll have to talk to Corporal Pfeifer. He's the one arranging everything." When Tor didn't react, Torger leaned forward. "You know who he is, right? Friedl Pfeifer?"

"Him? He's here?" Tor looked around the mess hall as if the man might stand up and wave. "I've never met him, but I've certainly heard of him."

Tor returned his attention to Tokle. "He was the first Austrian to win the Arlberg-Kandahar championship."

"Yep. And you probably never met him because he left Austria in thirty-eight to come here and compete. He's an American citizen now." Torger finally ate the eggs off the fork he had been waving for emphasis.

Tor understood the man's leaving Austria the minute he had the chance—Hitler had that country in his sights from the beginning. But he still had a problem with Tokle bolting from the neutral Norway.

Not now.

"So he organized the ski team once he joined the Tenth," Tor clarified. "How can I get on it?"

"I'll talk to him," Torger offered.

"Can I compete in Salt Lake City, do you think?"

Torger chuckled. "That's less than two weeks away."

"Twelve days." Now Tor leaned forward. "I'm serious. I need to go."

The other man raised one brow. "Need?"

"You know what it's like," Tor prodded. "Flying down the mountain. The wind. The snow. The challenge of the competition. There's nothing else in the world like it."

Torger's expression shifted from bemused to understanding. "I do. Yes."

"I haven't had that for four years, Torger. Four *years*." Tor was surprised at his surging emotions; if he couldn't join the team he thought he might go mad. "Not since Norway was occupied. So yes, I need to go."

Torger nodded. "I get it, Hansen. Let me see what I can do."

"Thank you." Tor held out his hand. "You have no idea how much I appreciate it."

Tokle shook his hand firmly. "What about your translator?"

Tor took a chance. "I won't need her. If there's anything I can't figure out, you can explain it."

Torger looked unsure. "I guess."

"And I speak German," Tor continued to press his case. "So I can talk to Pfeifer without a problem."

That seemed to ease Torger's mind. "All right, then."

"A ski race is a ski race," Tor stated as he stood. "I just need to know how and when to get to the top. I can handle things from there."

ᴎ ᴎ ᴎ

Kyle watched Tor make his way back to his own breakfast, now cold and looking pathetic on his abandoned plate.

"What was that about?" she asked when he reclaimed his chair.

"The Camp Hale Ski Team." Tor shoveled a forkful of cold scrambled eggs into his mouth. "I saw it in the *Ski-Zette* last night."

"And you could read the article?"

How?

Tor looked up from his plate. "I read the headline. Camp Hale Ski Team is Camp Hale Ski-*Teamet*. Not at all hard to figure out, Lieutenant."

True.

While Tor continued to wolf down his unappetizing food, Kyle tried to remember seeing the article but without success. Apparently the headline made no impression on her.

"What did Sergeant Tokle say?"

Tor spoke with his mouth full. "He's going to talk to Corporal Friedl Pfeifer and see if I can join. Do you know him?"

Kyle shook her head. "There are over eight thousand soldiers here, remember."

"But this guy's famous." Tor swallowed and washed it down with cold coffee. "He joined the staff of Hannes Schneider's Austrian ski school when he was only fourteen."

Kyle shook her head. "I never skied before you showed me how, and I've never lived in Europe—or even visited, for that matter. How could I have heard of him?"

Tor's movement stilled. "You need to go to Norway."

That will never happen.

"Maybe."

Tor waved his empty fork over his head. "When all of this is over, you need to go, Kyle."

"When all of this is over..." Kyle mimicked his gesture with her empty hand. "I'm going back to Minnesota to be married."

Tor looked stricken. "You don't know what you're missing."

Kyle felt punched in the gut. "I'm not you, Tor. I can't just pick up and run halfway around the world on a whim."

The captain's gaze fell to his plate and he ate the last of his eggs in silence.

"How can you eat that?" Kyle asked, changing the subject.

"When you live in a country occupied by greedy German bastards, you get used to eating what you can, when you can."

Tor looked at her again. "Eggs are a luxury."

Chastised, Kyle pointed at her unfinished breakfast. "Do you want mine?"

Tor laughed. "No. But thank you."

Glad to see his mood shift, Kyle asked, "What happens if you do get to join the ski team?"

"I hope I get to compete in Salt Lake City in twelve days."

Kyle startled. "Would I go with you?"

Tor shook his head. "I'd have Tokle to translate if needed. And I can speak to the Austrian corporal in German."

Kyle was a little disappointed, and surprised that she was. Was it the prospect of traveling to another place that pulled her? Or the fact that the captain would be gone for a length of time?

It can't be that. It just can't.

She tried to look unconcerned. "If you think that will work."

"I do." Tor pushed his empty plate away. "But it makes me think of something else."

"What?" she asked warily.

He smiled at her. "I think I should learn English."

Kyle felt another gut-punch. "Why?"

His brow twitched. "Why?"

"No. No. You're right," Kyle back-pedaled. "It would be helpful for you."

Tor looked at her and his expression had gone soft. "Should it be our secret, then?"

"Secret?" The word sent a frightening little thrill through her belly. Tor was already her secret.

"So you can stay on as my translator, of course."

Of course.

"If you want." She tried to sound noncommittal. "Sure."

"Then that's that. Because I do want you to continue being my own personal Lieutenant." His smile lit up his eyes in a mesmerizing way. "I like being with you."

Don't say it back. Say something else.

"Well, I guess I find you tolerable."

Tor laughed and pushed his chair from the table. "Time to hit the slopes. Let's talk about the lessons while you drive me."

И И И

Tor was a wreck all day, wondering how soon Torger would talk to Pfeifer and what the Austrian's answer would be.

He tried to soothe his nerves by taking several high-speed runs down the mountain on his own, but the resultant heart-pounding adrenaline surging through his veins only made him more determined. If Torger didn't have an answer for him at supper, Tor would find the corporal's barracks and talk to the man himself.

He and Kyle agreed to hold his first English lesson tonight, but the question of where was a problem. If the fact that he was "learning" English got out, it could risk Kyle's assignment—and that was the last thing he wanted to do. They needed to find someplace public but private at the same time.

And because of the frigid winter weather, it needed to be indoors.

"We could sit in the jeep like we were just having a conversation," Kyle suggested. "Though we couldn't keep the engine running and use up the gas. So no heat."

"If we dressed warmly, I think we'd be fine." He looked at how she was dressed now. Her military-issue wool coat and trousers seemed up to the task. "Do you have another idea?" Her brows pulled together. "I thought of the chapel, but the chaplains are usually on duty."

"Does the library have private reading rooms?"

Kyle wrinkled her nose. "Yes, but they aren't soundproof. We'd definitely be seen and probably overheard."

Tor spread his hands as Kyle stopped at the base of the mountain. "Let's try the jeep tonight and see how it goes," he suggested. "And in the meantime, could you look around the camp for another option?"

"Sure."

Tor came off his final run after he'd dismissed his men with the reminder that their test was in three days. He always hated reaching the bottom of the slope because that meant the ride was finished.

Heaven must consist of eternal mountains, he decided. And unending snow to fly over.

I'd rather have that than angel wings.

He stowed his skis and poles, and opened the door of the jeep, dropping into the passenger seat.

"How was your day, Dear?" Kyle teased.

"Traffic was terrible," he teased back, then, "Was your search successful?"

She shook her head and hit the gas. "This camp is too darn full of people. Turns out they're everywhere."

Tor sighed. "So the jeep it is."

"Yep." She glanced sideways at him. "Your place or mine?"

✎ ✎ ✎

Torger was talking to a tall dark-haired man with prominent eyebrows. When he saw Tor, he beckoned him from across the mess hall. Tor waved back and looked down at Kyle.

"Go on—you don't need me to talk to them." She grinned and winked at him. "Good luck!"

Tor nearly sprinted through the maze of tables, chairs, and

bodies. Obviously, Torger had already told Pfeifer about Tor because when he reached the pair, the man who must be Pfeifer laughed and addressed him in German.

"If you can slalom on snow as well as you navigate the mess, then I think you'll be great on the team." He saluted Tor, who saluted back, then stuck out his hand. "Corporal Friedl Pfeifer, sir."

Tor shook it vigorously. "It's a pleasure to meet you."

"The pleasure is mine, I assure you. Until I saw the article in the *Ski-Zette* yesterday I had no idea you were in the camp."

Tor was taken aback. "You know of me?"

Pfeifer nodded. "Sure. You made the Norwegian Olympic team for the cancelled games four years ago. Downhill and slalom, if I'm not mistaken."

Tor couldn't hold back his smile. "That's right."

He wanted to ask the question of the hour right away, but told himself to be patient. So far, the interview was going better than expected and he didn't want to jinx it.

"I may be an American now but I still keep a close eye on all of the Alpine races," Pfeifer explained. "I was very curious to see how you would do."

Now.

"Then let me show you in Salt Lake City."

Pfeifer laughed again and turned to Torger. "I like him," he said in English.

"He's a good man," Torger responded. "Straight arrow, you know? And skis like the devil is on his tail."

Tor had to pretend he didn't understand their exchange but he could feel a revealing blush heating his cheeks.

Pfeifer winced a little. "But he doesn't have English…"

"I can translate for him when you aren't around to speak in German," Torger offered. "But as he told me, all he really needs to know is how and when to get to the top of the mountain. Said he'd take from there."

Pfeifer laughed yet again. The man had a good sense of humor.

I like that.

The corporal turned back to Tor and spoke in German once

again. "Captain Hansen, would you be interested in joining the Camp Hale Ski Team for our upcoming competition?"

Tor beamed. "Yes, I would. Very much so."

"Do you have your own equipment?"

Uh, oh.

"No. My skis wouldn't fit in my duffel," Tor joked, hoping that Pfeifer's sense of humor held strong. "All I have are the Army-issued skis and poles."

Pfeifer frowned. "Of course you can use those. This is an official camp team, so there's no problem with that. I'm just worried about speed."

"I did some downhill runs today," Tor offered. "And I timed myself."

Pfeifer straightened. "What were your times?"

When Tor told him, the Austrian-born corporal and captain of the Camp Hale Ski Team clapped his hands and then shook Tor's shoulder.

"That will do, Sir," he effused. "That will do very nicely indeed."

Torger smacked him on the back. "Welcome to the team!"

Tor punched the air and let out a *whoop* that made everyone in a thirty-foot radius jump. He didn't care.

He was going to race again.

CHAPTER FIFTEEN

Giddy.

That was the only word that accurately described Tor's mood that night. Kyle couldn't help but smile at his childish enthusiasm. And aside from being absolutely engaging, it took her mind off the chill inside the jeep.

They were parked outside Tor's barracks, dressed warmly in their reversible Army issue ski parkas and white snow pants. The plan was to spend one hour a night working on Tor's English.

"He was worried about using the Army skis, thinking they might not be fast enough," Tor said. "But when I told him my times he was astounded!"

"I'm happy for you, Tor. And I'm glad you get to go to the competition." Kyle jabbed a stiff finger, hidden by her mitten, on top of the dashboard. "But we're here for English."

"Yes. Okay." Tor bounced a nod. "English."

"I assume you've picked up some words just by being here," Kyle began. "Can you tell me what you already know?"

"Sure." Tor listed the words in English. "Please, thank you, hello, goodbye, good morning, good night, come, go... Army, Mess Hall, barracks, jeep... Ski, poles, boots..."

"That's a great start," Kyle complimented. "And here, I

made these."

She handed him a thick stack of three-by-five note cards. "Each one has the Norsk word on one side and the English word on the other side. I want you to attach them to the items in your room so you can learn the words."

Tor looked through the cards. "I'll say the English and you tell me if I'm saying it right."

She grinned. "Good idea."

Tor went through the cards, saying the words out loud. "Bed, mattress, pillow case—"

"That's pronounced *case*, not *cahsuh*."

Tor repeated the word and continued through the stack. Kyle corrected the words he pronounced like they were Norsk and was pleased to see him apply what he learned from one word to another with similar spelling.

"The next step is just memorizing them," she said. "And then start listening for English words that sound like Norsk."

"Like good morning," he offered.

"Exactly."

"But I can't use them," he sounded like he was reminding himself, "because my learning English is a secret."

"At least for now…" Kyle chewed her lip in thought. "Maybe once the snow starts to melt and the instruction switches to mountain climbing and ordnance training I could officially ask to teach you instead of just translate for you."

Tor looked hopeful. "I would like that. Then I could practice openly."

Kyle pulled back the cuff of her parka and looked at her watch. "It's getting late and I can't feel my toes."

Tor tucked the note cards inside his coat. "Before I go, how do I say *I'm going to kiss you now?*"

Kyle's heart skipped. She said in English, "I'm going to kiss you now."

Tor leaned toward her until his lips met and claimed hers. She welcomed the kiss and allowed herself to sink into it completely. When he finally pulled away, she was breathless and could hardly open her eyes.

He rested his forehead against hers.

"Good night, Lieutenant," he said in English. "Thank you for the English."

"You're welcome, Captain," she answered in kind. "*Sov godt*. Sleep well."

January 20, 1944

Testing day for the soldiers who began their ski training eight weeks ago started at first light. Each platoon was assigned a time to take the T-bar to the top and begin their staggered descents to the valley. The qualifying time for making the mile-and-a-quarter downhill run was four minutes.

Tor expected eleven of his fifteen remaining skiers to qualify, including the entire band of five who were keeping his secret. Four of the novices were still struggling, and of course Kossin was still in the hospital.

Tor went to the top of the mountain with his and First Lieutenant Frank Collins' men. Collins' crew went first as they were expected to be the faster skiers, and Tor sent his men three at a time when it was their turn.

When the last three skied out of his sight, Tor started his stopwatch and pushed off.

Now that he had an opportunity to compete again, this run wasn't just for fun. He pushed himself hard, slaloming from side to side, crouching low over the skis, keeping his elbows tucked close to his body and his eyes focused on the slope in front of him.

God, I love this.

The same exhilaration that he always felt when he was flying over the snow suffused his frame, making him feel invincible. He caught up with his last three trainees and shot past them, their whoops of encouragement following after him like the vapor trail of a jet plane.

When he reached the bottom, he cut a quick half circle sending a spray of snow over the men waiting for the T-bar and shut off his stopwatch.

"What's the time?" someone shouted.

Tor lifted his goggles and looked for the voice. It was Freidl Pfeifer, waiting at the end of the line with the next platoon. *"Wie schnell bist du gegangen?"* he shouted in German. How fast did you go?

Tor grinned. *"Zwei Minuten, zweiundvierzig Sekunden."* Two minutes and forty-two seconds. "Slalom."

Pfiefer gave him two thumbs up.

и и и

In the end, two of Collins' men didn't qualify, both because they fell. One sprained his ankle, the other only his dignity.

With Kyle at his side, First Lieutenant Collins and Tor agreed that Tor would only work with the seven men who didn't qualify—including, surprisingly, the radio tech from his band of five—until they made the qualifying time and moved up with the rest of the platoon.

"That gives you time to train," Collins said with a crooked grin. "Make us proud in Salt Lake."

"Yes," Tor ventured in English, then added, *"Takk."*

"When do you leave?" Kyle asked him when the meeting in the officer's club was finished and they were walking toward the mess hall.

"We board the bus at eight in the morning on the twenty-sixth. Pfeifer said it's about eight or nine hours through the mountains if the roads are clear."

She squinted up at him, the day's bright sun on her face. "When is the actual competition?"

"We have the twenty-seventh to take practice runs and get familiar with the course," Tor explained. "And on the twenty-eighth and twenty-ninth we compete."

"Do you come back on the thirtieth, then?"

He shrugged. "I guess so."

Truthfully he had been so focused on getting to the competition he hadn't given any thought to when they'd return.

"So you'll be gone five days." Kyle frowned a little. "I wonder if I should request leave and go home while you're gone. There won't be anything for me to do here."

Tor didn't respond at first. For some reason, he wanted her to stay at the camp. If Kyle was at Camp Hale, then the only life she led was here. Nothing—and no one—outside this valley mattered.

"You want to see Erik," he forced himself to say.

"I've never been away from home before and it's been a long time since I left," she deflected. "My basic training started in September, and then I waited a month here for you to arrive." She counted on her fingers. "Five months. And I missed Thanksgiving and Christmas."

"But you do want to see Erik," he pressed.

"Of course I want to see my fiancé," she snapped. "But that's not the only reason to go."

"You feel guilty for missing the holidays with your family. I can understand that."

She wagged a negating finger. "No. Guilty isn't the right word. It insinuates that I did something wrong by enlisting."

"That's fair," he conceded. "And I know what you mean. I've missed a lot of time with my parents and my brother."

"I'd have to fly from Denver to Fargo, North Dakota," she mused aloud. "And then it's about three hours' drive north from there…"

Tor figured it couldn't hurt to point out the flaw in her plan. "With three days off, you'd travel for two days and only have one day to spend with them."

"And two nights. But you're right."

"Is it worth it?" he prodded.

"No."

Tor relaxed. "So you'll stay here."

"No." Kyle squinted up at him again. "I'll ask for five days' leave."

Well that took an unexpected turn.

"And because I stayed through Thanksgiving, Christmas, and New Year's, I bet I'll get it." She grinned. "Especially since you'll be gone at the same time."

Yeah, you probably will.

Tor sighed. "When will you put in the request?"

Kyle stopped short and looked at her watch. "Right now. If I make it to headquarters in three minutes, they'll still be open."

"Better run," he muttered.

She was gone before he said *run*.

ᚾ ᚾ ᚾ

Kyle banged on the door when she heard the knob rattle. "Please? I just need to turn in a form!"

She heard the groan from the other side, but the lock flipped. She pushed the door open and faced the disgruntled receptionist.

"I need to fill out a request for leave."

The WAC scowled. "You said turn in a form, not fill out a form."

"It will only take two minutes, I promise!" Kyle crossed her heart.

"Since it'd take me longer than that to have you forcibly removed, I might as well let you. Come on." The pudgy gal led Kyle to her desk and the stacked tray of forms.

She pulled one out of the third tray and handed it to Kyle. "I suppose you need a pen."

"Please."

That came out of her collar.

Kyle was true to her word and filled out the form in a flash. Luckily, she knew the exact dates because Tor had just told her when he was going to be gone.

"Here. And thank you!"

"I'd say *anytime*, but I'd be lying." The WAC set the paper on her desk and tucked the pen back inside the front of her uniform. "Now get out of here so I can lock up."

Kyle obeyed.

She walked back to the mess since there was no need to run. The sudden inspiration to ask for leave and go back to Viking made all the sense in the world. With five days off, she would have plenty of time to spend with Erik and her parents and the two days of travel would be worth it.

Once the request was approved, she'd write to Erik and ask him to pick her up in Fargo. That would give her a chance to talk to him privately when she first arrived and not have to be

awkwardly kissing him hello in front of her parents.
I hope it goes through.
She found Tor inside the mess hall talking to Torger Tokle.
"That was a great run if you slalomed the whole way," Torger said. "You'll be in the thick of the competition."
Tor turned to her. "Did you make it in time?"
"Yes. Barely."
"Good."
Was it her imagination, or did he look irritated?
Tor returned his attention to the other Norwegian. "My translator has decided to ask for leave while we are on the trip, instead of sitting around camp and twiddling her thumbs."
Yep. Irritated.
But why?
"Oh, I'd do much more than just sitting around and thumb twiddling," she retorted. "I'd lollygag and fidget. Stare at the wall. Maybe even brush up on my shenanigans."
Torger Tokle guffawed.
Tor scowled. "I get your point, Lieutenant."
Kyle smiled overly sweetly. "I knew you would. Not one wasted brain cell in that skull."
Torger was still chuckling. "You two sound like an old married couple."
Tor threw up his hands. "Heaven forbid!"
All of Kyle's happiness at the prospect of getting leave crashed and splintered around her feet. She couldn't even think of anything to say.
Her expression must have screamed something because Tor was immediately contrite. "I'm sorry, Lieutenant. That came out wrong."
Kyle tried to smile but couldn't make her face cooperate. "Of course. You weren't saying that marriage to *me* would be horrible. You were saying that marriage *in general* would be horrible."
"Well, I—"
"Because you have plenty of fish in *this* sea." She glared at him. "And you know how to cast a line."
Tor shook his head. "No, I—"

Kyle turned to Torger who stood silently with his hand over his mouth, his brows in his hairline, and his gaze shifting back and forth.

"The Captain may not have told you, Sergeant," Kyle said slowly, "but I am engaged. I'm going home to spend time with my fiancé, whom I haven't seen in five months."

Torger's hand lowered. "That does sound like a better choice than twiddling to me."

"Thank you. I agree." She hooked a thumb over her shoulder in Tor's direction. "This one will be your responsibility while I'm gone."

She took two steps away from the men before she turned back around. "Try not to lose him. He doesn't speak English."

With a wave of her fingers, she left the mess. She didn't have an appetite anymore.

CHAPTER SIXTEEN

January 26, 1944

Kyle sat across the table from Tor at breakfast on the morning they were both leaving Camp Hale. He had apologized profusely for his spontaneous reaction to Torger's comment, and continued to do so even after Kyle assured him she wasn't mad any more.

"It just sounded bad, like there was something wrong with me as a person," she kept telling him. "It doesn't mean I want to marry you or anything like that."

She thought the matter was finally put to rest and she focused her thoughts on Erik, not Tor.

Because Erik is the man I love.

Why did it feel like she was trying to convince herself?

She gave the man across the table a good, hard look. What she saw was the raw beauty she noticed when she first saw him: sandy hair, bright blue eyes, a tall frame with just the right amount of noticeable muscle. But now that she knew him, she saw another layer.

He was intelligent. He was kind—their recent kerfuffle notwithstanding. He was amazing on skis. He was quick to act when Kossin was injured, and strong enough to carry the private to safety. And Tor visited him in the hospital, assuring the soldier that he would not lose his chance to be part of the Tenth. His only fault was that he was temporary. When the Tenth Division shipped out, Tor would be gone from her life forever. And Kyle would eventually return to her normal life. That was what was going to happen. Nothing was going to change that for either of them.

"What are you pondering so intently?" Tor asked.

Kyle yanked her thoughts back into the mess hall. "Nothing. Just that I'll be home today."

"I was afraid you were still upset," he admitted. "You looked so serious."

Kyle decided to let that slide rather than get into it all again. "I'm hoping that the weather in Minnesota doesn't prevent Erik from getting to Fargo or us from getting back to Viking."

Tor chuckled. "There was a time when *getting back to Viking* had a whole different meaning."

Kyle rolled her eyes. "I know. Viking is a verb. And you think it's a stupid name for a town."

Tor shrugged and pushed his clean plate forward. "Wish me luck?"

She smiled. "I do. I hope you make Camp Hale proud."

"I hope I make Friedl Pfeifer proud," Tor countered. "I need to stay on the team."

Kyle noticed that Tor often used the word *need* in reference to skiing. The man really loved the sport and it showed.

"I have full confidence in you, Captain Hansen."

"You know, in days of old a lady would give her favor to a competitor before he entered the competition." Tor's blue eyes sparkled. "Might I receive your favor, my lady?"

Kyle laughed at his silliness. "Why good sir, what sort of favor does thou wish for? A kiss?"

Why did I say that?

"That would be most enjoyable and I shall claim it." Tor's gaze softened. "I was thinking of a token."

Kyle stared at him, curious. "Like what?"

Tor tapped his chin with the spoon he stirred his coffee with. "It needs to be something small enough to fit inside my shirt."

Kyle reached into the pocket of her trousers.

"Like a handkerchief? Wasn't that the usual token?" She handed Tor the plain white square of cotton. "It's not embroidered or anything. But you can have it if you're serious. I have plenty more."

Tor took it from her. "Of course I'm serious. Why wouldn't I be?"

Kyle's face warmed. "Well, isn't it usually a love thing?"

"Sometimes, sure. But it's more a symbol of support. Loyalty. That sort of thing." Tor tucked the folded square into his own pocket.

"I do hope you ski well," Kyle said. "And I can't wait to hear about it."

"I'm sure I will, now that I have my own good luck charm." He grinned impishly. "From a real Vikinger."

N N N

Kyle settled into a window seat of the airplane and fastened her seatbelt. Her WAC uniform seemed to be garnering attention and she really just wanted to be left alone.

On the three-hour ride to the Denver airport it felt weird not to be the driver, but she had no complaints about the private from the motor pool completing the task. She took the front passenger seat and was surprised when a sergeant opened the car door and climbed into the back seat.

He introduced himself as Sergeant Camden and said he was going to Denver to pick up a special piece of equipment for the camp dentist rather than wait for it to be shipped to the camp.

"Doctor McDavid is eager to get his hands on it," the sergeant explained. "But I have no idea what it is or what it does. Just that it's new and expensive."

"Well I'm glad for the company," their driver said as he headed out of the camp. "Three hours with only myself to talk to gets boring. Turns out I'm not a great conversationalist."

Kyle smiled at the jest.

A man dropped into the aisle seat across from Kyle and stared at her. "You in the army?" he asked abruptly.

Kyle turned to look at him. "Women's Army Corps. Yes." He shook his head in disgust. "Women are meant to serve in the home and in the family. That's their rightful place."

Kyle turned to look out the window and didn't say anything. She'd heard it before, and nothing she could say would change his mind.

"You mean to tell me you can do what a man does?" he challenged.

"Hey, buddy," the man behind him said. "Leave her alone."

Oh, no.

"Don't tell me what to do."

A middle-aged woman sat next to Kyle becoming a buffer between her and the loud-mouth. Kyle offered a brief smile and turned back to the window.

"She's serving the country," her defender said. "The uniform deserves respect no matter who's wearing it."

Kyle's new seatmate leaned against her shoulder and whispered, "What's he on about?"

Kyle drew a steadying breath and faced the woman and whispered back. "He says women should be in the home, not in the army."

The woman snorted. "Idiot."

"Serving the country?" the first man sneered. "Or *servicing* the soldiers?"

Kyle doubted the man saw what was coming.

Her middle-aged seatmate had a very large purse on her lap, and it made a very satisfying sound when she swung it across the aisle and flattened the offender's nose. Kyle clapped her hand over her mouth to hold back her laugh.

"That's for every woman serving in this war!" the woman shouted. "They're doing more than you are!"

Passengers in nearby seats heartily applauded.

"Hey! By dose is bleedink!"

A stewardess rushed forward with a towel. "Fasten your seatbelt sir. We're getting ready for take-off."

He pointed at the woman with the purse. "But she hit be!"

"You deserved it," the stewardess said bluntly. "And I'll throw you off the flight if you continue to be rude."

The man grunted and held the towel to his nose.

Kyle's grinning seatmate turned to face her. "My name's Mary. What's yours?"

N N N

Tor watched the scenery moving past the window as the rumbling Army bus wound its way through the Rocky Mountains, carrying the eleven-man ski team on the four-hundred-mile journey to Salt Lake City. It felt like home.

The soaring, snow-covered peaks and the narrow valleys cut between them reminded him so much of Norway that his chest tightened with longing.

When would he be able to go home again, he wondered. And what would he find when he did?

Thinking about Norway made him think of his parents and he said a quick prayer for their safety and health. And he also thought about his younger brother, Teigen, whose wartime experiences in Nazi-occupied Norway had been much harder than anything Tor had gone through up to now.

Teigen had been arrested, imprisoned, and spent seven months in a German labor camp in Kirkenes—a small northern Norwegian town deep in the Arctic Circle and bordering Russia. When Tor looked for Teigen before leaving Norway, he found his brother in Bergen.

Teigen had joined the resistance by then and was working on the ground to disrupt German activities.

Tor made a point of telling Teigen that he was proud to be his big brother.

Teigen's surprising response was, "Thank you for saying that. Your shoes are hard to fill."

Startled, Tor replied with, "Don't follow me, Teig. Walk your own path."

The brothers had hugged then, with the solid kind of hug that, if they never saw each other again, they would not find this moment lacking in any way.

I love you, Teig. Stay strong.

Tor stretched, scratched his head, and turned away from the

window to look at the other men on the bus.

If he could speak English without risking Kyle's assignment, he would confess to being star struck by the skiers whose names he recognized. Several of America's champions—also denied their Winter Olympics—had enlisted to be ski instructors at Camp Hale.

"How're you doing?" Torger sat in the seats behind Tor. "Does this make you homesick?"

"Are you reading my mind?" Tor joked.

Torger chuckled. "Don't have to. I feel it myself."

"Will you go back?" Tor asked. "When the war ends?"

Torger looked wistful. "I don't know, to be honest. I guess I'll have to decide when the time comes."

Tor had a different plan. "Norway is my country, and I expect to go back as soon as I'm able."

"You forget, I've been living and competing in this country for five years." Torger looked apologetic. "They have so many opportunities here that aren't available back home."

Tor smiled. "You still call it home."

Torger shrugged. "We don't always live at home, though, do we?"

That's an interesting concept.

"No," Tor conceded. "I don't suppose we do."

✣ ✣ ✣

Kyle waited until the rude man with the bloodied nose got off the plane in Fargo before she even stood up. The last thing she wanted right now was another reason to be anxious, so letting him withdraw seemed the wisest choice.

"God bless you dear," Mary said before walking to the airplane's door and disappearing from sight.

Kyle let a few more passengers go by before she stepped into the aisle. As she followed the line toward the exit, she reminded herself to be thankful for the blindingly white day.

At least we can drive on clear roads.

Kyle felt the blast of icy wind before she reached the stairs that led down to the tarmac. She slid her hands into her leather gloves and wrapped her scarf around her neck. Sunny as the day was, it was still well below freezing outside, and the wind intensified the chill.

She gripped the collar of her woolen coat closed and, with one hand holding her uniform's hat in place, began her careful descent to the ground. The tarmac was cleared of snow and ice so she was able to walk quickly to the terminal door without fear of slipping.

The sun reflecting off the surrounding snow was so bright that she wished she had the green ski goggles with her. Once inside the stuffy terminal it took a few minutes for her eyes to adjust to the darker interior.

Kyle swept the crowd with a glance, looking for Erik. When she didn't see him, she looked more carefully.

What'll I do if he's not here?

Not panic yet, for starters. She decided to follow the other passengers to where the bags were being delivered, thinking he might be waiting for her there.

When she rounded the next corner, she stopped.

There stood Erik with an armful of red roses and a grin that split his face in half. "Hello, Kyle."

Kyle ran forward and threw her arms around him, crushing the roses and pinning his arms to his sides. "I'm so glad to see you!"

When she loosened her hold, he leaned forward and kissed her. Disappointed that it was more perfunctory than passionate, Kyle slammed down the comparisons with Tor's kisses and smiled.

"How are you?" was the first thing she thought to say.

Erik held the flowers away from his chest. "Better than my roses, I'm glad to say."

Kyle looked at the expensive offering, horrified at the damage she'd done. "We'll get them trimmed and in water," she said confidently. "I'm sure they'll be beautiful the whole time I'm here."

Erik looked resigned. "Let's get your suitcase."

"Duffel." Kyle tucked her arm through Erik's and started walking toward baggage claim.

"What?"

"It's my duffel bag," she clarified. "Not a suitcase."

Erik frowned. "Why would you pack in a duffel bag?"

Kyle was confused by the question. "Because that's what I was issued. What else would I use?"

Erik stopped walking. He turned to look at her as if seeing her for the first time. "Are you wearing your uniform?"

Kyle unwound the dull green scarf from her neck, unbuttoned the calf-length double-breasted brown wool coat, and pulled it open to reveal her short olive-drab jacket, pleated trousers in the same color, and beige blouse.

"Is that a man's tie?" Erik looked horrified.

"No. It's a WAC tie," Kyle said evenly. "I'm not a man."

"Why are you dressed like that?"

"Because I'm a soldier on leave. It's what we do."

Erik stared at her. "Are you going to be dressed like that the whole time?"

"No, of course not. Only on my way from camp and on my way back." Kyle peered hard at Erik. "Does my uniform bother you?"

He huffed through his nose and resumed walking. Kyle had to trot forward a few steps to catch up. Determined not to start a fight before their three-hour car ride from Fargo to Viking she slipped her arm through his again.

"I just wasn't expecting to meet a soldier here," he grumbled. "I was expecting to meet my girl."

Kyle clenched her jaw for a moment before she answered. "I *am* your girl, Erik."

He sighed. "I just wish you looked like it."

CHAPTER SEVENTEEN

January 27, 1944

Kyle woke up at six in the morning without setting an alarm. She turned over and snuggled under the blankets to try and go back to sleep. It had been months since she had the luxury of sleeping late and she intended to take advantage of the opportunity while she was here.

Walking into the bedroom that she'd slept in all her life was unsettling. It felt like a stranger's room. Kyle wasn't prepared for that.

Have I changed that much?

Erik seemed to think so.

Steering their conversation in the car away from Tor had proven impossible.

"He *is* my job, Erik," Kyle said multiple times. "And if it makes you feel any better, I'm teaching him English so I'm working myself *out* of that job."

"That does make me feel better," he admitted. "How long will it take?"

"I don't know. But he's an intelligent man"—*I'm sorry, Erik, but he is*—"so hopefully he picks it up quickly."

Erik grunted. "Then what?"

"The talk among the officers is that the Tenth's mobilization will take place this year, so the fighting will be next winter."

Erik glanced at her hopefully. "Does that mean that you'll be home by Christmas?"

"I can probably be on leave next Christmas," she clarified. "But my enlistment doesn't end until June of nineteen-forty-five."

"Even if your job ends?" Erik scowled. "What will you do?"

"I'll be assigned to another unit."

"Doing what?"

"I don't know," Kyle said honestly. "I could even be moved to another camp somewhere."

When Erik drove up to her parents' house she did feel a surge of warmth and familiarity. But she realized that she thought of it as her parents' home—not hers. She told herself that was because she was between homes at the moment: her parents' house, her barracks at Camp Hale, and Erik's house.

Erik's house is my future home.

Kyle stretched under the blankets and turned over again. Her mind was awake but her body was in strict disagreement. She closed her eyes even though the room was still dark, in an effort to convince her brain to be quiet.

She had three days ahead of her to reconnect with Erik and rekindle their spark. And three days to explain to her parents exactly what she was doing in Colorado. That seemed like more than enough time for both.

I wonder how Tor is doing.

※ ※ ※

Tor finished his seventh practice run on the slalom course, exhilarated by the excitement of tomorrow's competition. Every fiber of his body zinged with the long-familiar movements and strained to go faster.

Snow thrown up by the skiers in front of him hit his face and made him feel alive. The skin below his goggles tightened with sunburn and windburn. His thighs ached with exertion.

There was no feeling like it.

"That was a good run, Hansen," Pfeifer complimented in German. "Are you saving anything for tomorrow?"

"Yep." Tor grinned as he unfastened his skis from his Army boots. "I'm just warming up."

He rested his skis and poles on his shoulder and walked to the bus that would take the soldiers back to their hotel. Inside, he stowed his equipment on the rack above the passengers then dropped into the seat in front of Tokle.

"How's it going for you?" he asked in Norsk. Remembering which man he spoke which language to was becoming tiring.

I'll be glad when I can speak English openly.

"Good... But downhill really isn't my strong point." Torger made an unconcerned gesture. "Next month we're going to the Steamboat Springs Carnival, and there'll be ski jumping there."

Tor grinned. "We already have another competition set up?"

"We do. And another in April. At Pike's Peak."

The heavens have opened up.

As the bus wound its way to the hotel, Tor realized he had been thinking he would tell Kyle about the two additional competitions when he got there.

Then he remembered she wasn't there.

Yesterday and today were the first days since arriving in Colorado that she wasn't by his side and he felt the lack in his core. He was a little off-balance somehow. Not physically, but emotionally. His anchor was gone.

He wondered if she missed him in any way.

Probably not.

She was at her childhood home and with her family, a place that wouldn't make her think of him. Plus, she was presumably spending time with her fiancé. Erik.

If he was in Arendal, would he be thinking of her?

Yes.

Damn it.

What sort of magic had the Second Lieutenant worked on him? And why was he disappointed that she wasn't waiting at the hotel for him so he could tell her his news?

Am I falling in love with her?

That was the ultimate dead end. On the way here he heard

the men discussing the division's deployment. The consensus was that the summer would be spent doing mountain climbing and ordnance training. In the fall, they would brush up on their skiing before being sent to Italy to fight.

"Gone before Christmas," one man said.

I can't fall in love with Kyle.

And she was engaged to Erik. There was no future for the two of them together.

Tor stared out the window, his mood completely quashed.

January 28, 1944

Kyle sat at Erik's kitchen table peeling potatoes while Erik talked about last year's crops and what he was planting in which fields in the spring. Earlier today she trudged through the frigid northern Minnesota air across crisp snow to the barn and helped him milk the cows.

By lightening his workload, Kyle gave Erik the chance to just sit with her in his kitchen and talk while they made supper together.

He smiled at her. "This is the Kyle I know."

She looked askance at the bowl of peeled potatoes. "The one who's good with a peeler?"

"The one who's comfortable in my kitchen. The one who milks cows." He blushed a little. "The one I can talk to."

"You can always talk to me," Kyle scolded. She stood and crossed to the stove where a large pot of water was heating.

As she sliced the potatoes into the pot Erik said, "I haven't felt that way lately. Not since you left."

"Why not?" Kyle looked over her shoulder. "What's stopped you?"

Erik's mouth twisted. "I'm scared, I guess."

"Scared? For me?" Kyle turned her attention back to the potatoes. "I'm perfectly safe, Erik. I'm not going to actual war."

"It's not that…" Erik's voice trailed off.

"Then what is it?"

When he didn't answer Kyle dropped the last of the potatoes

into the hot water and turned around.

"What are you afraid of?"

Erik looked embarrassed. "I'm not sure how to say it, but there's been a lot of talk since the war started about how men—and women too, I guess—aren't willing to go back to their hometowns now that they've seen the world."

Kyle opened her mouth to disagree but stopped herself. Erik had a valid point.

"It does change a person's perspective of the world," she admitted.

"See?" Erik pushed back his mop of dark hair. "And you're there with literally thousands of men from all kinds of interesting places."

"It's the army, Erik," Kyle reminded him. "Not a social club."

"Do you expect me to believe that the soldiers and the WACs aren't dating each other?" Erik shook his head. "If you do, then you're a fool."

Kyle sat back down at the table. "Of course. Some of the women are dating some of the men. That's only natural. But those women aren't engaged."

"Out of sight, out of mind," he countered. "And that goes for men *and* women."

"I thought absence makes the heart grow fonder," Kyle challenged.

Erik stared at her. "Is your heart fonder of me than when you left?"

Kyle recoiled. "That depends. I'm out of your sight. Am I out of your mind?"

Erik stood and walked to the oven without answering. He opened the door and peered at the roast inside for a moment. Then he closed to door and faced her again.

"I have never been unfaithful to you, Kyle."

His statement punched her in the gut as Tor's face appeared in her head. "I never thought you were. Why would you say that?"

His brow twitched. "I thought that's what you meant."

"No. I only meant that clichés aren't the best way to judge

things. Because there's one for every side of an argument."

"Oh. Okay." He pushed his hair back again. "Do you still love me?"

She swallowed her doubts. "Yes. Do you still love me?"

"Yes."

Their eyes locked and she asked, "Then why are we fighting so much?"

His expression hardened. "Because you decided to enlist instead of planning a wedding."

January 29, 1944

Yesterday the Camp Hale ski team won four out of the five giant slalom events, with Tor and Torger each scoring one of the victories. The day's top honors unsurprisingly went to the Austrian, Corporal Friedl Pfeifer, Camp Hale's international champion.

The second day of competition was dedicated to downhill racing—Tor's favorite. He and Torger paced at the bottom of the mountain, waiting for their chance to ride to the top. As it was yesterday, Kyle's handkerchief was tucked inside his shirt over his heart,

"How about a side bet?" Tor suggested.

Torger laughed. "No chance, Hansen. I got lucky in the slalom, but there's no way I can beat you in the long course downhill."

"Pfeifer will beat me, I think," Tor said. "He's had more practice in the last five years than I have."

"Maybe."

Tor looked at his countryman, surprised. "You think I have a chance to beat him?"

Torger shrugged. "There's always a chance."

Tor chuckled. "I'd make a bet with you, but I don't know if I'd bet for myself or against!"

"National pride would make *me* bet that the Norseman would beat the Austrian. But if *you* bet on the Austrian, then you'd lose on purpose." Torger grinned. "It's a fool's wager."

"It's not." Tor smiled evilly and his tone was intentionally menacing. "Because I would never *ever* lose on purpose."

※ ※ ※

Tor stood at the top of the course on the same mountain as yesterday and adjusted his green Army goggles. He had already checked the bindings on his skis. The straps of his poles were wrapped around his wrists.

He settled into position and waited for the crack of the starting pistol at the bottom.

Pop.

He was off.

The snow was icy and ridged by yesterday's slalom competitions—corn snow as it was called. Melted and refrozen on top. Tor used an entire stick of the yellow wax formulated for these conditions when he prepared his skis this morning.

Times overall would be slowed by the rougher course, but at least it was the same for every man.

Tor's knees flexed as his skis bounced down the slope. The skill required to keep up his speed challenged and invigorated him. His concentration was so keen that he was surprised when he suddenly crossed the finish line.

Skidding to a stop, he lifted his goggles and squinted at the leader board, waiting for his time to be posted. When it was, he beamed.

He was in first place.

January 30, 1944

In the end, Tor took second in the long course downhill race behind Friedl Pfeifer. The team did so well overall that they went out to celebrate that night.

"Here's to one night when the war does not exist," Pfeifer toasted. "And to the best men I have ever skied with."

"Hear! Hear!" the rest shouted.

In the company of his co-athletes Tor drank more than he

usually did, and found himself struggling between his three languages—two he knew and one he wasn't supposed to.

He finally stopped talking altogether and simply enjoyed the camaraderie of the group of first-rate skiers who understood and shared his passion.

Getting on the bus this morning was not nearly so pleasant. His head pounded and his stomach decided breakfast wasn't such a good idea. Thankfully, there were so few men on the bus that he could stretch his legs across the aisle and lay down.

Judging by the drawn looks of his teammates' faces, they planned to do the same. In spite of their triumphs, their raucous celebration ensured that the day's ride back to camp was going to be a quiet one.

N N N

Kyle kissed Erik goodbye outside the Fargo airport. It wasn't a passionate kiss, it was a friendly kiss. Their deeply passionate exchanges had been shared the night before.

As a result, she was leaving Viking with renewed resolve to focus on her relationship with Erik. In spite of her misgivings about living the rest of her life in the small town, she knew it was her destiny. She had to come to terms with that and make the best of it.

That meant no more kissing Captain Hansen.

Kyle would miss that aspect of their friendship, but it was always meant to be a temporary working relationship, not a social relationship. She knew she had to push Tor in his English lessons so that she could be released as his translator and assigned to do a different task in a different location.

Then all of her problems with Erik would disappear and her life would be peaceful again.

Lacking the excitement of the gorgeous Norwegian's attention, true. But peaceful and back on track.

That solidly resolved, Kyle wiped a tear from her cheek as she walked into the airport terminal alone.

CHAPTER EIGHTEEN

January 31, 1944

Kyle picked up Tor for breakfast at seven o'clock in front of his barracks the morning after he returned from his trip and she returned from her leave, just as she always had. But something about her was different today.

Tor wanted to hug her hello, but that was hard to do inside the jeep, so he settled for taking a firm hold of her hand.

"It's good to see you, Kyle." He smiled warmly. "I missed you."

She slowly pulled her hand from his and shifted the jeep into reverse. Her smile seemed strained and she didn't meet his eyes.

"How did you do?" she asked as she backed up the jeep.

Tor watched her carefully as she shifted into first and pressed the gas. "I took first in one of the slalom runs and second in the long course downhill, after Pfeifer."

"That's good!" Her tone was happier than her face.

"Yes. I was satisfied." Tor leaned forward to see her better. "What's wrong?"

A little crease formed between her eyebrows. "Nothing."

"Don't lie to me, Lieutenant," Tor said gently. "Something happened in Viking."

"Nothing happened, Captain," she insisted. "I just realized where my responsibilities are."

Tor's spirit sank. "With Erik."

"Yes."

Tor sat silently in the passenger seat wondering if there was anything he could say to her. All he had were questions.

"What does that mean?" he asked.

She glanced at him. "It means no more kissing."

Damn.

He'd miss that for sure. "Anything else?"

"You need to get serious about your English," she stated.

Tor knew what that meant. "So you can be transferred."

She nodded, her eyes still looking through the windshield.

"Why are you afraid of me?"

Kyle's head swiveled and her eyes were huge. "I'm not afraid of you."

"Then why is being with me upsetting you?"

She jammed on the brakes and Tor threw his arms forward to keep from hitting his head on the windshield. "What on earth—"

Kyle's chest was heaving and her chin was quivering. She stared at her lap.

"I'll tell you, damn you."

Tor knew better than to say anything at that moment. He shifted back onto his seat and waited.

"You're incredibly handsome. And charming. And smart. And heroic. And everything about you is attractive to me." She ran one gloved finger under her dripping nose. "In a different world, or at a different time, I'd want to pursue a relationship with you. But that's just not possible here and now."

Tor was having trouble drawing a breath. He needed to speak. He needed to say something. The truth.

"I feel the same way about you, Kyle."

Her shoulders began to shake and her face disappeared into her gloves.

He didn't touch her. He didn't try to comfort her. He just let her cry.

ℵ ℵ ℵ

They never made it to breakfast. Instead, Kyle drove the jeep away from the center of the camp where they parked and talked.
Well, he talked.
She cried.

Knowing that Tor was as attracted to her as she was to him was a double-edged sword of the cruelest kind. On one side of the blade it was comforting to know that the attraction was shared—she wasn't just experiencing a ridiculous crush on a man who barely knew she was alive.

But the other side of the blade wounded deeply: the possibility of love dangled in an impossible situation.

"You know what you thought of me when we first met," Tor said. "That I was just a panty-chaser. That I *know* I'm a catch, as they say. And that I'd take advantage of that."

Kyle nodded. "And now I know differently."

"Well, the other side of that is that I've never been in love. So I never gave much thought to getting married. To settling down. Having a family."

"The war got in the way," she offered.

"It did. That's true." He paused, seeming to search for the right words. "But it's more than that."

"Tell me," she whispered.

He looked at her, his expression tentative. "I think I assumed all those women were no more than flirts. There was nothing substantial about them."

Kyle sniffed. "Maybe."

"But with you—you didn't flirt."

She was horrified at the thought. "Of course not!"

Tor waved his hands as if he could erase that statement. "No, I mean you were yourself. You were Second Lieutenant Kyle Solberg. A beautiful woman who wasn't throwing herself at me."

He thinks I'm beautiful. "And?"

"And..." He ran his hands over his face. "I began to feel like I could... fall in love. For the first time."

Kyle's tears refreshed themselves, rolling hot and wet down her chilled cheeks. "Oh, Tor. What's to become of us?"

He looked stricken. "I'll go to war and you'll go back to

Viking. That's obvious. The only other choice would be to have an affair."

Kyle shook her head. "I would never risk the rest of my life on a fling!"

Tor rested his hand over hers. "And I would never ask you to. Or even let you, should it come to that."

Kyle reached for her handkerchief but it wasn't there.

"Here." Tor pulled the one she gave him out of his pocket. "I needed to return it anyway, now that it's done its job."

Kyle accepted it and lifted it to her nose.

It smells like him.

She blew her nose self-consciously and then asked, "What now?"

"We're still good friends. We won't kiss anymore. And I'll work on my English."

She peered warily into his eyes. "That's it?"

He shrugged. "What else should it be?"

"Nothing, I guess."

Kyle didn't want to start the jeep and drive away. When she did, then this whole mess with Erik and Tor and herself would be decided and done. But the beautiful Norseman would always be a regret in her life—brought together by war and held irrevocably apart by the same damned war.

She reached for the key.

Tor stopped her.

She looked at him, her expression somber.

"I have one last thing to say."

She gave him a hint of a nod.

"I think I'll always regret not meeting you under different circumstances. You're an amazing woman, Kyle. Never forget that."

"Thanks," she whispered and turned the key.

✈ ✈ ✈

After supper that night Tor decided to check in on Kossin and see how the private was coming along two weeks after the accident. He told Kyle he'd walk from the mess hall and released her for the night. He really needed to be away from her for a little while.

Funny how not being able to have her made him want her even more.

Tor took long leg-stretching steps as he traversed the huge camp, using both the exercise and cold air to clear his head. He'd mentioned the option of an affair to Kyle with half-a-hope that she'd consider it.

Of course, he knew in his heart she wouldn't. And he knew that was the right response.

Damn this war.

And God damn Adolf Hitler.

When he reached the hospital he walked two laps around it before he felt calm enough to enter. He climbed the stairs to the second floor and walked into Kossin's ward.

Marguerite was on duty again. She just smiled at him and put a finger to her lips, then pointed down the ward.

Kossin was sleeping.

Tor nodded that he understood, then walked quietly to the private's bed. Sitting with the injured soldier would give him the peace he needed to release the rest of his disappointment.

Because he was disappointed. Kyle's kisses proved that under the starched WAC uniform of the farm girl from Viking beat a very passionate heart. When Kyle loved, she would love with her whole being.

He just wasn't convinced that she loved Erik that way.

Stop it. That changes nothing.

Another member of the Terrible Trio—Flo—entered the ward.

"Can you talk?" she asked Marguerite softly. Marguerite must have pointed at his back because Flo said, "He doesn't speak English, remember?"

"Oh. Right."

Tor held still and breathed through his mouth. Whatever was about to be said was secret and he didn't want to miss a word.

"I'm going to visit Luddy tonight, and Frances is going to meet Fred. Want to come along?"

"Gerry's not expecting me." Marguerite sounded tentative.

"One of the guys could go fetch him."

"Okay." Marguerite sounded a little more certain. "What time?"

"You get off at ten, right?"

"Yes. I'll meet you at the rock right away."

The rock?

The rock near the POW enclosure was the first thing that popped into Tor's mind. Were these the women Tor saw visiting the Germans three weeks ago?

No. They couldn't be.

Could they?

There's only one way to find out.

"Great. I'll see you later." Flo's footsteps receded.

Tor heard Marguerite approach and turned a little to smile at her. He lifted his brows in question and used the same thumb signals to ask how Kossin was doing. This time, Marguerite gave him a thumbs up response.

Tor nodded and smiled again. Then he looked at his watch, pretending to be surprised at the time.

He pointed to himself, yawned, and mimed sleep by resting his head against his hands.

He stood, touched his finger to his lips, and tiptoed out of the ward.

И И И

Tor was hidden near the path to the POW camp by nine-thirty. He was dressed in the white snow camouflage parka and pants again and hunkered down behind a bush. If the nurses were meeting American soldiers, they wouldn't be anywhere near here tonight.

But if they *were* meeting American soldiers, why the secrecy and worry about being overheard? And why sneak out at night? There were more recreational options at Camp Hale than any small town like Leadville had to offer. A guy and his gal could date openly, and many of them did.

At least he didn't need to stay out as long as last time. If the three nurses weren't here by ten-thirty, then they were headed somewhere else.

But if they were coming here, he'd need an explanation for why he was here before he told Kyle. He couldn't say he overheard Marguerite and Flo because officially he didn't speak English, and his lessons with Kyle hadn't progressed far enough for him to have followed the hushed conversation.

I'll just say I couldn't sleep and came back to spy on the Germans.

Since he'd done it before, it made sense for him to do it again. Of course he was getting an annoying reputation with the Major General, but that man's opinion of him didn't matter. Not if anything Tor saw turned out to be important.

Giggling.

Coming from the left.

The sound of a dove cooing, coming from the right.

Footsteps tromping through the snow like elephants.

If the nurses had basic training, they didn't learn anything about secretive operations, that was for sure.

"Luddy?" *That must be Flo.*

"Over here." The low voice was German-accented. "Who is with you?"

"Fran and Marguerite."

"Gerry is in his bed," another voice said. "Should I get him?"

"Yes. Thank you, Fred." *That was Marguerite.*

"I miss you, my dearest Flo. Do you have a note for me?"

"Of course I do. Here." There was a pause. "Do you have one for me?"

"*Mein liebchen*, of course I do."

"Oh, Luddy. I love it when you talk German to me."

As Tor listened for the next twenty minutes, he heard expressions of love and devotion and ridiculous promises on both sides of the prisoners' fence that all started with *after the war.*

Tor was gobsmacked. These three nurses were obviously carrying on little love affairs with the German prisoners of war. How did such a thing even begin?

Were the men injured at some point?

It was more likely they faked an illness to meet the women. It wouldn't take much investigation to know the WACs were stationed at the camp—and figuring out that one of the roles they'd taken on was nursing was mere childsplay.

If that was the case, the wooing would be easy. In spite of the ratio of men to women in the camp, lots of the women were lonely. An exotic foreigner with a sad tale would be intriguing.

Did it never occur to them that they were fraternizing with the enemy? That was court-martial worthy behavior. These three nurses had made some very bad decisions.

And Tor was going to assure that they got caught.

After what the brown-uniformed Nazi bastards did to his beloved country and to his younger brother, Tor had zero compassion for any of the men imprisoned here.

These soldiers were captured in Africa, part of Rommel's Afrika Korps—they were disciplined, arrogant, and proud. Their deceptions and manipulations of the gullible women were right in line with their belief that they were genetically superior to the rest of the world and had the right to do whatever they wanted.

Tor stayed put until goodbyes were said—were those *kisses* through the fence?—before he straightened and stretched his cramped legs. As he walked back to his barracks across the camp he wondered how he would tell Kyle that her roommate and two other friends were in deep, deep trouble.

CHAPTER NINETEEN

February 1, 1944

"Why are you so fidgety?" Tor hadn't held still since Kyle picked him up before breakfast. "What's wrong?"

The captain flashed a contrite smile and swung his forefinger in an inclusive circle next to his head. "I can't tell you in here."

"Then why didn't you tell me in the jeep?"

Tor looked uncomfortable. "I hadn't figured out how yet."

Kyle's shoulders slumped. "It's bad news, isn't it."

"It's not happy news," Tor conceded. "But neither you nor I are directly affected. Well, you are, but only a little."

Curiosity pushed Kyle to ask more questions, but the fact that Tor wouldn't meet her eyes told her to wait. She applied her efforts to polishing off her oatmeal.

"I'm done," she declared before gulping the rest of her coffee. "Let's go."

She stood and Tor stared up at her. "Can I finish?"

Kyle looked at her watch. "Not if we want time to talk."

Tor grunted and took an enormous bite of sausage. He stood, his chair sliding backward on the floor with a rumbling whine, and wiped his mouth on a napkin.

Kyle climbed into the driver's seat of the jeep waiting

outside the mess hall and started the engine while Tor folded himself into the seat besides her. Kyle pressed the gas pedal and set the vehicle on a random path around the camp.

"Okay," she said. "Talk."

Tor cleared his throat. "I went to see Kossin last night, but he was sleeping. So I decided to go to the POW enclosure."

"Oh, Tor." Kyle sighed. "If anything was going on I think it would be discovered by now."

"Something is going on." Tor paused. "And now I know what. And who's involved."

Kyle was skeptical. "All right. Tell me."

"Your friends the nurses, Marguerite and the other two, are enjoying a secret flirtation with the Germans."

Kyle hit the brakes hard and the jeep fishtailed a little on the slick path. She stared at Tor, incredulous. "Prove it."

"I saw them approach the fence last night—it must have been between ten and ten-thirty—and there were three POWs waiting for them."

Kyle scowled. "That's it?"

Tor shook his head. "They exchanged notes, and they kissed through the fence."

Kyle felt the blood drain from her face. "Did you hear any names?"

"Fred. Gerry. And…" Tor rubbed his chin. "Something that didn't sound like a normal name."

No. No no no.

Kyle thought her hasty breakfast was going to make an undignified exit. "Was it Luddy?"

"Yes. That was it." Tor tilted his head. "How did you know?"

"I've heard them talking about those men but I assumed, of course, that they were American soldiers." Kyle rested her forehead on the steering wheel. "This is terrible."

"I knew it would upset you. I'm sorry."

"I just can't believe it…" How could those women be so stupid?

"We have to tell Jones."

Kyle's head popped up. "No—let me talk to Marguerite first.

Maybe this is all a misunderstanding."

Tor's expression turned as hard as the granite surrounding them. "You can't do that, Kyle. If you do, the women will destroy any evidence."

"Does that matter if it makes them stop?" Kyle was stricken.

"It might," Tor said sternly.

She knew he was right, but she still asked, "How?"

"We don't know what they've told the men about the camp," Tor pointed out. "What if they help the POWs escape and then they blow us up?"

"Would they really help the men escape?" That sounded awfully far-fetched.

"Lonely women do stupid things if they think love is involved. Have you heard of the Germans' *Lebensborn* project?"

Kyle answered warily, "No."

Tor's expression softened a little, as if he was sorry to have to give her more bad news. "It's Himmler's idea. *Lebensborn* encourages officers to impregnate 'racially pure' unmarried women, and then adopts their children into Nazi families."

Kyle was horrified. "And the women go along with it?"

"They get special privileges until the babies are born, and I think they expect to marry the fathers of their babies after the war."

Kyle scoffed. "One randy officer could easily have a dozen wives if that was the case."

"So you can see my point." Tor looked like he was trying to appear empathetic but failed. "Those nurses could be cooking up anything at all in the hopes of living happily ever after."

He's right. "They're caught up in the excitement and intrigue…"

"Believing every word the prisoners tell them…"

"Because they have their own plans and are using the women—*damn* it." Kyle pounded on the steering wheel. "How could they be so gullible?"

Tor circled back around: "We have to tell Jones."

Kyle capitulated in the face of his indefensible volleys. "Yes. We do."

"And after I tell him what I saw, you'll have to tell him the names of everyone involved."

"We'll go when you finish training today." Kyle started driving again. "I'll make an appointment after I drop you off so we won't have to wait."

Tor reached over and squeezed her hand. When she looked at his hand and then at him, he said, "Relax Lieutenant, it's not a kiss. It's just an encouragement from a friend."

Oh. Right.

February 2, 1944

Major General Lloyd Jones was not in his office that day, but Kyle secured the first available appointment the next day. When she and Tor were seated in the general's office, Kyle took a deep breath and started with the thing she knew was going to annoy Jones the most.

"Captain Hansen was outside the POW enclosure again and he witnessed three American women—nurses—interacting with the Germans in romantic ways."

She thought the man might have a stroke on the spot.

He glared at Tor. "What are you trying to do?"

Kyle translated Tor's answer. "With all respect, sir, I wanted to see if I could gain any more information about what might be going on with the prisoners."

"And once again, you were the one who happened to be there?" Jones scowled. "How do I know you aren't the one involved in these theoretical goings on?"

Tor looked like he might explode with more force than the general. "Translate every single word," he growled with out looking at Kyle.

"I will."

"My country has been overrun by these bastards. Their puppet-leader put my brother in a labor camp in the Arctic Circle for seven months. I don't care if you believe me or not,"

Kyle gave Tor a look that tried to say *be careful* when she finished his words.

Jones glared at Tor. "You don't *care?*"

"No. I only care that you investigate, sir. Because if you do, you'll see that I'm telling the truth." He pointed at Kyle. "My translator's roommate is one of the nurses in question. If that puts Lieutenant Solberg in jeopardy, then I want her protected."

Kyle didn't react outwardly, but inside she was shrieking, *why did you pull me into this?*

The Major General narrowed his angry gaze. "Who are the WACs in question?"

Tor looked at Kyle. "You tell him."

Kyle faced Jones. "Privates Frances Bundorf, Florence Pechon, and Marguerite Franklin, sir. Franklin is my roommate."

"And have you witnessed anything that would corroborate the captain's story?"

"Only that the names that Captain Hansen overheard do match a conversation I was involved in four weeks ago."

"What names?"

"Fred, Gerry, and Luddy."

The general steepled his fingers and his tone remained intense. "Tell me about the conversation, Lieutenant."

Though she hated to betray her friends' trust, Kyle couldn't condone their actions or allow them to continue. "They were planning to go out for the evening and they were talking about their boyfriends. They said the men weren't going out with them because their situation was complicated."

"Is that all?"

Kyle shook her head. "They said they're all just engaging in a little wartime fun. They called it romantic and said it gives them all a diversion."

The general's pointed finger tapped his lips. "Go on."

"They talked about passing notes and called the men just pen pals at the moment."

When Kyle stopped, Tor offered, "I saw them all passing notes back and forth."

Kyle turned to look at Tor. Was that comment coincidentally timed? It had to be. Their English lessons hadn't progressed far enough for him to understand her.

She translated his words.

The general appeared to be considering his next action.

"This is what I'll do," he began slowly. "I don't want to pull our WACs under suspicion without due cause. But I will order a search of the POW quarters of any prisoners whose names could be Fred, Gerry, or Luddy."

Tor nodded his satisfaction when Kyle translated.

"In the meantime, Lieutenant, you are under orders not to say anything about what you've told me to Private Franklin."

"Understood, sir."

"You and the captain are dismissed."

"Will he tell us what the search turns up?" Tor asked Kyle as they rose from their seats.

"I doubt it," she answered honestly. "But if Marguerite is arrested, I guess we'll have our answer."

February 14, 1944

Tor concentrated on his new group of trainees and told himself not to think about what Jones was doing—or *not* doing—to find out about the romantic interactions between the nurses and the prisoners.

"Almost two weeks," he grumbled to Kyle after supper as she drove him to his barracks. "I don't think Jones's searching for anything."

"There are hundreds of names to go through and match before the searches start," she reminded him. "And who knows how many of the prisoners will ultimately be targeted."

Tor scrubbed his face with his hands as if he could wipe away the apparent fact that his warnings had been ignored by Jones. Again.

He looked at Kyle. "We leave for the Steamboat Springs competition early tomorrow morning. I need to focus on that anyway."

She didn't react, so he continued. "Pfeifer told me that there might be as many as hundred-and-fifty soldiers there from Camp Hale and Camp Carson." Tor snorted. "I don't think there are any American skiers left who haven't enlisted."

"Doesn't seem like it." Her voice was flat.

Tor looked at her more carefully. "Is something wrong?"

She shrugged. "Erik's not very good at keeping up his half of the letter-writing."

Tor pressed back the words he really wanted to say. "Of course not. He's a man."

"But it's Valentine's Day."

Tor's gut clenched. It certainly was. February fourteenth.

He had been so careful not to undermine Kyle's declaration that they were nothing more than friends. He hadn't tried to hold her hand or kiss her or say anything to her that spoke of more than a professional working relationship on very good terms.

But damn it, if she was his girl he would never have made such a mistake.

"I'm sorry, Kyle. I know that disappoints you."

Kyle stopped the jeep in front of his barracks.

"Maybe something will come tomorrow." The pained hope in her expression made his heart hurt.

Tor clenched his fists and fought the urge to reach over and touch her cheek. "Maybe there was a bad snowstorm that prevented the mail from getting through."

Her lips pinched in a tiny moue. She nodded.

A crazy idea popped into his head. "Can you come watch the competition tomorrow?"

That clearly sent her thoughts in a new direction, and she looked at him in surprise. "I don't know."

"Have you been given any other orders for tomorrow?"

She shook her head.

"Then come. Be my translator," he urged. "We aren't staying overnight—and it's only two-and-a-half hours north."

Her brows pulled together. "Would I ride the bus with you?"

"Yes," he decided on the spot.

Kyle looked a little sheepish. "I admit, I have been curious about what it's like."

"Then consider it done." Tor held up his left arm and pulled back his sleeve to expose his watch. "Now go get some sleep. We leave at five o'clock."

Before the desire to kiss her overwhelmed him, Tor opened

the jeep's passenger door and hopped out. He stuck his head back inside and said, "Don't forget a handkerchief. It worked for me last time." With a broad grin, he shut the door and ran up the steps to the barracks' door.

N N N

Kyle's spirit was lifted more than she thought possible. Tomorrow would have been a day off with Tor gone, but now she'd be at his side in her military capacity. And that meant going in uniform.

And watching him ski.

The few times she'd watched him she was transported by his strength and grace. The idea of spending a day doing just that was making her unexpectedly giddy.

She opened the door of her shared room to find Marguerite at the desk, bent over a sheet of paper.

Kyle's mood dropped again with the reminder of what her friend was doing.

Marguerite looked over her shoulder and grinned. "Hi! Did you have a Happy Valentine's Day?"

"Not yet." Kyle moved to the closet and hung up her coat. "Either Erik forgot, or something kept the mail from getting through."

"Oh, I'm sorry." Marguerite made a sad face.

Kyle pointed at the desk. "Is that for your guy?"

"Gerry? Yeah." Marguerite turned back around. "I just need to finish it up and deliver it."

Kyle took a deep breath and kept her voice light. "I have to go to bed early. Captain Hansen wants me to go with him to the competition in Steamboat Springs tomorrow."

"Sounds like fun," Marguerite said to the desk.

"I hope so." Kyle picked up her alarm clock and turned the knobs to set it. "When you get back, please try not to wake me. I'm getting up at four."

CHAPTER TWENTY

February 15, 1944

Tor grinned as he watched Kyle. She was like a little kid on Christmas morning, not knowing what to pay attention to first.

They boarded one of the three buses of soldiers in the pitch black pre-dawn of the icy winter's morning. Tor made certain that both Tokle and Pfeifer were on the same bus as he and Kyle. Though most of the soldiers settled in for a two-hour nap, Kyle was full of questions.

"Keep your voice low," he said. "We don't want cranky competitors."

"Do you know all these men?" she whispered.

"A lot of them are ski instructors, I know that. But we haven't spoken."

"Obviously."

Tor hesitated. "Right. And some names I recognize from skiing competitions."

Once they were at Steamboat Springs, Tor pointed out the ski jump. "That's what Torger does best."

Kyle's jaw dropped. "He jumps off of that?"

"And he's one of the best in the world." Tor pointed to another slope. "Over there is the downhill and slalom. Those are

my events. They'll be in the afternoon."
"What's first?"
"The jumps." Tor took Kyle's arm. "Let's go get a seat."
When the competition started at nine, Kyle was gobsmacked by what she saw. "I can't believe they just fly into the air! Are they crazy?" She turned to him. "Would you ever try that? Or have you?"
"No. And I won't." He smiled at her excitement. "I prefer to fly lower to the ground."
"When will Torger jump?"
"At the end because he's expected to go farthest." Tor pointed at the lit sign that displayed the distances for each jump. "If you notice, the numbers keep getting higher."
Two hours into the competition, Torger Tokle was finally set to jump.
"There are the standings." Tor pointed to the leader board. "Corporal Zoberski is in first place with a distance of two-hundred-and-one feet. Hudspeth from Steamboat Springs is in second with one-hundred and eighty-seven feet."
"So Torger has to jump at least two-hundred-and-two feet to win." Kyle drew a deep breath. "Go Camp Hale!"
The crowd stilled when the horn blew, indicating that Torger had started his descent. Kyle leaned forward in her seat, her mittened hands clenched in front of her. Tor held his breath.
When Torger reached the end of the jump and launched himself into the air the stands were silent. Tor watched his countryman with a mixture of awe and pride; Torger's flight was mesmerizing to behold.
When he landed on the earth, knees bent and arms wide for balance, all eyes went to the display and waited.
Two-hundred-and-twenty-six.
The spectators, breathless for the last several seconds, broke out in raucous cheers. Kyle jumped to her feet and added her own voice to the cacophony.
Tor stood as well and leaned down to speak in her ear. "Let's get something to eat. The slalom starts at noon."

⚔ ⚔ ⚔

Kyle settled into a seat to watch the slalom. Tor had given her a pair of binoculars so she could watch the skiers farther up the mountain more clearly than with her naked eyes.

"I'm near the end as well, because of how well I skied in Salt Lake City," Tor warned her as he handed her a scalding cup of hot chocolate. "So stay warm and patient."

She beamed up at him, thrilled to be here. "I will. Do you have my handkerchief?"

Tor patted his chest. "Next to my heart."

The surge of pleasure that suffused Kyle's core was disturbing, but she decided to ignore that. The handkerchief she gave him this morning was an embroidered one that one of her aunts gave her when she was twelve. She always thought it was too pretty to use so it stayed at the bottom of her drawer, but for this occasion it seemed perfect.

As the competition went on, Kyle kept an eye on the times posted. When Tor was finally announced as the next skier, Camp Hale men were in the top three slots: Knowlton, with a time of one minute, fifty-eight seconds, Stingl at two minutes flat, and Pepin in third with two minutes, three seconds. Kyle raised the binoculars to her eyes and adjusted the focus.

Come on, Tor.

The horn beeped his start. Kyle held the binoculars steady until he skied into her view then she followed him the rest of the way down.

The man was glorious.

She loved Erik, she knew she did, but nothing her fiancé had accomplished so far was as amazing and impressive as this. Tor's entire body flexed as his balance shifted quickly from one ski to the other, sending him in opposite directions around the poles.

When he crouched low and shot past the finish line, Kyle dropped the binoculars and turned, breathless, to the time display.

Two minutes, four seconds.

Kyle tried not to be disappointed. She hoped Tor wasn't. Camp Hale secured the top four slots and he should be proud.

Besides, he always told me downhill was his strength.

Kyle watched Tor's expression carefully as she met up with him beneath the bleachers. He looked nothing like disappointed. He looked exhilarated.

"God, that was fantastic!" he enthused.

"You're not upset you got fourth?" she asked.

"Well, sure, I'd like to place higher. But there are more Hale skiers here than in Salt Lake so the competition is stronger." Tor lifted a mug of something hot and downed a gulp before he continued. "Besides, I haven't trained regularly since I joined the Norwegian Army four years ago. The fact that I was as fast as I *was* is great."

"And you said downhill is your strength anyway," Kyle reminded him.

He nodded. "And I have the chance to fly downhill everyday at camp."

"Might you win?"

Tor laughed. "I doubt it. But that's not why I ski." His expression shifted to an almost dreamy one. "I ski because it's life."

N N N

The downhill races were run late in the afternoon and the six-hundred-yard course was a little rough from wear. But it was a mere third of the distance that Tor trained his men on at Camp Hale, so he knew the run wouldn't tire him out.

He'd go all out from top to bottom, he resolved.

I'll fly as fast as I can.

Kyle was waiting in the stands below, binoculars in hand when he left her to ride the tow to the top of the run. He waited again for his name to be called near the end of the competition. The sun was low, hovering just over the top of the mountains.

"Hansen, you're up."

Tor skied to the starting line and felt his blood start to sizzle with anticipation. He flexed his knees, held his poles at ready and waited.

Three. Two. One.

Beep.

He was off.

The run was swift and short, but Tor relished every split second of his flight. He felt alive and challenged and the challenge was met.

As he skidded to a stop at the bottom, he watched the results along with the rest of the crowd.

Twenty-three point five seconds.

Tor nodded his satisfaction. There were three more skiers after him, so he'd have to wait with the rest of the spectators and competitors to see where he'd fall.

※ ※ ※

Private Cremer from Camp Hale took first with a time of twenty-three seconds flat, putting Tor in second place. Tor shook the man's hand in congratulations.

"You're a formidable competitor, Hansen," Cremer said. "I'm proud to have you on our side."

Tor nodded his thanks, glad that no one seemed to notice his understanding of the compliment, but not risking an answer even so.

"Half a second is not more than hitting an extra mogul," he told Kyle later. "Besides, the Camp Hale team scored fourteen-thousand-eight-hundred points today and won the trophy. Camp Carlson only scored eighty-four-hundred."

Kyle laughed at that. "I suppose that is what counts."

The men boarded the buses that would return them to Camp Hale after they had a chance to grab a quick supper at the Winter Festival. With his belly full and his body alive with the exertion, Tor was in a very good mood.

"So—did you enjoy the day?" he asked Kyle as the bus rolled onto the south-bound highway.

In the dark bus only the light from oncoming headlights showed him her expression. It was jubilant.

"More than I even imagined," she said. "It was thrilling."

Tor reached into his shirt and pulled out the embroidered handkerchief. "Even though I'm not disappointed with my places today, I think maybe the plain one was a better favor."

Kyle held out her hand. "I'll keep that in mind for the next time."

Tor laid the folded linen on her palm. "Athletes do tend to be superstitious creatures. Winning isn't always under our control, so we grab onto anything else that might influence our outcomes."

"And here I thought it was because we were friends."

In the quick light of a passing car, Tor saw a hint of sadness in Kyle's expression. "It is because we're friends that I asked for your favor to begin with."

Kyle didn't say anything.

Though it killed him to mention it, Tor offered, "Maybe when we get back, there'll be a letter from Erik."

Kyle still didn't say anything and he couldn't see her face at the moment.

Tor didn't know what to do. Should he continue to try and make conversation? Or should he leave her to her thoughts, whatever they were.

Pfeifer came up the aisle and sat next to the man in front of Tor and Kyle. "Well done today, Hansen!" he said in German.

"Well done all of us," Tor answered, taking his attention from Kyle. "We beat Carlson like they weren't even there."

He thought Pfeifer was smiling, although with him facing backward no light shown directly on his face. "It was a good day, wasn't it?"

"Torger did all right, didn't he?"

He could see Pfeifer nodding. "That jump was spectacular."

"Of course. He's Norwegian," Tor teased.

Pfeifer patted Tor's shoulder and moved to another seat to talk to Cremer.

"What did he say?" Kyle asked.

"Just congratulating the men on their places."

"Oh." Kyle yawned.

"You're tired. Rest your head on my shoulder."

She turned to face him. "I don't think I should."

"It means nothing, Kyle. I offer because my shoulder is more comfortable than a cold, hard metal window frame."

She glanced at the rattling window in question and then turned back to him. "What will the men think?"

"Do you care? Because I don't. Come on." Tor put his arm around her and pulled her close. "Relax, Kyle. Sleep if you want."

He felt her slump against him, her shoulder tucked under his arm and her head against the side of his shoulder.

Tor rested his cheek on top of her head and inhaled the scents of the day that were trapped in her hair: snow and wood smoke. He was content.

This is where she belongs.

February 16, 1944

"Major General Jones wants to see the two of you immediately."

Kyle looked up from her breakfast and glanced across the table at Tor before she answered. "What's wrong?"

The corporal looked flustered. "I'm not at liberty to say any more."

Kyle pointed at her and Tor's trays. "Are we allowed to finish our breakfast first?"

Now the corporal looked embarrassed. "He didn't say."

"What's going on?" Tor asked.

"Jones wants to see us right away," she said in Norsk.

The captain lifted a forkful of eggs. "Can we finish first?"

"He didn't say, apparently." Kyle saw the look in Tor's eyes so she added, "It doesn't matter how much you dislike him. He is the camp's commander."

"I never said I didn't like him," Tor objected. "I just don't like the way he mistrusts me for no reason."

"Lieutenant Solberg?" the corporal interrupted. "Is there a problem?"

Kyle decided to take control of the situation. "Yes, Corporal, a small one. You see, Captain Hansen and I returned rather late last night from a skiing competition in Steamboat Springs, and had only a light supper before boarding the bus for our three-hour ride back to camp."

"Oh." The man glanced nervously from Kyle to Tor and back. "What should I tell the Major General?"

"Tell him we'll be on our way shortly and will get there as soon as we can."

The corporal looked relieved. "Yes, Lieutenant." He saluted and Kyle saluted back, then he hurried out of the mess hall.

Kyle translated her response for Tor and lifted a spoonful of oatmeal. "I am curious. I wonder what happened while we were gone."

Tor shrugged with one shoulder. "One can only imagine."

※ ※ ※

Tor sat, stunned to his core, as Major General Lloyd Jones told him and Kyle what transpired the night before.

"Two German prisoners escaped from Camp Hale last night with Private Dale Maple."

Tor wanted to shout *I told you so*, but managed to restrain himself and look no more than concerned until Kyle translated the general's words.

After that, however, he showed his anger. "I did tell you something was going on."

Kyle translated hesitantly.

"Yes, Captain Hansen, you did."

That was it?

Irritated, Tor looked at Kyle. "So what does he want from us now?"

The general looked pained. "Tell me more about the nurses."

CHAPTER TWENTY ONE

Tor repeated his story of seeing the three nurses whom he recognized chattering with three German POWs called Fred, Gerry, and Luddy.

He ended his retelling with, "What were the names of the escaped prisoners?"

"I already thought of that," the general replied. "But their names were Heinrich Kikillus and Erhard Schwichtenberg, and apparently Maple picked them up from a work detail without anyone noticing."

Tor agreed that they were probably not the same men. "Besides, there we
re three of them with the nurses."

Jones looked at Kyle. "Have you heard or seen anything since we first discussed this?"

Kyle's expression was somber and she nodded. "Private Franklin was writing a letter to Gerry when I returned to my barracks last night."

The general reached for a paper on his desk. "I now have a list of every German prisoner in the camp. Would you please mark any who you believe might be Gerry?"

Kyle translated while she looked at Tor adding, "You know

German. Would you recognize German nicknames?"

"Sure," he answered. "As long as they're using their real names."

"Then help me." Kyle put the paper between them. "Tell me which ones to mark."

Tor and Kyle bent over the list.

"Gerhard. Friedrich. Georg. Ludwig. Fritz. Franz. Lutz. Ferdinand. Friedhelm." Tor looked at Jones. "There are some first names used by more than one man."

Kyle translated.

Tor handed the paper to the general. "But there's a start."

The general looked over the list. "Can you make any guesses as to the ages of the men? Or what they look like?"

"No. I'm sorry. It was dark and I was behind a rock."

His brow twitched. "Understood."

"What are you going to do?"

Kyle translated Tor's question.

Jones looked at him as if deciding whether or not to answer before offering, "First we'll search all of these men's bunks. If we find anything, the path is clear."

It was Kyle who asked, "And if you don't?"

"We'll search the nurses' quarters." The general laid the list on his desk and considered Kyle with a stern expression. "I'm sure I don't need to reiterate my order, Lieutenant, that you are to say absolutely nothing to the women involved."

"No, sir." Kyle heaved a jagged sigh. "Considering last night's events, the severity of the situation can't be overstated."

"There's one other thing."

Kyle looked worried. "Yes, sir?"

"We are not letting the civilians know what's happened until Maple and the Germans are caught. There's no need to alarm them unnecessarily in the meantime, because they *will* be caught." Jones straightened in his chair. "Our conversation here is classified. Do you both understand?"

Kyle translated, and Tor answered as she did.

"Yes, sir."

"Good. You are dismissed."

Tor rose slowly and stared at the general, waiting until the

man met his eyes.
When he did, Tor lifted one brow.
The general looked puzzled for a moment until understanding dawned. "Oh. And, uh, thank you for your help."
Tor saluted him.

ᚾ ᚾ ᚾ

Kyle didn't want to go back to her barracks in case Marguerite was there, so she spent a good part of the day in the valley's flat fields watching Tor work with his novice skiers. Her own lessons had been inconsistent due to his competitions and her five days of leave, but she was learning more just watching him.
It really is about showing, not talking.
Their English lessons had suffered from the odd schedule as well, but they had moved on to simple phrases. She just hadn't been successful at getting Tor to try any of them in public. One thing that he began doing, however, was asking her, *did he just say…?*
His skill at connecting words and their meanings was impressive even if he refused to speak them.
He does have Norsk and German, she realized. And if he knows any Latin from school, he should be advancing soon.
He's holding back so I'm not reassigned.
Again she felt an unwelcome surge of affection for the Norseman.
Damn it.
Kyle started the jeep, determined to go to the postal building and see if anything had come for her.

ᚾ ᚾ ᚾ

When Kyle picked up Tor at the end of training, she was snorting fire.
"I didn't do it," he said.
She frowned at him. "Do what?"
"Whatever it is that's making you so fierce."

Kyle made a disgusted face. "I don't want to talk about it."

"About what?" Tor ventured.

She turned to look at him, her expression incredulous. "I *said* I don't want to talk about it."

"That's fine." Tor shrugged and one corner of his mouth lifted. "I just want to know what you don't want to talk about so I don't bring it up."

"Don't bring anything up!" she snapped. She drove the jeep toward his barracks, her jaw clenched.

Tor poked the bear. "Have you seen Marguerite today?"

"No." she shot him an irritated glance. "Didn't you see me? I was watching your training."

"Is that what you don't want to talk about?"

"What? Marguerite?" she squeaked.

"Yes."

"No."

"Then is it the training you don't want to talk about?" Tor shifted in his seat to see her better. "Or maybe you have questions."

"Neither," she growled. "Just stop. Please."

Tor drummed his fingers on the dashboard. "The weather was nice today."

Kyle said nothing.

"I wonder if we'll have meatloaf again tonight."

She grunted.

"You know what meatloaf is, don't you?" Tor snickered. "It's like Swedish meatballs that are the size of a shoe."

Kyle's lips pressed together like she was killing a smile.

"Do you *like* Swedish meatballs?" Tor continued his inane conversation. "Because I think the only thing that makes them better…"

Tor held curved hands in front of him about a foot-and-a-half apart. "…is making them as big as an Army boot."

Kyle snorted and then sniffed to camouflage it.

Encouraged, Tor sat back in his seat. "Yes, indeed. A huge Swedish meatball as big as my head. That's just the thing."

"Well I have a Norwegian meatball the size of a captain in my vehicle right now," Kyle barked.

"Welcome back, Lieutenant." Tor laughed. "Do you want to talk about meatballs, too?"

"Will you *please* shut up?" Her words were sharp, but she displayed the hint of a reluctant smile.

"Absolutely, Lieutenant. I would be happy to shut up. You won't hear another word out of me. I promise, cross my heart."

He did so with exaggerated movements. "I'll be shutting up right now."

Kyle grunted again.

"Unless..."

Her arm shot sideways and she thumped him hard in the middle of his chest with a tight fist. Tor flinched out of reflex, but she didn't hurt him.

He rubbed his chest. "Feel better?"

"Yes." She pulled the jeep to a stop in front of his barracks and turned to glare at him. "Can I hit you again?"

"Yes." Tor spread his arms and offered her a target. "Go ahead."

Kyle recoiled. "What? No."

"You can't hurt me," he said wondering if she actually might. "And if it helps you get over whatever has set you on fire, then do it."

Her eyes narrowed and filled with tears. She punched him again, but not as hard.

"Keep going." The reason for her anger suddenly thumped him as hard as she did. "Hit me until you forgive Erik."

Kyle's face crumpled and a raw sob burst from her. She pummeled Tor's chest with her right fist—the only one that could reach him when she was behind the steering wheel. He let her hit him a dozen times before she tired.

Then he grabbed her arm. "Better?"

She slumped in her seat. "No. But yes. And no."

"Perfect answer." Tor opened his door and stepped out of the jeep. "I'll walk to supper. See you there."

He strode into his barracks wondering if staying just friends with the lieutenant was going to be possible.

※ ※ ※

Kyle drove away from Tor's barracks so confused that she couldn't think straight. Nothing had arrived from Erik yet, and that upset her deeply. He was her fiancé after all. Why wasn't he acting like one?

And then the captain provoked her so ridiculously until he made her laugh—at least on the inside. But when she lost her temper, he offered himself up as a sacrifice.

Hit him until she forgave Erik? What sort of man does something like that?

How he figured it out in the first place was obvious—after she told him nothing had arrived from Minnesota on Valentine's Day, he'd asked her to go with him to the competition in Steamboat Springs. She knew he did that just to distract her. But she was so glad that he did.

Now Erik's apparent disregard of her was standing in direct contrast to the Norwegian's kind considerations. That was not helping her hold to the only resolve that made any sense.

Kyle stopped the jeep in front of her own barracks and wondered if she had the strength to go inside and face Marguerite, knowing what she now knew beyond a doubt.

Nope.

Kyle reengaged the jeep and drove toward the POW enclosure, curious if any hint of a search was evident. As she drew closer and parked, she saw the prisoners standing rank and file in the exercise area under flood lights. All of the single-story housing units were lit from the inside and she could see movement in the rooms.

She sighed, glad on one hand to see the activity and wondering what might be found. On the other hand, she felt like she was waiting for something big and horrible to fall from the sky. Being around Marguerite and Flo and Frances was wearing her down.

After a few minutes, Kyle drove away. She'd know what she could know when it was knowable. Until then, she needed to focus on her job.

She left the jeep in its regular spot outside the mess hall and went inside to get a pre-supper cup of coffee. She was surprised to see Tor was already there, talking amiably with Torger and

Frank Collins.

When his eyes met hers, he rubbed his chest and winked. Kyle knew she blushed. She went to get her coffee and added cream before joining the trio.

"Tell them what you thought of the competition," Tor said without preamble.

Kyle had to smile at that. "It was incredible. I've never seen anything like it." She turned to Torger. "I can't believe what you do—aren't you afraid to jump like that?"

He shook his head. "No. My Norwegian skull is too hard for thoughts like that."

After a few more minutes of pleasantries, Kyle addressed Tor in Norsk. "Can I have a minute before supper?"

"Sure." He turned to his friends and said in English, "Excuse me."

Torger grinned and answered in that same language. "Of course."

Once there was enough distance between the two pairs of soldiers, Kyle stopped and faced Tor. "I drove by the POWs."

She clearly caught his attention. "And?"

"And they're searching every unit. All the prisoners were standing at attention in the exercise field. There were lights everywhere."

Tor nodded. "After last night's escape, I'd do the same thing."

"Then why ask about the names this morning?" Kyle asked. "Just to search those parts extra carefully?"

"And more specifically," he clarified. "They'll be looking for anything suspicious in the general search, but for signed love notes in those cases."

Kyle shuddered. "I hope this is over soon."

Tor's smile was grim. "It's bound to be."

February 17, 1944

Kyle was sleeping, dreaming of skiers who were flying away with German POWs on their backs when a knock at the door woke her.

Marguerite groaned and asked, "Who is it?"

"Military Police, ma'am."

Kyle gasped and sat straight up. Her pulse roared in her ears. She turned on the light and grabbed her clock.

Five a.m.

Marguerite squinted and sat up as well. "Did he say Military Police?"

Kyle nodded and reached for her robe. "I'll get it."

She slid her feet into her slippers and donned her robe as she walked to the door. She heaved a breath and opened the door with a shaking hand.

Two massive MPs faced her, unsmiling. "Private Marguerite Franklin?"

Kyle shook her head and stepped back, opening the door wider. "Come in."

The officers looked at Marguerite who still sat in her bed, wide-eyed and looking confused.

"Private Marguerite Franklin?"

She nodded. "Yes…"

"You're under arrest for fraternization with the enemy. You'll be held in the Camp Hale prison until your court martial, an which time you'll be found either guilty or not guilty."

Marguerite stared at the MPs. "What did I do?"

"You exchanged love notes with a German prisoner of war named Gerhardt Schilling."

"Gerry?" Marguerite turned frantically to Kyle. "What do I do?"

Kyle chewed her lower lip, feeling sorry for the gullible and clueless woman. "Get dressed, Marguerite. You need to go with them."

CHAPTER TWENTY TWO

"We'll be waiting outside, ma'am." The MPs backed out of the room and pulled the door shut.

Marguerite still hadn't grasped the severity of her situation. "Can't they come back later? The sun's not even up."

Kyle sat on the foot of her own bed. "That's not how getting arrested works."

"This has to be a mistake," Marguerite insisted. "It's just love notes."

Kyle tried not to look at Marguerite like she was the epitome of stupid, but it was a struggle. "That's what fraternizing *is*. And you did it with the enemy of our country while we're at war."

"But I never told him anything military," she objected.

"Are you sure?" Kyle pressed. "How do you know that something that seemed like nothing to you wasn't a detail that would help them escape?"

Marguerite scowled. "He wouldn't escape. He wants to marry me."

"I wouldn't mention that if I were you," Kyle warned. "It would prove your guilt."

A soft knock on their door was followed with, "Are you about ready?"

Marguerite was still in bed. "This *has* to be a mistake…"

Kyle sighed. "Mistake or not, I think you'd better get up and get dressed before they drag you out of here in your nightgown."

That possibility seemed to get through Marguerite's fog. She threw back the covers and jumped out of bed, hurrying to her closet. She pulled her nightgown over her head and reached for her bra.

"So…" she said with her back to Kyle. "Do you think they know about Flo and Frances, too?"

"I would assume so."

"What about Jane and Helen?"

Kyle startled. "There were more of you?"

"Jane and Helen just started talking to the men a couple weeks ago." Marguerite continued getting dressed, but she turned back to face Kyle, her confusion clear. "How do you think they found out?"

Kyle wasn't about to confess her or Tor's part in that. "I drove by the POW camp last night. All the lights were on and they were searching the barracks."

"Really?" Marguerite's movement stopped. "Why?"

Kyle couldn't tell her about Private Maple and the escaped German prisoners because the Major General specifically ordered her not to.

So she just shrugged. "Maybe something happened…"

Marguerite finished dressing and sat down to brush her hair. The MPs knocked on the door again.

"Private Franklin!"

Kyle stood up and went to open the door. "Come in. She's ready."

The MPs entered the room again and Marguerite rose.

"Hold out your arms."

She did, seeming to be unaware of the reason. But when the MP who'd done all the talking clamped handcuffs on her wrists she burst into tears.

"Do you have to do that?" she asked, sobbing.

"Yes, ma'am."

The second MP opened the desk drawers and shuffled through the papers inside. Then he threw back Marguerite's bedcovers and shook them out. He pulled the cover off her pillow. Then he lifted her mattress. Kyle's heart lurched when she saw the messy pile of notes stashed under there.

When he began to collect them Marguerite cried, "Those are mine!"

The MP shot her a severe look, straightening the wad of notes in his hand. "Not anymore. Now they're evidence."

He handed the stack to the other officer before he made a perfunctory search of Marguerite's dresser. Finding nothing else, he nodded to his companion.

The MP who handcuffed Marguerite took hold of her elbow. "Let's go."

*   *   *

Kyle couldn't go back to sleep after such a deeply disturbing interruption, so she got dressed for the day. When she finished, she still had half-an-hour before she needed to go get her jeep and pick up Tor, so she sat down and started a letter to Erik.

> *A very disturbing thing happened before dawn this morning—my roommate was arrested for fraternizing with the enemy! She and some of her friends had been visiting the POW enclosure here at Camp Hale and talking to the Germans imprisoned there. They were writing love notes back and forth, and even went so far as to think that the Germans would marry them when the war ends. Who would want to marry a Nazi?*

Kyle stopped, wondering if she should mention not getting anything from him for Valentine's Day. Maybe he did send her something, but it got lost for some reason. If that was the case, he'd want to know.

And if he sent her nothing, then he might be prompted to make up for the oversight now.

> *I hope you got my card for Valentine's Day. I sent it early so it would arrive on time. I thought I would hear*

from you, but nothing has come yet. I hope it hasn't been lost.

"That should do it." Kyle folded the letter she'd finish later and tucked it in the desk drawer before she considered Marguerite's disheveled half of the room.

She couldn't live with such a messy reminder of the nurse's indiscretions, so she bundled the linens for the laundry and folded the blanket, which she stowed under the pillow at the head of the bed on the bare mattress.

Marguerite's dresser drawers were closed, so whatever disarray was created inside wasn't visible.

Kyle donned her coat and left the room. It was finally time to pick up Tor and tell him what happened.

✄ ✄ ✄

Tor climbed into the jeep. The look on Kyle's face startled him. "What happened?"

"Marguerite was arrested at five o'clock this morning." Kyle's expression was an odd combination of excitement and despair. "Fraternization with the enemy. She'll face a court martial."

That was a lot of information to receive at once. "What about the other two?"

"I assume Flo and Frances received the same visit. But—" Kyle gave him a knowing look. "There are two *more* WACs involved."

Tor's brow shot upward. "Two more nurses?"

"I don't know if they're nurses or not. All Marguerite said was that their names are Jane and Helen."

"Five, then?" Tor wagged his head. "I hope they didn't give away too much information."

"The MPs found a bunch of notes under Marguerite's mattress." Kyle's lips twisted. "I guess they'll find out when they read them."

That's certainly true. "How'd she react? When the MPs came?"

Kyle huffed. "She didn't understand how serious it was until they handcuffed her."

He coughed a rough chuckle. "That would convince anyone, I'm sure."

"You were right about the activity at the POW camp last night resulting in something like this. They must've found notes with the women's names on them."

Tor nodded his agreement. "Couldn't arrest them without that I wouldn't think."

Kyle's expression turned pensive. "I wonder if they found anything connected with Maple and the escape."

"If they did, I doubt Jones will tell us," Tor answered truthfully. "Are you going to tell him about the other two WACs?"

"I don't know..." She sounded sadly resolved. "I suppose I should."

"I agree. Even if all you have is first names, there might be evidence of their involvement in the other notes."

Kyle shifted the running jeep into gear. "I'll go after I drop you at the mountain."

February 21, 1944

The secret of the POWS and their assisted escape was revealed in the *Ski-Zette* four days later. Kyle translated and read the article to Tor that afternoon when she picked him up from training.

Camp Hale Private Caught With Two Escaped Nazis

Private Dale Maple of the 85th Mountain Division was arrested on February 18th when he and two German POWs were caught crossing the border into Mexico.

Maple purchased a 1934 REO sedan in preparation for the escape. On February 15th he picked up Afrika Korps Sergeants Heinrich Kikillus and Erhard

Schwichtenberg from a work detail. After thirty-six hours of driving, they were within seventeen miles of the Mexican border when they ran out of gas.

The trio then covered the remaining distance on foot until they entered Mexico, where they were arrested by a Mexican customs official and turned over to American authorities.

Maple has been identified as a Naziphile and was often seen near the POW encampment where he conversed with the men in German. He is currently being jailed in Albuquerque, New Mexico and has been charged with treason.

The escaped prisoners are being returned to Camp Hale, where they will be held in solitary confinement for the remainder of the war.

Kyle looked at Tor. "At least we don't have to keep that secret any longer. But I still don't understand how he could do such a thing."

"Or any of them, for that matter." Tor's blood heated whenever he encountered anyone who was sympathetic to the Nazis and their darkly perverted cause. "I can only think that they're ignorant of the unconscionable crimes that Hitler and his filthy henchmen are committing all across Europe."

"It's harder here," Kyle admitted. "None of us has seen it for ourselves."

"Pray that you never do," Tor replied stiffly. "Because that would mean we couldn't stop them."

March 7, 1944

Two weeks later, Kyle translated the *Ski-Zette* to Tor again as they sat down to supper.

"It says that the Army convened the court martial and, instead of treason, they charged Maple under the 81st Article of War for relieving, corresponding with, or aiding the enemy."

She looked at Tor. "They called it the closest equivalent to the charge of treason."

Tor scowled. "Why did they do that?"

Kyle's eyes skimmed the paper. "It doesn't say. Maybe it's easier to prove."

Tor grunted. "Was he convicted, then?"

Kyle nodded. "He pled innocent, but was found guilty and was sentenced to death by hanging."

"Good. He deserves it," he stated without a trace of empathy.

Kyle turned the page. "Oh! Here's an article about the nurses involved with the POWs."

Her brow lowered as she read and translated. "Frances, Florence, and Marguerite were all found guilty of fraternization with the enemy and sentenced to twelve months in prison, to be followed by dishonorable discharge."

"What about the other two?"

"They aren't mentioned." Kyle looked up at Tor. "But wait until you hear this: the *Denver Post* reported that military officials seized three or four stills and forty to fifty gallons of liquor from the POWs here."

"What the hell is going on?" Tor pounded an angry fist on the mess hall table, causing their silverware to jump and tangle. "Is this camp just a resort for the Germans?"

"Easy, Hansen." Torger Tokle slid into the seat next to his. "What's got your Norwegian up?"

Tor gave Torger a brief rundown of the three articles, none of which showed Camp Hale in the best light.

"Well, then…" Torger grinned. "You should be happy to remember that once again the champion skiers of Camp Hale have a chance to redeem the camp's tarnished reputation."

The thought of skiing competitively always lifted Tor's spirits. "At Pike's Peak? When?"

"April twenty-third." Torger tapped the *Ski-Zette* in Kyle's hand. "It's on page one."

I need to read that for myself.

Kyle closed the paper and handed it to Tor. "I think your English might be good enough for you to pick out the important parts."

Torger looked at him in surprise. "You finally learning

English?" he asked in that language.

"I speak a little English, now," Tor replied, feeling like a complete fool. "But please speak slowly."

"Good for you!" Torger pounded his shoulder then returned to Norsk as he pointed at the paper. "See what you can work out on your own, and ask me about what you can't."

"I will." Tor smiled. "And thank you."

When they were alone again, Tor asked Kyle, "Have you heard from Erik lately?"

His obsession with her relationship with her fiancé wasn't healthy and he knew it. Neither was his hope that the engagement would end. In spite of that, he asked as sincerely as he could, knowing he wasn't in a position to offer her any alternative.

She lifted one unconcerned shoulder. "Yeah. I sent him a letter after Marguerite was arrested and added a comment that his Valentine's card never arrived."

I bet he never sent one.

"What was his response?"

Kyle made a disgusted face. "The first page-and-a-half was all about how he wasn't surprised at the WACs' behavior and that the women didn't understand *why* they shouldn't become involved with the men."

Tor was aghast. "He did not."

"Yes, he did."

I'd deck him if he was in front of me right now.

"And then," she continued, "the next day I got a card. But the postmark on it was after he got my letter."

"Do you think he forgot?" Tor poked.

"I don't know. He says it was the second card he sent and that the first one must have gotten lost."

Tor's delight stabbed him with guilt. He held up the folded *Ski-Zette*. "I'm going to go decipher the English. Wish me luck."

"Do you want me to drive you to your barracks?"

Tor stood, knowing that the precarious mood he was in at the moment made that unwise. "No. I want to walk. I'll see you tomorrow."

⁂ ⁂ ⁂

The headline read: *Many Camp Hale Skiers Submit Entries for Pikes Peak Ski Tournament* and the subtitle below claimed: *Will Be First of Kind to Be Held in U.S.*

Tor read the article with increasing excitement. The competition was to be held way above timberline on the snow-covered north face of Pikes Peak. It said that the list of men who submitted entries for the meet was increasing daily—*thank God I'm not too late*—and many were members of the Mountain Training Group.

Corporal Friedl Pfeifer was the first name listed.

Tor scanned the list of names for Torger, but he wasn't there. The disclaimer, *many more men from the Tenth Division have entered the meet, but it was not possible to get their names for this week's issue of the Ski-Zette* settled that.

The article said that the meet would consist of a controlled downhill and slalom race on a brand-new course which started at thirteen thousand feet and dropped to Glen Cove—one-and-a-half miles and a thousand feet below.

Tor was practically salivating. He felt the fizzy tingle of anticipation flood his veins. Such a challenge was irresistible to him. He must talk to Pfeifer first thing in the morning and find out how to enter. He had to be there. He *needed* to be there.

CHAPTER TWENTY THREE

March 23, 1944

With the mountain shrouded in clouds, training today would consist of military tactics required once the soldiers reached their objective. Tor showed his trainees how to change the cable location on their skis from the rear to the side of the toe piece, converting the binding from downhill to cross-country allowing the heel to lift during the stride.

Private Keith Kossin was assigned to Tor's group again but would train on a limited basis. Nine weeks after Kossin's fall the pins were removed and his leg was still in a brace, but the doctors wanted him to put weight on it and start moving again.

Tor was happy to have the man back under his tutelage and hoped he could build on what the hapless private already knew. Kossin was beaming, clearly ecstatic to be back.

Kyle was with him this morning to translate the day's instructions since they were doing something new.

"We're going to cross-country ski quite a way out to the training grounds," Tor began. "There's an enemy tent out there and men dressed in enemy uniforms. Once we get close, we'll take our skis off because they'll make noise in the snow."

He paused until Kyle finished. "Does everyone have their show shoes?"

All eighteen heads nodded.

"Good. Now when we approach the tent, there will be absolutely no talking. None. Is that understood?"

Again, all heads nodded.

"You are to slip up on the enemy, put your bayonet to their neck, and say *if you make a noise, I'll kill you.*"

One brave recruit raised his hand. "Shouldn't we say that in German?"

Tor smiled. "*Ja.*"

He turned to Kyle. "Tell them to say this: *mach ein Geräusch und ich werde dich töten.*"

Kyle did her best. Tor had the men repeat the phrase several times until many of them got it, but assured them all that for today's exercises the English equivalent would be fine.

"As for speaking German," Tor continued. "When we get to Italy, the men who are fluent in German will be assigned to enter the Germans' tents and take the officers prisoner. They'll also be the ones who'll have to read over enemy files and retrieve any essential documents."

When Kyle was done translating, Tor asked. "Any questions?"

No one raised a hand.

"Good." Tor looked at Kyle. "Would you like to come with us?"

※ ※ ※

Kyle looked up at Tor in shock. "Me?"

"Sure. You've kept up your required physical training, haven't you?"

"Well, yes, but I don't have any skis."

"There are three extra pair right over there." Tor pointed to a rack of skis and poles. "And this will be easier to master than going downhill."

Kyle was warming to the idea but, "Then I'll have to ski back too, won't I?"

"If you want to," Tor said. "But a Weasel will be bringing lunch to the training camp. You could ride back with them."

Kyle looked at the skis. "Maybe."

"Or." Tor leaned closer. His smile was trouble. "I could carry you back."

Kyle tried to keep her expression appropriate in front of the eighteen soldiers who were watching their Norsk exchange with curiosity. "That won't be necessary. But, yes. I think I'd like to try."

Tor faced his men, grinned, and said in broken English, "Lieutenant Solberg comes with us."

The soldiers found that amusing, judging by the looks they exchanged.

Tor obviously noticed because, still grinning, he scolded them. "Do not have her come in front of you."

The idea that she might startled many of them and the teasing stopped.

Kyle walked to the rack of skis and laid a pair on the snow. She fastened the bindings to her Army boots the way Tor had just shown the trainees.

"I don't have snow shoes," she reminded Tor.

"You don't need them. You're not going into combat," he replied. "When we get to that point, you'll wait behind until the exercise is completed."

Kyle wrapped the straps of her ski poles around her wrists.

"Ready?" Tor asked.

"Yep."

He faced his troops.

"Follow me!" he said in English.

Kyle's worries about keeping up were quickly proven unnecessary. She had been at Camp Hale for over six months and had become accustomed to the ninety-two-hundred-foot altitude.

The new trainees, however, were still adjusting.

As she skied behind Tor, the eighteen men trailed out behind her, many falling far behind.

"The conditions in the mountains don't discriminate between men and women," Tor observed when he stopped to allow the stragglers to catch up. "I think they'll have more respect for you and the other WACs now that they've seen that for themselves."

Kyle shot him a skeptical look. "Is that why you asked me to come along?"

"In part, yes."

"And in the other part?"

"I wanted you to see what I do all day."

That was not the answer she expected. It must have shown on her face because Tor chuckled softly.

"I also enjoy your company," he confessed. "And this pack of clueless chumps is driving me crazy."

Kyle laughed. Hearing that he enjoyed her company meant a lot to her, because she enjoyed his. Tor had become a special friend over the months and she felt comfortable and safe when he was around. He'd also kept to his word and had not tried to trip her up with inappropriate statements for her to soften and translate.

"I'm glad you asked. And I'm glad I came. This is actually fun."

"Fun for you." Tor's gaze rose over her head and his smile disappeared.

"Come on!" he shouted in English. "The lieutenant wants to go!"

✳ ✳ ✳

When they reached the point where the enemy camp was visible, everyone except Kyle took off their skis and strapped their bearpaws to their boots. Tor hefted his skis to his shoulder and the men followed his example. Then in single file they made their silent approach.

Tor told her that she could follow on her skis if she stayed fifty yards back.

"We aren't taking them by surprise," he pointed out. "They know we're coming at some point. So as long as you're out of the way you can get closer and watch."

As she did, it was soon obvious which of the men had hunting experience and which ones had only hunted for food in a grocery store aisle. That gave her an idea.

She unstrapped one ski and sank her boot into the snow to test its depth.

Nope. Can't do that.

She refastened the binding and settled her skis into the single line of tracks left by the nineteen pair of bearpaws that went before her. The snow there was already broken up and made no sound as she glided forward on her skis.

Kyle watched the men dressed in German uniforms as they were taken by the recruits. Some seemed to be giving up far too easily. True, it was cold and miserable out here and the play-actors had been here for weeks while various platoons took their turns at the training.

But these men needed to be adequately prepared. No Nazi was going to give up that quickly or easily.

Kyle spotted one brown-clad soldier sneaking around the edge of a tent. His clear aim was to grab an American from behind and turn the tables on him.

Good for you.

Kyle slid forward with slow smooth movements. She wasn't dressed in the head-to-toe white snow camouflage because she hadn't known she'd be here, so she paused behind trees and watched for opportunities.

The first man jumped a recruit but another took his place. Kyle continued to stalk him like she would prey in the woods of northern Minnesota.

When she skied up behind him and grabbed him she shouted, "*Mach ein Geräusch und ich werde dich töten!*"

He spun out of her grasp so quickly he fell on his rear, gaping up at her like she was an apparition.

"What the *hell?*" he bellowed.

Tor ran around the far edge of the tent, stopping when he saw her standing over her prisoner on her skis.

"I got one!" She pointed at the fallen man with a ski pole. "I didn't have a bayonet, but he is on the ground. Does that count?"

И И И

Tor recounted Kyle's victory to Torger at supper that evening wiping tears of laughter from his eyes.

"I wish you could have seen it!" he managed between guffaws. "That guy was furious. Couldn't believe he didn't see her coming!"

Torger was suitably amused. "I would have loved to see that! But I bet your men weren't happy about being beat."

"None of them were, to be honest." Tor hooked a thumb in Kyle's direction. "To be shown up by a woman? Grated on their egos, that's for sure."

"They started grumbling about women in combat," Kyle added. "Tor simply said that the best soldiers would win the day. So—*be* the best soldiers."

"This group needed a kick in the ass, to be honest." Tor's admiring gaze moved to Kyle's. "Never occurred to me to let a woman teach the lesson."

"Did you ski back?" Torger asked.

"No, I rode in the Weasel." Kyle gave a little shrug. "It seemed best."

"Probably was," the Norseman agreed. "Men with bruised egos can be rough."

"You're going to the Pikes Peak tournament, aren't you?" Tor asked him. Kyle suspected he was changing the subject and wondered why. "I didn't see your name on the first list."

Torger shook his head. "There aren't any jumps."

"Come for the fun of it," Tor urged. "Take a downhill run at least."

"I might. When's the deadline to sign up?"

"Two days before. April twenty-first."

Torger gave a non-committal nod. "I'll think about it."

"Do." Tor pushed away from the table and looked at Kyle. "Ready?"

"Sure." She stood and lifted her tray. "Let's go."

и и и

When Kyle stopped the jeep in front of Tor's barracks, he didn't get out right away.

"Is something on your mind?" she asked.

"Yes." Tor looked like he was scanning his thoughts for the right words. "First of all, you showed some impressive skill today, sneaking up on the man and surprising him."

Kyle smiled. "Thank you."

"And if you were in battle with a bayonet, you would've had him." He paused. "The thing is…"

Kyle's smile faded. "What?"

Tor twisted in his seat to face her. "You're a woman. You won't ever have a bayonet or be in battle."

She frowned a little. "Why does that matter?"

"It matters because it made the men angry." Tor put up a hand to halt her retort. "But they needed to be made angry. They haven't been putting in the effort they should be. These guys are nothing like my first group."

"So what's the problem?"

"A lot of men think the WACs are unnatural. Women shouldn't be in the army. They wonder about some of you."

Kyle was confused about what he meant by that. "Wonder? About what?"

"If you even… like… men."

It took a moment for Tor's meaning to become clear before Kyle's cheeks flamed.

"Aren't there enough camp romances around to answer that question?" she snapped.

Tor looked apologetic. "And that's the other side. That the WACs are here to pleasure the men."

Kyle wanted to hit something but Tor was her only—and thoroughly undeserving—target.

"UGGHHH!" she shouted instead.

"Today you showed them that maybe you deserved to be here under your own merit, and that will take time for them to accept."

"*Maybe?*" she yelped.

Tor threw his hands up. "Don't shoot me. Remember Norway has women in the Milorg working alongside the men."

Kyle crossed her arms angrily. "So what now?"

"There's nothing for you to do. Except don't do it again."

Kyle clenched her jaw. "Fine."

Tor's expression softened. "And now that I've said that, I can tell you the truth. I was so proud of you today."

Kyle looked sideways at him. "You were?"

"Completely. You did exactly the right thing."

Kyle's body relaxed some. "I've gone hunting with my father."

"It showed." Tor grabbed the jeep's door handle. "And to be honest, I'd be glad to have you by my side anytime. You're a force to be reckoned with."

Kyle flushed with pleasure. "That means a lot to me, Tor."

He smiled softly. "Good night, Kyle."

When he got out of the jeep and walked away she felt like her heart was trailing along the ground after him.

CHAPTER TWENTY FOUR

April 2, 1944

Tor had his men back on the slopes again after a week of combat training. Their moods had settled with regards to Lieutenant Solberg and some even joked about it, though not everyone laughed.

Today they were halfway up the slope and off to one side to work on turns.

"Look!" Tor barked as he demonstrated where to put their weight on the skis to change direction. "Here."

He pointed to the uphill and inside edges, then swung his skis in the opposite direction. "And then here."

He had begun using very simple English with this group to ensure they understood him.

"Now I do." Tor side-stepped up the slope several yards and slalomed down, making four quick turns.

"Yes?" He pointed at the men. "You do. Down."

The men lined up and started their downhill runs one at a time, practicing the maneuvers. Tor watched from his vantage point, overall not too disappointed. He followed the last man down and led the group back to the T-bar.

"Again."

He rode the T-bar up first, deciding how far to go. There was a point where a clearing in the trees would let the men ski down without blocking the main run and that's where he headed now.

He sent the men down as they arrived at the spot. Before they pushed off he gestured with a horizontal circle and said, "Go again."

Kossin stood next to him, clearly nervous. "Should I try it?"

Tor shook his head and motioned a straight line.

Kossin was relieved. "Okay."

The men were on their fourth cycle. Kossin was beside him in the trees again, working up the nerve to take another easy run. A man named Hackles was walking to his starting spot on the slope.

Tor heard a soft crack from higher on the slope. Adrenaline flooded his body.

No!

"Hackles!"

The soldier turned to look at him, and then he was gone. There was nothing in his place but a mound of snow.

"Oh, God..." Kossin moaned.

Tor cupped his hands around his mouth and shouted down the mountain. "AVALANCHE! AVALANCHE!"

Then he smacked Kossin's arm hard and reached up to pull a dead branch from a pine tree. "Help me!"

Kossin yanked another branch down and followed Tor who was already poking the branch deep into the snow. "Find Hackles!"

Poke. Nothing.

Poke again. Nothing.

Poke yet again.

Nothing.

Kossin was frantically poking the snow downhill of where Hackles had been standing.

"I can't find him." he cried.

"Do not stop!" Tor barked.

Men started arriving with shovels, jumping off the T-bar in pairs.

"How many?" the first one asked.

"One." Tor pointed. "He was there."

Men swarmed around him and Kossin, digging like a life depended on it. Because it did.

Tor hit something. He poked his branch in again and hit it again. It was too soft to be a rock.

"HERE!"

The rescue crew moved to his side and dug. Their wide, lightweight shovels sent sun-reflecting snow crystals flying in all directions—an incongruently beautiful sight in the life-and-death situation.

If Hackles hadn't been wearing his snow camouflage the task would be easier; as it was no flashes of color under the white layer would guide the men.

Suddenly an arm jutted up from the snow.

Three men dropped their shovels and grabbed it. They pulled upward until Hackles' face appeared.

The man sucked a loud, raw breath. And then another.

"Where are your feet?" one of the rescuers asked.

Hackles pointed up the slope.

Working more carefully now that Hackles could breathe, the men shoveled snow away until the private was completely uncovered.

One of his skis had been knocked off his boot, but the other one was still in place. Hackles' foot was twisted outward and away from his body.

"Is your leg broken?" a man with a red cross on his sleeve asked.

"I don't think so."

Tor laid belly-down on the snow at the edge of the hole and reached down to unfasten the binding on the remaining ski. The three men who started the job pulled Hackles free of the snow.

A toboggan appeared, having been dragged up by another man with a red cross embellished armband.

Hackles was helped onto the toboggan and the medics strapped him on in preparation to ride him down.

He looked up at Tor. "You saved my life, Captain. You poked an air hole for me. I don't know if you can understand me,

but I thank you."
Tor nodded but didn't say anything. The private saluted him, and Tor saluted back.
Thank you, God.

◢ ◢ ◢

Kyle's jaw dropped. "An avalanche?"
"Not a big one, but tell that to the man who almost died." Tor slumped in the passenger seat of the jeep. The rush of adrenaline and subsequent physical exertion of the rescue had left him drained.
Kyle's expression as she drove toward his barracks showed her confusion. "I thought avalanches were big loud things with massive amounts of snow falling down the mountain."
"They can be. But more often they're smaller slips." Tor heaved a deep breath. "Snow builds up in some spot but it's not stable. A shift in temperature can be enough to make part of it melt and then the whole chunk slides down."
Kyle glanced sideways at him. "Did you hear it coming?"
"I heard the crack. It wasn't very loud but I knew what it was." Tor took off his hat and scratched his head. "I shouted to Hackles, but it hit him before he could move."
"What did you do?"
"Shouted a warning down the slope. Grabbed a branch. Started poking the snow to find him."
Kyle looked at him like he was some sort of wizard. "I never would have thought of that."
"Norway has plenty of mountains and plenty of snow. You know we invented skiing, right?"
She rolled her eyes. "Of course."
"So we had to figure out what to do when the snow fights back."
"So poking around with a stick so you know where to dig?"
Tor smiled at her naïveté. "Ramming a branch into the snow hoping to find him—or at least open an air hole in the meantime."
"You've saved two lives now." Her tone sounded awestruck.

Tor didn't say anything. He'd only acted in the same way that was expected in his home country. Just because Kyle had no experience with such things didn't elevate his actions to heroic, whatever the *Ski-Zette* said.

"I'm exhausted."

Kyle stopped the jeep. "Will you still come to supper?"

"I think so." Tor looked at his watch. "I'm going to catch a nap in the meantime."

Two hours later when Tor entered the mess hall behind Kyle applause broke out. He waved it away and told her to keep moving.

Though she led him quickly toward the food service line some men, and a lot of women, were pushing past her to shake his hand.

"Save me," he begged her in Norsk.

"What can I do?" She smiled at him like she loved every uncomfortable minute of the impromptu show of appreciation. She picked up a tray and started moving down the line. "People are glad Hackles isn't dead."

April 18, 1944

The United Service Organizations—USO—was performing at Camp Hale this weekend and Kyle was clearly excited about going to the show.

"They're performing tomorrow night at seven in the lounge of the new Station Complement Service Club," she read from the Ski-Zette. "And on Sunday it's at two o'clock in the Red Cross auditorium at the hospital."

"Gee. It's too bad we don't have any connections with the nurses anymore."

She lowered the paper and glared at him. "Not funny."

"Sorry."

She returned her attention to the newspaper. "Here's the line-up. First is Ramee Sami, a magician who'll do a comedy burlesque of fortune tellers."

"Never heard of him."

"It says he was formerly associated with Houdini and has forty years of show business experience."

"Oh, wait..." Tor tilted his head. "Nope. Still never heard of him."

Kyle stuck out her tongue. "How about ventriloquist Dick Bruno? His dummy was made by the same studio as Charlie McCarthy."

"I've heard of Charlie," Tor offered. "Is he the dummy or the puppet?"

"Stop it, Tor." She was clearly trying not to laugh. "These are legitimate entertainers who volunteer to support our armed services."

"Okay. Who else?"

Kyle consulted the paper again. "Murray King, an accordionist who solos—"

"Oh, no. No accordion solos. Huh uh." Tor shook his head. "I'd rather have my eardrums punctured."

Kyle looked desperate. "Betty Wilson, petite dancer from New Jersey? Radio songstress Georgette Starr? She's been on Broadway."

"So I'd have to suffer through a magician, a ventriloquist, and an accordion player to get to them?" Tor's mouth twisted. "How much alcohol is available?"

Kyle folded the paper angrily. "You're impossible."

"*I'm* impossible?" Tor waved a negating finger. "No. What's impossible is the idea that America is at war on both sides of the world, but we're sitting here in safety and relative comfort with second-rate performers deigning to come entertain us."

"Well what would you have us do? Just twiddle our thumbs?" Kyle glared at him. "You know what you're all preparing to do!"

Tor put his hands up. "All I can say is that in Norway—"

"Would you please shut up about Norway!" Kyle jumped to her feet. "If it's so wonderful being occupied and worrying the Nazis' heels like a disobedient dog then why did you even come here?"

Tor gaped at her. "That's not—"

"I don't care!"

Kyle whirled around and stormed out of the mess hall.

Torger Tokle watched her go as he sauntered over to Tor's table. "I was coming over to tell you that I entered the Pikes Peak tournament, but it looks like you might have other matters on your mind."

"Yeah." Tor huffed and stood. "I guess I better get going. Looks like I have to walk to the mountain today."

April 19, 1944

Tor suffered through the magician, the ventriloquist, and the accordion player to get to the dancer, Betty Wilson, and the singer Georgette Starr, but admitted to Kyle after the show was over that it was better than he expected.

"I appreciate you coming with me after all," she said for the third time. "And I'm really sorry about what I said about Norway."

He opened the jeep's door for her in an intentional display of chivalry. "You're Norwegian, but you're not. I understand."

He closed the door after she climbed in then went to the passenger side and joined her. "Because we speak Norsk all the time—and you're so fluent—I forget that you're actually American."

She started the engine. "I haven't been in the best mood this week."

That, he knew. "What's going on?"

"I still don't have a roommate, so while that seems like a luxury, the truth is it's lonely." She looked at him, the full moon shining through the windshield onto her face. "I spend most of my time with you, and because of what happened with the POWs I don't have other friends anymore—or the time to make any."

Tor bit his tongue but couldn't stop himself from asking. "And Erik?"

She was quiet for a while, finally offering, "It's so hard trying to maintain our relationship when we're so far apart."

"Especially when he's not happy at the reason you're gone."

Stop trying to sabotage her.

"Sometimes I wish I could just get a discharge and go home. But then I get to go to an amazing ski tournament in Steamboat Springs and I actually know the competitors." Her expression brightened in the moonlight. "Or even a night like tonight—I'd never get to see a show like that in Viking. Probably not even in Fargo."

Her words made Tor feel worse about his attitude than he had before. He was so focused on the idea that Americans were at war without actually suffering that he forgot that there were millions of Americans whose horizons were being broadened by the world-wide conflict.

"I travel countries like you travel states."

Kyle's brow furrowed. "What?"

"As a European I forget that your country is as big as my continent. You can travel as far as I do, but you're still in America."

"Um, yes. But—"

Never mind," he interrupted. "It was just a random thought. I'm very glad you enjoyed the show."

"Oh. Okay."

"So will you come to the Pikes Peak tournament?" Tor smiled encouragingly. "Torger finally signed up."

Kyle smiled. "I'd love to."

Don't kiss her.

Tor leaned forward.

Kyle's eyes widened but she didn't pull away.

Don't kiss her mouth.

Tor's lips brushed her cheek.

"I'll take the plain handkerchief this time," he whispered.

Kyle turned her face to his.

Don't—

Her lips briefly met his, sending a jolt of surprised pleasure through his frame before she pulled away. She shifted the jeep into first gear and drove to his barracks in silence and without looking at him.

CHAPTER TWENTY FIVE

April 23, 1944

"*The Tournament of Superlatives* is what they're calling it." Kyle read the paper to Tor as they rode the bus to Colorado Springs. "It's the first of its kind ever to be held on America's best-known mountain peak, an all-military event, open only to members of the Army, Navy, and Marine Corps."

"That's interesting." *And another example of America's odd response to war.* "It must be true that the best known skiers in the world are in the American armed forces."

Kyle looked up from the paper and over the seatback between them. "You're here, aren't you?"

"I'm not known outside of a very small group of skiers who competed to make our Olympic teams," he demurred. "And that was over four years ago. I'm nobody now."

Kyle gave him a disbelieving look. "You're not nobody. At least not to Kossin and Hackles."

Tor sighed. "I only did what I was supposed to do, and it worked. I'm not a hero."

"Well if people want to think you are, you can't stop them."

Kyle's attention returned to the paper. "Do you want to hear more?"

Tor watched her for a moment. The early morning sun cast a rosy light on her hair from behind as she leaned against the side of the bus. She was a very beautiful woman, more beautiful than when he met her. Was that reality? Or the result of his growing affection for his spunky sidekick?

She looked at him again. "Yes? No?"

"Yes."

Her eyes dropped to the paper and she scanned for the spot she left off. "Looks like they plan to make this an annual event. It says one perpetual trophy will be awarded, with the winners' names to be engraved each year, while six trophies and ten prizes of skiing equipment will also be awarded."

"Skiing equipment?" Tor grunted. "That would be worth winning. Much more useful than a name on a trophy."

Kyle laughed. "For a world-class competitor you don't have much of an ego."

"I told you, Lieutenant, I ski because I love it. And because I love it, I got very good at it." Tor looked out the windows on the opposite side of the bus. The passing mountain peaks were topped with sunrise-colored snow. "Skiing is life."

N N N

Kyle examined Tor's profile. He was just as handsome as the day she met him, but now she knew that his attractiveness was as strong on the inside as it was apparent on the outside.

She was angry at herself for kissing him the other night, albeit briefly. But he was right there. And the evening had been so delightful. Kissing is what people did at the end of a date.

Even if it wasn't a date.

Not officially, anyway.

Kyle's heart was waging a battle with her brain, and so far her brain was still winning. When summer ended and the weather changed the men of the Tenth Division would be sent to Italy to do what they'd been training for: knock out the Nazis by attacking them in the Alps.

It was obvious that she'd never see the Norwegian captain

again once he left Camp Hale. She wouldn't even know if he lived or died there.

But...

There was no but—she made a promise to Erik to be his wife. Kyle had no intention of breaking that promise.

But...

A brief affair of the heart didn't mean she would have to break that promise. As long as she remained a virgin, then she could return to Viking unsullied and walk into Erik's arms without guilt.

Could I really?

Kyle pretended to read the *Ski-Zette* while she thought about the startling thought.

That kind of arrangement between them meant getting Tor to agree on strict limits to any physical play between them. That would be a hard line she must hold to. It was not negotiable in any way.

Her virginity was the one thing she would give Erik without question, even if her heart had been temporarily distracted.

Erik's birthday was coming up. Should she request leave and go see him before she decided? May was a busy time for him, getting the livestock and their newborns out of the barns and into the pastures, and plowing and fertilizing the fields in preparation for planting.

Erik was twenty-eight, three years younger than Tor who'd quietly turned thirty-one back in January. And much like the Norwegian, he never liked to celebrate the occasion.

"I got born and survived this long," Erik always said. "A toast with my friends at *Viking Arms* is plenty of fuss for me."

Kyle could either write to her fiancé and ask if he'd like her to come home, or she could just show up and surprise him. If she surprised him, that meant enlisting her parents to pick her up in Fargo.

And hope Erik has time to take me back.

Kyle wished she had someone—besides Tor, of course—whose advice she could solicit. Maybe she should write to her best friend from high school. Heidi got married at nineteen and her three young children ate up all of her time now, but she still lived in Viking and knew everything that happened in the tiny town.

Heidi it is.

The bus slowed down and made a westward turn.

"Are we there?" she asked Pfeifer who was sitting a couple rows ahead of her.

"Not yet." He pointed out the side of the bus. "We need to climb that mountain. Pikes Peak's at the top."

ᚾ ᚾ ᚾ

Tor retrieved his skis and poles from the bus and walked to the base of the runs to see if snow conditions were posted. They were. The board stated there was a six-foot base of packed snow covered with four to five inches of dry powder.

Perfect.

Tor slapped Torger on the shoulder. "Times today will be fast. Maybe set a few records."

Torger squinted at the hazy clouds overhead. "As long as the weather holds."

"It will." Pfeifer stepped up behind them. "Those are stratocumulus clouds. Nothing there but a welcome lessening of the glare off the snow."

Kyle returned from the restroom facilities, set up for the large tournament crowd already milling past a multitude of food vendors. "How's it look?"

Tor grinned at her. "Like iced lightning."

She loosed an appreciative chuckle and shaded her eyes. "Where is the run?"

Tor led her back to where the spectator bleachers were set up. Then he turned around and pointed. "Up there."

Kyle looked alarmed. "Are you skiing straight down?"

"Looks like that from here. But no, there's a slope. Do you have the binoculars?"

"They're inside my coat." Kyle looked at him again, this time with fear in her eyes. "I'm scared for you."

"Don't be. These are new runs, but the men setting them up had to ski down them many times before they were decided on," he assured her. "And I've skied where runs hadn't been created. Just like we will in Italy."

Kyle didn't look placated. "Please be careful."

Careful wasn't the issue. Skill was. And he had skill to spare. "I'll be fine."

Army trucks were lined up and waiting to carry the skiers to the top of the peak. After the men checked in and got their assigned times they knew what time to catch the ride—an hour before their scheduled races.

Tor saw that he wasn't racing at the same times as Torger or Pfeifer, which meant that with no witnesses present he could converse with the other skiers and officials in English. That was going to make his day easier.

The tournament started promptly at nine. Since Tor had some time to spare, he and Kyle walked back to the vendor area and bought a second breakfast; their first one was five hours ago. Then he settled her in the stands, retrieved the blue wax from his bag, and headed for the trucks.

Tor climbed into the canvas-covered back of the army truck and took the farthest forward seat on the bench. The mood among the competitors was jubilant—obviously he wasn't the only man itching for the challenge of the steep slopes.

"Where you from?" one man asked him.

"Tenth Division, Camp Hale," he answered.

Someone else said, "You have an accent."

Tor smiled. "I'm Norwegian. I came to teach skiing to the American soldiers."

"*Er du Tor Hansen?*" came a query from the back of the truck.

Tor leaned forward. The man's face was familiar. "Einer?"

"Yes, it's me. I haven't seen you in five years!"

"That's because you left Norway before we were invaded, you cowardly bastard," Tor teased.

"That's smart bastard to you." Einer laughed. "When'd you get here?"

"November."

"Welcome. You shipping out with the Tenth?"

Tor nodded. "I expect to, yes. Somebody has to lead these

guys to the Nazis!"

When the truck squeaked to a stop at the top of the run the men filed out of the back two at a time. Once on the ground, Tor retrieved his skis and turned around to look for a spot to sit and wax them. What he saw claimed his ability to breathe.

He was standing on top of the world.

At well over thirteen-thousand feet, and about a thousand feet below the rocky top, he had a nearly three-hundred-and-sixty-degree view of the mountains around him.

He drew a deep breath of the thin, frigid air, and thanked God he was there.

Then he brushed the snow off a small boulder, sat down, and began waxing his skis.

N N N

Kyle waited in nervous anticipation for Tor's name to appear on the board. Several men had already successfully skied the terrifyingly steep course without incident, so she was a little less apprehensive than when she first saw the steep run.

Even so, the times posted for the mile-and-a-half downhill course started in the two-minute range.

That's forty miles per hour.

Kyle wrapped her hands around her cardboard cup of coffee and watched the skiers' times shrink with each competitor.

One minute and forty two seconds was the time to beat when Tor's name was announced as next.

Fifty miles per hour.

Kyle set her coffee down and fished the warm binoculars out of her coat. She pressed them to her eyes and turned the focus knob until she could see him. Even on the highest setting, Tor was nothing more than a featureless figure at the starting line.

He pushed off before the faint pop of the pistol reached her. She followed him the best she could while refocusing the binoculars as he skied closer. He was moving impossibly fast.

God keep him safe.

When he reached the bottom he skied in a snow-throwing semi-circle to stop but hit the barrier before he could and he fell to the ground.

Kyle gasped.

Tor unfastened one ski then stood up and waved.

The crowd cheered.

They cheered even louder when his time was posted on the electronic sign: one minute and thirty-four seconds.

Almost sixty miles an hour.

Kyle cheered louder than anyone.

※ ※ ※

"Are you hurt?" Kyle's expression was etched with fear.

"Not badly," Tor said. "Just a little sprain. It happened when I hit the fence."

"You're limping."

"I know. It hurts."

Kyle slid her arm around his waist. He thought it was cute that she thought she could hold him up.

"These boots are only ankle high," he said pointing at his feet. "They don't offer a lot of support for edging purposes. When I hit the fence one of my skis slipped."

She peered into his eyes. "You aren't going to ski again, are you?"

Tor flashed a resigned expression. "No. I'm done for the day. No slalom for me."

"You're in first place right now," Kyle offered.

He nodded. "Then I have a chance of placing. I think Pfeifer is the only one who might beat me."

Tor limped with Kyle to the organizers' tent. One of the medics there wrapped his swollen ankle in an ACE bandage. He pulled his sock and boot back on, thanked the man, then hobbled back to the bleachers with Kyle.

"You stay here," she ordered her commanding officer. "I'll get your skis and poles."

"Thanks." He watched her walk away and wondered at her sudden change in mood. Was it because he was injured, even slightly?

Ever since she kissed him she had been more subdued in his

presence. Not cold, not grouchy. Just more quiet than usual. He wanted to know her thoughts but was afraid to ask. He didn't want to embarrass her and figured that if she wanted to talk about it, she would.

But since arriving at the tournament today, Kyle was back to her former self. She even tucked the handkerchief into his shirt herself with an impish smile and a, "Good luck, Captain."

It might have been his imagination, but he thought she almost kissed him again.

Kyle came back with his skis and poles over her shoulder and waved to him. "I'll take them to the bus," she called out in Norsk.

"Thank you," he called back in English.

When she returned from that task, she climbed to their seats with two steaming cups. She handed him one, smiling.

"We have to keep you warm, sir."

Tor stared at her, confused but very pleased. "Thank you, Lieutenant."

"You're welcome." Her eyes smiled at him over the rim of her cup as she took a sip.

ℳ ℳ ℳ

In the end, Tor took second to Friedl Pfeifer just as he predicted. Pfeifer beat him by two seconds.

Tor accepted his prizes—a small trophy and a new pair of civilian skis and boots.

"I appreciate the gifts," he said to Kyle on the way to the bus. "But I can't take the skis or boots to Italy. The skis and poles aren't white, and the boots aren't any good for mountain climbing. But that doesn't mean I won't enjoy them while I'm training."

"After your ankle is healed," she reminded him.

"That should only take a few days."

Kyle doubted that, but the stubborn Norseman was going to do whatever he wanted to do. "Just don't make it worse."

"I won't." His expression was confident. "I've had plenty of sprained ankles before."

The men of Camp Hale boarded their buses with tournament food in hand. The drive back was almost four hours long and waiting until nine o'clock for supper was more than their audibly rumbling stomachs could handle.

Kyle settled in front of Tor again so she could turn sideways in her seat to talk to him but not start rumors by sitting in the same seat as he.

If she did propose a fling, those rumors would probably surface at some point. There was no point in hurrying them along.

The sun sank behind the mountains as the bus wound it's way back to the camp. Conversation was lively at first, but as the sky grew dark it seemed to prompt snores.

"Are you tired?" she asked Tor.

"A little," he admitted. "It's the adrenaline mostly."

"What do you mean?"

"The challenge of making it down a slope as fast as you can sends adrenaline throughout your body. A man named Walter Cannon from America's Harvard University discovered it about twenty-five years ago. He called it fight or flight."

"I've heard of that." Kyle pulled faint facts from her memory. "The adrenaline enables your muscles to work fast and hard."

"Exactly," Tor said. "And afterwards, you feel drained. The more physical you are, the more you drain your reserves."

"Go ahead and nap if you want," she offered, grinning. "I promise I won't let them leave you on the bus."

"That's what friends are for, right?" He settled into the corner of the seat, stretched his legs into the aisle, and crossed his arms.

In less than five minutes he was snoring.

CHAPTER TWENTY SIX

May 21, 1944

Kyle sent a letter to Heidi the day after the Pikes Peak tournament. She started it with general news, including the gossip (which was how Heidi would see it) about the three nurses and their love affairs with the German prisoners of war.

Kyle went ahead and spiced up the telling a little so it would hold Heidi's attention, but she was sure to point out that the women were arrested, sentenced to a year in prison, and would be dishonorably discharged once they were released.

She decided not to talk about the escaped POW because she didn't want Heidi to panic. People who'd lived their whole lives in tiny Viking tended to worry about the outer world more than Kyle ever would again.

Then she casually mentioned that Erik's birthday was coming up and she was thinking about requesting leave so she could come home and celebrate.

The thing I can't decide is whether or not to try and surprise him if I do get leave. I'd have to have my parents pick me up in Fargo and ask Erik to drive me back afterwards... What do you think?

Heidi's answer took two long weeks to arrive, and when it did it was frustratingly vague:

I think the idea of surprising Erik is so cute and romantic. But I'm not sure he would appreciate the surprise since he's so busy getting the farm going for the season. Maybe it would be better if he knew you were coming.

Kyle thought about that for a couple days before she decided to go ahead and request leave. Three days was the minimum that would get her to Viking and back with a full day to spend with Erik, but she requested four. When the four days were approved, she sent a letter to Erik.

Only then did she tell Tor.

"I'll be fine, don't worry about me," he insisted with a little more enthusiasm than felt right. "You go and spend time with your fiancé."

Kyle had been holding back on her plan of enjoying a fling with the captain until she had some sort of answer about her possible visit to Viking.

Now she wondered if his overly bright reaction might be an attempt to hide a jealous streak.

I hope so.

"I might not go," she said. "It's not set for sure."

His expression shifted but she couldn't read its meaning. "Why wouldn't you go?"

She tried to sound unconcerned. "He might be too busy to take time off."

Tor lifted a brow. "I'd make the time."

Kyle met his gaze. "You're not a farmer."

He didn't reply verbally, but his expression made his opinion of that excuse very clear.

Yesterday Erik's answer came.

Kyle tore open the letter not wanting to wait until she got back to her barracks.

Dear Kyle,
Thank you for thinking of my birthday. That means a lot to me.
Unfortunately, your plans have come too late...

Kyle stopped reading. She refolded the letter and stuffed it back in the envelope. She said nothing to Tor and pretended like everything was fine. She didn't retrieve the letter until she was alone in her room and had gotten ready for bed. Only then did she feel like facing Erik's words.

Unfortunately your plans have come too late for me to take any days off for weeks to come. If you had written two weeks ago and had made plans to come then I might have been able to find the time. As it is now, it's just not possible.

Kyle put the letter in the desk drawer without reading the rest. There was no point. And today, after she dropped Tor at the gun range, she would go back to headquarters and cancel her leave.

Her first reaction to Erik's words was guilt. She was a terrible fiancée. Was she going to be a terrible wife as well? She didn't deserve Erik, who was working so hard to keep his farm productive so that he could provide for her and their children.

But when she went to headquarters to cancel the leave, she started to get angry.

I'm serving my country, damn it. Our country.

She wasn't free to come and go at will. She'd joined the WACs and her schedule was at the mercy of the United States Army. She made that choice willingly.

One of us should serve.
We are at war, after all.

Kyle never begrudged Erik staying home. She understood that as the only child and sole support of his aging parents he was needed at home. Not to mention the food he provided in

place of the farmers who were able to go off and fight.
But it seemed to her now that he felt bad that he was still at home, and he was taking that resentment out on her.
I don't deserve that.
"Are you sure?" the clerk asked Kyle. "You want to cancel your leave?"
Kyle nodded. "My fiancé isn't able to take time off to be with me, so there's no point in my going home."
"Why don't you go somewhere else?" she pressed. "Go to Denver for a couple days. Get away from this place for a while."
"By myself?" Kyle made a face. "No thanks."
"Well I'm not going to file this until tomorrow, in case you change your mind." She opened the center drawer of her desk and dropped the cancellation form inside. "You have until tomorrow at four."
Kyle gave the gal a polite smile and then left the office.
It's time to talk to Tor.

и и и

When Kyle picked him up from the munitions range Tor felt nervousness radiating off of her with palpable force. He considered her expression carefully, wondering what had happened since he saw her this morning.
"Kyle?"
She glanced sideways and flashed a nervous smile. "Yes?"
"Is everything okay?"
She bounced a quick nod, her eyes staring through the jeep's windshield. "Uh huh."
Her silent fidgeting screamed its contradiction of her words. "Kyle, what's going on?"
"I, um, have something I want to talk to you about."
"Go ahead."
She glanced sideways again. "Can we go somewhere and talk?"
Tor waved at the landscape around them. "Pick a place. The weather is beautiful. We should enjoy the moment."
Kyle drove the jeep to the bottom of the mountain. No one

was there since the snow had melted and the recruits' training had shifted from skiing to mountain climbing. She parked the jeep and opened her door.

Tor opened his and got out of the jeep. "Want to sit on the bench by the T-bar?"

"Sure." Kyle jammed her hands into her pockets and walked toward the base.

Tor followed with absolutely no idea what she was about to say. He sat next to her on the bench and turned sideways on the bench to face her.

"Sorry if I smell like sweat," he offered. "It was a hard day."

She waved a hand. "You're fine."

He waited a minute while Kyle chewed her lower lip and took deep, gulping breaths.

Finally he reached for her hand. "Just say it, Kyle."

Her words came out in a rush. "I'm not going away on leave after all."

That surprised him. "Why not?"

"Um..." She swallowed thickly and stared at her knotting fingers. "Erik can't take any time off right now, what with getting ready for the spring planting."

Why—does the man work twenty-four hours a day?

Stop it.

"Will you go later, then?"

She shrugged. "Maybe. We'll see how things go."

Something about her tone made Tor ask, "What things?"

"That's what I wanted to talk to you about." Her eyes lifted to his. "I'm still going to marry Erik and you're still going to Italy."

Tor waited. There was nothing he could say to contradict either one of those statements.

"But—and please tell me if I'm wrong—I think we still share an attraction..."

The tentative way her sentence trailed off made her statement a question. His pulse stepped up its cadence.

"Yes, Kyle. I believe we do."

She seemed to gain some confidence from that. "I still think you're handsome and interesting and smart." Color rushed into her cheeks until they were as red as berries. "And you kiss really well."

Tor smiled self-consciously. The compliment was not one he'd heard before. "What are you suggesting?"

She drew a ragged breath. "I'm suggesting a fling."

Tor's veins fizzed with the thought. "How—intense—of a fling?"

"I absolutely draw the line at giving you my virginity." The berry red in her cheeks deepened. "That belongs only to Erik."

"I agree…" Tor was stunned by her suggestion. Happily stunned. "What… why…" He couldn't even make a sentence.

"Because I don't want to regret you for the rest of my life." She pounded a fist on her thigh. "There. I said it."

He watched her carefully. "Regret me?"

Kyle smiled at him with trembling lips. "I think could fall in love with you, Tor. If there wasn't Erik."

"But there is Erik."

"Exactly. So in the meantime, I want to be your girl."

Tor's smile grew without him thinking about it. "I'm honored. I mean that."

She looked like he slapped her. "Only honored?"

"No! I mean, yes. To everything." He grabbed her hand and unfolded her fist until he could kiss her palm. "I would like nothing more than to spend my remaining time in America with you as my girl. My only girl."

Kyle stared into his eyes. "And you agree. My virginity remains mine."

Tor crossed his heart with his free hand. "I'm a gentleman, Kyle. You know that."

"I do." Her lips curled slowly. "Kiss me."

He frowned. "I've been training all day."

"I don't care."

She didn't need to ask him twice.

***

After a shower, clean clothes, and supper, Tor snuck Kyle away like they were errant teenagers. They left the jeep outside the mess hall and walked to the camp's perimeter behind it. If he had been thinking clearly, he'd have brought a blanket.

But he wasn't.

He was still in shock and wondering what this fling thing would be like.

Kyle stopped walking and turned to face him. The three-quarter moon peeked between the pine branches above them, adding slices of blue light to the yellow glow of the camp's lamps.

She lifted her chin and stared into his eyes. "What now?"

Tor slid his hands under her arms and lifted her from the ground until her face was in front of his. Kyle wrapped her legs around his hips and looped her arms around his neck.

"Hi," she whispered.

"Hi," he murmured back.

His lips claimed hers in a tender trap, searching, teasing, and testing. He wanted to make the moment last—like Christmas Eve, knowing that the next day was going to bring happiness and extending the anticipation.

He pulled away and sighed. "You taste wonderful."

"It's cinnamon," she teased breathlessly. "I had the apple pie."

Tor laughed softly. "That must be it."

He kissed her again, this time going deeper. Her lips opened and his tongue met hers.

She moaned a little. Her breath was warm on his cheek.

It was intoxicating.

Tor turned slowly and leaned his back against a tree, so consumed by the feel of her mouth against his that he was afraid he might lose his balance.

Kyle's legs tightened around him and she pushed herself upward until her face was above his. She took control of the kiss and he let her. Her passion was almost aggressive.

His arousal was inevitable.

She pulled away and looked down at him, breathing heavily, her eyes lidded. "I've wanted to do this for so long."

"So have I," he admitted.

She sighed and relaxed a little until her face was even with his. "It's going to be hard, isn't it?"

He flashed a rueful smile.

It already is.

"I care for you, Kyle. You know that."

"And I care for you." She gave him a soft kiss. "And we know how this will end."

"Don't fall in love with me," he warned.

She chuckled. "And don't *you* fall in love with me, Captain."

Tor felt his chest tighten and he wondered about the wisdom of their new game. Would he be able to walk away from her when the time came? To blithely hand her over to the farmer who couldn't make time for her now?

Maybe she'd change her mind. Maybe she'd wait for him to come back for her.

Even as the thoughts formed in his mind he knew they were futile. He was the one who was going to get hurt in the end.

At least he'd be the one leaving. He'd board a transport and travel back across the Atlantic Ocean to fight his battles abroad in Italy. There wouldn't be time for him to miss her, he rationalized.

Thinking these things, and accepting them as inevitable, released Tor's fears. He would fully enjoy his time with Kyle for the months they had left here in this valley. The risk she was taking demanded that of him.

Because I don't want to regret her for the rest of my life either.

CHAPTER TWENTY SEVEN

June 21, 1944

Exactly one month had passed since Kyle asked Tor to engage with her in a secret affair. Being with him was absolute bliss—as long as she kept Tor and Erik in separate compartments of her heart.

Erik was a solid house. Tor was a tent pitched in some wild wood. In the end, the tent would be taken down and the house would survive.

They quickly fell into a pattern, retreating into the woods around the camp after supper and finding sanctuary away from curious eyes. Tor brought a blanket the second night and Kyle left it in the jeep so they always had it. They spread it on the fragrant needle-covered ground and laid on it together.

Their kisses moved to touches. The touches became more intimate. Tor seemed to be letting Kyle set the pace and she took him forward bit by bit. The first time she reached inside his trousers was an amazing night.

She'd never taken hold of Erik so she had no frame of reference, but Tor's manhood fascinated her. Hard, yet covered in softness at the same time. Sensitive and powerful. Pulsating with his release.

"My turn," he whispered.

When Tor's hand moved between her thighs the heavens above opened up, leaving Kyle stunned and boneless. Still panting and quivering, she pulled him close and cried, her face pressed to his neck.

"I—I never..."

"So I gathered." He kissed her hair. "I hope that was all right."

She didn't move. She couldn't move. "More than. It was wonderful."

After that evening they found pleasure and release with each other nearly every night. Afterwards they would lay side-by-side on one blanket and covered against the night chill by another, watching the sky, and talking.

Kyle found that almost as pleasurable as their sex play.

"Tell me about your home," she asked one night. Her nether parts were still throbbing, her panties damp, and her blouse unbuttoned and open.

Tor was shirtless, the fly of his trousers gaped wide, and the waistband of his boxers rested just above the nest of coarse hair that housed his manhood.

"What do you want to know?" His voice held a post-peak smokiness that she loved.

"Everything."

Tor sighed and rubbed his forehead. "We're an old family. Hansen Hall goes back to the Vikingers."

"Hansen Hall?" Kyle was impressed. "Is it a mansion?"

Tor snorted. "No. But it's good sized."

Kyle turned on her side to face him and tucked the top blanket against her back. "What does it look like?"

"Well in front and to one side is the original round Vikinger tower from, I don't know, a thousand years ago or so."

"Are you serious?" Kyle was shocked; nothing in America touched that ancient age. "A thousand years?"

"Yeah. We only use it for storage now." Tor moved his hands in the air above them, creating an imaginary drawing of the house. "Attached to that is the medieval section, which was built in the late twelve hundreds, I think. It's very typical of the era, with a huge Great Hall, enormous stone fireplace, and a stone staircase to the sleeping chambers on the upper floor."

His hands moved farther to the side. "Then the modern addition was added." He turned his head and winked at her. "A little over two hundred years ago."

Kyle was astounded. "What's in the modern part?"

"Indoor kitchen. Huge dining room. Back staircase. More bedrooms. And eventually indoor toilets and showers."

Kyle thought of her parents' cozy little home and Erik's two-story farmhouse and they paled against Tor's description of his ancestral estate. "Well it sounds like a mansion to me."

"It looks a little odd on the outside," Tor admitted. "But inside the different parts aren't noticeable, thanks to generations of clever Hansen women and wives."

"I wish I could see it," she said without thinking. "It sounds amazing."

Tor's hands lowered to his waist. "Maybe someday you and Erik can visit Arendal."

Kyle felt a stab of guilt and her mood cooled. "I don't think so."

Tor shrugged. "You don't know. In twenty years maybe you'll come visit me and my wife and our dozen children."

That made Kyle laugh. "Yes, maybe we will."

"I'll leave a light in the tower so you can find me."

For some reason that silly promise tore at Kyle's core and brought tears to her eyes. She refused to wipe them so Tor wouldn't notice them.

Change the subject.

"Can you trace your family back to the Vikingers, then?"

"Not quite. They didn't write anything down back then." He turned his head to look at her. "The really solid information starts in the mid-thirteen hundreds with a man named Rydar, who had a Scottish wife named Grier. He reestablished the family after the Black Death."

Fascinating. "How'd he get a Scottish wife?"

"The story is that he lived in the Greenland settlement from the age of ten to thirty, then sailed back to Norway picking up a wife along the way."

Kyle was intrigued. "Nothing in my past is this interesting. My family all came from little Solbergelva west of Oslo. Do you know anything else about him?"

"A little. I know he was the one to add the chapel to Hansen Hall so the family could celebrate the Mass at home. He, Grier, and their children are all buried inside it."

Six-hundred-year-old graves aside, Kyle was surprised by the chapel's purpose. "Are you Catholic?"

He wagged his head on the blanket. "Not now. But in the thirteen hundreds you were either Catholic or pagan."

"Oh. Right." She had learned that in her Lutheran catechism.

"And we know from documents that my mother found in the tower that the Hansens became Christians back in ten-seventy when King Olav the Second declared Norway a Christian country."

"I love hearing all this," Kyle said truthfully.

She laid on her back again and snuggled closer to Tor, closing her blouse and buttoning it. Even in June the nighttime temperatures at this altitude were chilly.

Tor also pulled his clothes together. "Are you cold?"

"A little."

"Let's head back to the jeep." Tor climbed to his feet and helped her up.

He pulled his shirt on over his head and shook out the blankets while she ran her fingers through her hair and smoothed her uniform. "Will you tell me more stories?"

"Sure. If you're really interested."

"I really am." When he looked at her, his skeptical expression visible in the dim light, she said it again. "I think it's incredible that you know all this."

"Okay. Well," he scratched his head. "I guess I'll go chronologically."

As they walked back Tor told her about Jakob Hansen, the Renaissance knight who served King Henry the Eighth.

"No!" Kyle said. "Really?"

"Yep. Married Queen Catherine's lady-in-waiting. In fact—watch your step here."

Tor took her hand and helped her over a fallen log before he continued. "She was Spanish and she owned her own trade ships. Her contracts with my Hansen ancestor helped make our family's shipping business successful enough to survive all these years."

Kyle shook her head in awe. "Amazing."

Tor was clearly warming to the subject. "Then in the mid-seventeen hundreds, Martin Hansen moved to America. He married a woman he met on the ship."

Kyle smiled at that. "How romantic!"

"I guess." Tor cleared his throat. "Their son fought in the Revolutionary War and then married the granddaughter of King Christian the Sixth."

"More royal connections," Kyle observed. "I'm impressed."

Tor grinned at that. "It gets better. After Norway was taken away from Denmark and given to Sweden in eighteen-fourteen, their son Nicolas candidated for a reclaimed Norwegian throne."

Kyle looked at Tor in disbelief. "But he was American—wasn't he?"

"He was. But he was also fully Norwegian and had royal blood." Tor looked down at her. "He didn't become king."

She laughed. "Obviously. What happened to him?"

Tor frowned. "I think he ran for some office. I don't remember."

"I think this is fascinating." She made a face. "Nothing in my family is half so fascinating."

Tor stopped next to the jeep. "I almost forgot Brander Hansen. He was Martin's uncle."

Kyle looked at him across the open-topped vehicle. "What did he do?"

"He was deaf." Tor grinned. "But that didn't stop him from becoming a private investigator who worked for King Christian the Sixth."

"The same one whose granddaughter married the soldier?"

"Yep. Now remember…" Tor opened the jeep's passenger door. "Norway's not a big country. There are more connections than you'd believe."

As she took her spot behind the steering wheel Kyle couldn't help but wish that Tor's fascinating family could somehow be hers. "You said your mother found documents in the tower."

"She did. She's been digging through there for the last few years. I think she means to write a book about the Hansen's history."

"I'd like to read that." Kyle started the engine. "I know that sounds crazy, but if I give you my address in Viking will you send me a copy if she does?"

"Sure." Tor's expression was unreadable. "But don't hold your breath. Even if she does manage it, it'll be a few years."

Kyle smiled at him. "I'll wait."

July 4, 1944

"It's our Independence Day, so of course the Army makes a big deal about it." Kyle winked up at Tor. "You have a relative that fought in America's Revolution, so you should be proud, too."

She had a point, except that, "He was a different branch of the family. I descended from his brother."

"Close enough." Kyle turned her attention back to the main street of Leadville. "Just be glad you don't have to march in the parade."

Tor eyed the Pastime Bar across the street. It was the same one where Dale Maple accosted Kyle many months ago.

"Do you remember that?" he asked her. "I knew then that the guy was trouble."

Kyle's expression hardened. "He'll get his due. He's been sentenced to death."

Tor leaned down and spoke in Kyle's ear. "Interested in a beer?"

She looked over at the tavern. "Do you think they're open?"

As if to answer her the front door opened and a pair of soldiers walked out.

She looked up at Tor. "Let's go."

They settled at a small table by a window so they could watch the parade from inside the cool bar instead of standing along the crowded main street in the strong midday sun.

Tor ordered two pints of stout and pulled out his wallet. "Do you want any food?"

"No, thank you. But you go ahead if you want."

He did want. Tor ordered a brisket sandwich and fries.

Kyle's glance swept the front room in the tavern. "This is actually the only local bar I've been in since I came to Colorado."

Tor laid a few bills on the table. "With so much to do at the camp there's not much reason to come into town."

"Only two that I can think of." Kyle held up one finger. "You're a guy looking for a gal and a good time, or..."

She held up a second finger. "You scored an overnight pass and don't have to be back at Camp Hale by eleven."

Tor laughed. "Which is actually helpful only if reason number one works out."

Kyle smiled. "Point made."

Tor's sandwich arrived at the table just as the parade began. It was a patriotic mix of civilian and military talents with band music, precision drill demonstrations, floats sponsored by local businesses and—of course—a parade queen and her court sitting atop hay bales on a flatbed wagon, waving and throwing kisses and candy at the enthusiastic crowd.

"I'm looking forward to the fireworks later." Kyle snatched one of Tor's fries and bit it in half. "They're always fun."

"I'm looking forward to them too." Tor lowered his voice. "Our fireworks are always spectacular."

Kyle's eyes widened briefly when she caught his meaning and her cheeks turned an adorable shade of pink.

"You're incorrigible."

"Thank you," he answered mischievously. "I do try my best."

Kyle's eyes narrowed. "Is that your best?"

Challenge accepted.

"Just wait until tonight," he growled. "I'll have you begging for mercy."

Kyle put the rest of the fry in her mouth, her gray-green eyes bright with anticipation.

CHAPTER TWENTY EIGHT

July 25, 1944

Kyle swatted another mosquito while she waited in the jeep for Tor to return from overnight mountain climbing maneuvers. She had the top put back on the jeep to protect her from the blazing sun, but the damn mosquitoes weren't deterred at all.

The weather during the day was a pleasant seventy degrees—when it wasn't raining—but the nights still dropped below forty before the sun came up. Kyle and Tor knew to grab the hours right after sunset for their wooded trysts. And they always kept most of their clothes on because of the cooling air.

Somehow that didn't dampen any of the mood, but for Kyle it lessened the intimacy. In her mind, if they weren't naked, it wasn't a serious relationship. That fit her personal definition of a fling perfectly.

What she hadn't counted on, however, was how well she had gotten to know Tor. Their private talks under the trees, changing moon, and stars had reached depths that she never discussed with Erik. In truth, she'd had more conversations with Tor during these past two months than she'd had with Erik over the last two years. She told herself that was because she'd known Erik all her life and there was little she didn't already know about him. Tor was an exotic stranger who came from a different world. That didn't explain away his telling her his deepest fears, though.

"I was never as good in school as my younger brother Teigen," he admitted one night. "So I decided to excel in things he wasn't as good at."

"Like skiing?" she asked.

"Yes, but that came easy to me. I was stupidly fearless when I was younger, so I learned at the risk of my life at most times." Tor chuckled softly. "Please don't tell my mother."

"I won't." Kyle crossed her heart in mock solemnity. "In twenty years when I visit you and your wife and your dozen children, I promise not to tell your elderly parents anything about your reckless youth."

"Thank you." Tor's sigh was nostalgic. "When I saw Teigen last, he said my shoes were hard to fill. He has no idea how hard I ran to stay ahead of him."

Kyle had propped her head on one elbow to look at him. "You're a very intelligent man, Tor. I don't understand what you mean."

He smiled crookedly. "Teigen is school smart. He went to university and got a degree in chemistry and became an upper-level school teacher."

The respect in Tor's voice tugged at Kyle's heart. "I didn't go to university. Instead I worked and trained and competed my way into the Winter Olympic Games that never happened."

Kyle understood Tor's disappointment. "But you still achieved something that *very* few people in the world could match, Tor. And it's obvious that the other competitive skiers here respect you a lot."

"I know…" There was nothing conceited in his tone. "I joined the Norwegian Army as soon as we were invaded because my opportunities disappeared overnight with the Nazi occupation."

"It may have been the only path you thought was open to you at the time," Kyle countered, "but you are a damn good leader and your men respect you."

Tor looked at her then, his eyes wide and his cheeks drawn. "So what will I do when it's over?"

She still didn't have an answer for him.

The platoon appeared around a curve in the road, marching toward the jeep at double-pace. The soldiers each carried a pack with their sleeping bag and tent, and they all had their skis strapped on their backs as well. Even though they weren't skiing now, they would have to carry their skis with them when they climbed the Alps.

Tor jogged alongside his men. The bulk of his arms, whose contours she had become so familiar with, were on display in his short-sleeved summer uniform and he was taller than all but one soldier in his squad.

Kyle sighed as she watched him approach.

He's so sexy.

And, for now, he was all hers.

ᚿ ᚿ ᚿ

Today was Saturday and most of the soldiers were heading into town after supper. They invited Tor—who was using more and more English when he wasn't around Kyle—to come along.

"I have decided to go into town with the men tonight," he told Kyle as he climbed into the jeep. "We'll take a bus in after supper."

She started the engine. "That sounds like fun."

"I'm sorry, but I wanted to tell you right away in case you wanted to make plans of your own."

Kyle shot him a sideways look. "One of the rules of a fling is that individual plans *can* be made separately."

Tor lifted one brow. "Did you just make that up?"

Kyle shifted gears. "Yep."

Tor approved. "I think that's a very good rule as long as the majority of the trysts aren't overshadowed by the individual plans. Don't you agree?"

Kyle laughed. "You sound like a lawyer negotiating terms of a contract."

"And rightly so. This fling thing is serious business."

Kyle looked at him as if trying to figure out if he was mocking her. "Is it?"

Tor shrugged and smiled at her. "Seems to be. But what do I know? It's my first one."

Kyle dropped him at his barracks. "I'm going to check the mail and I'll be back to get you for supper."

"You don't need to. I want to walk tonight," he said. "It was a hard two days and I don't want my muscles to stiffen."

"Okay."

He leaned closer. "I'm a mess. Can you stand for me to kiss you?"

Her expression softened. "Always."

※ ※ ※

Kyle waited in line for her mail and was glad to see she'd gotten a letter from Erik. She hadn't heard from him in twelve days and was wondering if there was a problem at the farm like a bad storm or sick cows that prevented him from writing sooner.

She waited until she was alone in her room before she opened it, preparing herself for bad news and already crafting a sympathetic reply in her head.

Dear Kyle,

I had put off writing this letter, hoping there was a way to say this that won't hurt you, but I don't think there is. So, I might as well just say it. I'm breaking our engagement.

Kyle stared at the words in disbelief. She read them again to be certain she hadn't misunderstood. He was breaking off their engagement?

He was breaking off their engagement!

Why?

What happened?

You already know that it's been very hard for me to

> understand why you decided to leave Viking and enlist in the WACs, and while I've also tried very hard over this past year to forgive you, I just can't. Your decision hurt me more than you seem to understand.

Kyle's hands were shaking in rage. Forgive her? For enlisting and serving their country during wartime? What a selfish and small-minded reaction!

"So much for sympathy," she muttered. "I'll set him straight. This is ridiculous."

Kyle flipped the paper over.

> And I should tell you this next part myself, before you hear it from your parents or anyone else in Viking who you might get letters from. I have asked Ingrid Smelter to marry me and she said yes.

He'd already replaced her—and with Ingrid Smelter? The stumpy girl who was a year behind her in high school and took extra homemaking classes? The one who went to school dances with her cousin?

That Ingrid?

Kyle wasn't a vain woman, but she knew she was prettier than Ingrid. And looks aside, Kyle excelled in school and chose to take more difficult classes because they challenged her.

Maybe she couldn't make a perfect pot roast, but certainly that wasn't all that Erik cared about.

> Ingrid has assured me that she doesn't have any uppity ideas about a woman's role in this world. She will be very content to just be my wife and a good and competent mother to our children. I expect to have a happy and peaceful life with her.

Tears of anger and pain blurred Kyle's vision. Uppity ideas? And the implication that life with her would be neither happy nor peaceful?

"Am I really that unsuited to be a wife?" she asked the

empty room.

> The wedding will be the first weekend in August. I have to ask you to please not write back to me unless you want to extend your good wishes. Nothing you could say to me at this point could make me change my mind. I'm sorry everything turned out this way, but it is for the best.
>
> *Erik*

Kyle leaned against the headboard of her bed, stunned to her core. There were so many things she wanted to shout at Erik about his own personal faults—and if he was in front of her she would.

Her reactions bounced between rage at his judgment of her character and the idea that she would come crawling to him, begging him to take her back, to soul-deep disappointment that he just didn't love her any more.

Most of all she wondered how the man whom she loved and planned a future with could think so little of her.

What's wrong with me?

※ ※ ※

Tor was waiting in the Rec Hall for the next bus to take soldiers into Leadville and he was telling some of the other instructors a story in a mix of mime, English, and Norsk—which Torger was translating between his guffaws—about a sorry recruit's first day in his current squad.

"He and I were last and I said it was our turn to go down the mountain. So he starts and I see he has his skis straight. He's not guiding them or anything."

Tor mimicked the man's stance. "It looks like he's going to hit a tree, and I'm thinking of Kossin, and I'm scared he'll be hurt. So I follow him."

Tor started to laugh. "This guy is skiing in a straight line until he's about to hit something and then he falls on purpose."

Tor acted out his words. "Then he gets up, turns his skis and goes again!"

The instructors were all laughing, encouraging Tor on.

"He does this all the way down, and I can't believe it!" Tor wiped his eyes. "Then he tries to make a wide turn but falls in a snow drift and lands on his shoulders, head down and skis in the air."

Whoops of appreciation filled the room.

"I can just see it!" one American instructor said.

"I skied right to him and asked how bad was he hurt. He says he's not hurt." Tor spread his hands. "I said you hit that tree. How bad are you hurt? Did you hurt your leg, or what?"

The men grew quiet, waiting for the answer.

"Again he says he's not hurt, but I said he had to be. Then he looks up at me and says, I'm not hurt! I didn't hit the tree!"

Confused looks bounced among the men.

"So I said, if you're not hurt, then what are you doing down there?" Tor laughed so hard he had trouble getting the next words out. "And he—and he said—I'm down here because my skis are up there and I can't get them down here with me!"

The room exploded with laughter. Tor thought Torger was going to lose bodily control he was laughing so hard.

"That's the best story I've heard in a long time, Hansen!" the American instructor said between burst of hilarity. "You should win some sort of prize."

The bus pulled up in front of the door and the men, still chuckling, filed out of the Rec Hall and boarded in single file.

Tor was near the end of the line, still chatting with Torger when Kyle strode around the back of the bus and got in line.

It only took one glance for Tor to see that she had been crying. He excused himself and went to talk to her.

When she saw him, she shook her head. "Go ahead. I'll wait for the next bus."

"What's wrong?"

She wouldn't look at him. "Nothing. Go get on the bus."

"I'll wait and go with you."

She did look at him then. "Tor, get on the bus. Go with your friends. Let me be."

"Tor!" Torger shouted. "You coming?"
Kyle pushed him. "Go."
When he still didn't move she pushed him harder. "Get on the damn bus, Tor!"
"Last call!" Torger was hanging out the bus door. "Yes or no?"
Tor to a last look at Kyle's murderous expression and answered Torger. "I'm coming!"
He turned around and trotted to the bus and ran up the steps.
I'll wait for her in town.

CHAPTER TWENTY NINE

When Kyle saw Tor waiting for her to get off the bus she was angry. Of all the nights when she did want his company, this was definitely not one of them. Tonight she wanted to drink hard liquor and dance with strangers until her fury and pain were numbed enough that she couldn't feel them anymore.

She stepped off the bus and walked past Tor without looking at him or talking to him.

Of course he followed her. "Will you please tell me what's wrong?"

"No."

"Kyle—have I done something to hurt you?"

She halted and faced him. "This has absolutely nothing to do with you! Why would you even think that? UGH! Men!"

She turned around and kept walking.

Tor didn't follow her that time.

Kyle walked into the Pastime and marched straight up to the bar. "Rum and Coke, easy on the Coke."

The soldier next to her turned and gave her the once over. "Sounds like the lady has some forgetting to do."

"Yep."

Kyle pulled a bill from her pocket, but he stopped her.

"I'll get this one. And the next." He held up two fingers and the bartender set two rum and Cokes in front of Kyle."

She thanked the man who wasn't bad looking. *Good enough for tonight.* She downed the first drink and set the empty glass on the bar. Then she picked up the second one, smiled at her benefactor and said, "Wanna dance?"

ℵ ℵ ℵ

Tor watched Kyle from a distance, shocked at her behavior. He'd never seen her act this way, but he'd seen plenty of other women do it. She had all the earmarks of a woman scorned. One who planned to drown her heartbreak in booze and boys.

It had to be Erik.

What had the man done?

All Tor could do for her was stay in the background and make sure she didn't get hurt before she got back to her barracks later tonight.

Tor noticed after her first two drinks, Kyle slowed down on her third. She was obviously feeling pretty loose at the moment and was dancing with three eager soldiers who took turns holding her a little too close.

A pair of WACs joined the little party, necessitating another round of drinks. Kyle gulped the last of her third and took a hearty sip of her fourth before being swept back onto the dance floor.

After that, Tor stopped counting Kyle's drinks and watched her coordination instead. It seemed like she should be worse off than she was and he realized that the more the military men and women drank, the weaker their drinks were.

That lined the bars pockets while keeping the soldiers from getting alcohol poisoning.

Tonight Tor thought that was a fine plan.

Kyle seemed to be having a good time, laughing at the men's jokes and hanging onto their shoulders for balance. But every now and then her expression grew haunted and she ordered another drink.

Tor looked at his watch. It was nearly midnight and Kyle had been drinking pretty steadily for over four hours. Her gaze appeared unfocused and when she let go of any support she swayed like a pine tree in a strong wind.

One of her evening's companions slipped his arm around her waist and pressed his lips to her ears. Whatever he said made Kyle shake her head.

"I have t'go back," she said loudly enough for Tor to hear.

The soldier didn't seem to like that answer. He pulled her close and kissed her hard on the mouth. Tor moved through the crowd to get close to her.

Kyle almost fell backwards with the force of the kiss but caught herself on a table, spilling her drink. "Hey! Don' ruin ev'rything!"

The man pressed himself against her and ran his hands down her body. "Baby, you got me all wrong."

Kyle pushed his hands away and held her empty glass in his face. "Y'owe me a drink."

"I already bought you enough drinks, doll. Time for you to pay me back." He leaned in for another kiss when Tor's hand clamped down on his shoulder.

"Stand down."

He turned and sneered up at Tor. "Get your own girl."

Tor's fingers dug into the man's shoulder. "I said stand down, soldier."

The man grunted and let go of Kyle.

"You!" Kyle yelped. "What're you doin' here?"

"I'm here to take you back to camp."

She lifted her chin and glared at him. "What'f I don' wanna go back with you?"

"You don't have a choice, Lieutenant."

"See?" her accoster challenged and grabbed her again. "She wants to be with *me* tonight. And I bought her enough booze to earn it!"

Tor reached out and gripped the man's collar. "Well I say this is America in nineteen-forty-four and you can't buy women with drinks. That takes hard cash and a different sort of woman entirely." He twisted his wrist and tightened the man's collar against his skin. "So unless you want me to call that MP by the door over here to deal with you, I suggest you *stand down!*"

Tor's shouted command had the dual effect he planned. Not only did the soldier's aggressive attitude slip, but the MP by the door took a step in his direction.

He put up his hands. "Fine, you can have the bitch."

"Who you callin'—"

Tor released the man's collar and grabbed Kyle's arm. "Let's go."

И И И

Kyle's mind was fuzzy but she knew a few things. First, that man she'd been dancing with wanted a lot more than a night of fun. Second, Tor was here and he'd saved her again.

Third, she needed another drink.

"No." Kyle stopped and leaned away from Tor's grip. "I wan' another drink," she growled. "He made me spill mine."

Tor looked down at her. "Fine."

He ordered the rum and Coke and paid for it, then pulled her into a corner of the bar to drink it.

"This's weak," she grumbled.

"Just drink it."

She gulped it as fast as she could and held up the glass. "Satisfied?"

Tor took the glass and practically dragged her out the front door. When the cooler outside air hit her and the street began to undulate beneath her she felt ill.

"Wait." She reached out a hand and planted her feet. "I—I don' feel good."

Tor lifted her from behind and bent her over a patch of grass as she vomited.

И И И

Kyle sat on a bench in the little yard and cried. In between drunken wails and angry outbursts she told Tor that Erik had broken their engagement.

"For a dumpy little nothing who doesn't have uppity ideas."

Tor said nothing, just let her spill her guts verbally, now that the physical spill subsided.

"Why, though?" She looked blearily at him. "What's wrong with me?"

"Nothing."

"Then tell me this, if you're so smart..." She pointed a finger in his face. "Why doesn't anyone love me?"

Tor's chest tightened. "I do."

"What?" Kyle blinked slowly.

"I said, I do. I love you."

She leaned back and squinted at him. "I don' believe you."

He shrugged, doubting she would remember this conversation in the morning. "It's true, Kyle."

"Well guess what, Cap'ain." She poked him in the chest to punctuate each word. "I love you, too."

Tor chalked her words up to multiple rum and Cokes. "That's nice."

"It's more than nice. It's real nice."

Tor smiled and consulted his watch again. He wasn't too keen on pouring Kyle onto the camp bus in her condition, but he didn't have an overnight pass.

He saw a taxi drive by and waved it down. "Stay here."

Once he made arrangements for a ride, he collected Kyle and they got into the back seat. She dozed against his shoulder until the taxi stopped at the entrance to Camp Hale. He checked them both in and started the hike to her barracks, holding her close for support.

When they reached her barracks she stopped and shook her head. "I don't want to go to bed yet."

"What do you want to do?"

She looked up at him with a hunger that shot straight to his groin. "What we always do."

Tor measured his words carefully. "Okay. Go wash up first. Then come back down with your blanket."

She nodded. "Okay."

As he watched her stumble away, he planned to give her fifteen minutes to return. If she didn't, he would assume she'd passed out in her bed and he'd go claim his.

She was back in ten.

Her face was clean and her hair was damp and brushed. Kyle was starting to sober up.

"Here." She handed him several blankets. "I got them from the supply closet."

Then she took his hand. "Lead on."

※ ※ ※

The more the alcohol wore off, the clearer Erik's rejection echoed in her mind. All she wanted now was to lie in Tor's arms and feel his hands on her body. She desperately needed to feel loved.

Did he say he loved me?

Kyle watched while Tor spread the blankets over a soft pile of pine needles and she unfastened her trousers and the lower buttons on her blouse. When he turned to face her she reached for his belt and unbuckled it while he took her face in his hands and kissed her.

He still tasted like beer.

When the kiss ended, Kyle dropped onto the blankets and rolled onto her back. She held her hands up and Tor lowered himself over her.

His kisses moved to her breast and his attention there sent shivers over her skin. But when he began to move down her frame she stopped him.

"No. Not that."

He looked up at her. She could see his eyes by the light of the moon. "Why not?"

She sat up and pushed her trousers and her panties to her knees. "I want more."

Tor watched her as she fought her way out of the stubborn garments and then pressed his hand to the damp spot between her legs. "More…"

Kyle laid back down. "I want everything."

Tor's intense expression was clear even in the darkness. "What are you saying, Kyle?"

"I'm saying..." She choked on a sob. "I'm saying I want somebody to love me."

Tor stretched out on the ground next to her. "No. You've had a lot to drink tonight."

"I know what I want, Tor." She fumbled for the erection she knew was there as tears rolled across her skin. "Erik said he loved me, but I wasn't good enough for him."

She gripped him tightly and he gasped. "I need to know I'm good enough for somebody."

"Just somebody?" he challenged. "Then why not that man in the bar?"

"You." Her shoulders shook with her increasing sobs. "I want to be good enough for you."

"Kyle, I'm not sure—"

Kyle let go of his manhood and grabbed his head. She kissed him while she rolled on top of him.

He gripped her waist and tried to hold her still, but she ground herself against him anyway, making him groan.

"Please..." she whispered against his lips. "Please love me, Tor."

She reached down between them and took hold of him again.

※ ※ ※

Tor reached the breaking point. His defenses were blown through and he was Kyle's prisoner.

"Let me," he rasped.

He lifted Kyle's hips and aimed himself toward her, wiggling his tip into her. "Sometimes it hurts the first time..."

Kyle lowered herself slowly, moaning as she did, until there was no space left between them. She held still and the heat of her body consumed him.

"What now?" she whispered.

"One of us needs to move." He sat up and wrapped an arm around her waist. "Let me do it."

Tor lifted himself enough to roll them over so that he was on top. "Are you all right?"

"Yes. Oh yes." Kyle's eyes closed. "This is... so good."

Tor moved slowly at first, though there was no problem sliding in and out. Kyle was as ready for him as she could be.

"More," she whispered.

He obliged.

Soon, he was completely lost. Lost in the woods. Lost in her body. Lost in their joining.

Nothing existed for him but their point of intimate connection and the intense and lengthy eruption of pleasure that they shared as he emptied himself into her, heart and soul.

CHAPTER THIRTY

Tor helped Kyle get dressed and gathered the blankets under one arm. He tucked her under the other and supported her as they walked back to the barracks's door.

Kyle pulled his head down to hers and gave him a long and sweet kiss. Then she rested her head against his chest and whispered, "Thank you."

Tor rubbed her back. "Go on now. Get some sleep. It's Sunday so you don't have to pick me up in the morning."

Kyle leaned back and smiled dreamily up at him. "G'night."

Tor watched her climb the stairs. When she turned down the hall he stashed the blankets and left the building.

What have I done?

Well, he told her he loved her for starters. And he hadn't drunk enough beer for the alcohol to be the one choosing his words.

Did he love her?

If he did, that was going to be damned inconvenient come the winter.

He put no faith in her claim that she loved him. He doubted that she'd even remember saying it. And if that was the case, she probably wouldn't remember him saying it either. Tor decided to

never bring that subject up if she didn't.
As far as the sex was concerned, she was the one to press that forward. He tried to resist but she was so insistent, crying and begging him to make love to her.
And it wasn't just sex. It was making love.
Damn.
Tonight with Kyle was different from his other experiences. Probably because he knew her so well. And, to be honest, because he might actually love her.
I wish I knew what being in love felt like.
Tor reached his barracks and went up to his room. He stripped and climbed in to bed, only to find that sleep wasn't coming yet.
What have I done?

July 26, 1944

Kyle's tongue was stuck to the roof of her mouth and her temples felt like they were caught in a vise. She squinted one eye open. She was in her bed, in her room, in her barracks.
Why did she think she would be somewhere else?
What did I do last night?
She rolled over and laid on her back with one arm draped across her eyes while she tried to reconstruct the evening and figure out why she felt such a sense of dread.
The letter from Erik.
That was it.
Her engagement was over. Erik didn't love her, couldn't forgive her, picked another random gal to marry, and told her not to write him back if she couldn't be nice about it.
Kyle felt a renewed surge of anger which made her head pound.
How dare he? Who did he think he was?
Who did he think *she* was? Someone who wasn't good enough to be a farmer's wife?
Kyle sucked a breath as the realization hit her. She wouldn't make a good farmer's wife, not anymore. Not after this last year

spent in the company of men and women from all over the country—all over the world.

Tor's teasing about her coming to Norway started as a joke, but the more she played with it the more she began to think that she might actually go. Whether to see him or not didn't matter, it was her heritage and she was curious about it.

Before leaving Viking and joining the WAC the idea never occurred to her. Now a trip like that could be in her future.

Another stab of dread pounded in her head.

What was her future going to be now? When she finished her two year enlistment what would she do?

The thought of going back to live in Viking was suddenly very unappealing. Now that she wasn't going to marry Erik and live on his farm there didn't seem to be any reason for her to carve out a life there.

Maybe I could have a life with Tor.

Another surge of dread at that thought worried her. Something happened last night, and it had to do with Tor.

He was at the bar.

Kyle remembered her plan to drink and dance until she forgot about Erik, but she didn't mean to drink enough to forget what she was doing. She remembered some soldiers buying her drink after drink and taking turns dancing with her.

So far, so good.

Then she remembered one of the men kissing her when she didn't want him to. He spilled her drink. He wasn't being nice.

Tor told him to stand down.

Kyle smiled. *He rescued me.*

She remembered Tor taking her outside. And she was humiliated when she remembered that she threw up violently as soon as he did.

There was a taxi ride to camp. She'd washed her face and brushed her teeth. Then she went into the woods with Tor.

Oh my God!

Panicked, Kyle reached down and touched her nether parts to see if she felt different. When she probed herself, she felt bruised.

A flash of a memory burst into her mind—she was sitting

astride Tor, who was on his back on the ground, and she was trying to put his erection inside her.
Oh.
My.
God.
She had sex with Tor. He made love to her. She wasn't a virgin anymore. And he did it because she cried and begged him to. It wasn't his idea, it was hers.
Guilt mixed with fear flooded her. What would he think of her now? He had come to her rescue, saving her from who-knows-what, only to have her beg him to make love to her instead.
Wait.
Another zing of realization jolted her.
Tor said *stand down, soldier*. Not *stå ned, soldat*.
Was she imagining things? What else did he say?
I'm here to take you back to camp.
You don't have a choice, Lieutenant.
Was she so muddled by multiple rum and Cokes that she couldn't tell which language he was speaking?
Kyle knew she was speaking English, because the soldier understood her.
But he understood Tor, too.
When the jerk grabbed her and said something about Kyle wanting to go with him because he bought enough booze to earn her, Tor said it was nineteen-forty-four and that was a different kind of woman.
In English.
In perfect English.
Kyle dug through her foggy memories of the rest of the night, trying to remember their conversations.
After she threw up they were sitting on a bench. She told Tor that Erik had broken their engagement *for a dumpy little nothing who doesn't have uppity ideas.*
She was partly quoting Erik's letter. And she had no idea how to translate *dumpy* or *uppity ideas*.
She was speaking English the whole night. So was he.
Tor speaks English.

He lied to me.
He lied to everyone. From the first moment she met him. Another jolt of memory seared her skull, and this one made her heart pound and her hands shake.
She remembered asking Tor why didn't anyone love her.
He said, "I do."

И И И

Kyle stood under the hot spray of the shower until her fingers turned pruney. She couldn't stop crying. In the last twenty-four-hours she'd made a terrible mess of her life and had done it with the aid of a man who was completely untrustworthy.

How could she ever face him again?

But she *had* to face him again. At least long enough to confront him about not needing a translator so she could get herself reassigned to some other duty that didn't involve lying Norsemen.

Kyle knew that part of the reason for her unending tears was because she had feelings for Tor. She remembered poking him in the chest and saying that she loved him, too. That added a great big shovelful of manure to the stinking situation.

As long as she was engaged to Erik, she told herself she loved him. Erik and his farm were her destiny when Tor went off to Italy, and she held on to them as tightly as she could.

Then Erik cut her loose without warning and Tor came to her rescue when she was drifting in the storm without an anchor.

She probably meant those words last night, but that was before she realized Tor had been lying to her. The memory of her silly attempts to help him learn English—like making vocabulary cards for him to put up in his room—made her feel like an idiot now.

Especially since she had her first sex with him.

I'm not a virgin anymore.

Kyle let the water run over her knowing that when she turned it off she would have to face the world. For now the heat was soothing her aching head and bruised body.

There wasn't such an easy cure for everything else.

※ ※ ※

Tor saw Kyle from a distance before she saw him. She was wearing dark glasses and had her hands stuffed in her pockets. She was heading toward the mess hall for lunch and paying more attention to the road beneath her than to anything else around her.

He walked toward her and got in her path. "Lieutenant?"

Kyle's head jerked up and she stopped mid-step. "Um, Captain."

He hated that he couldn't see her eyes. "How are you?"

"I've been better."

"*Vi må snake.*" We need to talk.

Kyle huffed. "You can drop the pretense, Captain."

She remembered.

Damn.

He tried to look sincerely apologetic. "Then we really do need to talk."

She pointed at the mess with her chin. "I need to eat."

"I'll come with you."

"Please don't." Kyle resumed her pace and circled past him.

Tor caught up and fell in step with her, speaking in Norsk so their conversation would be private. "So much happened yesterday, Kyle. We do need to talk about it."

"I agree. I'm just not ready at the moment," she answered in the same language. "I'm starving and being with you will ruin my appetite."

Tor felt terrible. "Are you that angry with me?"

"Yes. Because you lied to me." Kyle opened the hall door before he could do it for her and stopped again to look up at him. "I wouldn't have done what I did if I'd known the truth."

Tor knew he wouldn't score any points by pressing the point here and now. "Where should I meet you?"

"I'll get the jeep after lunch. Be at your barracks when I get there."

She let go of the door and disappeared inside.

※ ※ ※

Tor was standing outside his barracks when Kyle drove up. He opened the passenger door and climbed in. She hit the gas before he got the door closed.

She drove to the pistol range and stopped the jeep facing the targets. A few men were practicing and he figured she picked that spot so the sound would cover the argument he expected they were about to have.

Tor turned in the seat to face her. "Where should we start?"

She faced him. "How about, you can speak English and never needed a translator in the first place?"

"Will you take off the glasses?"

Kyle hesitated. "Why?"

"I want to see your eyes when I talk to you." Tor reached for the dark glasses but Kyle took them off by herself. Her eyes were swollen and red.

"Satisfied?" she snipped.

"Yes. Thank you." Tor cleared his throat. "I trained in England for fourteen months and learned the language. But I do know it better now because I've been listening to it for the last eight months."

"But why didn't you tell me when I first met you at the airport?"

Her glare was so harsh that he felt like donning her dark glasses for protection. He pulled a breath then launched into his explanation.

"At first I was confused. I was sick on the plane, I hadn't slept well for thirty-six hours... I just wasn't thinking straight. And then when you spoke to me in Norsk, I answered in Norsk."

She looked skeptical. "So then why didn't you say something when we got to camp?"

Tor decided to jump in. "Because I liked you."

"Liked me?" she yelped. "What kind of an excuse is that?"

"An honest one."

Kyle snorted. "So now you're being honest? I suppose you thought it would be fun to see how far you could seduce—" Her words dissolved into a ragged sob.

"No. Never." He grabbed her hands and wouldn't let her pull them away even though she put up a good fight. "I swear to you,

"Kyle. It was never my intention to bed you."

She wiped her streaming cheeks on her shoulders because he'd imprisoned her hands.

"I found you intriguing and I wanted you around to help me adjust. Speaking a second language can be exhausting." He gave her a crooked smile. "That's all."

When she didn't say anything, he continued. "Last night wasn't my idea, you know that."

Her sobs got louder at the reminder.

"Don't misunderstand me, Kyle. I loved making love to you. It was amazing. And I think it was good for you too, wasn't it?"

She wouldn't look at him but she gave a tiny nod. "Was it making love, Tor?" she croaked. "Or was it just sex."

Now he didn't answer, panicked over what he should admit to.

She looked at him then with a myriad of naked emotions playing over her face. "Tell me the truth."

All in was all in. "I told you the truth last night, Kyle. Do you remember?"

"You said you love me," she whispered.

Tor's heart stuttered. "And you said the same."

Kyle seemed to grow calmer. "Yes."

Tor let go of her hands. "So what now?"

Kyle's voice was flat. "If I tell Jones you don't need a translator anymore, then I'll be reassigned."

"At Camp Hale?"

She gave a little shake of her head. "Not necessarily."

That was not good news. "Are you going to tell him?"

She stared at him, her eyes more gray than green at the moment. "I don't know. I'm still *so* angry at you. And at myself."

"Then don't do anything yet," he suggested hopefully. "Not until you've had a chance to think about everything for a few days. The situation may not look so dire in a week or two."

She sighed shakily. "Okay. I won't say anything yet."

Kyle put the dark glasses back on and restarted the jeep. "In the meantime, though, this fling is *over*."

CHAPTER THIRTY ONE

August 14, 1944

Kyle hadn't said anything to anyone about Tor's English skills for the last two weeks because she was tangled in such a messy mix of emotions that she didn't trust herself to be sane enough to take action at any given point in time.

She realized that even though she was furious at Tor—and had every right to be—she was more drawn toward him than ever before. That made sense, too. They'd each confessed to making declarations of love. And then they made love, forever changing who she was.

There was no going back on that.

So Kyle kept doing her job, translating for the captain as he and Frank Collins took their current platoon through training in the rifle and pistol ranges, grenade courts, gas chambers, and bayonet courses.

Truth be told, she found the training fascinating and caught herself wondering if there would ever come a time when women in the army would be issued firearms and be able to train like these men were.

In her current state of mind, she thought shooting at things would be very therapeutic. Maybe she'd ask Tor to teach her to shoot his pistol.

Once I'm speaking to him again.

So far, all of their conversations since that fateful night had been strictly professional and related to Tor's jobs; Kyle hadn't allowed herself to say anything of a personal nature to the captain. The drastic changes that took place in every aspect of her life during those hours had left her too fragile to reopen that door just yet.

But there was one result of Erik's breaking their engagement that surprised her: for the first time in her life she no longer saw herself as a future farmer's wife.

The freedom from that expectation both terrified and exhilarated her. When she lay in bed at night thinking about where her life might be headed now, she started to consider the idea of living some where other than Viking.

Where would I go?
What would I do?

She remembered reading in the *Ski-Zette* two months ago that President Franklin Roosevelt signed something called the *Servicemen's Readjustment Act of 1944*, but she hadn't paid a lot of attention to it at the time because she never thought it would apply to her.

In her current circumstances, maybe it did.

Today Tor was mountain climbing so she was on her own. After she completed her WAC required physical regimen, she decided to head over to Headquarters to see if anyone there had more information about it.

и и и

Tor had been the perfect picture of a gentleman since the night he made love to Kyle. The thing that was interesting to him was how easy it was.

Once he told her he loved her, he knew it was true. Futile, maybe, but true nonetheless. And she was definitely a woman he could see himself married to.

Tor's life hadn't been conducive to forming serious relationships since he reached adulthood. Training and skiing competitively meant he was on the move a lot. A flirtation here, a quick connection there. Fun, sure, but none of it lasting.

Those women were interested in him as an athlete who might be famous one day, and they made themselves available to him in the hopes that they could ride to the top with him. He knew it.

And, frankly, he took advantage of it.

And then that vile bastard Adolf Hitler invaded his neutral and peaceful country and Tor's life was changed irrevocably.

Now Tor would never ski in any Olympic games. Even if the pompous little asshole was defeated today it was too late to pull together games for nineteen-forty-four. That meant another four years of training if he wanted to qualify again and he was already well past thirty-one.

No, that dream was over.

Until two weeks ago, Tor hadn't given any thought to what he'd do once the war did end. He thought that if he was lucky enough to survive Italy he'd go home and figure it out then.

In the meantime he'd give serious thought to marrying Kyle.

If she'd have him.

Right now, that was a very large *if*.

※ ※ ※

"I have the information here," the receptionist said as she handed Kyle a printed flyer. "These benefits are available to veterans who've been active duty for at least a hundred and twenty days during the war and who haven't been dishonorably discharged."

That cuts out Flo, Frances, and Marguerite.

Kyle scanned the paper. "This does apply to us WACs as well, right?"

"I believe so." The girl shrugged. "Going into actual combat isn't required."

Kyle smiled at her. "Thank you."

Major General Jones came in the front door and stopped

when he saw Kyle.

"Lieutenant Solberg, I've been meaning to ask you to bring Captain Hansen in for a brief meeting."

As if he needs me there.

"Of course, sir. When would you like me to bring him?"

"I'll have my secretary set it up." Jones pointed at the receptionist. "Private Larson, would you please call Lieutenant Smith and ask him to arrange the appointment? I'll want a quarter of an hour. But it's nothing urgent."

"Yes, sir."

Kyle saluted Jones and he strode down the hallway. She faced the receptionist and held up the folded paper. "Thanks again."

She tucked the pamphlet in her back pocket and went out to the jeep. She drove it to the regular spot where Tor met her after their mountain climbing finished and parked under a shady pine. Then she pulled out the flyer and started reading.

As she did, her pulse surged with excitement.

"This is it," she whispered. "This is my chance."

She was so engrossed in the information and the sudden explosion of her options that she didn't notice Tor until he vaulted over the passenger door into the open-topped jeep.

"Easy there," she grumbled as the little vehicle rocked and groaned. She addressed him in Norsk to keep up the ruse. "How'd it go today?"

"It was a good day."

Kyle refolded the pamphlet and then looked at Tor. His blazing blue eyes, tanned skin, and wind-tousled hair did make him look like some grinning Nordic god. Her heart lurched a little, knowing he loved her.

"What have you got there?" he asked.

She handed it to him. "You can read it yourself."

Because you can *read it yourself.*

Tor read aloud, "The Servicemen's Readjustment Act of 1944?"

Kyle turned the jeep around and headed toward Tor's barracks. "From what I read, it gives the soldiers returning from this war some financial help to pick up and continue their lives."

"Because they were all interrupted," Tor murmured as he read. "Listen to this: you can get low-cost mortgages, low-interest loans to start a business, cash payments of tuition and living expenses to attend high school—wait."

He turned to her. "You finished high school."

"I did. But a lot of guys enlisted the day they turned eighteen. Before they graduated."

"Understood." He went back to reading. "Attend high school, college, or vocational or technical school, as well as one year of unemployment compensation."

"So they can live while they complete some advanced schooling." Kyle glanced at Tor wondering what his reaction would be. "And this applies to WACs, too."

He sounded surprised. "So you'll get all these things?"

"If I want, yes. I just have to apply."

"What about Viking?"

Kyle drew a deep breath and let it out slowly. "After the war ends, I don't think I'm going to live there anymore."

※ ※ ※

This changes everything.

Tor would never want to take Kyle away from these opportunities, but he certainly wanted to get her out of that stupidly-named village.

"Where do you want to go?"

She frowned a little. "Minneapolis, Minnesota I think. It's a big city so there'll be lots of school choices there."

Would I want to live in Minneapolis?

Tor didn't think so. But maybe Kyle would be willing to stay in Colorado. "What about Denver?"

Kyle looked at him as if he just suggested she become a brain surgeon. "Leave Minnesota?"

He wanted to say *I can teach skiing here* but caught himself. "There's skiing here."

She focused her attention back on the road. "I don't ski. Not really."

Tor let it drop. This was their first conversation about the

future since what happened and he didn't want to ruin it.
He folded the flyer. "Well, you have time to decide."
Her expression was unreadable. "Yes. I do."

August 15, 1944

Tor needed Kyle with him today because he had to explain how to properly don a gas mask before they entered the gas chamber.
"Tighten here." He demonstrated while Kyle translated. "This strap can save your life, or take it if it's not tight enough."
"I have a question, Captain."
Kyle said, "Go ahead."
"What do we do with our goggles?"
She turned to Tor. "He wants to know if your fly is open for a reason."
Tor glanced down reflexively, even though he knew that was not what the private asked.
"What are you doing?" he asked in Norsk.
She smiled evilly. "It's my turn now, isn't it?"
Tor's jaw clenched. "Tell him to strap his goggles where the gas mask was."
She did. "Any other questions?"
A private waved his hand. "Will they be using gas in the mountains?"
Kyle asked Tor, "If pigs could fly, would you ride one?"
"Maybe," he barked.
Kyle translated the terse answer.
"Ma'am?"
Kyle gave the soldier an encouraging smile. Encouraging Tor to strangle her, that was. "Yes?"
"Will there be more than one kind of gas? I mean like, some that can kill you, but some that just make you sick?"
Kyle nodded, her expression seriously grim and faced Tor. "If you only had one arm and one leg, would you prefer to be called Stump or Handy?"
Tor coughed to disguise his laugh. He stood with his mouth

covered by his fist for a moment, trying to hold onto a required shred of composure. Then he cleared his throat and gave Kyle an intense look.

"Tell him we don't know, so we'll prepare for the worst. And that I am going to kill you later."

She nodded, her eyes sparkling with amusement. "Yes, Captain."

August 20, 1944

The meeting with Jones had been delayed twice, but was finally happening. Kyle and Tor entered the Major General's office, saluted, and waited to be invited to sit.

Jones smiled pleasantly at Tor. "Captain Hansen, I wanted to let you know how pleased I am that you came to Camp Hale to train our soldiers."

Tor didn't react until Kyle translated. Thankfully she was on her best behavior today and promised no hijinks in the Major General's presence.

Tor dipped his chin. "Tell him it's been my honor."

Jones picked up a paper. "It's been brought to my attention that ninety-percent of the man in your squads have excelled in their qualifying tests, and that the remaining ten percent have passed after brief extensions of their training."

"They work very hard sir," he deferred.

"And I think they have a leader who inspires them." Jones's expression dimmed. "It's unfortunate that you won't be going to Italy with them."

Tor froze. Not going to Italy?

Kyle's eyes widened. She faced him when she translated, adding, "Did you know that?"

Tor was shaken. "No. Ask him why not."

"It should be obvious to *you*, Lieutenant," Jones said bluntly. "You aren't going into combat, of course, so Captain Hansen won't be able to talk to his men."

Tor felt like all of his bones had dissolved. Gnats danced around his vision.

No no no.
This can't happen.
"He can't lead men who don't understand his commands." Jones waved one hand toward Tor. "I'm sure the captain will agree."
Tor looked at Kyle. "I have to tell him."
"No. Don't. That would really make him angry—and you don't want that."
"What choice do I have?"
"I have an idea." She turned back to Jones. "I've been working with Captain Hansen on his English and he's coming along well. May I suggest a solution?"
Jones frowned a little. "Go on."
"An English proficiency test. If he passes, then he ships out with his men."
God bless her.
Tor watched the general carefully, trying without success to judge his reaction.
"Remember, the captain speaks German fluently as well," Kyle continued. "That would be helpful, wouldn't it?"
Jones nodded slowly. "I suppose. When will he be ready to take the test?"
"When do you need him to take it?" she countered. "I'll make sure he's ready."
Jones consulted a calendar on his desk. "October thirty-first is the absolute last day." He looked at Kyle again. "Can he do it?"
"Yes, sir," she answered confidently. "Maybe even before that."

CHAPTER THIRTY TWO

Tor wanted to kiss Kyle right there in Jones's office. Of course he didn't, but he barely restrained himself once they were in the hall.

"That was brilliant, Kyle," he effused. "You literally saved my career as a soldier!"

"I was trying to save us both." She waited while he opened the front door and they walked outside. "He would've been so angry at you if you told him the truth that he might have shipped you back to Norway on the spot."

True.

"And then he would naturally assume that you knew and went along with the deception," Tor added.

"Exactly." Kyle stood next to the jeep. "Do you need a ride?"

Tor wanted to be with her, but couldn't think of an excuse to prolong their time together. "No, but do I want to thank you."

"You're welcome." She watched him with a solemn expression. "Is there anything else?"

"Have you forgiven me yet?"

Kyle's brow plunged and she pointed at the building they'd just left. "Didn't I just save your stinking Norwegian hide in there?"

"Yes, you did," he said softly. "But I don't want to make any incorrect assumptions."

Kyle chewed her lower lip. "Yeah, I've forgiven you. Because it's too much work not to."

Tor watched her for a moment. "Then why do you still look so sad?"

Her eyes sparkled with unshed tears. "Because by doing so, I've just guaranteed that you'll definitely disappear from my life in three months."

И И И

Kyle didn't mean to cry. She didn't want to cry. But this tension between her and Tor had stretched her nerves to the breaking point.

"Get in the jeep," he said as he walked around to the driver's side. "I'll drive."

"You aren't authorized."

"I don't care."

Kyle wasn't up for an argument. She walked to the other side of the jeep and claimed the passenger seat.

"Do you know how to drive?"

Tor shot her a look that clearly questioned her intelligence. Then he started the engine and shifted into first gear.

"Where to?"

"Your barracks I guess," she answered.

Tor drove the jeep without effort—*of course he did*—and parked in front of his barracks's door. Kyle expected him to get out, but instead he shut off the engine.

They sat in a silence so thick that she felt its weight on her shoulders.

"There won't be any new recruits," Tor said out of nowhere.

Kyle knew that. "Because there isn't time to train them before the Tenth ships out."

"As soon as there's snow we'll go back up the mountain and practice what they know. Then we'll be ready to go." Tor drummed his fingertips on the steering wheel.

Kyle found the repetitive movement mesmerizing. "What are we going to do?"

"What are we *going* to do?" he asked. "Or what do I *want* to do?"

Good question. "Want, I guess."

Tor didn't hesitate. "I want to marry you."

Kyle scoffed. "Don't be ridiculous."

He turned to look at her. "You asked what I wanted, and that's what I want."

"Why? Because you took my virginity?" Kyle suddenly realized they were in an open jeep in front of a large barracks and her words could be overheard.

Tor looked at the few men and women walking by. "Don't worry. No one understands Norsk."

Kyle's face heated. "That's not a good reason, Tor."

"I agree. But that isn't the reason."

"Then what is?"

His expression was almost pained. "Because I love you. And because you are the first woman I've ever met that I wanted to marry."

"Oh, Tor." Fresh tears threatened. "It's impossible."

"I know. And it's completely selfish of me." He drummed the steering wheel again.

Kyle wondered if she would agree to marry Tor if he weren't headed to battles abroad in a few months. Or if he lived in America. Or if the war ended.

There are so many obstacles.

She wanted to tell him she loved him too, but the words wouldn't come out of her mouth.

"I guess in the meantime we'll work on your English."

He was clearly disappointed with her response, but she couldn't give him more at that moment. "And I'll take the test in eight weeks. A week earlier than Jones said. That should ease his mind."

Tor got out of the jeep and Kyle slid over to the driver's seat.

"I'll see you at supper," she called to his back.

He waved over one shoulder but didn't turn around.

August 21, 1944

The next day Kyle accompanied Tor to his training, but this time with a different purpose. At dinner last night Kyle pointed out that if Tor told his platoon that he needed to pass an English test in order to accompany them to Italy, that the men would help him become more fluent.

Or so it would appear.

And Tor's apparently easy grasp of the language would become more believable if he was forced to speak it all day every day around his three dozen tutors.

Tor thought it was brilliant.

Now he stood with Frank Collins in front of their platoon while Kyle took her place by his side.

"Say as much as you think you can in English," she told Tor. "And I'll step in when I need to."

Tor nodded and gestured to Frank that he needed a minute, then stepped forward to address the soldiers. "Good morning. I have something to tell you.

Surprised glances shifted from man to man as Tor addressed them in English.

"I am told—" *Keep the grammar simple.* "—that I must pass English test or I do not go to Italy."

More glances bounced through the men, these heavy with concern.

Tor turned halfway around and extended a hand toward Kyle. "Now Lieutenant Solberg teaches me English."

Kyle smiled and nodded.

Tor faced the men again. "I need help from you. Yes?"

Every man nodded.

Several men shouted, "Yes, Captain."

"Good. Thank you." Tor turned to Frank. "Now you."

Tor stepped back and stood next to Kyle. He watched the men as First Lieutenant Frank Collins gave the instructions for their bayonet practice. When the soldiers were released to ready their equipment, they swarmed Tor first.

"Don't worry, Captain. We'll make sure you pass that test."

"We aren't going to Italy without you, that's a promise."

"You can do it, sir."

"We believe in you."

Tor nodded and shook the men's hands. "Thank you. Thank you."

When the hubbub died and the soldiers got ready for the training, Tor finally looked at Kyle. Her eyes were misty.

"What makes you sad?" he asked in English.

Might as well.

"Not sad," she corrected. "I'm just so moved at the obvious respect and affection these men have for you."

Tor understood. Even without speaking to them most of the time, it was obvious that the young men under his command understood his dedication and his commitment to their training and safety.

"I'll pass the test easily and they'll feel like they helped." Tor smiled softly, glad for how spot-on Kyle's suggestions were. "It will bond us as a unit."

Kyle looked tired. "They do love you, sir."

"Are you all right?"

She waved a dismissive hand. "I didn't sleep well last night."

Tor glanced around to see if anyone was paying them any attention, then he switched to Norsk just in case.

"Why not?"

She appeared annoyed. "Your proposal."

Tor's heart stuttered. "Are you thinking about it?"

"Of course I'm thinking about it. About how impossible it is." She drew a deep breath. "I wish you hadn't said anything at all."

"I didn't intend to," he offered. "But when you asked the question…"

Kyle looked up at him. "Do you understand that by proposing to me, now I've lost *two* futures?"

That perspective had never crossed Tor's mind. Losing her future with Erik was obvious, but until Tor said he wanted to marry her, she had no future with him.

He created the possibility and it was destroyed in the same conversation. "I do now. And I'm sorry, Kyle. That wasn't my intention."

"I know." She shaded her eyes and watched the soldiers reform their platoon, bayoneted rifles on their shoulders. "I guess it's another casualty of war."

September 15, 1944

Tor and Frank's platoon was scheduled for orientation. They arrived at the theater early and the forty men filed into the seats.

"Where's your translator?" Frank asked.

"I'm listening in English," Tor explained. "I must practice for my test. So I can go to Italy."

"I can't believe you had the chance to get out of it." Frank shook his head. "Are you sure you want to do this?"

Tor looked at the faces of the soldiers he'd trained, and who were now training him. They were eager, earnest, and determined to a man.

Then he looked back at Frank. "I have to do this. For them, and for Norway."

Frank's expression showed his respect. "Yeah. I guess you do."

When the officer giving the orientation showed up, he was carrying a copy of U.S. News and World Report. He glanced through it and then started telling the group what it said.

"Do they just grab any guy and let him do orientation?" Frank muttered. "This is ridiculous."

"We could read that ourselves," Tor said. "But I don't think the men will."

"Good point."

When the magazine's information was apparently exhausted, the sergeant walked to the side of the stage where a stand and maps were waiting. He flipped a map over and showed the men where the allied positions were marked in blue.

"And here, in the red, are enemy's positions."

To Tor it was obvious that the red colored a lot more of the map than the blue did. The sergeant used a rubber-tipped pointer to explain where the Tenth would begin their attack and in which directions the three divisions would move to push the enemy back.

"So you all can see the importance of your mission," the sergeant concluded. "Train hard and make America proud. We're counting on you."

N N N

Train hard?

Tor looked around him as he walked to supper on that crisp mid-September evening. He still couldn't wrap his head around the luxuries these American soldiers enjoyed.

Sure, the Colorado Rockies had a way of knocking a man to the ground without warning. The soldiers' actual training was physically demanding and the strains of the high altitude divided the men from the boys in pretty quick order.

On top of that, the deep snow didn't forgive any mistakes, especially stupid ones.

But Camp Hale offered an embarrassing multitude of leisure time recreational facilities including auditoriums, movie theaters, service clubs, and field houses for all types of activities year-round. Not to mention hunting and fishing in the surrounding forests and streams.

Soldiers could participate in band or choral groups. They even created a musical production, *Hale and Hearty*, with WACs and soldiers performing original numbers.

To top that, Denver radio station KOA broadcasted the music programs performed by the Camp Hale Regimental Band.

Tor was afraid that when his men were faced with mortar and machine gun fire from an enemy hell-bent on killing every one of them that they might freeze and forget their training, frightened by the realities of blood-spattered friends dropping dead right next to them.

These soldiers were young, some barely eighteen, and the task ahead of them was daunting.

Please, God, help us get them ready.

September 21, 1944

Kyle awoke to a pale-skyed world covered in white. She pulled back the curtain in her room and watched as snow removal was already in full swing this morning.

"How does it look?"

"Cold," Kyle said over her shoulder to her new roommate.

First Lieutenant Sandra Weinstein had just transferred in from Fort Drum to assist in the administration of the WACs at Camp Hale. Once the Tenth was mobilized, the future of Camp Hale and the soldiers left behind needed to be decided.

Sandra threw back her covers and sat up. She pulled the curlers from her thick brown hair.

"Just like New York, I guess. Why couldn't I be transferred to a fort in Florida?"

Kyle smiled. "Just lucky, I guess."

As she dressed, Kyle wondered if the soldiers would go up the mountain today. She assumed they would if the T-bar was operating. They needed to freshen up on their skills.

She tried to focus on the beauty of the frozen day and not the fact that the snow brought Tor one step closer to leaving.

CHAPTER THIRTY THREE

October 24, 1944

Tor wasn't sure how the English test was going to be administered, but he entered the room with confidence. He took the chair indicated, and faced his three uniformed inquisitors.

"Good afternoon, Captain Hansen," one of the men began.

When nothing else was said, Tor realized he was expected to respond. He dipped his chin. "Good afternoon to you all as well."

"I'm Captain Despain of the Eighty-fifth Infantry," he continued. "On my right is Sergeant Wilcox, aide to Major General Jones. And on my left is Captain Brown of the Eighty-seventh Infantry.

Tor noticed that Despain did not physically indicate which man was which and assumed this was part of the test.

He looked at Brown first. "It will be an honor to serve alongside the Eighty-seventh, captain."

Tor moved his gaze to Despain. "And the same is true about the Eighty-fifth."

Last, he looked at Wilcox. "And I hope the sergeant will give a good report about my English to the Major General when we have finished." Despain looked impressed. "Well done, Captain. I'd say we're off to a good start."

For the next half hour, the three men asked Tor a multitude of questions, and when his answers seemed to surprise them, he expressed his opinions.

"I am worried about the soldiers here," Tor confessed. "I have not seen battle yet, but I have seen the enemy. I know what they are capable of. And they didn't train in a resort."

Despain's brow furrowed. "Do you think about Camp Hale as a resort?"

"Not in the training, no," Tor hastened to assure him. "But when we reach the Alps, there won't be theaters and field houses for their entertainment."

Captain Brown leaned forward. "I see your point, Hansen. And it's well taken. What I would say in our defense is this: we now have ten thousand men here who train for war every day. If we didn't give them someplace to cut loose and have fun, they'd be cannibalizing each other."

Tor lifted his brow. "What is cannibalizing?"

Despain smiled. "So you *will* ask if you don't understand."

That surprised Tor. "I would do that in Norsk as well."

The three men glanced at each other and Tor believed he had just scored more points.

"Cannibals eat each other," Brown said. "To cannibalize is the act of eating each other."

Tor thought the meaning would be something along that line based on how Brown had used the word. "I understand. Both the new word, and the reason why this camp has so many things to do."

Despain looked at the clock. "I think we've heard enough. Do either of you have any more questions for Captain Hansen?"

"No, I'm satisfied," Brown said. "You?"

"I'm satisfied as well." Despain turned to Wilcox. "Do you feel this interview has provided a fair assessment of the captain's English proficiency?"

Wilcox nodded. "I do."

Despain faced Tor. "Will you step outside for a moment,

Captain? We'll be out shortly with our decision."

"Of course." Tor stood and saluted. "Thank you for the interesting conversation."

He left the room, closed the door, and took a seat in the reception area. Less than three minutes passed before the trio appeared, smiling.

Tor stood.

Despain held out his hand and Tor reached for it. "The final decision is in the Major General's hands, but it will be our unanimous recommendation that you ship to Italy with your division. Congratulations, Captain Hansen."

Tor grinned. "Thank you. It'll be an honor to fight alongside the Eighty-fifth and Eighty-seventh."

N N N

"Passed with unanimous recommendations!" Tor looked like a kid who really did get a pony for Christmas as he climbed into the waiting jeep. "Jones has to make it official, but there isn't any reason for him to deny me now."

"Especially since you also speak fluent German." Kyle ignored the sense of dread that his words prompted and started the engine.

The outcome of his test was not a surprise based on his grasp of language, but nothing in the army was ever certain until it was certain. Whether she wanted him to go to Italy or return to Norway, however, depended on her ever-changing moods.

Tor interrupted her thoughts. "Will you go to the dance with me tonight?"

As was the case at almost all American military posts, dances were popular for both officers and enlisted men. The soldiers especially liked the dance competitions, though Kyle wasn't sure whether that was for the prizes, or the thrill of defeating competitors. Probably both.

"Sure." Kyle winked at him as she drove toward the mess hall between ridges of snow that could well remain until spring. "I'll save you from the civilians."

Since there were vastly more men than WACs at Camp Hale,

single women were brought up to the camp from Leadville to be dance partners for the surplus of men. A lot of wartime romances, and a few marriages, sprang up as a result.

Tor shrugged. "I'm not a great dancer but that doesn't seem to discourage them."

Kyle laughed. "Of course not. Have you looked in a mirror?" She parked the jeep and faced Tor, her dread intensifying. "Did they say what will happen to me now?"

Tor looked apologetic. "No. They didn't."

"Then I'll guess I keep doing what I've been doing until I get different orders..."

"With such a short time left, maybe they won't do anything until we're all gone."

Tor sounded hopeful, but that only made their impending separation more painful.

"Yeah. Maybe." Kyle opened the jeep door and got out.

Tor could be gone in six weeks. Nine at the most, based on what was printed in the *Ski-Zette*. One way or another, the Tenth would be gone before Christmas.

As she forced herself to eat supper, swallowing past the lump in her throat, an aide from Jones's office walked up to their table. He was beaming at Tor.

"Captain Hansen." He held out an envelope. "I have a message from Major General Jones."

Tor accepted the envelope and tore it open. A smile spread his cheeks and he looked at Kyle, his blue eyes twinkling.

"I passed my English test and am now set to ship out with the Eighty-sixth Infantry Division when they go to Italy." He shifted his attention to the aide. "Thank you, Sergeant Wilcox."

The grinning sergeant saluted Tor and Kyle before spinning on a heel and leaving the mess.

◆ ◆ ◆

Tor danced with Kyle all night. Even though that wasn't considered sporting with the ratio of men to women present, there was no way in hell he was going to let go of her.

"Rum and Coke?" he asked when they arrived at the Rec

Hall.

She looked nauseated by the suggestion. "No more of that for me. I'll have a plain 7-Up."

Tor claimed a small table off to the side of the dance floor. Tor downed his beer while Kyle sipped her soda. Most of the first songs were peppy and designed to get people moving. But at the first slow song, Tor grabbed Kyle's hand and pulled her on to the floor.

As they danced, Kyle leaned into him. He held her closer. He rested his cheek on the top of her head and inhaled the scent of her shampoo. He closed his eyes.

I never want this moment to end.

But it was going to end, and there wasn't anything he could do about it.

Tor decided to repeat his proposal, once he knew exactly when he was leaving. A last ditch effort to make Kyle his for the rest of his life. Faced with a definite date for his departure, she just might agree to marry him.

Where and how they would live when the war ended could be decided later. All he needed was to know she would be waiting for him.

Kyle lifted her head and looked him in the eye as if she heard his thoughts.

"I want to remember this moment forever," she said. "So after we both leave here, we can talk about this in twenty years."

Tor forced a smile. "In Norway with my wife and dozen children."

"Exactly."

Kyle tucked her head under his again, and Tor held her there.

November 2, 1944

Kyle went to the camp's doctor for her required annual physical. She knew she'd lost weight and might have to explain to him that she was depressed and why.

He's a doctor and what I tell him is private, she reminded herself.

Not that loving a man who was going into battle was unusual by any means. But loving a foreign man who was never coming back to the United States was one step farther down the path of futility. It had affected her both appetite and her mood.

Kyle was ushered into a chilly little room and instructed to undress and don a backless cotton robe. She did, keeping her socks on for warmth, and then perched herself on the examination table and waited.

A nurse came in and greeted her cheerily. "I don't blame you about the socks," she chirped. "Don't know why it can't be warmer in here."

After Kyle was weighed—down twelve pounds—and her blood pressure and temperature were logged, the nurse asked her several questions. Kyle was honest about her current emotional state, while insisting she could still do her job in spite of the malaise that stole her usually bright spirits.

"We're seeing a lot of that right now," the nurse said as she made notes. "The women here have made friends—and more—with the men. Knowing they're going into such a dangerous area has a lot of us worried."

The nurse set her clipboard down. "Doctor will be in shortly."

Going into such a dangerous area.

Kyle took deep breaths to keep from crying. She couldn't think about that now or the doctor might find her blubbering and say she's unfit for work.

Think about something funny.

Would you rather be called Stump or Handy?

Kyle laughed out loud.

A soft knock on the door preceded the doctor's entrance. He was a friendly-looking man with a horn-rimmed glasses and a fringe of red hair circling his scalp.

"Good morning, Lieutenant Solberg. I'm Doctor Kann. How are you doing?"

Kyle smiled a little. "I'm alright."

"Let's see here..." He lifted the clip board and read the nurse's notes while he made little humming noises. "Nothing here to cause undue alarm."

He set the clipboard down and settled his stethoscope into his ears. He stood next to Kyle and pressed the chestpiece to her back. "Breathe in."

Doctor Kann moved through listening to her breathe, testing her reflexes and shining lights down her throat and in her ears.

"Everything looks good. Will you lie down?"

Kyle did so. The doctor began to probe her belly while she tried not to laugh.

"Sorry," she giggled. "That tickles."

The doctor leaned over to consult the clipboard. "When was your last period?"

Kyle felt her face warming. "I don't remember, to be honest. I'm very irregular—always have been. I don't even pay attention any more."

Doctor Kann's lips pressed together and he looked at her kindly. "I'm going to do an internal exam. Just to be sure everything's all right."

"Oh. Okay."

The doctor washed his hands and asked Kyle to spread her legs. He slid his fingers inside her while he pressed on her belly. The pressure inside and out was very uncomfortable and she concentrated on breathing slowly and not tensing up.

When he removed his hand, he pressed his stethoscope to her abdomen. "Take a deep breath and hold it."

After half a minute he straightened. Kyle heaved a sigh of relief.

"You can sit up now."

She did, tucking the gown around her hips, while Doctor Kann washed his hands again. Then he turned to face her, his expression serious.

"Lieutenant, I'll need to run a test to be certain, but judging by the size and firmness of your uterus, I'd say you are at least three months pregnant."

Kyle didn't remember what happened next, but she awoke to the sharp smell of ammonia. She was lying on the examination table, covered with a blanket, while the nurse waved the foul-smelling capsule under her nose.

Kyle pushed it away. "Did I faint?"

"Yes." Doctor Kann shone little lights in her eyes. She squinted against them. She knew there was something she needed to remember, but it eluded her at the moment.

"Lieutenant, when did you last have sexual intercourse?"

Pregnant.

Oh, God... there has to be a mistake.

"I only did it once," she squeaked. "I can't be pregnant."

"Once is all it takes." Doctor Kann switched off his light. "When was that?"

Kyle tried to keep the panic from her voice without success. "July. Toward the middle. Or end. I think."

He counted on his fingers. "Three and a half months ago."

"This can't be right..."

"Can you sit up?"

Kyle nodded and the nurse helped her.

The doctor handed her a little glass cup. "I need a sample of urine in this. Try to fill it at least half way."

Kyle stared at him. "Why?"

"I'll send it to the hospital lab this morning and they'll run a hormone test on it. That will give us a definitive answer." Doctor Kann picked up the clipboard and made more notes. "But based on the information you just gave me, plus your symptoms and the physical exam, I'm pretty certain you are entering the second trimester."

Kyle was having a hard time breathing because her heart was bashing her ribs so hard. "When will the results come back?"

Doctor Kann handed the clipboard to the nurse and smiled kindly. "In five days. Come back then."

CHAPTER THIRTY FOUR

November 6, 1944

Kyle's life shifted into an unreal and often nightmarish state. Every time she remembered that she might be pregnant with Tor's baby, she panicked until she reminded herself that the test results weren't back and the doctor could be wrong.
Doctors are human. They make mistakes.
Maybe she had a tumor.
That possibility sent her into a different sort of panicked tailspin.
Luckily she didn't have to be at Tor's side hardly at all for the last four days because the entire camp was involved in a competition. Each platoon needed to complete a round of training exercises for each of the key skills they would soon be putting to use: mountain climbing, downhill skiing, rifle and pistol target practice, grenade targets, gas mask safety, hand-to-hand combat and bayonets.
The time it took each platoon to successfully complete each station was being logged on a huge board in the mess hall. The platoon with the shortest overall time was being rewarded with

two-day passes and an extra week's pay.

As a second lieutenant that would put an extra thirty-seven dollars in Kyle's pocket. She wasn't sure how much the privates were paid, but she guessed it meant an extra twenty-five bucks for them to blow during those two days of freedom.

The underlying reason for the competitive training shone over the camp like a klieg light: the time for the Tenth to ship out was drawing near. That seemed to put everyone's nerves on edge, either with eagerness to get on with it or with the fear of dying in battle.

This afternoon, after the training runs were finished for the day, the entire camp was called to attention in the center field. A stage had been set up along with a podium and a huge array of speakers and American flags.

The sun was trying to push clouds out of the way and having some success. Even so, standing in the boot-packed snow was chilly. Kyle took her place next to Tor, who grinned down at her.

"We have the best time in the downhill," he said under his breath. "And we're in second for hand-to-hand."

Kyle looked up into his beautiful blue eyes and her breath caught. She hoped their baby would have his blue eyes.

Stop it.

She smiled though her lips trembled. "Congratulations."

Tor's grin faded. "What's wrong?"

Kyle gave the same safe answer that she recently began defaulting to. "You're going to war."

Tor narrowed his eyes as he stared at her. "Why do I think it's more than that?"

The speakers came on with a loud crack. Kyle tipped her head in that direction and then turned to look at the stage—and away from Tor's probing. There was no point in saying anything until she was sure and tomorrow she would be sure.

"Attention!"

Ten thousand soldiers and two hundred WACs stiffened with the thundering thud of boot heels clomping together.

Major General Lloyd Jones stepped up to the podium and the men and women saluted him as one.

Jones saluted them back, holding the pose a beat longer than necessary. That little show of respect from their commander made Kyle's vision blur, and she blinked the moisture away.

He knows.

Jones leaned into the microphone. "At ease."

Another muffled thump filled the air as the soldiers changed their collective stance.

"First of all, I want to tell you how proud I am of the Tenth Division," he said slowly as his amplified voice bounced faintly off the surrounding rock. "You have trained hard, fought the fiercest elements, and become true warriors worthy of the task that lies before you."

He paused as if to give the soldiers a moment to digest his compliment. "To adequately signify all that you have done in this unique division, the Tenth Division is hereby re-designated as the Tenth Mountain Division."

Kyle saw heads turning and men grinning.

"You will all receive a blue and white tab embroidered with the word *Mountain*, which has been authorized as an addition for your sleeve insignias."

Though she was too far from the stage to be sure, Kyle thought she saw Jones smile.

"Well done, men." He saluted and held it again. "You are dismissed."

A roar of applause exploded from the soldiers.

November 7, 1944

Kyle sat in Doctor Kann's office literally shaking with apprehension. To pass time while she waited, she asked the nurse who showed her in what the hormone test for pregnancy involved.

"Your urine is injected into young female mice for five days." She sounded disinterested, like she'd said it a thousand times before. "Then they're killed and their ovaries are examined to see if their reproductive systems have reacted to the hormones in your urine. If they have, then the test is positive."

Kyle frowned a little. "Positive?"

The nurse sighed. "That means you're pregnant."

"Poor mice," was all Kyle could think of to say.

The door opened and Doctor Kann walked in. "Good afternoon, Lieutenant."

"Good afternoon," Kyle managed.

The doctor sat at his desk and picked up a folder with her name on it. He glanced over it and nodded slowly.

"Yes, the irregular periods."

Kyle wanted to scream at him *what's the result?*

He looked at her over the top of the folder and then laid it down slowly.

"You are definitely pregnant, Lieutenant," he said kindly.

Kyle started to cry. Deep gulping sobs racked her body even though she tried to hold them back.

Doctor Kann handed her a box of tissues and she pulled out a handful to mop her eyes and nose.

"Do you have a better recollection of the date that you had intercourse?" he prodded.

"Ju—july twenty-fifth," she stammered.

The doctor nodded and held up a little wheel. "If your menses were regular, that would put your period on July eleventh." He turned the wheel and squinted at it. "That means your due date is between April seventeenth and twenty-third."

This is real.

"Are you sure there's no possibility that the test was wrong?" she pleaded. "Could it be a tumor of some kind?"

Doctor Kann had clearly heard that before. "No, I'm glad to say you don't have cancer."

This is very, very real.

"Is the baby's father here at camp?"

Kyle nodded and blew her nose.

"Have you said anything to him yet?"

She shook her head and wiped her eyes.

"Is he married?"

Kyle gasped at the insulting implication that she was a home wrecker. "No! Of course not!"

"Then I suggest you have a conversation with him as soon as possible and get yourselves to a preacher before he leaves."

Kyle stared at him as the realization hit her.
I have to marry Tor.

"In the meantime..." Doctor Kann made another note in her folder. "You will receive an honorable discharge because of the pregnancy."

"When?" she croaked.

"You'll be released ten days after I file the paperwork."

Kyle wiped her eyes again, trying desperately to figure out what she was going to do. "When are you going to file it?"

The doctor looked at the clock on the wall. "The paperwork won't be processed until tomorrow, so I expect you'll be discharged on the eighteenth."

Kyle nodded her understanding, if not her agreement. She was numbed by the news. If she thought her life was turned upside down back in July, that was nothing compared to her current situation.

"Thank you, Doctor," she murmured and pushed herself up from the chair.

"Good luck, Lieutenant."

Kyle left the medical center wondering how her legs still held her up. She had one thought in her head.

I have to tell Tor.

ᴎ ᴎ ᴎ

Tor grabbed Kyle's arm the minute he saw her enter the mess hall for supper. Her swollen eyes were rimmed in red and her face was drawn and pale. He steered her toward the back wall.

"Kyle, what the hell is going on?" he demanded.

"Not here."

"Do you have the jeep outside?"

She looked up at him and nodded.

He still had hold of her elbow. "Come on."

Tor took the driver's side without asking. Kyle didn't object.

"Where should we go?" he asked.

She started to cry, obviously not for the first time that afternoon.

"Has someone died?" he asked gently.

"No," she croaked and pulled a handkerchief from her pocket. "It's nothing like that."

"Then what is it?"

Kyle waved the handkerchief at the windshield. "Go somewhere."

Tor started the engine and shifted into gear, racking his brain for the best place to go. He settled on the base of the mountain. Neither one of them spoke until he parked the jeep.

"Do you want to stay inside?" he asked.

"No." Kyle opened the door and stepped outside.

A light snow was falling but the clouds had trapped the coal smoke and its heat near the ground so the temperature was tolerable. Kyle walked to the bench by the unmoving T-bar and sat on it. Her face was in her collar and her hands were jammed in her pockets.

Tor sat next to her. "Tell me when you're ready."

She heaved a shuddering sigh. "There's no easy way to say this…"

Tor's gut clenched with dread. "Say what, Kyle?"

"I'm…" She gasped in a cry-induced hiccough. "I'm…"

Tor pulled one of her hands from her pocket and held it between his and forced his tone to sound kind. "You're what?"

She swallowed audibly before she whispered, "Pregnant."

Tor blurted without thinking, "Is it mine?"

Kyle's free hand rounded on him and slapped him so hard across his cheek that he saw stars.

"How *dare* you ask me that?" she shouted.

When she jumped up as if to bolt he tightened his grip on her hand. "That's not what I meant! I know it has to be!"

She glared at him in the dim cloud and snow reflected camp light. "Then why did you say that?"

"Because I was so surprised." He looked at her, afraid to believe her words. "*Happily* surprised."

"Happily?" Kyle recoiled. "Are you saying this is *good* news?"

Tor tried to sort through the emotions that were bashing him from all sides. "Will you sit down?"

Kyle slumped onto the bench next to him again.

"Now I am going to think out loud and ask questions," he said. "So please don't run away from me while I do. Will you promise me that?"

Kyle nodded a little.

"First of all, if you had asked me should we have a child at this point, I would have said no, obviously. I'm going into war. Does that make sense?"

Her voice was very small. "Yes."

"But it seems that God had other plans for us." Tor drew a deep and steadying breath of the icy air. "And now we are having a child together at this very uncertain time."

He looked into Kyle's eyes. "I've already told you I love you. And you said the same. I haven't changed. Have you?"

Kyle stared back at him. "No."

"I've also told you that I want to marry you, and long before either of us knew that our night together had started a life."

"Yes, you did." She seemed to be relaxing in increments. "But now it's real."

"It's true. What was just an idea is now in front of us." Tor slid off the bench and knelt in front of Kyle, still holding her hand. "I don't have a ring to give you tonight, but I am asking you, Kyle Solberg, if you will please marry me. And soon."

N N N

Kyle's heart felt like it was about to burst. "You want my baby?"

"*Our* baby. And yes, I want it very much."

Kyle knew she didn't have a choice. She had to marry Tor. She'd known other gals who got in trouble and married the guys, and not all of them were happy afterwards.

But we will be.

I love Tor with all my heart.

"I'll marry you, Tor. And I guess we'll figure the rest out as it comes."

He rose to his feet and pulled her into a long, deep, and consuming kiss. Her fears melted away while he held her so safely and securely.

And as the fear disappeared it was replaced with joy. She was going to be married to a man who adored and respected her for who she was and didn't resent her for it. And she was having a baby—Tor's baby. She was going to be a mother.

When Tor finally stopped kissing her and she caught her breath, she said, "We have a lot to talk about."

"I know. But all of that can wait until tomorrow." He kissed her forehead. "For now let me enjoy this moment, holding my wife and my baby in my arms."

Kyle leaned into his embrace. "I love you, Tor."

"I love you, Kyle. More than you know."

He squeezed her and tipped his head back, loosing a wolf-worthy howl. "I'm going to be a father!"

CHAPTER THIRTY FIVE

November 8, 1944

The next day was Saturday. Kyle and Tor went into Leadville together that evening and tried to find a place to eat dinner that wasn't completely filled with servicemen. Their time together was short and they needed to make plans for what was happening next.

"First things first," Kyle began after they ordered their supper and the waitress left the table. "I'll be discharged from the WACs in ten days because of the baby. So I think we should be married before that."

Tor looked concerned. "Is that bad?"

"No, it's an honorable discharge," she assured him. "I'll still receive all of my benefits because I've served long enough up to this point."

"That's a relief. That means you'll have a year's income to live on in the meantime." Tor huffed. "This war should be over before that."

Kyle was Lutheran but she felt like genuflecting. "Yes, God willing."

His eyes met hers. "What do we need to do to be married?"

"Get a marriage license," she answered. "I looked into it today and the requirements are simple: both of us must appear in person to apply and sign the marriage application, and we have to have some identification for proof of age."

Tor shrugged. "Our military IDs should do it."

"Exactly." Kyle smiled. "And then we can schedule the wedding."

"Good." Tor smiled at her, his eyes twinkling. "We'll get the license on Monday and get married on Tuesday."

Kyle's mouth fell open. "So quickly?"

"Why wait?"

She didn't have an answer.

Tor continued, "We'll get an overnight pass to stay in Leadville Tuesday night for our wedding night. Unless you think we could get more time?"

Kyle wrinkled her nose. "If I'm being discharged I expect they'll claim every bit of my remaining time as possible."

Tor looked like he was hatching a plan. "Then I should try to get three nights after you're discharged instead. We could spend it in Denver."

Kyle smiled. "I would like that. I hear the Brown Palace is a very popular hotel. And there are regular buses to Denver from the camp."

Tor nodded. "I'll work on that."

"So married on the eleventh and honeymooning on the eighteenth." Kyle suddenly realized she wouldn't be spending her days with Tor after that. "And when we return from Denver, I'll need to find someplace to stay in Leadville while you're at camp..."

Tor's mood visibly shifted. "We won't be together very much, then."

"I wonder if the camp would keep me on as a civilian until you leave?" Kyle was grasping at straws. "It doesn't hurt to ask."

"Yes. Do that."

Their food arrived and conversation halted while the plates were served. Then Kyle said, "We *could* wait and be married just before you ship out so we could still see each other every day..."

Tor shook his head definitively. "No. Absolutely not. Who

knows what could happen? An accident, a blizzard, a sudden change in plans—I'm not taking any chances that my son won't have my name."

"Your son, is it?" Kyle laughed. "All right, then. A boy it shall be."

"Tor Solberg Hansen." Tor lifted his beer in toast. "To my American Norwegian son."

Kyle lifted her glass of plain 7-Up, still laughing. "You do realize this baby is already a boy or a girl. What's the feminine of Tor?"

"There are too many to list." Tor waved a dismissive hand. "Make one up, if you want."

He clinked his glass against hers and drained it. Then he leaned forward. "Kiss me."

"Gladly." And she did.

November 11, 1944

Scheduling the chaplain and getting time in the chapel wasn't as easy as Tor thought it would be. Now that the Tenth Mountain Division was expecting their orders to come through any day, dozens of wartime couples were turning their romances into legal marriages while there was still time.

Tor had secured the four o'clock in the afternoon slot and he and Kyle had the chapel to themselves for half an hour before the last ceremony of the day would be performed.

He bought Kyle a wedding ring yesterday after they got the license—a gold band inlaid with three small diamonds—and he felt for it again, confirming it was still in his pocket.

He'd asked Torger to be his best man, but Kyle didn't have anyone as maid of honor, claiming she really didn't know any one at the camp who was special enough to her.

"It's fine," she insisted and smiled. "All that matters is that *you* are there."

They also agreed to wear their dress uniforms and not spend money on new clothing that she would wear once, and he would abandon when he was deployed. Tor smiled at the thought.

My wife is a practical woman.
A typical Norwegian.
His mother was going to love her.
Tor and Kyle really hadn't talked much about where they would live when the war was over. They agreed not to make any decisions about their future after the war until it ended and he came home.
Tor knew Kyle wanted to get as much as possible out of the Readjustment Act, especially since her permanent exit from Viking, Minnesota was being cast in concrete this very afternoon.
He could probably stand to live in America while she finished her education, as long as their eventual return to Norway was agreed on.
I want my son to understand where and who he comes from.
Tor and Torger entered the camp's chapel and waited in the narthex for the three-thirty ceremony to finish and those guests to leave.
The door kept opening and members of Tor's squad entered on blasts of winter air, accompanied by members of his previous training groups. Frank Collins was there, as well as Friedl Pfeifer.
A beaming Kossin walked up and slapped him on the shoulder. "Congratulations, sir."
"Thank you, private." Tor pointed. "How's the leg?"
"Good as new. Maybe better. I'm skiing like a pro now."
The door opened again and Kyle stepped inside. She wore her fitted drab-green four-button blazer with the calf-length flared skirt. Her blonde hair was rolled stylishly below her pipe-edge cap.
If Tor hadn't known she was pregnant, he wouldn't have noticed the slight bulge of her abdomen.
Now he wondered how he missed it.
He smiled at her. "My beautiful bride."
She smiled back. "My handsome Norseman."

ᛟ ᛟ ᛟ

Tor wore his drab-green Norwegian Army captain's uniform with its three-starred collars and King Haakon the Seventh's crest on his arm. Sewn to his sleeve below it was the barrel-shaped blue and white Tenth insignia with its two red crossed swords, topped by the new Mountain tab.

Kyle still couldn't believe that this six-and-a-half foot Nordic god—yes, she'd mentally succumbed to the annoying but accurate nickname—was about to become her husband. And that tonight she was going to be in his bed with every right to stay there.

They decided not to ask for an overnight pass for tonight, deferring their plans until she was discharged and only Tor needed to request leave. His three days had been approved and their reservation at the Brown Palace confirmed.

However, as soon as their ceremony was finished today they would drive into Leadville on a day pass and check into a cozy little inn where they'd have supper served in their room. Then they'd be all alone until they needed to drive back to Camp Hale and check in by midnight.

It wasn't a perfect plan, but it was a satisfactory one.

The door from the chapel into the narthex burst open and a couple ran out, laughing and holding hands while being chased by a dozen cheering well-wishers. Tor lifted one eyebrow and looked askance at Kyle.

"We'll be more dignified," she assured him. "We're Norwegian after all."

Torger went inside to see what was going on and then popped back out. "He's ready for us."

Tor offered Kyle his arm. She took a firm hold on it and smiled up at him, happier than she could imagine. Together, they entered the little church.

※ ※ ※

Tor repeated his vows with fervent sincerity while he held Kyle's hands and looked into her eyes which were mostly green today, either because of her green uniform or her happiness.

Most likely both.

If Teigen could see him now, Tor figured his brother would have a heart attack. Happily marrying the woman he loved? About to become a father? This was the last thing Teigen would expect from him. Teigen was engaged over five years ago and was supposed to be married in nineteen-forty. Sure, the war and his fiancée's politics caused him to eventually break the engagement, but Teigen was much farther down the marriage path than Tor had ever thought of being.

I can't wait to write him and tell him.

Tor would have smiled at the thought if he wasn't already grinning like a fool.

"I, Kyle Solberg, take you, Tor Hansen, to be my lawfully wedded husband."

Bliss.

и и и

Some jokers had decorated the sedan that Kyle and Tor were taking into Leadville. The window paint declared they were *Just Married* and empty tin cans were tied to the bumper.

"So much for dignity," Tor grumbled.

Kyle laughed. "This is the American part of the celebration."

Torger stepped in front of them. "Before you two go, I have a little surprise for everybody. Come to the Officer's Club."

Tor looked at Kyle. She looked a little guilty, he thought.

"Did you know about this?"

"Maybe. Some of it." She leaned closer and murmured, "Don't worry. We won't stay long."

When they entered a private room at the Officer's Club, Tor was dumbstruck. In the center of the table was a foot-and-a-half-tall *Kransekake*—a Norwegian wreath cake made from stacked flat almond cakes in decreasing sizes.

"Not only did your bride help me present you with a traditional Norwegian wedding cake..." Torger lifted a cloth napkin which was covering a bottle. "But I was able to get a very rare—in America—bottle of Linie Aquavit!"

Tor clapped his hands, thrilled to his core by Kyle and

Torger's efforts. "This day could not be better!"

Kyle and Tor posed for pictures by the wreath cake and fed pieces of it to each other for more photos, then toasted each other with the Linie.

"Tell me when you're ready to go," Kyle said. "Torger assures me he'll save anything that's left over for us."

Tor pulled his wife into a hug and a solid kiss. "I am a blessed man this day." He smiled at her. "Now let's get out of here."

ᛝ ᛝ ᛝ

Kyle's memory of making love with Tor in the forest was embarrassingly hazy but she remembered she liked it. The only thing making her nervous this afternoon was that, as intimate as they had often been, she was never completely unclothed in front of him.

When they arrived at the inn just after five-thirty, Tor asked that their dinner be served at seven.

"We have business to get to first," he whispered as they climbed the staircase to the second floor. "And possibly again afterwards."

A thrill of anticipation zinged through Kyle. She had no argument with his plans.

Now she stood in the bathroom wearing her only nightgown and nothing else. When her husband took it off her, she would be naked.

Would Tor be naked when she came out?

Only one way to know.

Kyle took a deep breath and opened the bathroom door.

Well look at that.

He is.

Tor turned around and faced her. He held out his arms.

Kyle walked across the small room and into his embrace. One passionate kiss later, her nightgown was on the floor and she no longer worried about it.

Whatever intimacy they had shared previously paled in comparison to the things Tor showed her today. He was tender, slow-paced, and paid attention to her entire body—until he finally groaned the end of his restraint and entered her.

Kyle was completely his, he made sure of it. When she peaked, she actually cried tears of joy. Nothing could have prepared her for the intensity of joining her body with a man she was deeply in love with, married to, and free to enjoy as often as she wanted.

She laid on the bed in his arms while he kissed away her tears. Nothing else that happened in her life would ever top this moment, she was sure of it.

"I love you, Tor," she whispered.

He nuzzled her ear sending a wash of gooseflesh over her skin. "And I love you, Kyle."

His hand slid over her tingling skin to her belly and rested there, warm and heavy. "I love both of you."

CHAPTER THIRTY SIX

November 20, 1944
Camp Hale, Colorado

Five days ago, the Tenth Mountain Division was told that they would ship out to Italy in stages. The Eighty-sixth Infantry—Tor's division—was leaving first.

On December first.

"That's eleven days after we get back from our honeymoon," Kyle said when Tor told her. "It's such a short time there's no point in my trying to find a room to rent. I think I should just stay in the Leadville Inn until you go so we can spend as much time together as possible."

Tor agreed. "Maybe you can leave your things there while we're in Denver and only take what you need for those three days with you."

That was exactly what she did.

Now she was alone in the inn at eleven-fifteen at night, looking at the neatly packed detritus of her last year-and-a-half, and wondering what her life would be like starting on December second.

Tor kissed her goodbye a dozen times before he headed to

Camp Hale to check in. Kyle held her sorrow back until he was gone, and only then did she allow herself to cry.

Denver already felt like a dream.

Three days together with no one else around them demanding attention or placing rules on their behavior was heaven. She and Tor never stopped touching each other—holding hands, arms around waists, kisses both affectionate and passionate—as if they were both trying to save up a lifetime of vivid memories while they could.

Kyle had deliberately not allowed her thoughts to plan beyond December first. She would take her marriage one precious day at a time after that. That was how war was. There were no guarantees.

I am blessed today, Lord. Thank you for my husband and his child.

Tomorrow she would go to the camp and see if there was anything she could do there for the next ten days. And she would miss Tor every night that she slept here alone.

Tonight, not wanting to sleep yet and with no reason to rise early in the morning, she decided it was time to write to her parents. She dug out a pen and stationery from one of her boxes and settled on the floor, using the oval coffee table as a desk.

There was no point in delaying her news or beating around the bush.

Dearest Mamma and Pappa ~

I am writing with the most startling news and I hope you will forgive me and be happy for me, because I could not be happier for myself.

I am married.

On November 11th I married the Norwegian Army captain, Tor Hansen, whom I came to Colorado to translate for. We fell in love months ago, but until Erik broke our engagement I wasn't free to accept Tor's proposal.

Tor is shipping out on December 1st to fight in Italy with the Tenth Mountain Division and we wanted to be married before he left.

There is more news that I hope you will welcome: you are to be grandparents.

I confess that the baby and the marriage were out of order, and I ask your forgiveness for this. When Erik's letter arrived in July, coldly releasing me from our promises and demanding that I be happy about his impending marriage, I found comfort with my dearest friend.

Once I discovered there was a baby on the way and I told him, Tor happily married me three days later. Your first grandchild ~ which Tor insists will be a boy ~ will be born in late April.

I have still more news.

Because of my delicate condition I have been honorably discharged from the army and will be coming home to spend the holidays with you. While I'm there I'll claim my benefits under the Servicemen's Readjustment Act, which I understand is generally being called the G.I. Bill, and decide where I want to live and what sort of education I want to pursue while I await my husband's return.

I'll call you on the phone when I know what time I'll land in Fargo on December 1st.

I love you and can't wait to see you both. I'm sorry there was no time for you to be at the wedding, but I do have pictures to show you. The army's demands in wartime are never convenient.

Please be happy for me.

All my love,
Kyle Solberg Hansen

N N N

Tor lay in his bed, in his room, in his barracks, and had never been more lonely in his entire life.

After almost thirty-two years as an intentional bachelor, it only took three days alone with his wife to transform him into a *husband*. And now he missed her soft warmth beside him so deeply that it hurt in his chest.

How will I survive leaving her?

The next ten days were going to require plenty of hard work and Tor expected that would distract him, at least during daylight. There was a lot to do to pack everything the division needed for the journey to war.

The first leg of that journey involved twenty buses carrying nine hundred Eighty-sixth Infantry men from Denver to Camp Patrick Henry in Virginia. They said it would take four or five days for the caravan to transport the soldiers the eighteen hundred miles.

There was nothing Tor liked better than folding his tall frame into bus benches for hours upon hours. It almost made him nauseated to think of it now.

From there the Eighty-sixth would board a ship to Italy. After that, he had no idea.

November 30, 1944
Camp Hale, Colorado

Tor and Kyle held on to each other as if their lives depended on never letting go.

Civilians were allowed into camp that night to say goodbye to their loved ones who were leaving in the twenty bus caravan before dawn the next morning and similar scenes were playing out all around them.

Kyle was determined not to cry. She didn't want Tor's last memory of her to be with a blotchy face and swollen red-rimmed eyes.

"I'll write if I can," he promised. "I don't know where we'll be or if there'll be any post offices nearby, but I'll try."

"I understand. And I won't worry if I don't hear from you." Kyle rubbed his cheek, enjoying the rasp of his days-old beard. "Unless some army guys show up at my door, I'll know you're still safe."

"Hopefully we can kick Hitler's ass soundly and get out of there fast." Tor's lips curved. "Like the sign says, we have a date with the son-of-a-bitch."

Kyle forced a smile. "That will be my daily prayer, I promise you."

Tor kissed her again, a slow tender sort of kiss. Then he sighed and rested his forehead against hers.

"I can't wait until our son is born and you can come with me to Arendal."

"And I can't wait to see Norway and meet your family," she whispered, not trusting her voice.

"They're going to love you."

Kyle swallowed and forbade any tears to appear.

The camp siren sounded eleven o'clock, calling the visits to an end. Tor put his arm around her and he kissed the top of her head.

"Let's walk slowly so you're on the very last bus to town."

They did.

When the line was nearly gone, Kyle threw her arms around Tor. "Thank you for giving me a part of you to live with. If I didn't have your son, I don't think I could say goodbye."

"So you're a believer now?"

Holding her close with one arm, Tor slid his other hand inside her coat. His broad palm and long fingers pressed against her growing womb.

"Take good care of him." His voice cracked.

Kyle laid a hand over his, tears rolling defiantly down her chilled cheeks. "He'll know you, Tor. No matter what. I promise you he'll know everything about his amazing father."

"I love you, Kyle." Tor sniffed and his breath hitched. "You're the only woman I've ever loved."

"And you're the only man." She looked into his eyes. "Now I *know* what love really is."

Tor kissed her one last time and then pushed her toward the bus. Kyle climbed the steps and took a seat near the back.

When she looked out the window, Tor was gone.

December 1, 1944
Fargo, North Dakota

Kyle saw her mother and father waiting inside the Fargo terminal. She thought she'd cried enough tears in the last twenty-four hours to have run out of them but clearly she was mistaken. She ran to her parents and was enveloped in their dual embrace. She couldn't speak for several minutes. She felt safe in their presence and knew that, even if they were disappointed in her, that their love for her wasn't shaken.

"Is he gone?" her mother asked.

Kyle nodded. "Before dawn this morning."

Her father looked concerned. "How are you feeling?"

Kyle tried to smile but failed. "I'm fine, Pappa."

"You sure?"

Kyle wiped her eyes. "It was hard, Pappa. Saying goodbye."

"Well, I wish we could have met him." He shrugged. "That's all."

Kyle curled up on the back seat of her parent's car and let herself relax. For the first time in three weeks she wasn't responsible for anything at all. She fell into a thankfully dreamless sleep during the three-hour ride to Viking and didn't awaken until her father shook her gently.

She sat up. The windows of her childhood home glowed their welcome. Her mother opened the front door and went inside while her father helped her out of the car.

"Be careful, it's slippery."

Kyle accepted his hand even though she didn't need it. "I've been living in snow, Pappa. I'll be fine."

"Well if you fall now, you're falling for two."

His logic was impeccable.

December 5, 1944
Camp Patrick Henry, Virginia

Tor's legs cramped as he stepped down from the bus at midday on their fifth day of travel. The weather in Virginia was cold, but it was a lot warmer than Colorado.

Camp Patrick Henry served primarily as a troop staging ground and, according to the sign at its entrance, operated under the control of the Hampton Roads Port of Embarkation.

Torger nudged him. "That's where we catch the boat."

Tor waited for his duffel bag to be unloaded. All of the ski equipment was being handled separately from the soldiers' personal things and they wouldn't see it again until Italy.

"Where do we go now?"

Torger shrugged. "Follow the line."

Tor trudged after the other men from his bus. They were directed to a huge barracks with dozens of bunks.

"Enlisted men to the right, officers to the left," a corporal repeated over and over.

The room on the left had only cots, no bunks. Tor and Torger dropped their duffel bags on two of them, then Tor began a series of ski stretches to relieve the stiffness in his legs.

As he crossed his legs and reached for the floor he asked Torger, "Do you think there is a telephone I could use?"

The ski jumper grinned. "Want to call the little ball-and-chain?"

Tor wagged his head at the stupid joke. "No, I want to call my *wife*. Let her know we made it here."

After lunch, Tor went in search of a phone and was directed to the telephone center in Area Two. Torger went with him as an excuse to explore.

"Rec Hall Number Three, Theater Number Four, Last Chance Nite Club," Torger read the signs as they passed the buildings. He smacked Tor's arm. "This place is gonna be fun!"

Tor turned a corner. "The telephone center's down this way."

For reasons he understood completely, the recreation options held no interest for him. Without Kyle at his side, the world seemed to have lost vibrancy.

Inside the center, Tor gave the operator Kyle's parents' phone number and then sat in a booth and listened on a handset while the call was placed.

The phone on the other end rang four times before a man

answered with, "*Ja?*"
"Mister Solberg?" Tor ventured.
"Ja. Who is this?"
"It's Tor Hansen, sir." *Should I have said I'm your son-in-law?* "Is Kyle available?"
"Tor—oh! Yes!" The voice moved away from the handset. "Get Kyle! It's her husband!" The voice moved back into range. "This is Ole Solberg speaking. I'm your father-in-law."
"*Jeg er bæret over å møte deg, sir.*" I am honored to meet you, sir.

There was click on the line as another phone was picked up. Tor kept going anyway. "*Jeg vet det er sent, men kan jeg ha din datters hånd i ekteskap?*" I know it's late, but may I have your daughter's hand in marriage?

"Tor?" Kyle's voice sounded like churchbells.

Tor smiled. "Hello, my darling."

"Yes," Ole said vehemently. "Yes, you may."

"*Tusen takk, Ole.*"

"I'll hang up now. God bless you both." Another click signaled Ole's exit from the conversation.

"Are you at Camp Patrick Henry?" Kyle asked.

"Yes, we arrived today. I'm not sure when we sail, but it should be within the week. How are you?"

"Better, hearing your voice."

"Did you have any trouble getting home?"

"No, the weather was fine, thank goodness. But it's been snowing for the last three days."

Tor wiped a tear. "I miss you, Kyle."

"Not more than I miss you. I pray for you every time I think of you." She laughed a little. "So by now your guardian angel is probably *very* tired of hearing from me."

Tor refused to face the possibility that danced around the edge of his thoughts. "Keep praying my love. And I'll keep praying for you and our boy."

"Thank you for giving him to me, Tor." She sniffed. "I know I said that before, but I really mean it."

"Thank you for accepting him. I don't think he was an

accident."

"No. He's a blessing from God."

A timer pinged. "I have to hang up now. I love you, Kyle. I'll try to call again before we leave."

"I love—"

The line went silent.

CHAPTER THIRTY SEVEN

December 10, 1944
Viking, Minnesota

The church service was focused on the many lives lost in Pearl Harbor three years ago. Kyle remembered it clearly. It was the act of aggression that drew America into the war and subsequently changed every single one of her citizens' worlds.

Getting dressed for the day had been a challenge. Now that she was four-and-a-half months along, none of her clothes fit. Kyle and her mother had spent the last six days at the sewing machine: expanding waistbands on skirts, opening pleats on slacks, adding vents and elastic wherever possible.

Her sweaters still fit, of course. But she was going to need a new wardrobe soon.

Kyle knew Erik and his wife Ingrid would be at the service, so she selfishly wanted to look sharp. She tried on several combinations of the altered items until she settled on a navy blue skirt, white blouse, and a cardigan in a traditional Nordic pattern.

"You look absolutely beautiful, Kyle," her mother gushed as Kyle donned her warm wool army coat. "It seems your condition suits you."

"About that..." Kyle went out the front door and climbed into the back seat of the car that her father had been running and warming up for the last fifteen minutes. She waited to continue until her mother was settled in the passenger seat and her father started driving.

"I want you both to know that I plan to be honest about everything that's happened to me in the last five months," she began. "But I just might fudge a little on the timing..."

Her father met her eyes in the rear view mirror. "Timing?"

Kyle's face tightened and her pulse beat in her ears. "I don't want to bring any more shame on you than I already have."

Her mother twisted around and looked her in the eye. "Answer me one question. Honestly."

Kyle nodded apprehensively.

"Who took your virginity?"

Kyle's eyes widened. "Mamma!"

Now her mother's face scarleted. "I just need to know. Was it Erik?"

Kyle could not believe they were having this conversation, especially in front of her father.

"No, Mamma. I swear to you." Kyle screwed up her courage to verbalize the answer. "Tor was my *first*, and my *only*."

Her mother's relief was clear. "All right, then."

She turned back around and heaved a big sigh.

Her father's kind eyes met hers in the mirror again. "That's a relief to us both, Kyle. And you aren't the first couple to jump ahead of the preacher, especially in wartime."

His eyes moved back to the snowy country road in front of them. "It's nobody's damned business when things happened. Only that you are married to the *one* man who could be father of your baby."

"Thank you, Pappa." Kyle knew he meant it because he swore on a Sunday. "But just so we keep our stories straight, please follow my lead."

"Will do, sweetie."

"What have you two told people so far?"

Her mother and father exchanged guilty looks.

"Nothing, actually," her mother admitted. "After we got your letter we decided to wait and talk to you before saying anything."

"So no one knows I'm back?" That would actually work in her favor.

Especially with Erik.

Her mother turned around again. Her expression was apologetic. "No, honey. I'm sorry."

Kyle smiled. "Don't be! This will be perfect."

א א א

Kyle stood in the narthex of the Viking Lutheran Church—now that she had Tor's opinion of her town's name in her head the ironic church title did make her grin—greeting longtime friends and neighbors. Flanked by her parents, Kyle repeated her story.

"His name is Tor Hansen and he's a captain in the Norwegian army. He was the officer I was translating for. After Erik broke our engagement, Tor proposed. I received an honorable discharge because of the baby."

Karster Olsen, Erik's dad, pinned Kyle's father with a skeptical stare. "Have you met him, Ole?"

"Sadly no," her father answered. "But we did speak on the phone when he asked for my permission to marry Kyle."

She smiled.

God bless you, Pappa.

"I'm afraid there wasn't any break in their training for a trip back, Karster," Kyle added. "The Tenth Mountain Division—Tor's division—has already left for Italy."

Do not cry.

Erik appeared in the edge of her vision. Kyle turned to look at him. Ingrid cowered by his side as if afraid Kyle might jump her, claws unsheathed.

"Erik! Ingrid!" Kyle flashed the couple a huge smile. Her eyes dropped to Ingrid's waist to see if they might have jumped ahead of the preacher as well, but saw no sign that they had. "I haven't had the chance to congratulate you two."

"Hello, Kyle." Erik pulled Ingrid forward. "I didn't know you were back."

"Yep. Got here six days ago. I waited until my husband shipped out before leaving Camp Hale."

Erik startled. "Husband?"

"Yes. After you dumped me, Tor proposed." Kyle rested her hands under her belly to accentuate her condition. "Turns out he's very strong…"

"You're having a baby? Already?" Erik glanced at Ingrid, whose face flushed alarmingly.

"Not until *well* into the spring." Kyle patted her little bulge. "But my husband is six-foot-six, so this little fellow is already growing like a weed."

Judging by Erik's uncomfortable expression, her words had the exact effect she hoped they would. "So what about you two? Starting a family soon?"

"Uh…"

"Don't worry." Kyle gave Ingrid a reassuring flip of her wrist. "Not everyone conceives so quickly."

"Are you going to live here?" Ingrid's tone made it sound like that was the worst possible scenario.

Kyle's plans solidified in an instant. "Oh, no. I'm planning on living in Minneapolis and attending the University of Minnesota."

"But you're having a baby…" Ingrid looked confused.

"I have the G.I. Bill. That pays my living expenses for a year and my tuition." Kyle gave a little shrug. "Hopefully the war will be over by then and I can join my husband."

Erik looked at her like he was seeing her clearly for the very first time. "I was wondering why I never heard from you."

Kyle spread her hands. "My marriage was a whirlwind. Tor's training stepped up. And I taught him English so he could go to Italy with his division. It just didn't seem important."

Kyle's mom touched her arm. "We need to go in. The service is about to start."

Kyle offered one last smile before turning away from Erik and Ingrid. She walked into the church with her head high and her dignity completely intact.

December 10, 1944
Camp Patrick Henry, Virginia

Once again Tor sat in the telephone center listening to Kyle's phone ring.

"Hello?" It was her mother.

"Hello, Kylli. This is Tor. Can I speak to Kyle?"

Tor heard a crackle in the line. Based on their last call it seemed that the need to be brief was understood.

"Tor? I'm so glad to hear from you!"

Tor experienced the same surge of emotion as last time when he heard his wife's voice. "Are you well?"

"Never better." She chuckled. "In fact I'm growing out of my clothes. What about you?"

Tor smiled.

My boy is big and strong.

"I've been so bored here that the days seem twice as long," he admitted. "But we are finally boarding the ship tomorrow—the *SS Argentina*—and sailing for Naples, Italy."

"I hope the voyage goes well. When will you arrive?"

"They said in a week-and-a-half if the weather is good."

"I'll keep praying for you."

"Thank you, sweetheart. I'm sure I can write to you at least once when I get there."

"Do what you can, my love. But stay safe first of all."

"I'll do my best."

"I went to church today. Now everyone in Viking knows you proposed after Erik dumped me and we're already having a baby."

Tor laughed. "I see you left out a few unnecessary details."

He heard the smile in his wife's voice. "To quote my father, it's none of their damned business."

"I expect your parents are happy to have you there."

"Yep. But I already filed for my G.I. benefits and I'm moving to Minneapolis in January. I'm enrolling in the University of Minnesota."

Tor knew this was her hope. "What will you study?"

"I'll start with basic requirements. When the war's over you

and I can decide if I continue or we move to Norway."
Tor honestly didn't know which path he'd choose. Luckily, that decision was months away at the very least.
"I love you so much, Kyle. And I'm very proud of you."
"I love you, Tor, more than I ever imagined I could."
"No matter what happens, I want you to remember that you are the most important thing in my life. Marrying you made me whole."
"I feel the same way."
The timer beeped.
"God be with you, Tor."
"And with you, my beloved wife."
The line went dead.

December 22, 1944
Naples, Italy

The *SS Argentina* edged slowly into its slot at the Port of Naples. Tor had never been so glad to see anything in his life as he was to spot the Italian coastline rising out of the horizon.

Their crossing wasn't considered rough, apparently, but the constant rocking and rolling of the ship made him queasy. Only lying on his back on the too-short bunks or standing in the wind gave him relief.

Now that his feet would be on solid ground again, Tor was looking forward to enjoying big Italian meals without his belly arguing with him.

Lots of them.

According to their briefing during the voyage, the Eighty-sixth Infantry was heading three hundred and seventy five miles north to Bagni di Lucca. That meant the nine hundred men on this mission would hike twenty-five miles a day until they got there.

"Thankfully there should be supply trucks doing the heavy lifting," their colonel explained. "But we can't risk a caravan of twenty buses attracting German attention, even if we *could* get a hold of 'em."

Then he grinned at the gathered soldiers. "But the scenery is absolutely beautiful, if that's any consolation."

Tor looked at the city of Naples from the deck of the shop. It was big enough and busy enough that he should be able to find a post office and mail a letter to Kyle before his platoon hiked out the next day.

Torger appeared next to him. "Ready to get off this bucket?"

Tor patted his midsection. "More than you know."

The men went below deck and joined the other troops. They shouldered their duffels and sat on the bottom bunks, waiting for their units to be called to the loading deck to disembark.

Torger's was called before Tor's was. "See you up top, old man!"

Tor gave him a lazy salute. Once the men were in public, saluting was forbidden. They didn't want the enemy to be able to tell by watching who the high-ranking officers were, thereby turning them into targets.

When Tor's platoon was finally called a half hour later, he gladly made his way through the crowd to the open loading bay. He gave his name to the guards who were checking the soldiers' names off as they exited, and walked across the swaying steel mesh gangway to the solid ground of the pier.

He wondered what people would think if he kissed the ground.

Tor smiled inwardly at that mental image and followed the line of soldiers to the end of the pier. Strangely, the ground still felt like it was moving.

"That's not uncommon," the man next to him said. "Shouldn't last more than a couple days."

Well that's just great news.

Something—or rather, someone—appeared in Tor's peripheral vision. He turned his head to see a man of his own height standing nearby, but dressed in the leathers and fur of the Viking era.

Tor looked away and rubbed his eyes, then looked back.

The Viking was still there and staring at him.

Tor looked around him. No one else seemed to notice the man.

I'm hallucinating. I need food.
Tor kept walking and ignored the vision.

✸ ✸ ✸

Torger and Tor went out to supper together, along with three other soldiers from their respective platoons. It was so good to sit in a restaurant and eat food that wasn't colorless, tasteless, and made in mass quantities.

"Another?" Torger asked the waiter and pointed at their empty wine bottle.

"Two!" one of the men barked and held up two fingers.

The opened bottles appeared immediately. The Americans who had arrived to fight the Germans were obviously welcome.

Tor pushed his plate away, the thin pasta and fresh fish in a creamy tomato sauce completely gone. "That was the best meal I ever ate."

"Agreed," Torger said with his mouth full of bread.

Tor stood and dropped some money on the table. "I'm going to take a walk and see if I can find a post office."

He winked at Torger. "Gotta write to the little ball-and-chain, don't I?"

The four men waved him off and Tor started walking. The Viking was soon beside him.

"What are you, my guardian angel?" Tor muttered.

"Something like that."

Tor stopped and stared at the man. "Am I going crazy?"

"No. I am definitely here." He shrugged. "But only you can see and hear me."

Tor looked up and down the nearly empty street. He waited while a man walked by him—in between Tor and the Viking—and didn't acknowledge the other man.

Tor looked him in the eye. "Are you going to follow me everywhere?"

"Yes."

"How long?"

"I do not know."

Tor rested his hands on his hips, disbelieving this

conversation, and sighed.

"Well... I guess I could use an angel."

He turned toward their accommodations for the night and walked in companionable silence with the Viking by his side.

CHAPTER THIRTY EIGHT

February 7, 1945
Minneapolis, Minnesota

Tor's second letter was dated January 9th, the same day Kyle moved to Minneapolis. Her mother forwarded it to her tiny new home.

Kyle made the six-hour drive from Viking, checked in to a motel directly across the Mississippi River from the University of Minnesota campus, and drove across the bridge to meet with the university's veteran's services people.

After a flurry of letters and phone calls with the veteran's services office throughout December, Kyle had been accepted as a freshman, her tuition was covered, and furnished housing was found for her near the campus.

Classes started the next week.

Because she was married and pregnant, she had to rent an apartment off campus, but that was fine. It wasn't a terrible walk and she still had her sturdy army boots and warm wool coat. Kyle had enough money in savings to get her started, and her first veteran's check for living expenses arrived last week.

Kyle set her textbooks on her little kitchen table and heated water for tea while she held Tor's letter against her cheek. The strong ink strokes on the front of the envelope made her so happy when she opened her mailbox. Now she wanted to savor the reading.

Once her tea was made, she carried the cup to the sleeper sofa where she sat, tucked her legs under her, and rested a hand on the shifting surface of her abdomen.

"Calm down, Thor," she said softly. "We have a letter from your daddy."

As if the babe understood, his movements stilled while Kyle read the necessarily cryptic letter out loud.

My dearest wife,

We finally made it to our destination yesterday afternoon after walking every day since my last letter to you. It was tiring, but the scenery here is beautiful. That helped.

Can you imagine this many men straggling in to an average sized village over the course of a day? The people here rushed to take care of us and told us they were glad we had come. Judging by the conditions here, these people have not had an easy time.

In fact, nowhere that I have seen in this country is unscathed. Torched and abandoned buildings litter the beautiful countryside. It's heartbreaking.

We have already started preparing for our battle. After five days here, we'll spend one day walking to the site of the offensive. We'll be making use of our training, that's for certain.

I wish I could hear from you. I want to know what your days are like. How much you are growing with my son. What the weather is like. When we are back together I will never spend a night away from you again.

I'm sending you and the babe all of my love. And please keep praying for me. I believe it's working.

Your loving husband,

Kyle read the letter out loud three times while she rubbed her stomach. Then she set it down and picked up her tea. She prayed silently while she sipped it in the silence of her cozy apartment.

Her decision to move and start college at this stage of her life was gutsy and she knew it. Not only was she seven years older than the average college freshman, but she was expecting a child. Kyle knew she would face opposition and she showed up ready for it.

She was a Second Lieutenant in the Army, after all.

Kyle started by making appointments to meet with each of her professors. Sitting across from their desks in their typically academic offices, she told them where she had been, what she had done, and why she was in their classes.

"If it's all right with you," she said, "I'd like to work ahead so when I miss a couple weeks with the baby I can still finish on time."

Three of her teachers were clearly impressed and offered to do what they could to help her complete her class load by the first of June.

Two weren't so eager.

"I understand that you *can* work on a degree…" Her stuffy English Literature professor spoke down his uplifted nose. "I just don't understand why you'd *want* to."

"That's a simple answer, sir." Kyle smiled sweetly. "Because someday you'll retire. And I expect you'd want your replacement to be well educated."

The man blinked. "Oh. Yes. Quite."

After their interview he wasn't overly helpful, but he did accept all of Kyle's extra papers for credit. She'd currently earned one-hundred-and-forty percent out of a possible one hundred in his class.

Her psychology professor's suggestions, however, were actually offensive. "Go home, Mrs. Hansen. Take care of your home and raise your baby. You're an embarrassment to your gender."

Kyle didn't answer right away. This pompous ass deserved a dressing down and she wanted to do it right.

"Thank you for your opinion, sir, but there are factors you

have not taken into consideration."

"Oh, really?" he drawled. "Such as?"

"For starters, I think I want to be a psychologist."

He lifted a brow. "Why?"

"Because the science of the mind fascinates me." She offered a mirthless smile. "And because there will be multiple thousands of men—and women—who will return from this war with something called *shell shock*." She looked pointedly around the smallish office. "Can you treat them all by yourself?"

"That's not the—"

"Not only that," Kyle interrupted, not believing what she was about to say. "But many *multiple* thousands of men won't come home at all, will they?"

"Now see here—"

"No sir. You see here." She kept her tone calm and civil. "My husband, my child's father, is currently fighting in Europe. Can you guarantee he'll come home?"

"Don't be absurd," he scoffed.

"I'm not. I'm being the opposite of absurd." Kyle fought the fraught emotions erupting in her chest and lifted her chin. "I am assuring that I can take care of our child, by myself, in case he doesn't."

That shut the man up.

He glared at her. "I won't grade you on a different scale than any of my other students. And attendance is part of that grade."

"In that case, I'll excel in all of my assignments and tests," Kyle countered. "Then even if you fail me in attendance, according to your syllabus I'll still receive a B."

She stood and extended her hand across the desk. "Thank you for your time."

The offer of a handshake seemed to confuse him. He rose slowly and accepted. "You're welcome, Mrs. Hansen."

Kyle walked to the office door, opened it and turned back to smile at the still standing professor.

"I believe I've just successfully completed assignment number fifteen: Deflecting Aggression Without Engaging, don't you? Have a great afternoon!"

February 18-19, 1945
Northern Italy

On the nearly vertical face of Riva Ridge near Mount Belvedere in northern Italy, Tor used his pick to test a crack before he pounded a steel piton into it and attached a snap link. Then he fastened the coiled rope he carried over his shoulder to the link and let it unwind down the mountain. Those who followed would use the rope to pull themselves up the face of the ridge.

The wind was wet and bitterly cold and Tor was constantly showered with ice crystals from above. With his skis and poles strapped to his back he felt like a bird with clipped wings.

The Tenth Mountain Division had launched their attack on the ridge after sunset under the cover of darkness, intending to surprise their German enemy. Their uniquely trained corps was the spearhead for twenty coordinated allied divisions who were pushing the enemy irrevocably north.

Climbing silently in the dark on either side and below him were dozens of men from the Eighty-sixth Infantry Regiment, creating a path for the rest. Along with the advance team, Tor reached the top of the Ridge just before midnight.

He and the others signaled to the units below that the remainder of the nine hundred men could begin their ascent in force, then started preparing the area for their coordinated attack.

Fortunately a haze hung over the lower elevations of the ridge and helped conceal the ascending mountaineers, though searchlights behind the combat area scanned the low-hanging clouds.

According to Tor's watch, by four o'clock in the morning all the members of the Eighty-sixth had reached their objective. Their counterparts in the First Battalion and Company F of the Second Battalion had also reached their separate objectives on nearby parts of the ridge.

None of them had been detected.

The Eighty-sixth soldiers gathered in their units and donned their skis. When daylight was near and Tor received the signal, he sent his men forward, armed with grenades and rifles with bayonets in place.

The German 1044th Infantry Regiment was taken completely by surprise, but that didn't make the battle any less bloody. With the sunrise the Germans launched counterattack after counterattack, accompanied by heavy artillery fire on the ridge.

When the Allies' counter-artillery repulsed a failed attack, the Germans came forward with their hands up in surrender.

"They are tricking you."

Tor heard the Viking's voice and carefully looked to his side. "What?"

"They plan to get close and attack you," the angel said. "Be ready to fight back."

"Be ready, men!" Tor shouted. "Don't trust the bastards!"

The Viking was right.

When the 'surrendering' soldiers dropped to their knees and started shooting, Tor's men responded with artillery fire and grenades and drove the Germans back, killing many.

At battle's end, Tor's platoon confirmed twenty-six Germans killed, seven captured, and more Nazis bleeding all over the snow than Tor could tally.

It was a good day.

February 20, 1945
Riva Ridge, Italy

Gaining control of Riva Ridge was a vital link to the campaign through Italy, and last night the Germans were taken completely by surprise as the Americans secured the ridge above their camp for today's battle.

How I wish I could tell you about this.

Kyle was never far from Tor's thoughts. He asked the Viking how she was doing, but apparently his guardian angel's powers only extended to Tor and his immediate vicinity.

What good was that?

The Tenth Mountain Division's Eighty-fifth and Eighty-seventh Infantry had arrived in Italy on January thirteenth, and were now in position to attack the Germans on Mount della Torraccia.

Thanks to last night's victory, the Six-hundred-fiftieth Artillery was setting up on Riva Ridge. The plan was for them to fire on Mount Belvedere and back up the Tenth in their assault of the German stronghold, while the Eighty-sixth launched a downhill attack on the Germans camp below the ridge.

"Come on, you ridge-running, stump-jumping, sons of bitches!" Tor shouted. "Strap on your skis and let's kill some more Germans today!"

Almost nine hundred members of the Eighty-sixth Infantry launched themselves down the hill, descending on their enemy like a flying plague of well-armed locusts. Dressed in white camouflage and gliding on white skis they achieved a modicum of surprise on the cloudy day.

Torger shot past Tor shouting, *"Die du drittsekkene!"* Die you sons of bitches!

Tor's competitive spirit prompted him to catch up with the ski-jumper but the thought of his wife tempered that urge.

Instead he shouted after his friend, *"Spar litt for meg!"* Save some for me!

The Germans knew the Allies were waiting at the top of the ridge and they were better prepared than the night before.

"To your right!" the Viking shouted.

Tor swung his rifle to the side and shot, taking down the German. "Thanks!"

"Watch for grenades."

"And you watch for everything else!" Tor countered.

He slid to a stop and shot into the forest before pulling the pin from a grenade and throwing it in that direction.

As he skied forward again Tor kept to the forest—for cover as much as to search for enemy soldiers. He dropped over a ridge and found himself on the edge of a blast hole. He skidded to a stop when he saw the white uniforms.

"Who are they?" he asked the angel.

The angel bent over the bodies and looked at the dead men, then he straightened and faced Tor sadly. "One of them is your friend."

"Torger?" Tor side-stepped forward on his skis until he could see the man's face. "Oh, no. Not you, Torger. You were too fearless, I think."

"Someone is behind you!"

Tor whirled around and shot the brown-uniformed soldier in the face.

He hesitated, then mentally shook himself. "Let's go." *I'll think about Torger later.*

He never heard the explosion.

ᛟ ᛟ ᛟ

Tor looked down at his shattered chest. There was no way he could survive such a devastating wound. He squinted at the Viking as he struggled to draw breath past broken bone.

"I thought you were my guardian angel." His voice was no more than a rasped whisper.

The angel looked as shattered as Tor's chest. "I could not save you this time. I am sorry."

A light began to glow in Tor's peripheral vision: bright, warm, and inviting. He glanced at it, torn by the need to remain here on the snowy mountain and fight the impossible battle to survive, and the desire to go forward and discover what awaited him on the other side.

He looked back at the Viking. Everything around the angel was growing darker, though the angel remained clear. "What am I supposed to do now?"

He smiled sadly. "Go to the light, Tor. You have fought valiantly and your reward is waiting."

"Am I dead then?"

"You are dying."

Tears filled Tor's eyes. "What will happen to Kyle? And our baby?"

The Viking's expression shifted. "I cannot see the future, Tor. But I do believe that she and your child will have a fine life."

Tor tried to grab the angel and surprisingly felt the man's hand. "Will you watch over them?"

If an angel could cry, Tor believed the Viking would be sobbing.

"I swear this to you: if there is any possible way for me to do so, I will."

Tor nodded, said one last prayer for Kyle and the babe, and then left his broken body on the mountain.

CHAPTER THIRTY NINE

February 27, 1945
Minneapolis, Minnesota

Kyle opened the door to her apartment in response to an unexpected knock. She glanced at the clock. It was two in the afternoon.

A pair of somber men in army uniforms stood facing her.

"Mrs. Tor Hansen?"

"No—please no—tell me he's not…"

"The army offers its condolences, ma'am."

Kyle moaned and sank to her knees. Sobs shook her shoulders and tears gushed from her eyes. This was every soldier's wife's worst nightmare.

No no no no no nooo…

She felt herself being lifted and led to the one upholstered chair in her home. Someone shut the door. Someone handed her a handkerchief.

"I'll make tea," a male voice said.

Tor is dead.

My husband is dead.

She lifted her head and stared at the officer sitting on her couch.

"How?"

"He was hit by a grenade on February twentieth in a battle below Riva Ridge in Italy."

The one making tea added, "Two days before that he heroically led a group of men up the side of Riva Ridge for a surprise attack on German forces."

"That made the Allied victory possible."

Kyle looked from one to the other, grasping at any straw of hope. "And you're sure it was Tor who died?"

The officer on the couch reached into his pocket and handed Kyle her husband's dog tags.

Fresh sobs overtook her.

Oh Tor.
Not Tor.
Please not Tor.

But it was Tor, no matter how hard she tried to will it not to be. She pressed one hand against her womb.

My poor baby...
You'll never meet your father...

The tea kettle whistled, pulling her attention back to her visitors. She looked from one to the other, not caring what they thought of her still-flowing tears.

"What happens now?"

"Your husband's remains are being shipped here, to Minneapolis. We can arrange for him to be buried in the Veteran's Cemetery with a military ceremony."

The tea officer set a steaming cup on the coffee table. "It's offered at no charge to military families. Unless you have other plans?"

Other plans? Why would she have other plans?

I never planned for this.

Kyle stared at the steeping tea while her thoughts whirled and tangled.

Her first thought was maybe she should have the Army send Tor's body back to his parents so he could be buried at home. His deep love for his homeland was one thing she always admired about him.

As if in response to that thought her baby moved with sudden force, and she knew in that instant that Tor needed to be buried nearby. Their child needed a grave to visit.

So do I.

"Yes. Do that."

The men sat with her while she drank her tea without tasting it. Even though they didn't say anything, just having them there was admittedly comforting. It kept her from going mad with shock and grief.

"Is there someone we can call for you?" the tea officer asked when she set the empty cup back on the table.

"My parents, I think."

Kyle couldn't imagine saying the terrible words out loud at all, much less hear her mother or father's initial stunned reaction to Tor's death. She would gratefully let the bereavement officer make that call.

"Do you have the number?"

Kyle pointed. "It's next to the telephone."

While the tea officer made her another cup, the other officer called her parents. Kyle tried not to hear what was said, but she couldn't help it.

A fresh wave of grief swamped her.

She sobbed into the muffling handkerchief, not wanting her parents to hear her crying.

The officer hung up the phone. "Your father said to tell you that he and your mother are on their way."

"They're coming?" Kyle sniffed and dabbed her nose. "Why?"

"I told them that your husband's service will be in two days, ma'am. And it's nice to have family around at a time like this."

Two days?

I'm burying my husband in two days.

Tea man set Kyle's second cup in front of her. "May I ask when your baby is due?"

Kyle lifted the cup to her lips and mumbled, "Two months."

"Congratulations, ma'am."

Her gaze flicked to his. "I served, too. I was a WAC. Second Lieutenant. Stationed at Camp Hale."

Both officers looked at her differently.

"We weren't told that. You were discharged?"

"Because of the baby. I'm attending the university here under the G.I. Bill."

That clearly surprised both of them. "Will you continue?"

She laid her palm over the spot where her baby was currently stretching. "I'm a widow with a child to support. We'll have to see."

※ ※ ※

The bereavement officers stayed another half hour until Kyle finally sent them away. It was time for her to grieve alone.

Before they left, the officer who had the dog tag reached into his coat pocket and handed Kyle an envelope.

"Since you were in the WAC you probably know that every soldier who is sent into active duty is required to write a letter to someone they're close to, in case the worst happens."

She did, but she hadn't been thinking clearly enough to remember.

She reached out her hand. "This is Tor's?"

"Yes, ma'am."

"Thank you." She set the letter on the coffee table.

It took her an hour to open it. And she only did it then because her parents would be half way to Minneapolis by now and she wanted to read it before they came.

Kyle turned on a lamp to read by, realizing that she was now sitting in the dark. When she unfolded the paper her heart clenched at the sight of Tor's strong handwriting.

With a sigh of determination, she read her husband's words.

December 10, 1944

My dearest darling Kyle,

I hope you never read this letter, because if you do that means I am gone. How fervently I've prayed that God will allow me to remain with you and our child, not for my sake but for yours. If you're reading this, then He must have had other plans.

First I want to tell you how to find my family: address your letters to Nikolai or Matilda Hansen, Hansen Hall Road, Arendal, Norway. Whatever you send there <u>will</u> reach them.

As for Teigen, he was traveling with the resistance when I saw him, so write to him at our parents' address until you hear that he has settled somewhere else.

Do write to them, Kyle, soon and often. I want them to know the amazing woman who won my heart and made what are now the last months of my life so worth living.

And please—take our child to Norway to meet them. Not right after the war of course, but don't wait too long. Our baby will have Norwegian citizenship because I'm a Norwegian citizen and we were married at the time of my death, so travel is simple from that standpoint.

You will have noticed I am saying our child, not our son. I do know that you may be carrying a precious daughter. Either way, I want you to raise our child to be fearless like you. Because you are fearless, Kyle, even if you don't realize it.

Now is the time for you to charge.

Take advantage of your Readjustment Act's benefits. Move to Minneapolis. Get your degree. You have been training for these things for the past year. My battles abroad are done. Yours at home are just beginning.

Don't let anyone stand in your way. Be victorious.

You will receive a death benefit from the American Army, and if you take our marriage certificate and my death certificate to the Norwegian Embassy you will receive my pension. I don't know how much this will add up to, but I hope it's enough for you to do what you need to do.

Last of all, my dearest wife, thank you for loving me. I've never been happier or more settled in my life than I have been with you. To say I love you is too weak, because what I feel for you goes so far beyond words.

That said, you are still a young woman, Kyle. You need to marry again. Our child needs a father who is in your home and can provide the steady assurance and protection that every child needs. Find him with my blessings. And then give our baby some brothers and sisters to play with.

It's so hard to stop writing this letter, because that will be the end of our connection. I don't know what the afterlife will be like, but if I can watch over you in any way, I will. At least until you marry again.

I can't say goodbye. I may have died, but my love for you never will.

Tor

Kyle sat in the upholstered chair reading Tor's letter over and over again. She could hear his voice in her head, speaking these English words with his mixed British-American-Norwegian accent. Then it hit her.

He wrote this in English.

Kyle realized at that moment that Tor wanted his American-born child to be able to read his final letter someday.

"He will, my love," Kyle whispered. "I'll make sure of it."

She folded the pages carefully and tucked them back inside the envelope.

CHAPTER FORTY

April 13, 1945
Minneapolis, Minnesota

Kyle's mother didn't leave after Tor's burial. He was even awarded a Silver Star during the ceremony for exceptional bravery.

Kylli was still in the little apartment six weeks later, cooking and cleaning for Kyle while Kyle strove to complete her schoolwork ahead of schedule.

"I never would have asked you to do this, Mamma," Kyle repeatedly told her. "But I am so glad to have you here."

Kylli smiled at her daughter as she tucked in the sheets and folded the sleeper sofa. "I would never leave you alone at a time like this."

Kyle tried to get her mother to sleep in the Murphy bed in the alcove off the living room, but her mother refused saying, "You'll be uncomfortable enough these next weeks. I'll be fine on the couch."

Kylli had been making subtle changes in the apartment as well. The walls now held framed photos from Tor and Kyle's wedding. Her mother snuck the negatives off to a camera shop and had the black-and-white enlargements printed and framed.

"He was a very handsome man, wasn't he?" Kylli sighed when she showed her daughter what she'd done. "I hope his son looks like him."

"Not you, too," Kyle groaned. "What if it's a girl?"

Her mother winked at her. "Then I hope she looks like you."

Kyle wasn't sure if seeing her husband's face on a daily basis was helpful or whether it reminded her anew of her loss. Her reaction seemed to depend on her mood which was as changeable as the April weather. This morning she stared into his eyes and felt like he was with her.

Kyle rubbed her lower back which was aching when she woke up. "I'm not sure that bed is much better than the couch."

Her mother looked at her in that evaluative way mothers have. "When did your back start hurting?"

"I don't know. In the middle of the night sometime."

Kylli approached and pressed her palm to Kyle's belly. "Any contractions?"

"Just the normal ones. But they're definitely getting stronger."

As if to prove her words, Kyle's womb tightened painfully. She put her hand on her mother's shoulder and breathed deeply until her body relaxed. "Ooh. That was a strong one."

Kylli returned to her morning clean-up. "Are you sure you should go to class this morning?"

"I have to." Kyle started gathering her books and folders. "I have to turn in my research paper in psychology so I can at least get a B in that class."

"I can take it for you," her mother offered. "Why don't you rest?"

The offer was more tempting than Kyle wanted to admit., but she couldn't afford to miss the class time. "Rest? I just got up. I'll be fine."

Another contraction squeezed her midsection. Kyle grunted, set her books down, and concentrated on breathing.

She felt a little shift in her belly. Water gushed onto the floor. Kyle's eyes flew open and she stared at her mother, surprised and terrified at the same time.

"I'm having a baby!"
Kylli already had a towel in her hand. "Yes you are. Let's get you to the hospital."

※ ※ ※

Ten hours later Kyle was in the maternity ward of the University Hospital staring down at the puffy-faced blond-haired baby in her arms. Her son, Thor Solberg Hansen, weighed in at an impressive nine pounds and two ounces and was twenty-two inches long.

Kyle loved him so much that she kept weeping.

Here's our boy, Tor.

Can you see him?

Kyle had decided to spell her son's name with an H so Americans would know how to say and he wouldn't have to correct them his entire life. She was sure Tor would understand.

"Thank you, Tor, for this incredible blessing," she whispered. "I will never be able to thank you enough."

Kyle rested as long as she could stand to—three entire days—before checking out of the hospital.

"Doctor says a week," the nurse scolded.

"I'm a farm girl," Kyle countered. "I know how all this birth stuff works. My milk came in this morning, so now I'm taking my baby and going home."

With a huff, the nurse waited for Kyle to settle in the wheelchair and pushed her to the front door of the hospital. Kylli followed with baby Thor in her arms.

Now the adventure begins.

September 9, 1945
Minneapolis, Minnesota

On the first day of the fall semester classes Kyle handed Thor to her roommate Beth when he finished nursing and then buttoned her blouse.

"I have three classes today, so I'll be gone about five hours," she said. "If he gets hungry you can make up a little of the formula, and I'll nurse him when I get back."

Beth nodded and rested a hand on her three-year-old daughter's head. "I saw the evaporated milk and Karo syrup on the counter. I'll boil some water just in case so it's ready and not too hot if he gets fussy."

"Thanks so much!" Kyle hefted her books. "Wish me luck."

"Luck?" Beth giggled, her rosy cheeks squeezing her brown eyes. "You've aced every class so far, so I don't think luck has anything to do with it."

Kyle would disagree, considering the pompous psychology professor had caved and given her the A she deserved. She kissed the top of Thor's blonde head and walked out the door of the Victorian duplex.

Once Kyle received Tor's death benefit she made a decision. She used the money as a down payment and got a low-interest loan through the G.I. Bill to purchase a fifty-year-old duplex near the campus. Then she spent the summer cleaning and repainting both two-bedroom, one-bathroom units.

She easily rented out one side for enough to cover the mortgage payment, and she lived in the other side. And after advertising in the newspaper for *a female roommate, free rent in exchange for babysitting*, Beth showed up at her door with little Greta in tow.

As she assumed, Kyle wasn't the only war widow with a child who was trying to survive on a limited income.

The arrangement was working well so far, and Beth was wonderful with Thor. Even Greta kept calling him her baby and fawned over him.

Thor, of course, loved the attention.

Just like his father.

As Kyle walked toward campus, the bright blue sky and balmy breeze pushing her forward, she realized that even though she only had a short time with Tor, he'd completely changed her life. And though the ache of her loss was still raw and prompted inconvenient tears at times, the fog was lifting and she could see forward.

It's time to send Matilda and Nikolai another picture.

Finding Norway

THE NORSEMEN'S WAR

Book 3:
Kyle & Dahl

CHAPTER ONE

July 2, 1950
Arendal, Norway

Kyle held five-year-old Thor's hand as they got off the bus in the town square of Arendal. The two days of travel, flying from Minneapolis to Oslo, spending the night in a hotel, then taking the four-hour bus ride to her late husband's ancestral home were as exhausting as they were intimidating.

What if they don't like me?

Little Thor had come through like a champ, fascinated by every aspect of the journey, and his dual citizenship with Norway and America made that part easy.

Kyle furtively looked over the people in the square while the bus driver unloaded their two large suitcases, wondering if Teigen Hansen remembered that he needed to pick her up.

"Thank you," she said to the driver. "We'll be fine."

At least I speak Norsk.

Making this trip was important to Tor, who in his active-duty survivor's letter asked Kyle to please stay in contact with his family and bring his son to meet them. The fact that she was full-blooded Norwegian but had never visited her own ancestral land made the journey all the more poignant.

"Where's my uncle?" Thor asked in English as the bus pulled away from the square.

Kyle wished she'd taught him Norsk, but with completing her bachelor's degree in psychology at the University of Minnesota and starting her master's program, she'd been far too busy.

Maybe I should have looked for a roommate who spoke Norwegian.

"He's on his way," Kyle said with a confidence she didn't have. "We'll just wait right here. Isn't this a nice town?"

It truly was.

Picturesque and sitting on the island-strewn southern coast of Norway, Arendal was protected from the North Sea by a multitude of rocky outcroppings. Tor explained that being only ninety miles across the sea from Denmark made Arendal the perfect location for his Viking ancestors to settle and later for his family's long-standing shipping business to thrive.

Kyle heaved a nervous sigh.

What if they don't like me?

She shaded her eyes from the bright summer sun and scanned the square again. Then she gasped. Her hand pressed against her mouth. Her heart pounded against her ribs.

A ghost was walking toward her.

"Kyle?"

Now that he was close enough she could see his bright green eyes. Not blue, green.

She nodded. "I'm sorry. I just…" Tears blurred her vision. "Tor always said you looked alike."

Teigen smiled his surprised understanding. "I didn't think about that. I guess it would be a shock."

"Mamma?" Thor's face was twisted in concern. "What's wrong."

Kyle quickly wiped her eyes. "Nothing darling. I'm just happy to meet your Uncle Teigen."

Thor looked up at his tall uncle. "You look like my Pappa."

"Do you know any English?" Kyle asked Teigen after she translated her son's comment.

"A little." Teigen squatted down so his eyes were level with

Thor's. "And you are just like your Pappa," he managed in heavily-accented English.

"Everybody says that." Thor pulled his hand from Kyle's and held it out to Teigen. "It's nice to meet you, Uncle Teigen."

Teigen laughed, sounding so much like his older brother that Kyle's chest tightened. He grabbed Thor's hand and shook it. "It's nice to meet you, Thor Hansen."

Then he straightened and looked down at Kyle. "Shall we go?"

***

Hansen Hall was built on the top of a bluff about a mile west of the center of Arendal. Looking exactly like Tor described, the structure was dominated by a round stone tower which stood three stories over the road. There were no windows in the tower, only the vertical slits which allowed archers to defend the inhabitants.

Viking archers.

Extending off one side of the tower was the two-story medieval structure with glass windows leaded in a multitude of small diamond-shaped panes. Peeking over the flat roof of the medieval façade were several tall chimneys and slanted slate roofs declaring the presence of the "modern" wing—built over two hundred years ago.

Kyle climbed out of the car and breathed in the salt air of the North Sea, wondering how far down the water was. The view from the bluff was spectacular. The sound of the big black sedan's engine seemed to awaken the old building and doors opened, spilling people onto the drive.

Kyle knew Matilda and Nikolai immediately.

Tor's mother was thin and a bit fragile looking, but she wrapped Kyle in a tearful hug that was surprisingly strong. "I am so happy you are finally here."

Kyle hugged her back. "As am I, Mamma Hansen."

Matilda loosened her hold and stepped back to look at Thor, who was walking shyly around the back of the car. She looked as shocked to see her grandson as Kyle had been to see Teigen.

"Oh my word. He really *is* the image of Tor at that age."

Kyle smiled at her mother-in-law. "I hope you have pictures. I'd love to see them."

Nikolai hefted one of the suitcases while Teigen claimed the other. "Welcome to Hansen Hall, Kyle. We have all been eagerly waiting for this day for a long time."

"Thank you, Pappa Hansen." She rested her hand on Thor's shoulder. "We are so happy to be here."

A petite woman with short, light brown hair and pale blue eyes stepped forward, smiling. She had a baby on her hip, and a pretty little girl held her hand.

"Hello, Kyle. I'm Selby." She lifted the hand held captive by her daughter. "And this is Torhild."

Kyle squatted down to her niece's eye level the same way Teigen had to Thor. "I'm your Aunt Kyle, and my son Thor is your cousin."

Torhild chewed a finger and looked at Thor who was now leaning on his mother.

"How old are you?" Kyle asked even though she knew the answer.

Torhild held up five fingers.

"Five years old? That's wonderful. Thor is five years old, too." Kyle put her arm around her son. "But he doesn't speak very much Norsk, so you'll have to teach him."

Kyle straightened and tucked her finger into the baby's hands. "This must be Jans. How old is he now?"

"Just turned four months. We waited to have him christened until his Aunt Kyle got here." Selby lifted her free shoulder. "We figured everyone would want to meet you, anyway."

Kyle looked around at the people gathered together: Nikolai and Matilda, Teigen and Selby, Torhild and Jans, and knew that she and Thor were exactly where they should be.

Teigen and Nikolai carried her suitcases to the door while Matilda linked her arm through Kyle's. "Let's get you settled."

Kyle took Thor's hand and walked into Hansen Hall.

We're here, Tor. We finally made it.

Now read the story of the Viking apparition and Tor's modern day great-granddaughter:

An Unexpected Viking
A Restored Viking
A Modern Viking

Sveyn Hansen was a Viking in 1070—until Norway's king declared the country Christian, sparking deep-rooted conflict. Sveyn, caught in a violent clash and run through by a sword, lay bleeding on the ground while at his head the priest gave him last rites. But at his feet, the devil was pulling Sveyn toward a different end. A blinding flash and deafening boom shook Sveyn to his bones. Once he could see and hear again, he wasn't certain what had happened. Only that he was not dead. And he was no longer alive.

Hollis McKenna's boss, insisting that she take a break after several grueling months at the Arizona History and Cultural Museum, banishes her to a relaxing weekend event. When Hollis arrives, she spies a cover model standing off to the side. Surprised that no one is conversing with the gorgeous six-foot-plus man wearing the Viking costume, she winds through the crowd to speak with him herself. He insists that Hollis hold her "lighted rectangle" to her ear while she converses with him. Frustrated at his repeated insistence, she holds out her phone and demands to know why.

"Because you are the only one who can see me."

NOTES ABOUT THE 10TH MOUNTAIN DIVISION:

AUTHOR'S CONFESSION #1: The American soldiers climbing Riva Ridge did not actually have their skis with them. But because those were Tor's final scenes, and the training info about Camp Hale focuses so heavily on the famous skiers that trained there, it felt wrong not to have Tor go into his final battle without his beloved skis. The same goes for Torger Tokle, who did die there.

AUTHOR'S CONFESSION #2: On June 22, 1944 the 10th Mountain Division was actually shipped to Camp Swift in Texas to prepare for maneuvers in Louisiana, which were canceled. Why the Army would send a ski-and-mountain-climbing patrol to this low-altitude and hot climate is unclear. I left it out intentionally because it didn't fit my plot. And frankly—it was boring.

NOW FOR THE REAL STUFF:

The creation of an elite ski corps was a national effort after Charles "Minne" Dole, founder of the National Ski Patrol, persuaded the U.S. Army in 1941 that they needed a division of trained skiers and mountaineers.

Camp Hale, constructed in 1942 at an altitude of approximately 9,300 feet, was located between Red Cliff and Leadville in the Eagle River valley of Colorado, as a United States Army training facility. Enough men were recruited to create three army regiments: the 85th, 86th, and 87th. They became the 10th Mountain Division and were deployed after training. By the time the division went into combat it had trained for 3 years and numbered over 10,000.

On February 18, 1945 in Italy, and under the cover of darkness, 900 men from the 86th Mountain Infantry Regiment used ropes to climb Riva Ridge in complete silence to surprise and capture the German lookouts. Once on the ridge, Field Artillery was able to fire on Mount Belvedere, aiding the 85th and 87th regiment in a successful assault on that strategic position.

By the time peace was announced on May 2, 1945 the 10th Mountain Division had outrun its supply lines and pushed the Germans into the Alps. The men of the 10th also paid the heaviest price of any U.S. Army division in Italy: 992 dead and 4154 wounded. The 10th Mountain Division served in combat for only four months, but had one of the war's highest casualty rates.

On July 1, 1943 with passage of the Women's Army Corps Bill, the Women's Army Auxiliary Corp (WAAC) became simply the Women's Army Corps (WAC) and gained full military status. Altogether, more than 400,000 women served in various branches of the United States Military during World War II.

The presence at, and contributions of, the two hundred women who formed the Women's Army Corps Detachment at Camp Hale have largely been lost from the historical record. The Camp was built and created for training elite mountain and ski troops, so the focus of the military and the media was the men's activities.

In 1914 the ACE ("All Cotton Elastic") bandage was invented by a group of scientists at Becton Dickinson Corporation. When writing historical novels, one has to research all sorts of random things. This was one of them.

Camp Hale was decommissioned in November 1945.

Early in the spring of 1959 Torger Tokle was elected to the Ski Hall of Fame in Michigan. Tokle came to America from Norway in 1939 and, after a spectacular career, laid down his life for his adopted country a short six years later at Riva Ridge.

WAC Armorers maintained and repaired small arms and heavy weapons, but WACs were not allowed to be trained in their use until 1978 and were not issued firearms until the 1980s.

Army Technical Sergeant Carl V. Cossin chronicled his experiences with the 10th Mountain Division and was the inspiration for the character of Private Keith Kossin, in addition to providing some anecdotal information included in this story:
http://www.mywarhistory.com/browse/printPreview.aspx?serviceH erold=78

THE HANSEN FAMILY TREE

Sveyn Hansen* (b. 1035 ~ Arendal, Norway)

***

Rydar Hansen (b. 1324 ~ Arendal, Norway)
Grier MacInnes (b. 1328 ~ Durness, Scotland)

Eryndal Bell Hansen (b. 1327 ~ Bedford, England)
Andrew Drummond (b. 1325 ~ Falkirk, Scotland)

***

Jakob Petter Hansen (b. 1485 ~ Arendal, Norway)
Avery Galaviz de Mendoza (b. 1483 ~ Madrid, Spain)

***

Brander Hansen (b. 1689 ~ Arendal, Norway)
Regin Kildahl (b. 1693 ~ Hamar, Norway)

***

Martin Hansen (b. 1721 ~ Arendal, Norway)
Dagne Sivertsen (b. 1725 ~ Ljan, Norway)

Reidar Hansen (b. 1750 ~ Boston, Massachusetts)
Kristen Sven (b. 1754 ~ Philadelphia, Pennsylvania)

Nicolas Hansen (b. 1787 ~ Cheltenham, Missouri Territory)
Siobhan Sydney Bell (b. 1789 ~ Shelbyville, Kentucky)

Stefan Hansen (b. 1813 ~ Cheltenham, Missouri)
Kirsten Hansen (b. 1820 ~ Cheltenham, Missouri)
Leif Fredericksen Hansen (b. 1809 ~ Christiania, Norway)

***

Tor Hansen (b. 1913 ~ Arendal, Norway)
Kyle Solberg (b. 1919 ~ Viking, Minnesota)

Teigen Hansen (b. 1915 ~ Arendal, Norway)
Selby Hovland (b. 1914 ~ Trondheim, Norway)

***

*Hollis McKenna Hansen (b. Sparta, Wisconsin)

Kris Tualla is a dynamic, award-winning, and internationally published author of historical romance and suspense. She started in 2006 with nothing but a nugget of a character in mind, and has created a dynasty with The Hansen Series, and its spin-off, The Discreet Gentleman Series. Find out more at: www.KrisTualla.com

Kris is an active PAN member of Romance Writers of America, the Historical Novel Society, and Sisters in Crime, and was invited to be a guest instructor at the Piper Writing Center at Arizona State University.

"In the Historical Romance genre, there have been countless kilted warrior stories told. I say it's time for a new breed of heroes. Come along with me and find out why: **Norway IS the new Scotland!***"*

Made in the USA
Columbia, SC
04 November 2017